The Spy In a
Catcher's Mask

THE SPY IN A CATCHER'S MASK

a novel by

Kurt Willinger

Sabre Press
Troy, Michigan

Printed in the United States of America

Paperback ISBN 1-879094-44-4
Hardcover ISBN 1-879094-45-2

97 96 95   3 2 1

Sabre Press
an imprint of
Momentum Books, Ltd.
6964 Crooks Road
Troy, Michigan 49098

Cover design by Tim Bodendistel and Donna Mattus

Library of Congress Cataloging-in-Publication Data

Willinger, Kurt
     The spy in a catcher's mask/ Kurt Willinger.
          p.   cm.

     ISBN 1-879094-45-2 (hc). --ISBN 1-879094-44-4 (pb).
     1. Berg, morris, 1902-1972--Fiction. 2. World War, 1939-
     1945--Secret service--United States--Fiction. 3. Baseball
     players--United States--Fiction. 4. Spies--United States--
     Fiction 5. Catchers (Baseball)--Fiction. I. Title.
     PS3573.I45646S68 1995
     813'.54--dc20   95-1867

For Sweenie, my best friend

Preface

This is a work of fiction. It is based on the exploits of a major league ball player named Moe Berg. An outstanding defensive catcher with a lifetime batting average of .248, Berg was the one who characterized the mask, chest protector, and shin guards as "the tools of ignorance." This athlete, a magna cum laude graduate of Princeton, could count some of this century's most famous people as friends, including Franklin Roosevelt, Albert Einstein, Babe Ruth, and "Wild" Bill Donovan. It was through Donovan that Berg became an OSS agent, parachuted into Europe, and gathered information about German atomic weapons development. This included a face-to-face encounter with Werner Heisenberg, Germany's leading nuclear scientist. These are facts, all the rest is fiction. But as Yogi Berra, that keen observer of the human condition, might have said, "If it ain't true, it ought to be."

Acknowledgments

To: Warren Rogers, advertising art director, who flew B-24s in WWII. Richard Mumma, business executive, who leaned out of drafty helicopters in 1951 to snap pictures of the North Korean landscape. Christopher (Kit) Mill, young entrepreneur and Princeton man. Dr. Gene Gurney, NASA public information officer, author, and pilot of nearly anything with more than one engine. Ferdinand Maggiore, construction czar and surfside raconteur. And Uncle Ernie Kahn, retired businessman, who served his country during WWII by interrogating captured Nazi officers.

Thanks, friends, for all the help, for answering all the dumb questions twice and sometimes three times, and for the loan of your names.

Part 1
Gathering Strength

THE HOUSE IN QUESTION stood on Dickerson Street in the Roseville section of Newark, New Jersey. It was a generously sized home in the Victorian style popular at the turn of the century, yet not so large as to command the description "stately." It was painted white with neat gray trim and wore decorative touches of gingerbread cutouts and fancy millwork. In its effort to be distinctive, it blended comfortably with the rest of the homes on the maple-lined street. But now there were rumors that the house had been sold and the new owners were planning changes. Change invariably foments disquietude, especially in a semirural, tree-lined community like Roseville.

First, the new owners put up a short stockade fence around the property. No other house on the street had a fence. Next, a wooden sign appeared in the middle of the front lawn proclaiming in both English and Hebrew that this was to be the new home of the Temple Beth-El Hebrew School. Now the two-story frame house on Dickerson Street stood out in some people's minds as if it had a red light above the front door.

"Can they do that?"

"There must be some ordinance against it."

Anxious inquiries downtown revealed that the area's zoning did permit such an establishment. But this information did little to placate agitated homeowners who were openly suspicious of the foreign-looking strangers in their midst. It was only when the rabbi invited a delegation of neighbors to inspect the school and meet the children that some of their disquietude faded. He explained that it was essentially old testament Sunday school except that classes were held in the middle of the week. "It's just Bible class," "They seem to be keeping up the place," "The kids are well-behaved," the visitors later explained to neighbors. Slowly their fears and xenophobia began to dissipate and the little Jewish school became an accepted fixture in the neighborhood. Change had come to Roseville, New Jersey, just as it had reached so many American cities in this first decade of the twentieth century.

In September Rose Berg brought her son, Morris, to be enrolled in the school. As she sat stiffly in the chair beside the desk of the bearded young rabbinical student who served as the school's administrator, she was finding it difficult to understand his reluctance to accept her boy. The soft-spoken woman listened intently as the administrator explained his position.

"Don't misunderstand me, Mrs. Berg. We like to start them early, but for your Morris it might be just a bit too early."

"But he's already to the kindergarten," Rose Berg offered, hopeful that this new evidence would sway the administrator.

The bearded scholar betrayed a hint of a smile at her naiveté. Reaching out and placing his hand on hers, he attempted to explain further.

"Mrs. Berg, kindergarten is more for the socialization of children. A preparation for the years of learning to come. They get alphabet and learn their numbers but it isn't for at least a year that they begin reading. And then, only the simplest of texts. Here at the Beth-El School, the boys read the Bible stories from the first day. So you see, not being able to read would put your son at an uncomfortable disadvantage. Perhaps next year, Mrs. Berg. Come back next year."

As he ushered Rose Berg to the door, he could see by the look on her face that she still did not comprehend. These greenhorns!

"But he reads!" Rose Berg said as she paused at the office door.

"He reads? What does he read?" asked the administrator, a touch of sarcasm creeping into his voice.

"He reads everything," Mrs. Berg replied.

"Like? . . . "

"Like the newspaper, books from the library, the Torah. Everything."

"He reads the Torah? Come now, Mrs. Berg."

At this the young man made no effort to disguise his skepticism. "You have an English-Hebrew bible at home you read to him, am I right?"

She nodded, not quite following.

"And he enjoys and understands the stories, is that what you're saying?"

"Oh, no," said Rose Berg. "It's only Hebrew and no one reads it to him, he reads it himself."

"I hardly believe that a child of . . . "

"He's right outside," said Rose, growing impatient with the young scholar. "When he reads you something, you'll believe it."

Little Morris Berg grinned as his mother emerged from the office. The boy had been sitting quietly as his mother instructed, but she'd been in that room an awfully long time and his good behavior was wearing thin. He was just about to peek into one of the several books piled on the low table in front of him.

"Hello, Morris," the bearded young man said, as he held out his hand to the boy. "I was wondering if you would try to read something for me. Could you do that?"

"'Kay!" said the boy.

The book on top of the pile was the Story of Moses in Hebrew, which the administrator handed to the child. Morris opened the book and began to read out loud. Perfect pronunciation. Unfaltering and remarkably erudite.

"I don't believe it!" mumbled the administrator. He then handed the child a random volume of Compton's Encyclopedia from the bookshelf.

The boy read: "Proust, Joseph Louis (1754-1826), French chemist. Originator of the law of definite proportions which offered strong support for the theory of Atomism."

He offered the child the next book in the stack, which happened to be a text in Russian. When the administrator noticed the title, he reached over to exchange it for another, but before he could the boy proceeded to read the cyrillic printing. The child could also read Russian.

After listening for several minutes the bearded young man instructed the boy to "keep reading, I'll be right back."

He returned with the rabbi and a volunteer mother. They sat, rapt, as if in a vaudeville theater, as four-year-old Morris Berg read paragraphs from five different books and the entire obituary section of the *Newark Star-Ledger*. The boy displayed such proficiency in Hebrew, English, and Russian that his audience was tempted to applaud. Little Moe had no idea what the fuss was all about but he basked in all the attention. He was accepted to the school. Rose Berg filled out the school's short admission form with the dignified air of a wealthy woman browsing through Tiffany's, content in the knowledge that she could afford anything in the place.

In a few months little Morris Berg managed to memorize most of the Torah and all the children's stories and continually amaze staff, visitors, and congregation members with his scholarly precocity. Visiting parents could barely hide their displeasure with their own offspring in the face of the Bergs' prodigy son. Morris wasn't very popular with his classmates at first, showing them up the way he did. Eventually he won them over with his cheerful nature and unpresupposing ways.

Morris continued his studies at the religious school for several years taking on a formidable schedule for a boy of such a tender age. Five days a week he attended elementary school. Monday, Wednesday, and Thursday he attended Hebrew School from 4:00 to 6:00 p.m., and on Tuesdays and Fridays he was inevitably found playing ball in Branch Brook Park. Moe handled his busy schedule effortlessly. Only when he was promoted into the class of older boys did some difficulty arise. These classes lasted an extra hour, so, instead of 6:00 p.m., Moe and the older group were dismissed at 7:00. As they left the school property a gang of neighborhood toughs was waiting for them across the street.

"Hey, Jew boy," one would call as the Hebrew students would head up the block.

"Yoo-hoo dirty Jew! Dirty Jew!" others would chant as the students continued, their pace quickening. The laughing, boisterous toughs followed, crossing the street to fall in behind the Jewish boys.

Both groups were dressed similarly: knickerbockers, high top leather shoes, cloth caps, and woolen coats. Except for the neckties worn by the Jewish boys and their slightly neater appearance, the youths looked nearly alike. Their differentiation was that one group had designated themselves pursuers and the other, the pursued.

Inevitably the Jewish boys, now including the youngest among them, ten-year-old Moe, broke into a run. Their tormentors gleefully quickened their pace, resulting in a pell-mell three-block sprint all the way to Market Street where the trolley tracks ran. Ignoring traffic, the young Jewish boys dashed into the busy intersection, often narrowly avoiding injury from a horse cart, motor car, or frantically clanging trolley. The toughs halted their pursuit at the curb, out of breath, laughing, shouting epithets of "Jew bastards," "Yellow!" and "We'll get you next time!" across the cobblestone gulf at their fleeing quarry.

This scene recurred nearly every evening. When some parents complained, an adult was assigned to convoy the boys for a block or so. While the adult was in evidence the gang remained on the opposite side of the street, whistling angelically and exchanging mischievous grins. Unfailingly, though, as the adult abandoned his charges, the chase immediately resumed.

Ten-year-old Morris Berg pondered this situation. He could not understand why he was being chased. He didn't even know why he was running. Tomorrow evening after school, he decided, I'm not gonna run.

The next evening all the elements of the regular scenario were in place--the Jewish students, the rowdy gang, the taunting, the stalking, the quickened pace, the frantic dash to safety. Only this time one element was out of place. One of the boys did not run. Moe simply continued walking. It was so unusual, most of the gang ran past him, but a couple pulled up and turned to face the little Jew who wouldn't run. This was annoying. He was acting as if he wasn't frightened--totally out of character.

"Hey, Jew boy, where you think you're going?"

Moe continued walking. The gang moved to surround him. Their leader, a stocky, redheaded boy wearing a frayed cap and heavy woolen knickerbockers torn at the knees, confronted him.

"I said," shoving his hand at Moe's chest, "where you think you're . . . "

Moe swatted the hand away and said, "Get out of my way!"

The surprised leader, fearful he was losing face, moved forward and shoved Moe with both hands. Moe was braced and the push had little effect.

"Leave me alone, I don't want any trouble with you," said the Jewish boy.

Moe was simply telling the truth but his tormentor interpreted his reticence as cowardice. The boy shoved at Moe once again and was brushed aside. The redhead then charged the smaller boy in an attempt to bowl him over, but Moe was too agile. He sidestepped the bully and his small fist landed a solid punch to the tough's cheek as he stumbled past. The mortified older boy sprawled on the sidewalk. As he rose unsteadily, his face smarting, he assumed a boxer's pose and postured as if to declare that now he really meant business. This action prompted encouraging shouts from his cohorts, who had now formed a circle around the combatants. Little Moe raised his hands for a moment and emulated his opponent's stance, then as if thinking

6

better of it, lowered his head and charged into the bully. The redhead doubled over with an "oof" of escaping breath as Moe butted him in the midsection. The momentum drove them both into the gutter. As they fell, Moe landed on top of his tormentor, whose head rebounded solidly against the cobblestone paving.

"Fight!" someone shouted.

As they wrestled in the gutter Moe could tell that most of the fight had left his opponent. Moe's primary struggle now was to disentangle himself from the bigger boy. At this point two large hands pried them apart and hoisted them to their feet by the backs of their collars.

"Knock it off, you hooligans!" ordered the big, red-faced cop. "Go on! Go home, there's nothing more to see," he barked at the bystanders who had been drawn to the ruckus. "On your way," he ordered the now scattering gang. "I know all of your names," he shouted at their retreating backs. "You better get some ice on that bump, son," he told the dazed redhead. "Off you go now. And you, you little sheenie," turning to Morris Berg, "I don't want to see you makin' trouble in this neighborhood again." He punctuated his remark with a firm poke of his billy.

When Morris arrived home that evening, dirty and disheveled, his parents showed great concern. When it became clear that their son was unharmed and his appearance was the result of a street fight, their concern escalated significantly. Bernard and Rose Berg were horrified at the prospect of their youngest child heading down the road of thuggery and ruin. They spent the next few evenings lecturing the boy on the evils of violence. Violence was equatable with stupidity. Violence was something that refined and intelligent people avoided at all costs. Violence was for goyim, not Jewish scholars.

On the next Monday evening, as the boys filed out of the Hebrew School, the gang of toughs was, as usual, loitering across the street. As they uttered their taunts, the Jewish boys began to run with the toughs in raucous pursuit as if some ancient ritual was being enacted. The two formations of boys sprinted all the way to Market Street, the pursuing toughs never quite overtaking their prey. Amid the breathless pack of fleeing boys was young Morris Berg dashing resignedly along with his frightened fellows.

Things were very different for Moe Berg on the ball field. There he could be himself. Once he displayed his ability, Moe ceased being the pint-sized Jewish kid who showed up in the afternoons. He was just a ball player like the rest of the guys. The bigger boys accepted Moe and permitted him to play catch and warm up with them but found it too humiliating to allow the little pipsqueak to play in an actual game. There were lots of afternoons, though, when teams were short a player and had no choice but to let Moe play. When shortstop Moe Berg took the field, it was a truly remarkable sight. He fielded ground balls flawlessly, covering the ground to his left and right with equal deftness. Moe instinctively kept his glove close to the ground, a technique even the best prospects don't master till well into their teen years. Word got around about the little squirt who could make the throw to first with remarkable strength and accuracy even when deep in the hole. "'Kid's got a gun for an arm," "A real howitzer!" the Branch Brook Park oldtimers, who usually were on hand to scrutinize the quality of play, would remark to one another.

One afternoon, Reverend Mulqueen, the coach of the Roseville Methodist Church team, happened by. Moe, dwarfed by the other boys, was in the outfield shagging flies. Mulqueen watched as the boy handled every chance hit to him. He had heard the talk of the remarkable little ball player and decided to see for himself.

Mulqueen, a pretty fair judge of baseball talent, borrowed a glove with the excuse of needing some exercise, and called Moe in. He then put Moe through a tryout for the Roseville nine. Mulqueen threw hard, soft, wide, and high. He even threw some crude curves. The boy handled them all. Mulqueen then bor-

rowed a bat and stroked some line drives, grounders, and dribblers to the boy; Moe gloved everything. Even a few that the clergyman thought he'd put past him.

Our regular shortstop is sixteen this year, Mulqueen was
thinking. I was planning to replace him with Johnson, the left
fielder, but the boy daydreams. This kid could play second or
even short.

This kid could be the answer to a young minister's prayer.

"Would you like to play on our baseball team? What's your
name, son?"

When Mulqueen heard the answers, he knew he should have
asked the second question first. A Jew? On a Methodist church
team? It just isn't kosher. Or is it? Isn't the purpose of the
activity program to engage community youngsters in healthy and
character-building sport? And to keep the little darlings from
breaking windows and setting fires and getting into God knows
what mischief during the long hot summer months? I think it is!
With that rationalization, the next hurdle would be parental con-
sent.

The brass bell on the door of the Warren Street drugstore
announced a customer to Bernard Berg, pharmacist and proprietor.

"Good morning. What can I do for you?"

"Good morning to you.

I'd like to talk to you about your son Morris."

Uh-oh, thought Bernard. "Is Moe in some kind of trouble?
What's he done?" trying not to sound overly distressed.

"Oh, nothing, nothing at all. On the contrary. He's a very
nice young man. Well mannered. Intelligent. And an excellent
ball player for his age. By the way, how old is he?"

Bernard hadn't figured where this conversation was headed.
"Ten," he answered.

Ten? thought Mulqueen. Oy vey was the first thing that came
to Mulqueen's mind. The top age limit for the team was sixteen.
None of the players were younger than thirteen.

When the purpose of Reverend Mulqueen's visit was finally communicated and Mr. Berg's low opinion of baseball was made clear, the discussion really got interesting. Back and forth they verbally tussled, the pharmacist only disengaging briefly to attend patrons. After more than an hour of argument, rebuttal, and counterargument, Berg threw up his hands in magnanimous capitulation.

"All right, all right, Morris can play. You have my permission."

Mulqueen was delighted. He believed his argument about teaching character to formative young minds who could otherwise get in trouble won the day, but it was really that Bernard Berg liked the minister and thought him refreshingly bright for a goy. It also didn't hurt when the clergyman bought a new electric vaporizer for the parish house. The only thing left now was to find a new name for the talented little runt.

Runt Wolfe of the Roseville Reds socked a triple with the bases loaded in the seventh inning of the St. Lucy game and ended the three-year schneider that Father Sabatino and the Loyals had smugly expected to go on forever.

That evening at dinner in the rectory, Mulqueen and the bishop were toasting their victory.

"A remarkable lad, that Runt Wolfe. And only thirteen years old."

If you only knew, your eminence, thought Coach Mulqueen. If you only knew.

Moe went on to attend Barringer High School and proved to be an excellent student, but to the annoyance of his parents, his passion for sport and especially baseball persisted. Moe became one of the premier players of the Barringer team and was instrumental in the Blue Bears winning the state championship. Bernard Berg, however, could not appreciate his son's athletic achievements. To say that he viewed his youngest son's involvement in sport with revulsion would be understatement, but in the light of Moe's acceptance to Princeton University, the pharmacist kept most of his objections to himself.

At Princeton, the world opened up for Morris Berg as he thrived on the physical and intellectual challenges.

2

IN THE EARLY 1930s, the city of Washington, steeped in southern gentility and framed by monuments, magnolias, and cherry blossoms, was an energetic, bustling work-in-progress. Its residents, justifiably proud of their burgeoning capital city, were also known to possess a wry sense of humor as evidenced by the popular motto, "First in war, first in peace, last in the American League." This motto was coined by Washington Senators baseball fans of a previous decade to express their frustration at being compelled to endure seemingly endless years of lackluster teams.

The outlook suddenly brightened for Washington fans as the Senators took the pennant in 1924 and again in 1925, but after that all too brief spurt of excellence, the team regressed and once again played uninspired ball.

The team's poor showing combined with the economic depression gripping the country dropped gate attendance to record lows. The franchise shortly found itself operating in red ink. In desperation, key players were sold outright to wealthier clubs to compensate for lost revenues. Players' salaries were cut and economies were sought in every quarter to help ride out the financial storm.

Although politicians, bankers, and newspaper chains were insisting that better days were just around the corner, the depression impudently ignored their exhortations and persisted. Over 15 million American men were out of work with little to divert them from their troubles save a baseball contest if by chance they could come up with the fifty-cent price of admission. Four bits, however, was considered far too costly for any man to spend for a ticket that guaranteed him an afternoon of hopelessly inept play.

Clark Griffith, the principal owner, concluded that a new manager might spark the team and thus improve the draw. The great former Senators pitcher Walter Johnson was promoted from the minor leagues and given the job. In his day, Johnson, dubbed the Big Train, had provided some of the rare bright spots amid scores of gloomy years. To improve the team, Johnson traded for sluggers Heinie Manusch and Buddy Myer. He then sought to further strengthen his club by improving its pitching staff. Because the Senators couldn't afford the price of proven veteran hurlers, he hoped to expedite the development of young arms from the minor leagues. With this strategy in mind, Johnson traded a pair of Class AA infielders for the Chicago White Sox catcher Morris (Moe) Berg.

Berg joined the team in spring training of the 1932 season. On the first full day of practice in the warm Biloxi, Mississippi, sun, with the heady fragrance of newly mown grass sweetening the air, Moe approached each of the Washington Senators veterans and introduced himself.

"Hello, Joe," he greeted veteran Joe Kuhel, "I'm Moe Berg," as he extended a friendly hand and enthusiastic smile. "You played a fair solid first base last year and I'm very pleased to meet you.

"You're Sam West, aren't you? I'm Moe Berg. Happy to shake hands with a fine hitter like you. Nearly had a hundred RBIs last year, didn't you? That's hitting when it counts!

"General Crowder, I'm Moe Berg. It's going to be a relief not having to face you again this year. Frankly, I think you're capable of winning more than twenty. Let's work on it.

"Buddy Myer, isn't it? I'm Moe Berg and I'm very glad to meet one of the league's premier second basemen. Wasn't it .293 with 173 hits and 114 runs scored?"

Myer nodded vaguely, choosing not to reveal that he was impressed. Yes, Berg did have the numbers right. The new guy seemed to know the stats of all his new teammates, something that would be taken as a compliment by any one of them. "Looks like our new backstop might work out just fine" was the early consensus.

By opening day, Moe's solid play and readiness to help teammates hone their skills had earned him the full acceptance of the players.

Manager Johnson was well aware of Berg's reputation for sure hands and clutch hitting but his interest was in the catcher's knack of rapidly bringing along young, inexperienced pitchers. It was said that Moe possessed a veritable green thumb when it came to the propagation of sprouting young arms, an ability developed during his tenure with the Chicago White Sox. If the Senators had any hope of making a move this year, Walter Johnson believed, it would take pitching, and Berg's extra savvy behind the plate could make an important difference.

Berg was big for a catcher. He stood over six feet, with a muscular frame of 185 pounds and dark hair and eyes that gave him an intense and exotic look. When the dashing athlete strode to the plate for his turn at bat, ladies day crowds could be observed leaning in toward the playing field to better observe this young Valentino in flannel knickers. Moe was quite aware of the attention and sometimes would respond with a trick--a little bit of showing off that he reserved for the occasion of ladies day.

When a batter popped up behind home plate, Moe would position himself under the ball and at the last moment duck his head to make the catch behind his back. This bit of showmanship was always sure to delight the spectators nearly as much as it annoyed the players on the visiting team. The first time Berg pulled his little stunt, the boys on the bench looked to Johnson for some response. Walter only rolled his eyes to the heavens, turned his back, and dipped another chew of Sweet Caporal.

Johnson figured if the man wants to give the ladies a thrill once in a while, it's okay by me, but, Mr. Vaudeville, you'd damn well better not drop that ball.

Once, early in the season, rookie pitcher Monte Weaver was getting tattooed pretty badly right from the start. The Browns seemed to have the kid's number. In the dugout, Johnson called Berg over with a tilt of his head.

"The kid got anything?" he asked.

"Monte's aiming the ball, Skip, trying to nip the corners. I can't get him to just rear back and let loose."

"Well, you'd better think of somethin' or he's comin' out. We're down four runs in the third and I'm not about to concede this game."

After the Senators got a run back in their half of the third, Moe and Monte returned to their respective battery positions. Browns outfielder Goose Goslin stepped in and impatiently thumped the plate with his bat. He'd already had two hits today and was eager to keep it going. Moe called for a fastball to get ahead in the count and Monte supplied a tentative offering way inside that the Goose clubbed down the third-base line, foul. He got a lot of wood on that pitch. Time out for a trip to the mound.

"I'm sorry, Moe. Can't seem to get it into high," the dejected rookie murmured.

"Don't worry about it. I'm gonna fix you up," said Moe as he reached for the rosin bag to dust the back of his hand. Moe then stepped closer to the young hurler.

"I've got these special baseballs. Five of 'em. Had 'em made for me in Cuba. They're four, five millimeters smaller than regulation. Give you a heck of a grip. The ballboy's about to bring 'em to the ump. You'll be able to throw those bb's through a brick wall."

"Hey, c'mon, play ball!" the umpire rasped, breaking up the tête-à-tête on the mound.

As Moe was returning to his position, he turned and told Monte, "Watch for the kid bringing the balls." Moe winked mischievously back at the mound as he pulled down his mask.

15

The next pitch was fouled again, this time straight back. The umpire threw a new ball into play and called to the home dugout for a new supply. The batboy sprinted out with five new balls, which the ump stowed in his jacket pockets. As he did, Moe pointed to the ump and nodded--those are the ones. The next pitch was chopped into the dirt foul toward the third- base coach, who made a nice pickup, perused the ball, then flipped it into the ump saying it was scuffed. The ump threw it out, then reached into his pocket and threw a new ball to the mound.

As it thumped into the glove and Monte grasped it with his right hand, he gasped. Oh, my God. It is smaller. He's crazy. This ball feels little . . . and light! I could throw this bean through the backstop.

"Let's play ball, fellas," the ump growled.

Moe then put down one finger for another fastball. This time the ball buzzed over the plate like a scalded hornet, at which the surprised Goose could only manage a late and feeble swing.

"Strike three! Yer out!"

The next two batters, Melillo and Ferrell, went down on a strikeout and a pop foul to the first baseman. Nothing across for the Browns.

The Senators eventually rallied to win that game, giving Monte Weaver, who pitched the next six innings brilliantly, his first complete game victory. It would be the first of twenty-two games the rookie would win that year. When Monte later approached Moe to ask him about the special balls, Moe made the rookie promise never to mention it again.

"I could get into some very serious trouble. Got me?"

"Got you!"

Moe banished the subject forever with a wink.

As manager Johnson passed Moe on the way to the club-house, he put his hand on the catcher's shoulder and said, "Nice goin', Moe."

"Thanks, Skip."

"Nice goin', Moe"--fine words coming from someone like the Big Train, one of the all-time greats of the game. At that moment, however, Moe experienced a pang of self-doubt. Sure, I helped the kid, but the talent was always there. But what about me? What the heck am I doing here, playing at a boy's game. I'm going to be thirty years old next year. Sure, I love the cameraderie, the excitement of performing in the arena, of testing myself every day. . .yet it seems there ought to be something more. Something important. Yet the honest truth is that I love it. Truly love it. The money's good and these days that's certainly nothing to sneeze at. So what am I complaining about? Stop thinking so much, Morris, you haven't got a care in the world. Moe jogged to catch up with his teammates on their way to the clubhouse.

"Hey, Moe," shouted Buddy Myer from the clubhouse entrance, "what's the capital of North Dakota?"

"Bismarck," Moe answered without losing stride.

"What's Hack Wilson's shoe size?" someone queried from the back of the locker room.

"Five and a half," said Moe as he placed his own 11½s in the cubby for the boy to polish.

"Who was the first vice president of the United States?" asked the batboy.

"John Adams," Moe shot back.

"What's the phone number of that flashy redhead in the stands behind third?" Whitlow, the third-base coach, threw in just for laughs.

"Evergreen 7682," Moe replied to the delight of the clubhouse gang.

"I wouldn't be surprised if that really was her number," Monte Weaver confided to his neighbor.

The game of endless questions was something the players never seemed to tire of playing. Especially after a victory. If Moe wearied of it, he never let on, nearly always answering swiftly and correctly.

17

Once outfielder Manusch asked Moe, "Don't you get fed up with the questions?"

"No, Heinie, not at all. For some of these mugs, it's the first time they cracked a book since their McGuffy reader."

Moe's seemingly unbounded stores of knowledge became a source of pride to his teammates, some of whom made money betting visiting players that they couldn't stump their erudite catcher.

Moe roomed at the Wardman Park, the Washington hotel that housed the team's bachelor players. His quarters could best be described as a cluttered monk's cell. It was not a small room but in conforming it to his needs, Moe had impressed every square foot of wall space into use for bookcases and bookshelves. There was a bed, a night stand, a small writing desk and chair, a chest of drawers, and except for a small, genuine Degas bought on his graduation trip to Paris, for decoration, the room was dominated by two and a half walls of books. A glance would suggest that there wasn't room for one more volume but this detail was never a deterrent to Moe. There was always room for one more precious find.

When a visitor would inquire if Moe had read them all, Moe would state solemnly, "I'm afraid I have."

Morris Berg accumulated books the way a miser collected gold--as if they weren't making any more of the stuff.

Moe was also an avid newspaper reader. Rising early each morning, he would walk to a newsstand specializing in out-of-town and foreign papers. Each day Moe would buy every paper he hadn't read. He inevitably befriended the proprietor, a man who had been wounded in the Great War.

"Hello, Henny!" Moe called into the shadowy recesses of the impossibly cluttered newsstand.

Henny Eckstein's face appeared in the opening. "So, boy-chick, I have your papers right here. Plus a last month's *Forwards*."

18

"Thanks, Henny. What do I owe you?"

"Two bits and two pennies for the stack."

Moe placed the silver quarter and shiny copper pennies on the counter and hurriedly gathered up the neatly folded pile of newspapers.

"So, boychick, you're running? Always, you're running. You can't spare a couple minutes to schmooze?"

"I've got a game today."

"Oh, a game! Then run. A game is important."

"So long, Henny," said Moe as he turned to leave with his papers.

"Tell me, boychick, when someday you got something even more important than baseball, how fast you gonna run then?"

"Henny, what could be more important than baseball?"

"You'll find out one day. Smart boy like you, you'll find out."

"Good day, Henny," said Moe laughing, then walked toward his waiting breakfast at the Wardman Park.

That old news dealer is more serious than any of my professors. I suppose he thinks I'm wasting my life, too. Well, can't worry about that now, gotta run.

Later, Moe rose from the table littered with breakfast dishes and a score of well-read newspapers and hurried downstairs.

In front of the hotel the station wagon waiting to ferry the players to the ballpark honked its warning. It always left promptly at ten.

For Moe, Washington was a marvelous city in which to play ball. The capital was a true international center and thrummed with intellectual activity. There were great schools, great restaurants, a symphony, complete libraries, and lots of bookstores--a cultural banquet for Moe. There were also plenty of conventional banquets in town and Moe made every effort to take full advantage of them too. Foreign embassies often invited professional athletes to their dinner parties as a sort of combination public-relations event and egalitarian diversion. They were

19

invariably delighted by a guest who was not only a professional ball player who owned his own dinner jacket but also could address them in their native tongue. This very evening another opportunity for elegant freeloading had presented itself.

A festive air presided over the baroque dining room of the Spanish Embassy situated off Sixteenth Street on Embassy Row. The opulent table, which seated nearly twenty fashionably dressed diplomats and guests, was lavishly appointed with flowers, candles, and gleaming silver. The scene offered a shuddery contrast to depression-rent America and the desparate squalor of the tattered bonus marchers huddling in their makeshift shacks just a short distance from the ornate embassy gates.

"You think these swells do this every night?" Heinie Manusch, currently the American League's leading batter, murmured to his teammate and fellow guest, Moe Berg.

"Dunno, Heinie, but I hope the ambassador's wife keeps a kosher kitchen," was his reply, causing both men to stifle an unseemly chortle.

Behind the ambassador, his wife, and two daughters, hung a portrait of Niceto Alcalá Zamora, the new president of politically unstable Spain. The painting occupied the place where only months before a likeness of King Alfonso XIII had graced the wall.

"Now, dear friends," the ambassador announced, rising to his feet, "I am happy to introduce our honored guests. To my right, Senor Albin Maitland, chairman of the great steamship line, and the charming Mrs. Maitland."

The couple rose and acknowledged the other guests with smiles. Mr. Maitland then offered a toast to the "legitimate" government of Spain and then, as glasses were raised, appended his salute by damning "those miserable Communists who desire nothing more than to ruin our two great countries." The toast was drunk by the other dinner guests, some of whom were officers of the embassy, with less than total enthusiasm. In Spain, leftist views were shared by a great many of the people and it might not be prudent to be observed publicly denouncing them.

The ambassador thanked the tycoon and his wife and quickly moved on to the introduction of his other guests. To the left of his own dear wife, he indicated the two professional baseball players.

"May I present Senors Morris Berg and Henny Manusch of the Washington Senators."

Moe and Heinie rose and bowed graciously to their hosts. Heinie then raised his glass and offered a toast to peace, a toast enthusiastically joined.

"If I may," Moe added, raising his glass, "I would like to offer a toast of my own. To the great literary genius, Miguel Cervantes."

"Certainly, Senor Berg," said the ambassador as he rose. "By all means to Cervantes, a most thoughtful and gracious toast, but if I may, I would like to know the motivation for your gesture."

"Mr. Ambassador, honored guests . . . " Moe paused dramatically.

Here we go, thought Heinie, Moe's gonna lay it on with a trowel like only he can.

"It seems to me that Cervantes in his great work, *Don Quixote*, has managed to capture the very essence of the Spanish character. Its nobility of spirit, its great heart, the courage to ceaselessly strive against all odds in defense of lofty principles. And of singular importance, the understanding that to fail is far less important than the grand and fervent effort."

The ambassador, his wife, and officers exchanged smiles, nodding at Moe's words. This baseball player seemed to know his Cervantes and possess considerable insight into the Spanish character. A delightful surprise, indeed.

"We find that there is a certain similarity to the Spanish character to be found in our own game of baseball."

The Spaniards looked a bit confused as Moe continued.

"It is the striving that wins the hearts of American baseball fans. A star batter only succeeds once out of three times, yet he is revered and rewarded. The 'nice try' is applauded. And a game well played, even in defeat, earns respect. With your permission, I would like to offer you an expression of this characteristic. It is in the form of a short poem called 'Casey at the Bat,' by Ernest Lawrence Taylor."

Then Moe began to recite the poem, speaking the words to the predominantly Spanish group in flawless Castilian.

> *The outlook wasn't brilliant for the Mudville nine that day;*
> *The score stood four to two with but one inning more to play*

The Spaniards beamed with delight as they listened to Berg's expert transliteration.

> *Then from 5,000 throats and more there rose a lusty yell;*
> *It rumbled in the valley, it rattled in the dell;*
> *It knocked upon the mountain and recoiled upon the flat,*
> *For Casey, mighty Casey, was advancing to the bat.*

The elegantly dressed and bejeweled audience hardly dared breathe as he continued.

> *And now the pitcher holds the ball, and now he lets it go,*
> *And now the air is shattered by the force of Casey's blow.*
> *Oh, somewhere in this favored land the sun is shining bright;*
> *The band is playing somewhere, and somewhere hearts are light,*
> *And somewhere men are laughing, and somewhere children shout;*
> *But there is no joy in Mudville--mighty Casey has struck out.*

The room quieted and then burst into laughter and applause.

"Bravo!" someone shouted.

"Well done, Senor Berg. Gracias."

"We must invite this Berg fellow to the embassy more often, I think," the ambassador said to one of his colleagues.

Later, as the evening was ending and the guests were being shown to their cars, the wife of the ambassador approached Moe.

"Senor Berg?"

"Madame Ambassador."

"I have a question if you don't mind my asking."

"Certainly not. Please."

"The mighty Casey? Exactly to where did he strike out?"

Moe graciously promised to explain next time.

Another characteristic of Washington that proved especially pleasing to Moe was that the city was a veritable class reunion of the students and professors of Moe's Princeton days. Because of this, the town abounded with faces familiar to Moe, many of them currently in government employ. More than any other citadel of learning, Princeton University served as an unofficial prep school for the U.S. State Department. Whether it was the school that happened to turn out exceptional candidates for the government branch or that senior officials were comforted by recruits who bore the names of friends and colleagues would be difficult to determine. In any case, the system seemed to work to the satisfaction of all.

It was therefore hardly a surprise that in the spring of his third season with the Senators, Moe bumped into a familiar face outside the ballpark.

"Kit! Kit Mill, great to see you. How've you been? You look wonderful!"

"So do you, old man. It's the absolute top seeing you again. I see you're still dressing like an undertaker," said Kit, referring to Moe's habitual preference for somber suits and ties. They both laughed as the shared old gibe was revived. Christopher Mill's characteristic broad grin was a welcome sight, thought Moe, as the two former teammates pummeled each other. The blond, blue-eyed Mill, stylishly appointed in a straw boater and white Palm Beach suit, had been the second baseman of the Princeton nine, the other half of the sterling double play combination that included shortstop Moe Berg. This was the legendary team that went two years without a loss--nineteen consecutive games, a collegiate record that stood for many years.

"Last time I saw you, you were headed to Brooklyn to play for the Dodgers."

"I was, Kitter," said Moe. "They lost both their shortstops to injuries so they were forced to call in a college man."

"And the pitching?" Kit asked almost solemnly. "Was it tough?"

"Let's say it was different."

"Different?"

"Yup, so different I had a heck of a time hitting it."

Both men nodded knowingly at that.

"But you didn't stay with the Dodgers . . ."

"At the end of the season I went to Paris to study French philology at the Sorbonne. Spent every nickel the Dodgers paid me."

"I read you were playing for the White Sox. How'd you wind up in Chicago?"

"They brought me up from Reading in the minors."

"I always liked Chicago."

"Chicago's great, and the White Sox organization, good people. They allowed me to report late for spring training so I could finish up my law studies at Columbia."

"Oh, so it's barrister Berg I'm addressing. I'm impressed."

"Aw, well . . . but what about you, Kit? What have you been up to all these years?"

"Oh, nothing very remarkable I'm afraid. Been with the State Department most of the time. Took the grand tour with a favorite aunt after graduation. Then a friend of my father's got me a junior position in State. I'm a supervisor now, it's interesting work. . ."

The two former teammates chatted enthusiastically as they walked away from Griffith Stadium along Florida Street in the warm early evening. As they renewed their friendship, the residue of years sloughed away and they once again became boys, strolling together along familiar tree-lined Princeton walkways.

"Those were good times, Kitter, weren't they?"

Moe had two great loves at college: language and baseball, and he applied himself to both. Possessed of a highly sensitive and discerning ear and a photographic memory, Moe was able to master twelve languages, including Sanskrit. He could speak German like a native Berliner or Frankfurter, speak Russian like a Cossack or a Muscovite, or converse with a Marseilles stevedore as effortlessly as he would with a Sorbonne scholar. Moe Berg had soft ears.

He also had soft hands, which allowed this twenty-year-old linguist to gobble up ground balls reminiscent of Rabbit Maranville. Not only was he a good defensive player, but Moe could also hit. He sustained a batting average of above .340 during his junior and senior years, when he was a mainstay of Princeton's most illustrious teams. As an outstanding scholar and athlete Moe became well known on campus. That's where the difficulty started.

Princeton had institutions called eating houses, a variation of the Greek fraternity system. During his first three years, Moe gave no thought to joining such an establishment. It would have been an exorbitant indulgence for a young man studying at the university on a shoestring. Because most of his teammates were members, Moe could dine as a guest. In his senior year, however, Moe decided that he would like to indulge in the extravagance of membership, so he made a formal request to join.

It must be remembered that the institutions of academia of the twenties, thirties, and forties were conservative, hidebound, and elitist, and, where social aspects came to the fore, downright snobbish. After all, who but the members of the upper classes could afford to send their offspring to a university? When it came to intermingling, exceptions might be permitted in the classroom but never at dinner.

The answer to Moe's request was delivered affably and most definitely.

"Why bother, old chum," said the eating-house representative, offering what he felt was his most sincere smile. "You're always welcome as a guest of one of the members. No point to joining up, really. I'm sure you understand. There's a good fellow."

Moe did not understand. He once thought of these young men as friends. Even years later the hurt was as evident as it was then. At the time, Moe made no response to the rejection. Instead, embarrassed and disillusioned, he tacitly accepted the decision and hoped that the matter would disappear.

But his friend and teammate Kit Mill elected not to be so accepting. Instead he was openly irate when he heard the news. He cornered the eating-house officers and insisted on a more specific explanation for his friend's rejection.

"Jewish, you know, that makes it impossible--the other chaps won't stand for it," was the answer.

Kit knew the answer, he just wanted to hear it spoken.

Young Mill promptly set out to organize a boycott of Princeton eating houses by athletes and other students. He received a surprising amount of support for his cause, so much, in fact, that the eating-house directors contrived a "provisional" membership to offer to the Semitic son of old Nassau. Moe accepted their compromise more out of desire to end the mawkish controversy than any sense of vindication.

This single, painful experience, which marred an otherwise idyllic four years at school, was vividly recalled. I had nearly forgotten, Moe thought as he walked with his friend. Those fellows, young men of privilege and breeding, they're just as narrow and prejudiced as the garden variety bigots one finds everywhere. They just had better manners. . .I just didn't realize it then.

"Sorry, Kit, my mind was wandering. What is it you just said?"

"I said that I have a confession to make."

The big man quieted, his dark eyes focusing more intently on his friend.

"Our meeting this afternoon wasn't a coincidence."

26

"Go on," nodded Moe.

"I've been sent to ask if you'd like to participate in the Major League Baseball Exhibition Tour of Japan this fall."

Moe's eyes brightened and he barely suppressed a grin.

"You speak Japanese, I understand."

Moe nodded that he did.

"So you might help out with the interpreting and such. So far, we've got Ruth, Gehrig, Foxx, and Simmons lined up to go. Charlie Berry of Philadelphia will be one catcher. You'll be the other. All expenses paid. A goodwill tour, about fifteen, twenty games. You know how they love baseball over there. What do you think?"

"I'd love to go," Moe answered without a moment's hesitation. "This is swell. I'd be honored to go. When do we leave? Sounds like great fun."

"I'm glad you're amenable," said Kit. "You'll get a formal request to join the team from Connie Mack. There's just one more thing. We'd like you to do us a little favor."

"Certainly, Kit, if I can."

"It might entail some personal risk," Kit said.

"Go on . . ."

UNDER GRAPHITE-SMUDGED SKIES and into a wind-driven, face-sting-
ing drizzle, the *Empress of Japan* departed Vancouver, British
Columbia, in late October 1934 and steamed into the angry
north Pacific destined for Yokohama. On board the *Empress*
were most of the stars in America's baseball firmament. There
was manager Connie Mack, Babe Ruth, Lou Gehrig, Jimmy
Foxx, Al Simmons, Charlie Gehringer, Lefty Gomez, Lefty O'Doul,
Charlie Berry, Earl Averill, Clint Brown, Frank Hayes, Joe
Carascarella, Ed Miller, and Earl Whitehill, just to name a few.
Most of them brought their families along on the generous invitation of Matsutaro Shoriki, owner of the Yomiura newspaper
chain that cosponsored the trip.

The cruise was one long celebration, toned down slightly by
the presence of the players' wives, but exhuberantly festive
nonetheless. Some rough weather during the first week of passage thinned the ranks of revelers, but as the seas calmed, the
party was fully joined by all.

It was generally understood that Moe Berg, backup to catcher Charlie Berry, was on the trip primarily for his ability to translate. The superstars of the game assembled on the ship were
aware of his status as a second eschelon player. The wives, however, viewed Moe as something very much out of the ordinary.
He was an educated man, something rare in the social order of
professional baseball, mannered, charming, and erudite compared with the rough talking, unlettered lads they had married.

There was one thing more, however, that fastened the attention of the players' wives on Morris Berg. He was a bachelor, and a good-looking one at that.

"What's a fella like you doing playing baseball?"

"Well, I . . ."

"And you're a lawyer, I understand?"

"Yes, I . . ."

"And, Moe, you promised me this dance."

"Did I? Oh, yes, of course I did."

It seemed that every player's wife viewed Moe as a genuine catch and was keen to help him straighten out his life, which meant in most cases urging him to find a nice girl and settle down.

"Jew husbands never beat up their wives," one would remark sagely, as the baseball wives gossiped into the wee hours.

"Yeah, and they're good providers, I understand."

The klatch nodded in assent.

One evening, after all the fox-trots had been trotted, the lindies hopped, and the ship was growing quiet, Moe retired to his cabin to contemplate the recent events and the peculiar attention the team wives had paid to him.

The ladies are a bit presumptuous and their flirting is certainly harmless but I wonder what it is that troubles them so. I suppose they'd like to see me living a more upstanding and conventional life. "You could do something important," they tell me, as if baseball wasn't important. It certainly should be important to them. In fact, several of them entered their husbands' lives as baseball Annies, the women who loiter around lobbies of hotels where the players stay. Strange how they seemed to be nearly frantic to turn me toward some ideal of propriety and respectability. Marriage? A professional career outside of baseball. I suppose one day I will practice law. . .when my playing skills have left me, but, heck, right now I couldn't be happier-- doing precisely what I want. Free as a bird. And, frankly, I haven't yet met the girl that I'd consider spending my life with. No, the well-meaning ladies are wrong! When the time comes to

29

settle down, I'll know it. In the meantime, I'm a baseball player. A major leaguer. I'm not wasting my life, I'm having the time of my life.

As the major leaguer shut his eyes and drifted toward the dreamy border of sleep, his final thought was: Tell me, old chum, why do you continually feel the need to convince yourself of that?

When the *Empress* docked, the entire city of Yokohama turned out to welcome the All-Stars. On the short ride to Tokyo, the road was lined with cheering school children who had been given the day off in honor of the occasion. Cheering throngs filled the streets as the convoy of athletes and wives entered the city in a blizzard of paper raining down from nearly every tall building in a remarkable imitation of a New York ticker tape parade. The Ginza district was so congested that no other vehicles could move for hours. Even Babe Ruth, who fully expected to be at the center of the adulation, was visibly moved by the outpouring. The next day at the official welcoming ceremony a commemorative scroll was presented to each player while floral bouquets were graciously proffered to wives and family members by kimono-clad daughters of the Japanese officials. The charming ceremony was punctuated by a thundering "Banzai Babe Ruth."

The Sultan of Swat turned to Moe Berg and said, "This has to be one of the greatest days of my life. Moe, could you tell them for me?"

Moe nodded, then stepped forward and conveyed his friend's heartfelt words into the public-address system. The crowd's response to the Babe's expression of gratitude was louder and more exuberant than before. The official goodwill delegation of American All-Stars and their families was warmly welcomed to the Island Empire of Japan.

Game twelve of the exhibition series was scheduled for Friday, November 29. It was to be played at the Omiya Grounds about a half hour's bus ride north of Tokyo. As the busload of athletes and retainers pulled away from the hotel, the still air and cloudless sky promised an unseasonably warm day for the game. The Bambino rode to the ballpark with a yellow paper parasol at his side. Later, when he took his place in right field, he would open it to shade himself from the sun and generate some good-natured chuckles from the fans. On this day Moe Berg did not board the bus to the ballpark. Charlie Berry would have to do the catching.

It was nearly noon when Moe emerged from the hotel. He was wearing a dark suit and a raincoat and carrying a bouquet of flowers. He strode out onto the Yasukini-dori and hailed a cab, directing the driver to take him to St. Luke's International Hospital a little more than a half mile from the hotel. It was a tall, strikingly modern building. Recently built, it was easily one of the tallest structures in the city.

Moe strode into the front entrance to the reception desk and, in perfect Japanese, requested the room number of Mrs. Lyon, the daughter of the American ambassador, Joseph Clark Grew. The young woman had recently given birth to her first child, Alice Emily. The Japanese receptionist informed Moe, in perfect English, of the number of Mrs. Lyon's seventh floor room and directed him to the elevator. When the doors opened on seven, Moe did not exit. Instead he pushed fifteen, the top floor. On fifteen, Moe stepped out. Beside the elevator was another door marked 'stairs' in Japanese. Moe glanced left and right, then hurried up the stairwell through a heavy metal door to the roof where a remarkable view was revealed, one that few westerners had ever seen. All of Tokyo radiated away from the tall building. To the left and right lay the crowded residential areas. One could clearly see the bay and distant Yokohama. Several warships lay at anchor. A cluttered shipyard was to the right of

31

some merchant ships. To the southwest were the rail yards and oil refineries beyond which lay majestic Mount Fuji. One could see the outskirts of town geared for industry--warehouses and factory buildings with tall smokestacks. There was a remote area where a web of electrical power lines converged, and farther west one could make out wide fields with aircraft lined neatly in rows. Due north was the Diet building, the seat of government, beyond which stood the Imperial Palace. All were revealed in crystal clarity on this cloudless autumn day.

Moe then reached inside his coat and produced a 16 mm movie camera borrowed from Lefty Grove's wife, Amelia, who had bought it for the trip. He raised the camera to his eye and slowly, very slowly, panned all 360 degrees of the view. As Moe completed the circle, he lowered the camera and was struck with a curious feeling of excitement, an exhilaration unlike anything he had experienced before. Was it the danger? The imminent risk of exposure? Perhaps. Moe also realized these stolen images represented an aggressive act in the interest of a just cause. He savored the feeling for a moment longer, then, changing the lens setting from f16 to f5.6, raised the camera to his eye and filmed it all again, just to make sure.

Moe stowed the camera away once again and, after retrieving the bouquet of flowers from the building's ledge, left the roof and returned to the elevator. The lift stopped on four, as a young Japanese woman carrying a newborn baby stepped in with her husband. With a polite bow, Moe offered the bouquet to the young mother. At first the new parents were reluctant, but then Moe said something in perfect Japanese that caused them to smile and accept the flowers. The gracious gai-jin and new Japanese papa exchanged bows once more. On the ground floor, Moe bowed once again to the couple, then strode out the front door of the hospital to a waiting taxi. Mrs. Lyon never knew that she had a visitor.

"Where were you today, Morris?" Connie Mack asked sternly that evening at dinner.

"I'm truly sorry, Skipper," Moe replied, "but I had to visit a sick friend."

A totally inadequate excuse, thought Mack, but Berg's always been fairly steady so I'll let it slide. Besides, we won 23-5 today with homers by Ruth and Gehringer.

Several months later a meeting in the Oval Office of the White House was concluding.

Bill Donovan, retired army colonel, Medal of Honor recipient, and former U.S. assistant attorney general, had been briefing the president on the status of American military readiness in the face of potential foreign belligerency. He made two important points. First, the state of America's military readiness was grossly inadequate and second, a need existed for an organization with the dual purpose of information gathering and the support of clandestine activities outside the continental United States. The other military men in the room took great exception to Donovan's findings. The president thanked Donovan and without comment adjourned the meeting.

"Mr. President, there's one more thing."

"Yes, Bill?" said FDR as he motioned to the doorway for Gus, his valet, to wait.

"I've been informed by the State Department that some valuable and rather fresh intelligence has been provided to us recently."

"Fine. That's excellent," the president responded, a bit puzzled by the seemingly routine news.

"It came from a most unusual source--the catcher, Moe Berg, on the Japanese exhibition tour."

"Really?" beamed FDR. "Our own Washington Senators Moe Berg?"

"Yes, sir. His information was extraordinarily comprehensive with exceptional attention to detail. The fellow seemed to instinctively understand what areas would interest us most."

"That's fine, Bill, fine. I remember the man. Threw out the first ball to him last season or the one before. Moe Berg, the catcher. And he did well you say?"

"Outstanding!" Donovan underscored as the brawny Gus Gernerich entered to whisk the president of the United States to his next appointment.

Over his shoulder, cigarette holder clamped at a jaunty angle, the president said, "Glad to hear it, Bill. When you see him next, please give the catcher my best regards."

4

SPRING WAS LATE IN 1941 and the opening-day crowd at Griffith Stadium was bundled up against the chill. The Senators were hosting the Red Sox and despite the temperature and the fact that both teams had finished in the second division last season, hopes were high in both dugouts that this would be their year. Eternally forgiving, spring holds out her promise equally to all.

Jake Early, the Washington backstop, tensed as the president raised the ball aloft and flashed his patented grin. He paused to allow the photographers to record the event. Sensing the press had enough time to reload for a second shot, Franklin Roosevelt made his throw. Despite his virtually useless legs and his bulky topcoat, FDR managed to put some vinegar into the throw. Even the Republicans in the crowd cheered appreciatively as the accurate throw thudded convincingly into the relieved catcher's mitt. Politics aside for the afternoon, it was comforting to all in attendance that this commander in chief was a kindred fan.

As the opening-day ceremonies were concluding, a message was sent to the Red Sox dugout by Bill Donovan, who sat in the presidential box beside FDR, that the chief would like to speak to Moe Berg. When Joe Cronin left Washington in 1935 to take over the reins of the Red Sox, he brought catcher Berg with him. A pleased but curious Moe Berg trotted out to the owner's box and shook hands with President Roosevelt, Wild Bill Donovan, the World War I hero, and club owners Tom Yawkey and Clark Griffin.

FDR then leaned toward Moe and said, "Moe, I'd be pleased if you would drop in to visit me at your earliest convenience. If you call Bill here, he'll arrange the appointment."

Donovan then gave Moe a calling card with a private phone number handwritten on it.

How wonderfully mysterious, thought Moe as he trotted down the left field line to the Boston bull pen with the card in his back pocket.

"Hey Moe, what'd the president want?" The Sox bull pen contingent was buzzing with curiosity.

"Does he wanna know how many Democrats on the team?"

That produced a collective chuckle.

"His son want a tryout?"

More dopey laughter.

"Or is he lookin' to be an umpire when he's finished bein' president?"

Guffaws all around.

"I'll tell you fellows," said Moe, affecting a confidential tone. "He was asking . . ." Moe looked furtively left and right, then leaned into the group, " . . . if we really needed all you men in the bull pen; y'see, he's awfully shorthanded for the draft. And he wanted to know if the team could spare a few of you able-bodied fellas."

At that the bull pen crew quieted, their wise guy grins faded as they eyeballed one another uncomfortably. Only when Moe broke into a broad "gotcha" smile and pointed at them did they realize they'd been yanked. A thin laugh of relief could be heard emanating from the visitor's bull pen.

The yellow cab dropped Moe at the southwest gate of the White House. He paid the fare and, nodding to the guard, headed up the long curving drive. The sergeant in the gate house eyed him suspiciously but made no effort to impede him.

As he walked along the asphalt, Moe pondered the irony of this son of an immigrant keeping an appointment with the president of the United States. His father, Bernard Berg, had walked out of the Ukraine as a young man and crossed the Atlantic in steerage at the end of the previous century. The elder Berg settled on the Lower East Side of New York as did so many of his fellow greenhorns. Once he managed to find steady work ironing shirts, Bernard sent for his sweetheart, Rose Tashker. Though the couple worked seven days a week, they somehow found time to have three children. Samuel, the firstborn, then Ethel and Morris. Bernard Berg aspired to become a physician but financial realities made that goal impossible. He did eventually graduate from night school at Columbia University with a degree in pharmacy and opened a drugstore in Newark, New Jersey.

The Bergs somehow managed to send their three children to college. Sam fulfilled Bernard Berg's dream and became a doctor. Ethel pursued the teaching profession; the baby, Morris, who seemed to possess the most promise of all, became a baseball player. Bernard Berg would never forgive his youngest child for frittering away his life playing a game. "A baseballer! A sport!" he would rail. "You're nothing but a playboy. For this you went to Princeton? Oi!"

I wish you could see me now, Pop, thought Moe, as he gave his name to the desk officer seated just inside the portico of the White House's west wing.

"Morris Berg? Yes, sir, if you'll please have a seat, someone will be down presently to escort you to your appointment."

"Thank you," said Moe as he sat down on a brocaded sofa against the wall of the foyer, more than slightly relieved that they had his name on the list.

As a slender redhead with pretty legs approached, Moe leaned forward attentively. When she briskly continued past, Moe sat back, a bit disappointed that she was not to be his escort. Moe always had a special weakness for redheads with nice legs.

A few minutes later, Bill Donovan emerged from the small lobby elevator. He limped slightly as he approached Moe. The limp was a souvenir of the Great War.

"C'mon, Moe," said Donovan, extending his large hand. "Let's go see the chief."

"Mr. President, Moe Berg is here," Bill Donovan announced as he ushered the ball player into FDR's small upstairs study.

"Ah, yes, how nice to see you again, Moe," the president said, flashing the patented smile that instantly put his visitor at ease.

Hurrying over to shake hands, Moe noticed sheets of postage stamps spread out on the large desk ringed by at least a half dozen bronze donkeys of various sizes. Politics was his life but philately was FDR's great diversion. The hobby allowed him to escape for a time from the unrelenting demands of world affairs.

"It's a pleasure to see you, sir," said Moe taking the chair opposite the president. Donovan quietly took a seat in a chair near the door.

"Well, Moe," said the president, "I'm glad you could come. What do you think of the Red Sox's chances for a pennant this year?"

"We measure up fairly well, sir, with Joe Cronin still effective in his player-manager role. Dom DiMaggio and young Ted Williams are certainly assets, along with pitchers Newsome and Wagner. I believe, sir, we are going to be quite competitive," Moe answered, knowing that baseball talk was hardly the purpose of this audience.

"That's fine, Moe, nice to hear. And how would you assess the chances of our Senators? I'd be interested in your point of view."

Moe then gave an objective critique of the Washington team.

"I doubt that Bloodworth will have as good a year as last but Travis's hitting and Case's base stealing should produce a fair amount of runs. And young Mickey Vernon has great potential. Your pitching's a bit suspect, sir, with the possible exception of

Leonard and Chase and Carrasquel in relief. I'm afraid, Mr. President, the Senators will be hard pressed to make the first division."

"Hmm," FDR nodded. "I'm afraid I'm inclined to agree with you. It's a pity. Now, if you don't mind, I'd like to change the subject. Sometime ago, Moe, I received a letter from Albert Einstein. He expressed concern that the Germans might be developing a superweapon, an atomic bomb. This device, based on uranium, is capable, they say, of generating far more energy than any conventional explosive and seems to be a natural extension of some new investigations in physics in which, I'm told, German scientists have a significant lead. Our best advisers consider such a weapon possible but highly improbable. My dilemma, of course, is that we cannot allow Hitler the exclusive franchise in this technology. Therefore we have initiated our own exploration into this new science. I trust you'll keep this knowledge to yourself. Now, I know you are not a scientist, Moe, but what I'd like you to do is visit with Professor Einstein at Princeton and perhaps you can bring us back a sense of how the Germans might be going about their exploration--making bombs and so forth. And then who, I mean the names of the scientists who most logically would be doing the work.

"You see I need an unbiased view. Someone with no preconceptions or political ideology to color his thinking. A person outside the inner circles of government or science. And as far as the military is concerned, I'm afraid many of our top colonels and generals believe that wars are won exclusively by men with rifles, new weapons being regarded as just so much frippery. Some of my other advisers believe that Einstein wants to nudge us toward action that might alleviate the persecution of so many of his people at the hands of the Nazis. I personally disagree with both views, but frankly it wasn't until my friend Alexander Sachs told me a rather inciteful story that I made my decision to investigate this capability for our United States. He spoke of a man who offered to build an armada of ships for Napoleon capable of cruising at high speed in any weather without the need of sail.

On the advice of his admirals, Napoleon dismissed that man. His name was Robert Fulton, the inventor of the steamship. Sachs's point, of course, was had Napoleon been a bit more visionary the outcome at Trafalgar would have been quite the opposite and our British cousins might be speaking decidedly frenchified English. Mais oui?"

All three men chuckled at the improbable image of an awkwardly Gallic Englishman.

"I would be very much in your debt if you would accept this errand, Moe."

"Of course, sir, I'll give it my best effort."

"Good, excellent! Thank you, Moe. We can help with the appointment and with your ball club. It's been so nice chatting with you and thank you again for coming so promptly."

It was clear that the meeting was ended as Bill Donovan rose stiffly from his seat and opened the door.

"Oh, sir, there's one more thing."

The president looked up a bit surprised as Moe produced a baseball from his jacket pocket.

"It's signed by the entire team. I thought you might like to have it."

The baseball fan in FDR surfaced with a grin.

"That's wonderful, Moe, how thoughtful of you."

"You are quite welcome, sir," said Moe. "You'll notice Ted Williams's signature there; he's generally a prune about giving autographs, but I managed to convince him."

As Moe Berg and Bill Donovan were leaving the private office of FDR, the president of the United States was installing his pince-nez to read the names on the American League ball. He had a broad, boyish grin on his face.

Joe Cronin, of the Boston Red Sox, was an autocrat. The fiery player-manager would instantly rail at anything that impinged on his authority. He believed a winning team could have only one leader and insisted on having the final word on all baseball matters. In truth, he was a lot less of a son of a bitch than his self-image allowed and his players respected him. His talent was that he focused primarily on the strengths of his athletes and payed far less attention to their shortcomings--accentuating the positive, as the song went, a strategy that never failed to get the best out of his men.

This morning he was in his clubhouse office, feet up on the desk, contemplating some lineup changes, when the phone rang. It was Tom Yawkey, the owner.

"How are you, Mr. Yawkey, uh, Tom," Joe responded, trying to sound as matter of fact as possible.

The communication was brief.

"One of your men, Moe Berg, needs to take off tomorrow. Let him."

"Sure thing, Mr. Yawkey."

"Thank you, Joe."

"No problem. Good-bye."

Cronin was glad he left out "sir" as he hung up the phone. He liked to think of himself as fearless but owners always seemed to intimidate him.

Later, in the clubhouse, as the players were engaged in their usual pregame routine--horseplay, dressing, and discussion of the sports pages for revealed truths and hidden meanings--manager Cronin walked in. He was wearing his new slippers, a recent gift from his wife, which were much too large. The slippers made a funny "shalaap shalaap" sound as he strode into the carpeted room. The players disguised their amusement. One did not readily laugh at manager Cronin's expense. Moe Berg was just removing his necktie and draping it neatly on a peg in his cubby.

"Skip," he said, addressing the manager. "I'd like to take off tomorrow, if it's all right with you. I've got some personal business."

The clubhouse got quiet. Those who had overheard got quiet. Those who had not, got quiet from the quiet.

"No problem," said Cronin, sounding impossibly affable. "I'll have Beezer go to the bull pen."

The exchange was over. Moe continued undressing and Cronin continued his floppity walk to the training table where he poured himself a glass of orange juice. As Cronin returned to the sanctuary of his office, the dressing room noises resumed.

"He must be getting soft," murmured Doerr to Peacock, who was double-knotting his laces.

The two looked at each other for a moment and then shook their heads in unison.

"Nah!"

THE APPOINTMENT WITH PROFESSOR EINSTEIN was scheduled for Tuesday morning. The fellow on the phone, Dr. Stoltz, administrative assistant to Dr. Einstein, didn't seem particularly keen on the idea. He was very protective of his famous charge. Stoltz believed that no intrusion upon the professor's valuable time could be warranted, especially an intrusion by the government, and he made these feelings clear. Because this request came from so far up, however, Stoltz's protests were waved aside. On the telephone he had made an issue of calling himself *Doctor* Stoltz. Moe wondered if the reluctance he sensed in "Dr. Stoltz" would be inhibiting in his meeting with Einstein. No outsider to academia, Moe could converse easily with the most pedantic of scholars.   He also knew that this kind of posturing was usually characteristic of academics who hadn't yet won their spurs.

It was a fine clear day that May afternoon in Princeton, New Jersey.   Moe, just off the train from Boston via Manhattan, decided to walk to the campus because he was early for his 2:00 p.m. appointment.   Above, a covey of white clouds played bumper cars in the bright blue backdrop, providing amiable company for his stroll. The school had changed little since Moe attended classes here as an undergraduate. It felt like a homecoming. The new Institute for Advanced Study was some three miles southwest of the main campus. Fuld Hall was built as a showcase for Professor Einstein and over the years had attracted some of the finest minds in physics and mathematics.

Einstein had no scheduled lecturing responsibilities. He divided his time between consultation with faculty and graduate students and personal work. His work methods at the institute could best be described as informal; he often wandered into an empty classroom and covered the blackboards with equations and other cosmic musings. To the horror of the institute's administrators, the chalk was usually erased by the professor who next occupied the room. Subsequently a graduate student was assigned to follow Einstein in his roamings and copy his chalky ruminations on paper. Who knows, perhaps somewhere in those scribblings lies the key to harness gravity or faster-than-light space travel.

As Moe approached the broad, grassy quadrangle of Fuld Hall, he noticed a person who appeared to be a caricature of the famous scientist walking toward him. Nah, couldn't be; but it is. Is it? Yes! He's certainly not very concerned with his appearance, thought Moe.

Albert Einstein, the world's most celebrated intellect, was wearing two sweatshirts against the chill, the top one inside out, tan corduroy trousers, tennis shoes, and no socks. His hair was long and frizzed, obviously not having this day engaged a comb, and he was sporting a two- day growth of graying stubble on his face.

"Professor Einstein," said Moe hoping not to shatter the great man's reverie.

Einstein looked up and said in an accent, "Hello, nice to see you," and continued walking.

Moe turned to keep pace with him and said, "Professor Einstein, I'm Morris Berg. I'm here on behalf of the White House. I would like to talk to you about your letter to the president."

Einstein slowed, folded down the corner of the equation he was exploring in his mind, turned, and then, smiling, gestured to a nearby bench.

"Morris Berg, the baseballer?" said the planet's resident genius.

Morris Berg never particularly held with humility. He viewed it as an affectation. All his life he had been the big engine that could. He knew what he could do, which was most mental and physical things, and he freely acknowledged the things that he couldn't. To be recognized by one of the most famous minds of all time, however--that was truly flattering.

They talked about the war in Europe, the health of President and Mrs. Roosevelt, and Einstein's satisfaction at having been invited to dinner at the White House next month. He confided to Moe that he planned to bring his violin and play for the presidential couple and their guests, and did Moe think Beethoven was inappropriate. They even talked baseball. Moe had written an article for the *Atlantic Monthly* delineating the requirements entailed in the positions of catcher and pitcher--a sort of in-depth job description. Einstein said he had not only read it but that he also enjoyed it very much. What else could Moe do but tell the physicist that he had read the paper on special relativity and "uh, enjoyed it very much." As he said the words, he realized how stupid it must have sounded considering only a handful of people in the world fully understood the theory. Einstein smiled, though, and seemed genuinely pleased with the compliment.

Moe Berg was a serious and gifted linguistic scholar but he was also somewhat familiar with the scientific principles associated with the paradox that Einstein had intuited in 1905: mass was energy and energy was mass, just as ice was water and water was ice, simply in a different form. This theory was fundamental to man's attempt to begin understanding the building blocks of his universe, which brought them to the potential device, the subject of Einstein's letter to the president. Yes, it was entirely possible, if not yet feasible. Certain obstacles had to be overcome, such as the refinement of enough uranium to obtain its more active isotope and the construction of the proper environment to foster a controlled and sustained chain reaction.

No, his letter was not a ruse to provoke U.S. intervention in the troubles of Europe--although Einstein doubted that Hitler would confine his aspirations to the European continent.

Finally Heisenberg's name came up. Professor Dr. Werner Heisenberg, brilliant, capable, ambitious--and nationalistic. This last trait was offered by Einstein with concern. The nationality of a scientist was supposed to be nature. Her discovered laws should never become the exclusive property of any group or country, especially Nazi Germany. Yes, Heisenberg, Germany's leading scientist, has the background, the brilliance, and the political acceptability to Hitler to develop a uranium weapon.

"I believe if you find Heisenberg, you'll know how goes the manufacture of the destructive device."

Einstein named a few others who might be involved in such a project but topping the list with three stars was Heisenberg.

"Please visit me again," said Albert Einstein to Moe as they stood up and shook hands. Then Einstein turned away, recovered his place in his interrupted musings, and continued his stroll past the far brown brick buildings and infinity.

Later, in the administration building, as Moe was having the receptionist call for a taxi, a short, fleshy-faced, baldish man accosted him.

"Are you Berg?"

Moe nodded, "Yes, I am."

"I am Dr. Stoltz. You are late! And therefore Professor Einstein will *not* be able to see you today. It is unfortunate but, you must understand, the professor is a very busy man. It's a pity that you missed your chance, Mr. Berg," the little man added smugly.

"I understand completely," Moe said graciously. "Good afternoon, Dr. Stoltz."

Moe turned and walked out of the building to wait for the cab, leaving the pompous academic standing puzzled and slack jawed on the marble foyer floor.

Back in Washington, Moe found that there was plenty of information available about Werner Heisenberg. Every up-to-date physics text included the man and his contributions to quantum mechanics. In European scientific circles, Heisenberg was considered a mathematical "wunderkind." He had won the 1932 Nobel Prize at age thirty-two, the same year a certain Moe Berg was hitting .236 for the Senators. Moe also discovered he was quite familiar with the writings of Heisenberg's father, August, who was professor of Byzantine philology at the University of Munich. The younger Heisenberg, it appeared, was fiercely nationalistic and supportive of the principles espoused by Germany's new chancellor, Adolf Hitler. Accordingly, his close relationships with many Jewish students and scientists now became a detriment and he found it expedient to all but turn his back on his former colleagues. Thus men of the stripe of Wolfgang Pauli, Otto Stern, and Max Born, giants of the new physics, were shunned and friendless in the new Germany. As Moe probed more deeply into the background of the young physicist, he was amused to find that even a true son of the fatherland was not immune to the excesses of the new order.

Back in 1937, the SS official newspaper, *SchwartzeKorps*, attacked Heisenberg for being a "white Jew" who had become contaminated by all his contacts with Jews and Jewish thinking throughout his academic career. An exceptional and most promising career might well have been over if his mother had not interceded. It seemed that Heisenberg's mother and Heinrich Himmler's mother were friends.

"I'd greatly appreciate it if you'd ask your son to stop those bullies from picking on my son," was the gist of their conversation. After several weeks, Himmler directed the SS magazine to cease its attacks and publish a formal retraction of the allegations against Heisenberg.

Moe learned that serious investigation into the atom began in 1938 when physicists Otto Hahn and Fritz Strassman working in Berlin bombarded the ninety-second element, uranium, with neutrons and produced three isotopes of the lighter element barium. Observation and the associated calculations confirmed the enormous energy release predicted by Einstein years before. The process, not immediately understood, was eventually described as being like the fission by which bacteria reproduce. This was nuclear fission, however, functioning within the once thought to be immutable heart of the atom. If the mathematics proved correct, this fission could produce a "boom" with "a million times as much energy per pound as any known explosive." That was the portentous description of Czech physicist Leo Szilard, one of the scientists who had urged Einstein to send the warning letter to President Roosevelt. Now every serious science facility in the world was turning its attention to this phenomenon. At Princeton, Berkeley, and New York, investigations were under way. The work in Paris, Holland, and Belgium, discontinued because of the German invasions, was mostly transferred to the safety of the American continent.

In Germany, the now-redeemed son of the fatherland, Werner Heisenberg, had been selected to create the sustained nuclear reaction that was expected to lead to an atomic bomb. Heisenberg, who achieved his preeminence in quantum mechanics, worried that experimental physics wasn't really his cup of tea, but in the interest of the needs of the fatherland, he would put forth every effort. What was troubling to him was that he, like many of his colleagues, believed that science ought to be its own master and never become subordinate to politics.

Yes, Einstein was correct. Heisenberg was unquestionably the man. This conclusion was further confirmed by secret documents smuggled out of Germany by an agent named Rosebud. Rosebud, it turned out, was Paul Rosebaud, editor of the German scientific journal, *Naturwissenschaften,* and agent of

British intelligence who further confirmed that the Germans were stockpiling uranium and expanding mining operations at the rich deposits in recently annexed Czechoslovakia.

All the facts that Moe gleaned from his interview with Einstein and his Washington research on Heisenberg pointed to the need for one more important piece of information to be gathered--firsthand knowledge of the implementation of the German uranium project. This was the conclusion of his comprehensive report to Bill Donovan to be passed on to FDR.

"Thank you, Moe," said Donovan. "This is mighty important work you've done. It clarifies several issues. I know the CIC will be pleased. America may technically be neutral at present but in view of the merciless beating the British are taking over there I can't believe we'll remain neutral. For the time being there's little we can do about it but step up our lend-lease program and prepare ourselves. But I believe that it's only a matter of time. Now, Moe, I've got to ask you, and you've every right to tell me no. And I'll understand if you do, but, if you're willing to go to Germany and personally assess this atomic situation for us, we'll get you in. We want a complete outsider for this job--a person without any associations with the State Department or the scientific community. Someone who can speak the language like a native--I understand that your German is flawless--but most important, someone who can handle himself in a pinch . . . like a professional athlete. So what do you say, Moe? I don't have to tell you how important this is." Donovan, unblinking, looked directly into the eyes of Moe Berg, lawyer, scholar, linguist, professional athlete, and awaited his answer.

Is he crazy? He wants me to go to Germany? In the middle of a war? Walk among those barbaric people? People who hate me simply because I'm a Jew. Probably would think nothing of killing me. But then, wouldn't it be exciting to face them. Look the villains in the eye. Maybe it's about time a Jew stands up on his hind legs and fights back. Yes, that would be something. That would be important. That would be worth the risk. And how long can I stay in baseball, anyway?

49

"Yes," Moe heard himself say as he nodded quietly, "I'll go."

With those words and a powerful handshake from a grinning Bill Donovan, Moe Berg added spy to his list of professions.

Part 2
Turning Toward Europe

BACK IN THE SPRING OF 1940, more Americans were concerned with whether the Yankees would repeat in the American League than with the troubles of faraway Europe. As Moe Berg crouched in the Red Sox bull pen warming up the day's starting pitcher, he had no way of knowing that in a year's time he would find himself playing a key role in what would soon become a worldwide struggle. The European war Germany began would eventually touch nearly all the beings on the planet, but for the time being most of the world's citizens continued living their lives with little or no concern for the imminent disruption waiting in the wings. Even the Nazis seemed content to pause and admire their almost effortless conquest of Europe's democratic nations.

In Paris, shocked citizens were subjected to the spectacle of German soldiers goose-stepping past the Arc de Triomphe. A few misguided Parisians cheered, some wept, but most simply stared at the frightful scene in stunned disbelief. How could this happen? How could this befall the invincible French Army, the most technically advanced, best-led fighting force in the world? Every Frenchman grew up believing in the supremacy of his country's military. When put to the test France's superannuated generals proved better at pomp and parades than repulsing an invading army.

Selma Wiener stood in the crowd that day and observed the gray uniformed intruders as they strutted up the Champs-Élysées. She was a young American who had come to offer her services to the refugees of Nazi aggression in the East. Now, ironically, she found herself in the very same predicament of those she sought to aid. She was in danger and she was frightened. Not until this very moment could she truly empathize with the terrorized people in whose behalf she had worked so diligently during the past year.

Upon graduation from Columbia University, Selma Wiener went to work for the New York branch of the European Refugee Relief Organization, which collected donations and clothing to send abroad. Some two years later, believing she could be of more value on the front lines of the battle, Selma announced to her family that she had booked passage to France. The constant stream of uprooted people fleeing the Spanish Civil War and then German aggressions had severely strained the altruism of the countries allied against fascism. As Hitler's war moved west, nervous Europeans turned away from charity, more than ever concerned with their own needs than the welfare of strangers. Thus the task of caring for the refugees fell almost exclusively to humanitarian organizations, such as the Salvation Army, Protestant charities, and the ERRO, the group Selma had joined.

While still in the States, several young people in Selma's group resolved to go to Europe in the interest of the cause, but as the departure date drew near the ranks of adventurous volunteers began to thin until only the headstrong and idealistic Miss Wiener remained. Her commitment to her cause still unshaken, the determined redhead resolved to go it alone. Her mother implored her not to go. Her father forbade her. Her little brother, who had always coveted her room in their small Brooklyn apartment, prudently kept his opinion to himself. Inevitably idealism prevailed and after a tearful farewell at a Brooklyn pier, Selma Wiener boarded the French liner *Jeanne d'Arc* and steamed toward the troubled continent. She made the trip armed only with her ideals and a generous measure of bravado.

Once in France, the gregarious redhead made friends quickly. Her irrepressible enthusiasm, so unlike some of the reserved and vapid American visitors they had met in the past, was a delight to her French colleagues. Selma rented a cozy Left Bank apartment above a butcher shop on the Rue St. Rustique near the Montmartre Cemetery, which she shared with a girl named Babette LaCroix. The two young women met at the relief center and became friends almost immediately. Selma's roommate was originally from the alpine western portion of France and had been staying with her married brother and his wife. She was happy for the opportunity to move from the cramped quarters. The blonde Babette helped Selma perfect her French while Babette in turn received a working knowledge of American English. Living and working in Paris, Selma came to know the French, their love of life, and their knack of living so zestfully. Even their arrogance in believing themselves to be the most refined and cultured people on earth seemed acceptable to Selma. Now, after nearly a year, she found it difficult to reconcile how easily her beloved French had been cowed by the Germans. These villains from the East were here, today, in the city of light, and few Frenchmen, it appeared, had the gumption to do anything about it.

"Is saving your skins all that important?" she railed at her refugee support group compatriots. Most of her young colleagues had been working closely together since Hitler's initial rampages. Perhaps some of them felt as she did, but none would meet her angry eyes. These young idealists who had worked so tirelessly in helping refugees in their flight to safety simply gave up. Until now it had all been a lark, providing food, shelter, clothing, and transportation for the displaced families. Today, however, borders were closed tight and there were far fewer travelers to shepherd.

"So easily you point the finger. You are not French, you are American. And not even Jewish anymore!" was the delayed retort from young André Froulet, a graduate student in finance

55

at the Sorbonne and member of Selma's organization. He resented her rebuke, though he knew there was more than a bit of truth in it.

André's countercharge stung. Six months ago, Selma had gotten herself a new passport. Selma Wiener, age twenty-four, from Brooklyn, New York, student on holiday, had become Sally Carlisle, age twenty-four, Park Avenue, New York, student on holiday. Her friends back home always called her Sally . . . Selma was so . . . old country. Many of her college friends would be surprised to know that her given name was Selma. Eventually all her French friends and colleagues called her Sally. So it's really not such a drastic change, she reasoned to herself unconvincingly. Her new papers had transformed a working-class Jewish girl into an Episcopalian socialite on tour. The change also afforded her a semblance of immunity from harm at this precarious juncture in time--the reason that the rebuke from her comrade cut so deeply.

The new identity seemed like a good idea at the time, but now she felt craven. Sally had to pay dearly for it too. A price that made her rethink just how thoroughly liberated a woman she was.

It was nearly six months ago. Her friend Babette had picked up new passports and papers for a family of five hoping to reach the safety of England. The husband was the editor of a small weekly newspaper in Austria whose editorials were openly critical of his countrymen's rapturous welcome to the Nazis. They fled the country in the nick of time. Counterfeit papers were provided by Sally's group. They were remarkably authentic-looking documents that assured that border crossings would be much safer for these wanted persons. That's when Babette conceived of providing Sally with a new identity. As a Jew in an occupied country her movements would be restricted and bound to become even more so. As an American "shiksa," the girls reasoned, she could function with relative impunity. Plus, to be truthful, it was a little uncomfortable being Jewish in 1940s Europe. So Sally agreed to buy a set of forged documents.

The price was set at a little more than a thousand francs. The "little more" turned out to be much more than Sally wanted to pay. Sally had twelve hundred francs with her when she entered the flat of the forger's go-between, Maxim Vernay, who worked in the Palace Hotel and provided the originals for his forger associate to counterfeit. The documents he borrowed from the hotel safe were always returned promptly. The originals, used as models for style, texture, color, and printing, produced nearly undetectable facsimilies. Vernay took the thousand francs from Sally, showed her the U.S. passport and New York driver's license of a Miss Carlisle, and then took Sally's hand. At that instant she knew what the full price would be for her new identity.

Sally wasn't a virgin. She had engaged in her share of coed petting and gropings. Then there was her anthropology professor at Columbia. She had a crush on him from the first moment he entered the lecture hall and wrote "Asst. Prof. Alex Tarkman" on the blackboard. He was so. . .worldly! She went to his flat for an extra assignment and wound up drinking Chianti from a wicker-encased bottle and losing her virginity. It was so wonderfully romantic--real sex with no clothes on, on a bed and at that moment passionately in love with the man and with life. Flesh to flesh. Real adult stuff. He was a gentle and considerate lover and made her feel amazingly free, aware, and invigorated. She was buoyed by the realization that she now possessed one of the great secrets of the universe, while her dear teacher, Assistant Professor Tarkman, napped in flaccid contentment beside her.

"God, I love finally being a woman," thought Sally then.

Well, woman, here you go again. Only this time it isn't with a dashing and brilliant man of letters, it's with an uncouth, unshaven, unappealing, bellboy who never brushed his teeth.

Oh, yuk, thought Sally, as she stepped out of her dress and then her slip. I've turned whore to save mankind.

He embraced her roughly and maneuvered her onto the bed. When he started grabbing at her underpants, she took them off fearful that he would tear them. After a while he grasped Sally's hand and placed it on his penis. She grabbed it and brought him quickly to climax. For a moment she thought the ordeal was over but soon realized she wasn't going to get off that lightly. He obviously had ideas of making an entire romantic evening of it as he began kissing her stomach.

Oh, dear, thought Sally as Maxim continued heading south. I was hoping to save this for someone special. Mr. Wrong applied himself to the task with great zeal. The pig, thought Sally, as the word *ambivalence* flashed in her mind. She had learned the word in college but not until this moment did she fully comprehend the concept. She bucked and squealed and in all respects presented an Academy Award climax. Faking it seemed the best way to get this over with, but dirty Maxim had other ideas. It was now to be her turn in the barrel. He moved up on the bed and shoved his penis at her face. Repulsed, she kept her mouth closed, which only made him rougher.

"Uh-uh," Sally shook her head. "Don't want to."

Maxim shoved her backward, then reached over to the dresser and picked up the passport. He bent back the thick cover and held the pages with thumb and forefinger of each hand as if to tear them in half as he looked Sally in the eye. She understood the message and submitted to the process, which took much too long and made Sally's jaw ache. At last he reached orgasm in a spastic quiver and wilted back onto the bed. Sally spat emphatically in disgust. The insult was lost on the oblivious clerk. He had just made good his fantastic boast to the other young men of the group that he would one day have the pretty American. Sally dressed quickly, picked up her new identity papers, and hurried home. She wanted a bath, badly.

The German occupation of Paris was surprisingly low key. Except for the diminished traffic, the streets of Paris looked remarkably normal. Now and then a car conveying German officers rumbled past often followed by a truck filled with armed troops. Generally, however, the lack of overt military activity made it difficult to sustain a sense of trouble. Even the German swastika gently fluttering on its staff in front of the Hotel Crillon seemed less hateful than it ought to be.

Most Parisians were concentrating on getting their lives back to normal. For Sally, however, there was no normal life to which she could return. She was stuck, she realized, no longer in the refugee travel agent business, no longer able to return to her home in America. Should she escape to Spain? Stay and hide? She certainly could never embrace the Germans as so many French seemed inclined to do.

One hundred fifty kilometers west, in a small Breton village called Locminé, a tall, slender, old woman was talking to her priest. She was concerned for her son.

"He is in the army, you know, and these Germans, they," she shuddered, ". . . so brutal and unprincipled."

The priest tried to comfort her, to assure her that things would work out. Privately he feared the godless Nazis even more than she did.

"Madame de Gaulle! Madame de Gaulle!" A little boy in shorts and sandals came running across the square. "Madame de Gaulle, your son, on the radio!"

A bulky radio was lifted to the windowsill of a nearby house so that she could hear. She heard only the last part of the broadcast, about how the French must continue to fight wherever they are in the world under the tricolor of the Free French. Then the transmission from London was over. Not many Frenchmen heard the impassioned broadcast of Charles de Gaulle, forty-nine-year-old brigadier general, but in time his voice would become the rallying point for the liberation of France.

The officers of the German Occupation Command who had monitored the broadcast simply laughed. They were presently negotiating for all the oceanfront property in the country in return for an armistice--a deal that included all the ships of the French fleet docked at ports all over the world.

Some of the French who heard the broadcast were heartened by it. They in turn passed on the words of the general. Those words gave birth to the resistance movement.

Sally Carlisle heard those words and suddenly the question of what to do was answered.

"I want to be part of the fight," she announced to Babette. "I want to join the Free French."

Babette stared at her friend for a moment, then slowly nodded. Only days before, she had come to the very same decision.

One hundred fifty kilometers west, Madame de Gaulle kissed the hand of the young village priest and with head erect and a purposeful stride belying her advanced years took the rutted path back to her home. She wasn't much interested in the coming maelstrom. Perhaps she sensed that she would not live out the month. She was content, though, because she knew her beloved Charles was safe.

7

TwENTY-FOUR-YEAR-OLD ERNST KAHN tore open the envelope addressed to him from the local draft board. "Greetings . . ." it began. Four years earlier, Ernie, his mother, and two brothers left the farm the Kahn family had occupied for several generations and with a few suitcases and bundles of household goods turned their back forever on the old world to seek the free air of America. The Jewish family from the Mosel River area of Germany had somehow foreseen the inevitable acceleration of Nazi persecution.

On the day Ernst had been directed to appear for his physical examination, the slightly bewildered young man found himself standing buck naked amid dozens of other bewildered young men in the large drafty room on an upper floor of Manhattan's Grand Central examination center. A brown medical folder provided his sole concession to modesty. As he walked self-consciously along a raised runway past two seated men in white smocks, he was ordered to stop, turn, and face front. The condition of the inductees' feet was of immediate concern. A bandy-legged fellow beside Ernie was asked to step forward and hand over his folder so that the first white-coated inspector could make a notation. The young man was then ordered back into line. Never once did either foot inspector glance up above their subjects' ankles. They were locked almost hypnotically to a world consisting solely of feet.

Ernie had good arches, good hearing, good eyesight, and when groped by the doctor and directed to "turn your head and cough," presumably good testicles. The immigrant Kahn family, currently living in Washington Heights, was greatly dismayed by the imminent conscription of young Ernst; it had been an all too similar process that deprived them of husband and father some twenty years before. Their father, Julius, died of wounds incurred in the Great War, leaving the young family to be raised by Emma, their mother. The loss of her husband had hardened the once-handsome Emma and made her suspicious and cynical. Despite their fresh start in the new world, Emma could not dislodge the feeling of imminent disaster. Ernie, however, viewed his conscription as a potential for great adventure. It would give him the chance to escape the restrictive clutches of a family that focused too much upon itself. In America there was opportunity and the possibility of fulfillment beyond the limiting jurisdiction of family, and Ernie was eager to experience it.

Ernie was short--barely five-foot-three--but he was blond and blue eyed and powerfully built, a virtual poster boy for the Third Reich. His heavy German accent often caused strangers to do a double take--"you sure you're on the right side, pal?"

The Kahn boys grew up in a town called Bullay on the Mosel. It harbored a small population of Jews, a handful of families that had lived and worked there for generations. The town got along with its Jewish neighbors because the Jews of Bullay were never fancy. The Kahns were farmers who raised and sold cattle and dealt in wholesale meat. They were hardworking, serious, scrupulously clean, honest people, and shared the values of most of the folks in that little backwater from world politics. It had been Bullay's mayor, a Nazi party member, who warned the Kahn family about the coming escalation of persecution. He predicted that no place in Europe would be safe for them and urged that they leave not only Germany but the European continent as well. When the Nazis inevitably did come to round up the remaining Jews, there was little joy in Bullay.

Ernie was classified 1-A and two weeks later reported for induction and training. Basic was tough, but Ernie, a canny farm boy, soon figured out what the Army expect of him. After a few weeks of basic he was singled out as one of the platoon's soldiers to be trusted with greater responsibility. When he was put in charge of the guard duty rosters and detail lists, he was scrupulously fair about assignments, giving his best buddies an equal share of the dirty jobs. This earned him the respect of his peers and the acknowledgment of his noncoms of his potential for leadership.

Once, early in basic, a former ash hauler from Brooklyn named Bulowski decided that he didn't like the little Kraut named Kahn. Ernie stood right up to him telling the Polish Goliath where he could get off. Goliath shoved. David swung. The right cross struck the big man square in the jaw. Unfortunately this only enraged the truculent Polack, who proceeded to beat the living crap out of little Ernie. That beating, however, further endeared him to the rest of the platoon.

Ernie's NCOs liked him. "Good attitude" was their way of describing the little squad leader. "Can speak German fluently" was another of Ernie's capabilities that was brought to the attention of the captain. Captain Moroz had been in charge of a loading dock in civilian life. Somehow this qualified him for an officer's commission.

"Should I inform battalion about Ernst Kahn? Maybe Intelligence could make use of 'speaks German fluently.'"

"Nah!"

This training command is too cushy a job, thought Moroz. "Don't make waves. The army needs forty cooks. The next forty jeeps become cooks. Including Private Ernie Kahn." And that was that.

Just to cover his own backside, Captain Moroz had the company clerk note "speaks German fluently" in Private Kahn's permanent file folder.

Some months later, an olive drab Dodge sedan picked up Moe Berg in front of the Wardman Park Hotel. It was the same hotel in which he stayed when he was playing ball for the Senators except that this time he occupied a spacious front room and wasn't required to share a bath.

Inside the staff car were two soldiers, the driver, a Major Welch, who was Moe's assigned liaison man, and a young two-striper in the rear seat.

"Morris Berg, Corporal Ernie Kahn," said Welch as he gestured with his head toward the back seat. A week before, Moe had selected him from a dozen German-speaking soldiers. Although the corporal was not the best educated or most accomplished of the group, a quality of optimism about him appealed to Moe.

"Pleasure," said Moe from the front, reaching to shake hands. "Nice to see you again."

"Yes, sir, same here, sir," responded the young soldier. Basic training had conditioned him to sir everybody as often as possible.

Moe recognized the German accent.   From somewhere around the Mosel valley, he judged. The car raced through town making very good time in the prerush hour Washington morning and headed north to the Maryland countryside. Corporal Kahn was enjoying the luxury of sitting in the back seat of a plush new staff car chauffeured by an officer; it was a damn sight cushier than anything he had yet encountered in his brief military career. When the car turned off the main road to a gate house about forty-five minutes later, Ernie sighed. The joy ride was over.

The sign declared that this was Ft. Holabird, U.S. Army. The corporal at the gate scrutinized the typewritten orders handed to him by the major along with his ID.   He then waved the car in, popping a salute as it sped past. The other gate guard, who was taking his time opening one side of a wide double barrier, had to move quickly to keep both himself and the gate from getting run down by the car. Major Welch had little patience for sloth in enlisted men, Moe observed.

They drove through rough countryside for what seemed at least another half hour, stopping finally at two wooden towers each about forty feet high. One of the towers had a facsimile of an aircraft fuselage at the top. It was complete with an opening the size of the exit door of a C-47. A weapons carrier with two soldiers seated in it was parked next to the tower. A staff sergeant and a corporal stepped out as the sedan pulled up. These two had the hardened look of fighters, thought Moe--coordinated, lean, and tough.

Parachutes were pulled out of the back of the GI truck, at which time some no-nonsense instruction on fit and adjustments were given by the NCO.

"Make sure your family jewels are tucked safely out of the way or you *will* be singing soprano *all* the way to the ground." He made his point, most persuasively, Moe thought.

Moe and Ernie learned about the D ring of the main chute and the mechanism for the auxiliary chute. After being shouted at a few times, they usually reached for the proper handle when ordered to do so.

Next they removed their chutes and were given a pair of coveralls. Moe's was snug over his suit jacket; Ernie's was huge on him. It occurred to both of them that they ought to swap for a better fit but neither said a word, not wanting to incur the ire of the prickly sergeant. They then laced up high brown boots, which, surprisingly, fit perfectly.

The retired major leaguer and the young corporal then strapped on their chutes once again and climbed up the wooden steps to the top of the tower. After being given instructions on how to position hands and legs, Moe stood in the door for a moment, then jumped. He was surprised at the sudden jolt even though he was expecting it. As the cable slackened and his feet touched down, he gave a thumbs up and shouted "O.K." in what he realized must have been a near contralto. Back up the tower for a next try went Moe as Ernie took his turn. Inexplicably Ernie pulled his auxiliary chute D ring and the silk billowed out as he was lowered to the ground. The sergeant rolled his eyes as they repacked the smaller chute and sent him back up the platform. Each man made at least five more jumps; Ernie concentrated more on keeping his hand away from the auxiliary chute than watching the horizon and rolling on landing. They concluded that they both passed the course when the paratroop instructor nodded to the major, collected his equipment, including the boots, threw it all into the back of the weapons carrier, saluted, and drove off without another word. Moe and Ernie were quite pleased with themselves.

Obviously two hours on a training tower hardly prepares a man to jump behind enemy lines, do a bit of spying, and get out to tell the tale. The logic went like this: what's the point of real practice jumps when there was a high probability that they would break a leg or sprain something? Why not just give them a thorough check-out on harness and fit and then simply do the jump? The odds were better on surviving one real jump than several practice jumps and then the real one. Plus there's the fear factor, which doesn't really kick in till the third jump anyway.

"Let 'em think they've got it made," the major told the jump instructor before he drove off. "It's really safer that way."

Welch then opened the trunk of the Dodge to reveal a small arsenal. Pistols, rifles, submachine guns, hand grenades, and ammunition, in all languages. Away from the tower, Moe and Ernie proceeded to shoot at a steep dirt berm aiming at paper targets held down with rocks. It was fun popping off all that ammo. Each tossed several grenades from behind a concrete wall, both U.S. and German types.

Later in the day Welch took three new guns out of the trunk of the Dodge: a .32 caliber Beretta, a Walther PP, and a Schmeisser M38 submachine gun.

"These are going to be yours, " he said. "And if I were you, I'd learn to shoot them. Well!"

Ernie Kahn had qualified with a Garand and fired the Browning .30 caliber machine gun with good accuracy, so the Schmeisser didn't look too difficult. Moe, like most scholars, disliked guns, believing that firearms have been on the side of every lost argument since the invention of gunpowder. It might be fun to fire off a mess of ammo with cotton plugs in your ears, but it was quite another thing to seriously practice to become deadly.

In the following weeks, Moe and Ernie spent many hours on the FBI indoor range in Washington. Ernie's proficiency rose quickly, allowing him to stay consistently in the black with all three weapons. Moe, however, didn't improve. He was flinching, hearing the bang even before he pulled the trigger. The target practice did little for Moe except to bring him and his partner closer.

Both were from the New York area, Ernie from Washington Heights in Manhattan, Moe from Newark, New Jersey. Both were from Jewish immigrant families who revered education and culture and achievement. Both were far from their own--point guards in a universe of strangers.

Sitting in the range coffee shop, the two men chatted about themselves.

"My big brother is a butcher," confided Ernie.

Moe laughed. "So's mine." Then he explained that his older brother was a physician, a highly accomplished one at that.

"I bet your father's proud," Ernie asked, sure of the answer.

"Of Sam, yes! Very proud. But he thinks I'm a bit of a bum."

"Even when he saw you play ball? You must have played in Yankee Stadium. He must have seen you play the Yankees?"

"He never saw me play," answered Moe. "He just didn't think sport was appropriate for a grown man."

"Too bad," said Ernie.

"Yeah," answered Moe.

"I mean for him," corrected Ernie. "Wow," said Ernie, completely distracted by the blonde vision of a WAC sergeant sauntering by. "Hubba, hubba!"

Moe had to agree, the tall, stacked young woman was indeed "hubba, hubba."

When she was gone, Ernie turned serious. Moe smiled.

"Moe, you know more about this than I do, I'm sure. I just volunteered for a mission. I speak German, you know."

"Yeah, I know."

"So we must be going to Germany. But for what?"

What the hell, thought Moe. We're old paratrooper buddies. Might as well tell him a little.

"We're going in to find a scientist who may be building a secret weapon for Hitler. Our job is to find out how far along it is and gum up the works if we can."

"Do we have to kill the scientist?" asked the corporal.

"Well, maybe that too." Moe acknowledged.

"Good," said Ernie, thinking about it. "With a really terrible weapon they could do anything they wanted. They could kill people. Kill us. And nobody could stop 'em. If *we* could stop them we could save a lot of lives."

The pure honest logic struck Moe. Until now, he had treated this like a challenge or an adventure--just another complicated and difficult personal test, like a chess game or politics, only more important. Ernie had brought it down from its pedestal. It was simply good against the vilest kind of evil. It was moral.

"Hey, Moe," said Ernie slyly, being completely aware of the big man's ineptitude with the firearms, but too polite to have mentioned it before, "why don't you put the face of that big scientist in the bull's-eye next time you shoot. Maybe you'll hit something."

Next Tuesday night at the range the pale visage of Werner Heisenberg shimmered in the black area of the paper target. It was projected from Moe's memory of a photograph taken at a Swiss symposium of European mathematicians. Werner never even flinched as he took five slugs between the eyes.

"Better," murmured Welch as he stood at the back of the range behind the shooters.

68

SECOND LT. EUGENE GURNEY was receiving training in a squadron of P-40 Warhawks out of Amarillo, Texas. The instruction came easy to him and he was quickly singled out as a natural pilot. After three weeks he was designated flight leader. That meant leading a group of three or more planes on the daily training missions they flew, which usually consisted of shooting landings, strafing some junked cars out in the desert, or taking on another fighter squadron in the mock dogfights called "pin the tail on the Warhawk." Sometimes training took the form of a simple cross-country exercise. Second louie Gurney excelled and earned his silver bar in the minimum time--hardly surprising because Gene had learned to fly at age twelve.

His father had a medium-size farm in Missouri that grew alfalfa and soybeans. On a grass field near the edge of the farm, the elder Gurney permitted a crop duster to keep his patched-up, aging Jenny. Pilot Harry M. Smith was in the big war. Fought the Germans in the air. A hero, most likely. You could tell because he didn't talk much about it. He was a nice guy, too, but he drank. He taught the Gurney kid to fly. The kid proved to be a natural, all instinct, no fear. Comfortable in the air. When young Gene got into the army air cadets program, the training was a piece of cake. Easier in fact. Easy as pie. Once, while on a practice flight, his Boeing-built Stearman trainer threw a wheel. The left main just fell off on takeoff. Gene felt it go, then turned to see the tire bouncing along the runway behind him. He bought some altitude, turned hard right, then turned into a shallow approach and greased the good wheel down on the grass while he worked to hold the wheelless side up for as long as possible. By the time the left wheel strut caught the turf and spun the Stearman into a ground loop, there wasn't much momentum left to do any real damage. "Excellent flying skills and instincts. Cool under pressure" was noted in the file folder of First Lt. Eugene Gurney.

Gene was truly happy now that the government had given him a powerful aircraft and let him fly it as often as he wanted. There was little more he could ask for in life but to zoom endlessly through the cerulian Texas panhandle skies.

The orders to fly to Washington came out of the same blue.

"Take everything. You may be back, you may not" was the advice of the squadron adjutant. It was obvious that he knew as little about the assignment as Gene did.

He got a hop on a transport to Washington National Field. He was told at ops to sit tight and wait to be interviewed. After lunch at the Officers' Club, he checked back at ops and was directed by the sergeant to report to the athletic field. At the far end of the field a softball game was in progress. On the opposite diamond were two men having a catch. One was wearing a white shirt and dark pants, the other in a T-shirt and khakis. As Gene approached, the two stopped their activity, walked toward each other, and shook hands. The T-shirted soldier then turned and with his uniform shirt over his arm walked toward the ops building. As he came abreast of Gene, the soldier shrugged his shoulders and rolled his eyes to the heavens as if to say, "Don't ask me, buddy." Gene walked up to the big man; a hand and a smile were extended.

"Gene Gurney? I'm Morris Berg. Nice to meet you. You can call me Moe."

"Nice to meet you, sir. . . Moe," replied Gene.

"I thought we'd talk, have a catch if you don't mind. After all, it's such a nice day."

Am I trying out for some nutty baseball team? thought the young lieutenant.

"First of all, where you from?" Moe flipped him the baseball underhanded.

"You finish college?" Easy throw.

"Are your people poor, rich, or in the middle?" Underhand throw in the air.

"How do you feel about rich people?" Ground ball. Easy hop.

"Did you hear Churchill's speech? Do you think he really meant 'they'd fight them on the beaches'?" Hard throw--that stung!

"What's your nationality? You know, where are your people from?" Soft throw bit over his head. Leap. Off the fingers.

"What's your mother like?" Grounder again, only faster.

"And your father?" High throw into the sun. Juggled but caught.

"What do you think of the Germans?" Hard grounder. Right through his legs.

"Do you know anything about Hitler?" Easy flip.

"What do you think of the pope?" Hard grounder with lots of spin. Bad hop comes up and hits him on the arm. Gene picks up the ball and returns it very hard.

"You got a girl?" Easy throw but way to his right. Gets to it but drops it.

"Are you a virgin?" Over his head. Can't reach it.

"Are you hoping to get a medal?" Nice easy throw.

"Do you think Negroes should be allowed to fight?" Grounder to his left. Nice catch.

"How about Negro officers?" Another nasty grounder. Hard and squiggly. Gene blocks this one with his chest, then picks it up and throws it back with just a bit of extra zip.

"What kind of plane do you fly?" Nice easy throw.

"How much money does your dad have in the bank?" Another easy throw.

"Why did you volunteer to go on a dangerous mission?" Short throw making Gene run in.

"What's your favorite baseball team?" Another short throw making Gene come closer.

"The Cardinals! You gotta be kidding!" At which point Moe sticks out his hand, smiles, and shakes good-bye to Lieutenant Gurney. "Thanks for the catch, Gene. I enjoyed it See you around."

The next fellow to be interviewed was just arriving as Gene picked up his khaki shirt and began to walk back to the headquarters building. He could only offer the new guy a puzzled shrug and eyeroll as they passed. As Gene Gurney was tucking in his shirt going up the wooden steps of the operations building, he thought to himself, What the heck was that all about? I'm not sure I want to be on this baseball team. I should have lied about being a virgin. Damn! I know I didn't get it.

"I'll take Gurney," said Moe to Major Dineen. "He's smart but not intellectual. Decent and shows some guts, but he's not mean. And he can get riled but still control it. Good self-discipline, and he learns fast. Can't play ball worth a damn though, but still, I want Gurney."

THE LONE AIRCRAFT EXECUTED AN ADROIT TURN from base leg to final approach, aligning itself to the exact center of the long runway at the Biggin Hill Royal Air Force Base. Its landing lights sparkled in the fading light as the twin-engined transport flared out expertly and settled gently onto the concrete landing strip as if its cargo were freshly laid eggs. Near the end of the runway, the driver of the "follow me" jeep acknowledged the landing with an approving nod, then flashed his headlights and bade the C-47 give chase to the operations area. There the shiny new Dakota, as the Douglas DC-3 was called by the Brits, was chocked and shut down, its four thousand-mile transatlantic journey, by way of Keflavic, Iceland, finally concluded. The aircraft and its cargo of medical supplies, lubricants, electrical generators, Spam, toilet paper, and one carefully crated jukebox containing the latest hits from the States were all part of the burgeoning lend-lease program flowing from America.

Three passengers aboard stepped down to the ramp from the aluminum steps provided by the flight engineer--three civilians, from the way they were dressed. One was bigger and looked a bit older than the other two. When the rest of the crew deplaned, the three passengers and their transportation team gathered and shook hands in a little postflight ceremony.

"Good-bye."

"Thanks for the ride."

"So long."

"Good luck, fellows."

"You too, Peggy."

The one unusual thing about the scene was that the pilot of the Dakota was a woman. Actually more girl than woman. And pretty, too. Any base personnel who happened to observe this scene would have wondered what in blazes was the U.S. Army coming to. Women in the air? Although that was a fairly nifty landing. Most likely, the copilot brought 'er in. Yeah, it had to be.

Moe, Gene, and Ernie were met by a young British foreign office aide and shepherded to Claridge's where they were shown to a suite of rooms usually reserved for visiting maharajahs or Arab sheikhs. These days in crowded London, modest lodgings were nigh impossible to find and therefore there was little choice but to impress some of the city's luxury accommodations into service.

"Not too shabby, huh, fellows?" Moe observed to his thoroughly impressed teammates, neither of whom had ever seen rooms so extravagantly appointed.

There was a note for Moe from Bill Donovan, which requested his presence at a meeting at the American Embassy at eight tomorrow morning. "By the way," the message concluded, "welcome to England."

Bill Donovan's large, ursine hands enveloped Moe's and pumped it enthusiastically in a hearty greeting.

"It's damn good to see you, Moe," said Wild Bill. "Good trip? Great!" said Donovan before Moe could respond. "Oh, this is Robbie Robertson. Professor Howard Robertson, meet Morris Berg."

Robertson, who had only recently met Donovan, was just learning to cope with the big man's exhausting brand of enthusiasm. As the threat of Nazi invasion became increasingly imminent, Britain's nuclear development program was packed up lock, stock, and barrel and moved to the safety of the States. In return for the technology, the United States and Britain agreed to an open exchange of scientific information and military intelligence. FDR had placed Bill Donovan in charge of the two-way flow of secrets. Robertson, the American physicist, was serving as scientific liaison to the United Kingdom's community of physicists. He nodded to Moe, offering a faint smile as he shook hands.

"Moe here has just been visiting Professor Einstein at Princeton. Straightening him out on a few of his theories, I would guess. Right, Moe?"

Robertson was impressed. He had never met Einstein himself but had thrilled to the purity of thinking provided by the legendary mathematician throughout his own years as a student. It was a giddy thought to have just clasped the hand of someone who had recently touched his hero. So he impulsively reached out and shook Moe's hand a second time.

"Good, good," said Donovan. "I see we are all going to get along just fine. Now, first I want to make something clear. Your team has been excluded from this meeting simply in the interest of streamlining our talks. Anything conveyed here or in your subsequent talks with Robbie, you are free to share with them at your discretion, okay?"

Moe nodded.

"I've got to return to the States this evening. The president's given me a big job to do and I've got to get back to start the ball rolling. I'm really glad that I was able to greet you properly and personally introduce you to Robbie here. His job over the next few weeks is to give you a cram course on the atomic business--splitting atoms and all that. And all I can say is you'd better get started soon because there's no way of knowing how much time you'll have to learn your lessons. Robbie, he's all yours. Now, if you'll excuse me, I've got some homework to finish before I hand it in to the CIC."

Donovan then abruptly turned his complete focus to the papers on his desk as Moe and Robbie quietly exited the room.

In the hall, Robertson asked, "When do you want to start?"

"How about right now," was Moe's response, as the two men left the embassy and headed toward Robertson's offices at the Imperial College.

"So, Berg, what do you know about the atom?"

The physics lessons had begun.

Robertson's background was in mathematical physics, which he tempered by acquiring a down-to-earth understanding of physical processes. This made him an ideal tutor for agents such as "the catcher" who would be best served by a broad technical picture rather than attempting a mastery of the rather daunting calculations. His lessons amounted to a cram course in nuclear physics with an emphasis on the practical side and, most critically, its attending hardware.

Instruction began at an office in the Imperial College of London University, but, because both men were avid walkers, soon adjourned outdoors into the brisk London springtime. Each day in all but the most inclement weather student and teacher could be found roaming the footpaths of Kensington Gardens, engrossed in the principles of nuclear physics, bomb building, and becoming good friends. Moe's forte was language, not science, but with Robertson's artful and energetic didactic, the lessons began to take. Moe learned of the hypothetical function of an atomic pile and the yet-unachieved goal of initiating a sustained chain reaction. He also learned what physical form such a device might take sitting in a laboratory somewhere in the Reich. The function of a cyclotron was explained along with the configuration necessary to generate the magnetic fields required to direct atomic particles into near light-speed collisions. Moe learned about uranium and its isotopes and the likelihood of the creation of entirely new transuranic elements in the search for more readily fissionable substances. The catcher was beginning to acquire the scientific patina that would permit him to engage in all but the most complex discourse in nuclear physics.

"So, then, deuterium isn't an element at all, it's simply an odd version of hydrogen . . ."

"An isotope," Robertson corrected.

"An isotope," Moe continued, "which happens to be carrying a spare neutron in its nucleus."

"Correct, Moe," said Robertson.

"So, when ordinary oxygen combines with that 'heavier' form of hydrogen. . ."

"It forms deuterium oxide . . ." Robertson explained, hoping his student was following, ". . . also known as . . ."

"Heavy water!" Moe grinned as he made the connection.

"But what role does the heavy water play in the atomic pile?"

"Fermi showed that if a neutron could be slowed by a moderator, it would have a better chance of dislodging other neutrons--in much the same way a bowling ball thrown too fast, even though at the perfect one-three pocket, will often fail to generate the necessary action to knock down all ten pins. A neutron fired at a uranium nucleus will incur more collisions if it is slowed and caused to rebound. A neutron-rich moderator will facilitate those extra collisions."

"And without it?" Moe asked.

"Without it," answered Robertson, "a great many neutrons would be lost to the air and the reaction would quickly stop."

"So heavy water is a necessary part of a chain reaction."

"Yes," said Robertson, "but there is evidence that other substances might do as well."

"Such as?" asked Moe.

"Paraffin or maybe pure carbon--still quite theoretical. . .yet to be tested out, but these substances show promise."

"But," Moe continued, "why worry about other moderators when you already know heavy water will work?"

"Because," Robertson explained, "heavy water is very rare and extraordinarily expensive to produce. There may not even be fifty gallons in existence. For a chain reaction, hundreds of gallons might be required.

"Got it. I think I understand it now."

"I think you do too, " said Robertson. "So how about some lunch? Teaching the mentally deficient is hungry work." With that he put his arm around his prize pupil's shoulder.

The two sat eating their sandwiches on a bench facing the green. Today's dreary overcast had miraculously opened up to offer evidence to Londoners that the sky was indeed blue. Britains needed all the reassurance that God could muster these days. On the pitch beyond, a pick-up game of cricket was beginning.

"Howard!" one of the young men on the green shouted. "Come and play."

The physicist and his student walked over to the players.

"Not me, by any means, but Berg here is something of a sport, I hear. Why don't you give it a go. All work and no play . . ."

Moe halfheartedly agreed. "Sure, what the heck. Where do I stand?"

He was positioned in the field and the game commenced. Much like baseball, the pitcher threw a ball and the batter tried to hit it. If successful, he would then run to a designated base. That, however, is where the similarity ended. The slightly smaller ball came in on a bounce, from a stiff-armed overhand throw. The batters didn't always swing hard; more often they seemed content to simply deflect the pitched ball to the side. They would then run past the pitcher's rubber to the opposite batter's box. A round-trip meant a run. In cricket lots of runs are made. The outfielders seemed to have very little to do--mainly stand around or retrieve dribblers that had gotten through the close men.

So far, cricket is for the birds, thought outfielder Moe Berg.

Suddenly the batter cracked a pitch to Moe's right; it was a slicing line drive worthy of Jimmy Foxx. Moe saw it all the way and got a good jump. I'm not gonna dive for it, thought Moe, these are my best pair of pants. Moe, running at full speed, stretched out his hand and with an audible smack made a one-handed shoestring catch.

Ow! Am I crazy? Catching a hardball with my bare hand? In flexing, it didn't seem broken but it sure throbbed like mad.

"Nicely caught."

"Well played" was the response of his teammates.

"Thanks," said Moe. It really wasn't such a big deal, he thought to himself. With a decent glove it would have been a fairly routine catch.

"So, when do I get to bat?" asked Moe.

"You're eleventh," said one of his teammates. "Probably won't come to bat today."

"Oh, let him bat," said one of the other players. "He can take my place. But he's got to wear a box."

In the bushes, Moe put on the "box," a groin protector like the American protective cup. As he emerged from cover, a teammate struck the ball solidly for four big runs. When the batsman finally made out, it was Moe's turn. Don't allow the ball to strike the wickets was the instruction given him by his captain.

Oh, so batting is a sort of defensive action, Moe realized. Well, let's see if I can change that notion.

It must be revealed that Morris Berg--scholar, raconteur, professional athlete, and secret agent--had a vanity. It was his hitting ability. This man, who was possessed of more gifts than God grants most men, was hopelessly vain about his batting average. Years before, in a scouting report, Mike Gonzales, of the White Sox organization, sent a telegram to the home club assessing a young minor-league player named Moe Berg. It read economically, "good field, no hit." This terse description subsequently entered baseball lore as the label for many a slick-fielding, weak-hitting prospect, but to Moe the summarial critique was unfair and inaccurate. Another similarly demeaning assessment of Moe was attributed to Casey Stengel, who stated cynically, "He can speak twelve languages but can't hit in any of them."

"I nearly hit .300 in '28" Moe would lamely offer in his own defense.

"Everybody hit .300 in '28" was the inevitable cynical come-back.

Moe even came to make jokes at his own expense. Once, when asked by a teammate's wife when he was going to get married, he replied that he would marry when he batted .300.

So here he was. In a foreign country with a bat in his hand. An oddly shaped bat, to be sure, but a bat nonetheless.

The first pitch came in a lot faster than expected. Moe was lucky to get a piece of it and dribble it to the left. It had lots of spin and eluded the fielder. He ran to the other wicket and then back to his own for a run.

"Well done!"

"Good show!"

Are they kidding? Well done for a foul ball?

The next pitch came in slow but with lots of rotation on it. Moe hitched, then swung and struck a dying drive past the fielders. The bat split lengthwise along the hitting surface. Everyone gathered around, staring at the two pieces of wood. They acted as if they had never seen a broken bat. Moe had no way of knowing that a broken cricket bat was about as rare as a triple play.

With a new bat (their only reserve) he stepped in against what the fellows called a googly bowler. The next ball headed toward the wickets with a wicked spin. When it struck the ground it took a veering bounce. This time Moe kept his hands back . . . waited, and stroked the orb deep toward the bleachers, if in fact there had been bleachers. The players acted as if it were a grand slam home run. In fact, it was better. A grand slam is only four runs. This shot went for six. Moe was slapped and pounded and well-done-old-chapped all over the field.

"Take that, Mike Gonzales," Moe shouted to the heavens. "The last laugh is mine. See that, Stengel. This Jew can hit after all."

Isn't it strange how vanity turns intelligent men into loonies now and then?

"I daresay, you enjoyed that bit of exercise," Robertson remarked to Moe as he helped the new cricketer on with his suit jacket.

Moe simply continued to grin. He had often referred to baseball as "my theater" when people outside the national pastime had queried him about the paradox of an educated man playing a boy's game. Now, as he and his new friend walked through the park, Moe understood his own rationale even more clearly: his athlete's body simply craved challenge and approval.

"Why, you old ham," he muttered to himself.

"What was that?" Robbie asked. "With all that noise, I didn't quite catch what you said."

Ahead, at the entrance to the park, a group of Londoners was gathered around a fellow on a soapbox who was shouting and gesticulating. Some of the crowd was heckling him and others were shouting down the hecklers. It was a harsh contrast to the tranquil park meadow they had just abandoned.

"All Hitler wants is to stabilize Europe. Those stupid countries are always fighting each other. He wants peace. Isn't that what Britain wants too? Then let us give him a signal that we agree with him. The divisive Jews are at the bottom of all of Europe's troubles. Jews! They've been stirring things up for centuries."

"That's right," someone in the crowd added. "They're the moneylenders, right?" "And when do they do the most business? When there are wars!"

"That's right, the Jews love wars."

"And it's our sons who have to go and die," another voice added.

"Do you want your son to die for the Jews?"

"No!"

"It isn't fair."

Moe darted forward through the crowd toward the speaker, leaving his surprised friend behind. A moment later, Robertson followed. The speaker, meanwhile, had now changed his tone from ranting outrage to calm reasonability.

81

"The only thing to do is to round up the Jews of Britain and send them to Hitler. As an offering of good faith. In the name of peace. Then Hitler would understand that the people of . . ."

The speaker suddenly disappeared from view as a hand reached up from the crowd and grabbed his necktie. Moe managed only one punch before Robbie reached him, pinned his arms, and pulled him away from the center of the crowd. With surprising strength the scientist bodily extricated his friend from the now pushing and shoving crowd and directed him to the relative tranquility of the busy London street. After they walked a couple of blocks in silence, Moe stopped and apologized.

"Sorry, Robbie, I just saw red. Sorry."

"Don't let it trouble you in the least, Morris, although my experience has shown that cricket usually has the exact opposite effect."

10

IN THE SUMMER OF 1941, Britannia had only three things going for herself: the dogged leadership of her prime minister, Winston Churchill; her rich Uncle Sam across the waves; and the "finger" that her people frequently displayed in contemptuous salute to the blustering Nazis throughout the darkest nights of the blitz. It proved to be all they would need. Even as the bombs fell, the staunch Britains were finding new ways to demonstrate their defiance.

The economic minister, Hugh Dalton, was appointed by Churchill to head the SOE, Special Operations Executive, a new organization created to support the resistance movement throughout France and the Low Countries. The resultant sabotage and harassment of the Germans would prove invaluable to the ultimate goal of "driving the Hun back to the dark recesses that spawned him" as Churchill had vowed.

Airdrops of arms and shortwave radios were arranged. Resistance groups were organized under the very noses of the overconfident Germans, who were occupying Paris as if they were on holiday. The conquerors could be observed visiting the museums, strolling in the parks and boulevards, and taking coffee in the sidewalk cafés. Overconfidence breeds carelessness-- exactly what the resistance was hoping for.

André Boudreaux was an airplane mechanic by trade. He had served his apprenticeship at the local airfield where he learned to maintain and repair engines and airframes, many of them relics of the Great War. The slender, craggy-faced, twenty-six-year-old had touseled blond hair and bright, mischievous green eyes. He had the face of a friend. Most people thought of him as "handy." Given enough time, there was no piece of machinery that he couldn't fix. To André, there was little difference between a sewing machine and an airplane. "A machine is a machine." During the past year little recreational flying was going on in France so the young man repaired farm machinery, automobiles, even leaky roofs. Whatever needed mending. He often received payment in food--vegetables, lamb, an occasional ham, or, more frequently, a chicken whose laying days were over. Bright, friendly, and well-liked, André's one fault was that he didn't possess an ounce of ambition. Easygoing André blithely faced each day as it came. When the Boshe invaded his country everything changed. The once mild-mannered young man burned with outrage. He vowed to help liberate his country and joined the French Resistance, eventually becoming one of its leaders. André Boudreaux had transformed himself into a cold, calculating monkey wrench thrower. Wearing a beret, grimy scarf, and glowering look with the inevitable cigarette dangling from the corner of his mouth, he looked like a comic synthesis of Humphrey Bogart and Maurice Chevalier. Ugh! What a mess! thought Sally. The fellow could be good looking if only he'd clean himself up. André's impression of Sally was even less complimentary and he didn't mind saying so.

"Even if there were such a thing as the resistance, why would you, a spoiled American idler, want to join them?" He spoke with the most disdain he could muster.

"Because I am against the Germans and what they have done. And I want to help. I can't just sit still and do nothing. It was just too easy for them. Somebody has to stop them, make them pay. Show them the world won't stand for . . ."

André and his two cronies listened, smirking with unconcealed contempt.

She felt the tears well up and she strained to suppress them. I'm not going to cry in front of these clods. And what a pathetic resistance movement it must be anyway with grinning fools like this in charge.

"And I'm Jewish, so you see . . ."

As this new information registered, the cynical smiles were replaced by utter hilarity. This redheaded, green-eyed, button-nosed, hoity-toity American was Jewish!

"Of course, and Himmler is an Eskimo."

They all laughed even harder at the joke their leader had made. Their leader seldom joked. What happened next happened fast. André amid ridiculing Sally and her professed Jewishness glanced at Babette, the sister of one of his most trusted lieutenants, who with a subtle nod confirmed Sally's statement. Sally never saw the exchange. She was drawing back a righteously indignant fist, which she delivered to the side of André's jaw, at the precise moment he had looked away. It was not a very hard blow but it knocked the man backward where he tripped on the fireplace screen, crushing it as he fell in a sitting position on the hearth. The group quieted so the only sound to be heard was crackling of the fire and Sally's short, quick breaths. When it looked as if André were not going to kill her, everyone began laughing. André rose, brushing himself off, trying to reclaim his dignity despite the smell of burnt corduroy. He said to Sally, "Can you drive a car?"

"What?" said the confused and tearful girl.

"Do you drive?" he repeated more slowly and impatiently.

"Yes. I drive," Sally blurted out.

"Bon!"

André turned to Babette and said, "Tell her where to meet. Tonight."

He then turned and headed to the door, doing his best to affect a manly swagger. As he exited, a wisp of white smoke from his singed pants trailed in the doorway. The others left at five-minute intervals. Probably by seniority or rank, Sally surmised, because she and Babette were last to go.

"Am I in?" asked Sally expectantly.

"Not yet," said her friend. "It depends on how you do."

They rode north for hours into the night. Their transportation, a dilapidated farm flatbed with truck tires that carried Sally, the old driver, and a solemn young man. The two horses providing the power were rejects from the German conscriptions of some weeks before. These plugs were so unsightly that even the Germans didn't want them, but they had heart and heart can often take you a long way--nearly all the way to Chantilly, the place designated for the airdrop, if, of course, there was no moon. Sally knew none of this until a few kilometers from the drop site. That's when the silent fellow riding next to her finally spoke and gave Sally her instructions. He informed her of where she was, how far from Paris, and her assignment.

"Stay with the cart and driver." Which would be parked a few hundred meters from the drop site close to the road. If she was needed she would be called. If not, go home. He would return with the others. Having said his piece, he jumped off the cart heading for the woods, an old double- barreled shotgun slung over his shoulder.

All the crickets and night chirpers seemed to stop at once. In the silence, a faint, distant hum grew into a mellow drone. Sally and the old driver looked at each other. She then leapt from the cart and ran toward the sound. Sally had been ordered to stay put but parked in the woods as they were she could see nothing. She needed to know what was going on. When the girl got to the clearing, she observed three lanterns set up in a triangle. A pointer! Sally realized. In the gloom her eyes could finally make out two poles about twenty meters apart. As her night vision improved, she could make out the slender line of a rope suspended between the uprights. The plane flew over loud and low, lining up on the pointer formed by the glowing lanterns.

"A package!" The plane had dropped a package, which was hurtling toward the meadow. Suddenly it slowed as a dark parachute blossomed above it. Package and chute lazily drifted the remaining distance to the ground. When the plane was nearly past the clearing, it pulled up and veered left. Sally saw another package fall from the aircraft. This one seemed to hesitate alongside the fuselage for a moment, then continue its plunge to earth. This time there was no chute--only a ragged streamer of dark cloth. The package missed the field and plummeted into the trees between Sally and the cart. Despite the engine noise, she heard the crash as it hit and tried to mark the spot in her mind.

Meanwhile the men in the clearing who had pounced upon the first package were still looking up. They were either uninterested in the second package or they hadn't seen it. Once again the quiet was disrupted by engine noise. "Here it comes again" as Sally put her hands over her ears. This time it zoomed even closer to the treetops. A weighted white line was trailing behind the aircraft. It snagged the line strung between the poles and snatched something off the ground. The plane nosed up as full throttle was applied and the trailing parcel and aircraft disappeared into the dark.

The lanterns were hurriedly extinguished, the poles uprooted and carried away. An eerie silence blanketed the clearing. Then, as if satisfied that the intrusion by humanity had ended, the orchestra of forest creatures resumed their concert.

They didn't see the package, Sally realized. She shouted, "Alors!" but got no reply. Sally then ran into the clearing to tell someone. The area seemed deserted. Sally ran through the woods toward the cart. She told Gramps, "Stay here, I will be right back." The old fellow didn't like it, but the determined girl gave him no opportunity to object.

Sally ran into the woods toward the parcel. Strange, she thought, it's not as dark as it was. She was either getting accustomed to the dark or it was growing light.

"Ooof." A thick branch in the ribs slowed her pace to a more cautious lope. She stumbled around for what seemed like an hour, tripping over stumps and roots, vines and thorns tearing at her face and arms, falling into soggy mounds of decaying leaves, thinking all the while, I'll never find it. Suddenly there it was, a white padded canvas duffel swaying silently at eye level.

On the long ride home the exhausted and very dirty girl found it difficult to stay awake as she leaned against the hay bales in the back of the flatbed. The contents of the package were stashed in three of those hollowed-out bales and the chute and harness were stuffed under the seat in a feed sack. The old man knew his missus would skin him alive if he left all that silk behind. At a tediously slow pace they clip-clopped their way back to the city.

A truckload of German soldiers waved and whistled as they overtook the horsedrawn wagon with the young woman on the back, but when the young Germans got a closer look at Sally's disheveled appearance, they grimaced and hooted. "What a pig!" one said, summing her up for his comrades. They shared a hearty laugh as they rumbled out of sight. They would have been much less lighthearted if they knew of the firepower accompanying the old farmer and his disheveled daughter.

Sally slept soundly on the remainder of the ride home. The farmer had to wake her so that he and his wife could unhitch the cart and put away the horses. Justifiably exhausted, Sally and the old-timer had together dragged a 250-pound sack of guns and ammunition through the woods and loaded it on the cart.

We did it. Grandpère and me. And where the hell were you, André Boudreaux? were her last wakeful thoughts as her head nestled into the down pillow in her cozy flat above the butcher shop on the Rue St. Rustique.

11

OF THE TWO BAGS DROPPED TO THE RESISTANCE THE NIGHT BEFORE, the second was by far the more valuable. It contained a transmitter, as in the first bag, but also a supply of precious spare tubes, three medical kits, two little sacks of some funny-looking spiky things that resembled oversized jacks, five Sten guns with magazines of ammunition, and three wooden crates of hand grenades--lots and lots of the palm-sized pineapples.

Sally got two kisses from each member of the team. There was never any doubt as to her loyalty; several inquiries had confirmed everything she claimed. The only question was about guts. American women traveling abroad were not known for their toughness. Sally wore the scratches to prove hers plus a canvas trophy case of priceless arms and supplies. She was delighted to find that she had been accepted as a recruit in the Maquis, a quasi-military organization devoted to sabotage, ambush, and general harassment of the occupying army. This secret army was headed by Vidal, formerly Brigadier General Delesraints of the French Army. He stayed in regular contact with de Gaulle in London and was kept constantly on the move, his nomadic life-style a direct result of the recent technological advances in German radio direction finders.

The group spent much of its time training, learning to field-strip weapons, and prepare explosives. Rank and chain of command was stressed. Their mission was considered far too important to allow individual improvisation. Sally applied herself diligently and learned quickly. The group's first operations consisted of little more than pranks: sugar in the gas tanks of trucks, switched road signs, ditches dug and covered in hope of disabling a vehicle and thus delaying a convoy. None of this activity did any real damage to the enemy. When a carburetor needed to be cleaned of sugar, the German mechanics set to it. They had their own maps and replaced road markers as fast as they were taken down. There was always plenty of manpower at hand to pull a truck out of a ditch and fill in the hole. At present the German Army was sitting idle. The armistice signed by Pétain ended all action. For the German officer corps, the response to petty sabotage helped relieve the boredom and would keep their men out of trouble. Eventually the petty actions subsided; London cautioned against them and, besides, sugar was far too scarce to be poured into some Boche gas tank.

Then word came from a contact at Villacoublay, a few kilometers south of Paris. The airfield had earlier been commandeered by the Nazis and a squadron of ME109s was stationed there. All civilian planes were ordered to either let the air out of their main gear tires or, in the case of solid rubber tires, remove their propellers--a reasonable enough request because the Germans obviously didn't want any unauthorized flying going on during their stay. Now a new order had been imposed on the French airport authorities: all planes were to be pushed or towed to a small remote area of the field. The implications were clear. The Germans needed the space. For? More planes! This was confirmed by the arrival of three new fuel trucks that would support the airport fuel truck previously commandeered by the Germans. "Keep watching" was the response from London. It was not a long vigil. Two days later the sky was blackened with aircraft. Bombers. JU 88s. It seemed like hundreds of them, but the Geshwader consisted of only sixty-six, made up of KG55, KG56, and KG77. A new bomber base was being prepared for them somewhere to the west. A shorter run to England, one presumed. They were stopping at Villacoublay to refuel and await the completion of their new air base. By the way they were parked, packed in, close together, in the grassy areas on both sides of the runway, it appeared they were planning to stay for several days.

Now here was a target of opportunity, thought André Boudreaux. A hundred German bombers destroyed. That would indeed be something. He still hadn't counted them and probably wouldn't. One hundred was such a glorious number to be inscribed on the back of his Legion of Honor.

The airport was well guarded. It would have to be a bold plan. With only a short time to pull it off. Those bombers might leave at any time.

Think, André, he said to himself, we have two cars and a lorry. We'll rush the gate. Crash through. Shoot the guards. Run to the aircraft and throw hand grenades and blow them up. We may not get all of them. But we'll get a few. What do you think?

This was the plan he presented to his lieutenants that evening.

"We'll never get past the front gate. And even if we do, on foot carrying all those hand grenades, we would all be Swiss cheese before one plane is reached."

The pessimistic assessment came from Jean-Marie Albion, the local knife sharpener. He had a bicycle cart that he would park, elevate the rear wheel, and engage a pair of grinding wheels. He did a brisk business in sharpening farm implements, plows, scythes, knives, axes, and even the cutlery for several Paris restaurants and butcher shops. He made a fairly good living with his sharpening--one of those rare humans who was content with what he had. Although few people knew him very well, everyone respected him. If he didn't like the plan, an alternative should be devised.

Hubert Fique, the area's veterinarian and André's third in command, agreed with Jean-Marie. He and Arnold LaCroix were the two university men in the group. André then looked to Arnold for some acknowledgment of the merits of his plan. LaCroix shook his head.

"All right," said André, raising himself up an indignant few inches. "Let's hear a better plan. I'm certainly willing to listen."

No better plan materialized that evening. They left, frustrated and dejected, at five-minute intervals.

Next morning, news of the big announcement was the topic of everyone's breakfast conversation. A soccer match was to be held next Sunday in the field near the church. German carpenters had already begun construction of stands with wood requisitioned from a nearby lumberyard—probably seating for their officers. On two sides of the flat field were little hills, creating a natural amphitheater for spectators. This field had been used each fall for the county fair. It was unlikely that there would be a fair this year. The real surprise was that the local residents were invited to the match. It seemed bizarre, the Nazis putting on an entertainment for the French. There were some French who were saying, "See, the Germans are not such a bad sort. Their only quarrel is with our government who gave them such a hardship after the war of 1914." To many it seemed reasonable. The truth was that the German commanders had several regiments of men to keep alert during this respite before the invasion of England. Besides, the two infantry companies had a couple of soccer professionals in their ranks and this diversion would offer a rare opportunity to bring those arrogant fly-boys down to earth. The commandant of the German rifle brigade, Heinrich Sicher, was an avid footballer, having been a second-string forward during his university days. As the years passed he had embellished his football prowess in his mind. He personally would coach the team.

One night later, mechanic, veterinarian, scholar, and knife sharpener sat down to devise a plan. The scheme they eventually concocted was so outrageous that it just might work.

Dieter Meineke was the commander of the Kampfgeschwader quartered at Villacoublay. He was delighted with the idea of a soccer match. He knew he had some good athletes among his own boys and with the men of three bomber squadrons now bunked in his hangars, there were undoubtedly more good players to choose from. Although the fleet commander outranked him (he was Obersturmbannführer and the bomb group commander was an Oberführer), he was technically base commander and therefore this event was his show.

The subject on Dieter Meineke's mind this morning was uniforms. Heinie Sicher had them for his infantry team. Elegant! White, knee-length shorts, trimmed with black piping and a black polo-type shirt with an eagle-swastika motif on the breast. The numbers on the back were black, outlined in white. He had no intention of letting his boys play in their regular-issue athletic outfits while their opponents were prancing around in such finery. No, they were going to compete in even finer uniforms than the damn ground pounders.

The young officer who had accompanied his commander to the tailor shop this morning finally conveyed this point to the proprietor. The tailor was at first relieved that the request was for sport outfits and not military clothing but then became even more agitated when he found out that the uniforms had to be ready in six days. The tailor explained to the lieutenant that this was virtually impossible. He in turn conveyed this to his chief. German officers of Dieter's rank are seldom told that their wishes were impossible. What he understood was that it couldn't be done for the regular price. So he instructed his interpreter to agree to an extra charge. During this exchange the tailor was rethinking his position. The pistols the two Germans wore were looking more ominous by the second. When he heard that he would be well paid for the work, he agreed quickly, much relieved.

I'll simply put a dozen people to sewing, including me; we should be able to just make it, he thought to himself. A reprieve can work wonders toward the development of a can-do attitude.

A red and black motif was selected. With silver piping. Very Luftwaffe.

"You see, Franz," the colonel said to his young companion. "With merchants, it's always money--you've just got to know how to deal with these types. Now, how about joining me for a coffee?"

"I would be delighted, Herr Obersturmbahnführer," said the lieutenant, surprised at the unusual expansiveness of his commander.

They sat sipping their coffee at a table in front of a small café. The passersby displayed little overt interest in their presence but in truth the sight made their stomachs turn. There was no more graphic symbol of their humiliation than two carefree Boche idling away the day on a Paris boulevard.

"You see, young man, the only place suitable for democracy is sport. In any other place in society it weakens a people."

The young blond lieutenant nodded in assent, having no idea what his commander was talking about.

12

＋—＋ 彑◊彑 ＋—＋

IT WAS A PERFECT DAY FOR A SOCCER MATCH. A brief thunderstorm the night before had scrubbed the morning air to a brilliant freshness. As the sun began to traverse its ancient arc in the cloudless sky, it bestowed its warm approval on the living creatures below it. Every small while a spring day gets lost and shows up in midsummer. Today was such a day. It made even the Germans feel good. The field was a bit damp and there was a soggy spot over near the church, but the grassy sloping spectator area was in fine shape. Blankets and oilcloth tablecloths were spread for seating. A band played a spirited selection of marches while the crowd was settling into their places. Soon infantry, Luftwaffe, and French civilians were eagerly awaiting the start of play. A rousing rendition of "Deutschland über Alles" wrenched some spectators back to the improbability of the situation but with the opening kick everyone seemed to relax again. The Maquis was also in attendance, widely dispersed through the crowd. If one knew who they were one would also have observed that some of the men were wearing bulky sweaters--a bit overdressed for such a pleasant afternoon.

The girls looked swell. Any French woman, if she puts her mind to it, can be a knockout. They had put their minds to it. The young German soldiers and airmen on the hillside had a difficult time concentrating on the game, hormones being obstinately oblivious to national disputes. With all the neck craning and sidelong glances, many of the distracted young people failed to notice the first goal put in by red and black Luftwaffe. The Maquis women were also strategically mixed into the crowd in pairs. Their task was to be as visible as possible, cheering and giggling noisily, while displaying as much bare leg as propriety would allow. Not to be outdone, many of the other young women entered this exhibitionistic competition. One had to sympathize with the French men in the stadium. They were bound to be unhappy whichever direction they faced. With so many distractions, few saw the tying goal by infantry making it 1-1 at the end of the first half.

The match continued evenly with each goal answered by a subsequent score by the opposition. Then one of the professional players on the infantry team fouled his man flagrantly, taking him down with an illegal tackle and necessitating the removal of the injured player on a stretcher. The pro was ejected by the official for rough play but substitutions were permitted to both teams. The infantry commandant was livid, looking as if he wanted to shoot the ref there and then, something that might well happen later because the ref was the colonel's chief clerk.

Luftwaffe eventually won the game, 7-5, the final goal coming in the warning seconds as infantry was straining to tie. There was applause for the victory and applause for the high quality of play. As the band played Strauss, the players shook hands. The soldiers, players, and girls mingled, joked, and flirted to the degree the language barrier permitted and then gradually dispersed. The crowd shielded the seven Maquis men in the stands who pulled off their sweaters and trousers, revealing Luftwaffe red and black uniforms underneath. They carried dirt in their pockets with which they smudged their faces and arms. Uniforms and legs were already dirty underneath their trousers and the sweaters had generated an abundant amount of perspiration. The Maquis "players" walking in the crowd looked exactly as if they had participated in a hard game.

The trucks were loading Luftwaffe troops to take them back to the airfield. The Maquis men, dressed as players each carrying a small standard light pack, ostensibly for field shoes and towel, cadged a ride on the many trucks. The elated and singing troops were happy to give a lift to members of their winning team. They were hauled on board, clapped on the back, and soon joined in the singing. Any conversation directed at any person was responded to with a sheepish smile and a raised hand as if to say, "Wait till I catch my breath." It provoked a laugh and "besides this is the best truck of singers in the Luftwaffe so let's prove it." Through the double gates rumbled the vehicles bearing men from three different bomber squadrons, all mixed together. The trucks disgorged their exhuberant cargo near the two main hangars in which the troops were housed. Many loitered happily outside their quarters discussing the match, their victory, and the pussies they had glimpsed in the crowd. Seven players carrying satchels and strolling toward the parked bombers were paid little attention except by an occasional perimeter guard who wanted to hear the score once again or simply exchange a wave with a member of their own victorious team.

Sally and Babette were taken by car a few kilometers south of the airfield. They had been instructed to leave before the match's end to reach their destination early. The driver of the ancient Citroen, which had once served as a Paris taxicab and was now relegated to suburban transport, backed it into the woods out of sight. He had agreed to provide the car, but no more. He was to drop off the girls, walk home, and report the vehicle stolen. His terms were acceptable to the group--one more case of a Frenchman who wanted to help while incurring a minimum of risk.

Accompanying the girls into the woods was fifteen-year-old Georges Lamont. Considered too young to fight, Lamont was permitted to serve as bodyguard to the girls. The pink-cheeked young man was armed with a Sten gun presented to him by André, the lad's hero and role model who had personally instructed him in its use. The girls took turns carrying a rucksack containing a pair of heavy wire cutters and a small light-duty cutter, two pairs of pliers, six hand grenades, and two pairs of work gloves.

The woods bordered the field. If the three kept a straight course for about three kilometers they would emerge directly behind the parked bombers. The Germans had erected three wire fences protecting the wooded side of the base. It was also well patrolled, particularly at night. The woods were to be the escape route for the team of sappers. The plan counted on the turmoil and explosions around the aircraft to draw off the guards.

Sally, Babette, and young Lamont finally reached the first fence, still a good twenty meters from the next fence. They immediately began cutting. A red light flashed on the board at the German mobile command post but there was no one on hand to see it. The lieutenant and corporal manning the console were at the doorway of the trailer cheering the boys outside, who were celebrating their victory over infantry. It was a great occasion. Beating infantry was much sweeter and a damn sight more difficult than beating France. Meanwhile the girls, working swiftly, cut through the first fence and made a five-foot-wide opening. They immediately set to work chewing at the second fence. It occurred to Sally that to cut only two sides then bend it back like a flap and secure it with a length of wire would save time. All three felt they weren't working fast enough. Then a dull thud was heard from beyond the woods followed in rapid succession by several more. It must be the men. They've gotten through to the planes.

JU 88s were parked on the grass in three tight squadron groups on both sides of the taxiway. Maximizing space, they were parked wing to wing, back to back. With typical German efficiency they were fully fueled and ready to deploy. André and the Vet took one group of planes, the others divided up the other two squadrons. As they sprinted down the line, a grenade was thrown at each wing root. André's first throw rolled against the fuselage and spun to stop. His second rolled off the wing onto the ground beneath the fuselage. The third grenade bounced once then rolled into the slot where flap met the wing. The other men ran, pulled pins, and threw frantically. There were so many planes. Before the fifth throw was off, the first grenade exploded. The small blast was followed immediately by an enormous detonation. The bomber lifted in the air like a flaming flapjack. Fire was everywhere, then black, acrid smoke. Similar explosions could be heard from the other two parking areas. The air was getting hot. In the middle of the conflagration five mechanics came running out from between the planes. They had been changing a set of sticky brakes. The pilot had logged the brake problem on landing and these men, squadron screw-ups, were made to work while everyone else got to go to the big game. As they appeared a light truck with four Germans armed with Schmeisers came roaring down the ramp. The terrified mechanics running out from amid the planes were gunned down by their comrades who believed they had flushed out the saboteurs.

The real saboteurs, now out of grenades, sprinted for the woods. André, however, ran in the opposite direction toward the approaching Germans. He gestured wildly and pointed down the line of burning planes as they came abreast of him. His soccer uniform continued to be an effective disguise. One of the last and slowest running Maquis, Jean-Marie, the knife sharpener, was struck in the back by a flying fragment of burning wing, killing him instantly. André kept running past Germans up the taxiway and across the runway to where the fighters were parked. He climbed into the first fighter and directed the surprised mechanic to start her up. He gave universal index finger up in a circle sign. The mechanic began cranking frantically spurred on by the emergency. Meanwhile André was trying to figure out the cockpit. He had never run one of these babies before but he managed to find the correct switches and grab the throttle when the mechanic gave him a heil, the Nazi equivalent of thumbs up. The Messerschmidt kicked over with a roar and André slammed the canopy closed. The mechanic removed the chocks and the aircraft went roaring out of the parking area.

"Mon Dieu," marveled André at the power of this machine. He had never taxied anything like it. The rapidity of the explosions had slowed now as black, greasy smoke obliterated the sky and made breathing nearly impossible. But André hardly noticed as he tromped on the left brake to spin the plane around and headed back toward the dumbfounded crew chief and the line of parked fighters. At full throttle he rammed the parked aircraft, managing to knock the tails off five of them before a burst of machine gun fire shattered his canopy and ended his life. At that precise instant André Boudreaux was thinking what an excellent plan this had turned out to be.

Georges Lamont and the perimeter guard spotted each other at the same moment. They both raised their weapons. The guard was faster than young Georges. The first short burst killed him. The next longer burst was a response to the spasming nerves and muscles of the dying boy. The guard stood over the body, transfixed by his handiwork. He didn't hear the pin being removed from a grenade a few feet away. Sally waited a few moments then heaved the live grenade over the fence toward the German. She threw too hard and the grenade struck the opposite fence and rebounded to land two inches from the sentry's left boot. As the danger registered in the soldier's brain the command to flee was dispatched down to his feet. They never had time to comply. The grenade exploded, flinging the young German against the opposite fence in a wet and writhing tangle of red-stained gray rags. Sally started toward the opening and young Georges when the first of her men appeared, sprinting away from the conflagration. Babette frantically waved to direct them to the openings in the fence and they sprinted through. Sally tried in vain to pick up Georges's sten gun but it was hopelessly pinned under him. She then looked toward the still form of the guard--a boy, hardly older than Georges, his face unmarked and peaceful. She left the two dead boys, dashed through the fence openings, and followed the remnants of the team as they headed for the car. The breathless seven piled in as Sally took the wheel and headed the car north at a slow, unhurried speed toward the remote barn with the hidden basement, which had been prepared to hide them till things blew over.

"Where's André?" Sally asked.

No one answered.

"And Jacques?"

"Jean-Marie?"

No one answered.

"Georges?"

As Sally shook her head, her eyes welled up with moisture. She tried to push the accelerator through the floorboard, and then remembered to slow down.

The box score for the day was as follows: Luftwaffe 7, Infantry 5. Eighteen JU 88s destroyed. Eleven severely damaged. Seven slightly damaged. Five fighter planes severely damaged. One slightly damaged. Five mechanics killed. One perimeter guard killed. One air crewman severely burned while towing a bomber to safety. Awarded the Iron Cross second class. One firefighter overcome by smoke after refusing to abandon a burning aircraft. He was mentioned in dispatches for special merit. On the next day one hundred French civilians were executed. One Paris tailor was interrogated and then shot. One taxi driver was shot while attempting to avoid arrest. Three days later, one Luftwaffe guard officer court-martialed and shot. One guard corporal court-martialed and shot. One crew chief court-martialed and shot. When Generalfeldmarschall Sperrle was informed of the fiasco, he ordered Obersturmbannführer Dieter Meineke court-martialed and shot.

Only the Maquis's report to London mentioned the four Frenchmen who had given their lives to free their homeland. Later when the details of the raid became clear and the full extent of André Boudreaux's heroic leadership was revealed, General de Gaulle himself signed the citation for four posthumous Legion of Honor medals, one of them first class. The

Legion of Honor, first class, is presented with breast star and red sash. This award is generally reserved for heads of state and visiting royalty, but during these times, de Gaulle determined, France needed heroes more than statesmen. If André Boudreaux had survived, there is little doubt that he would always be wearing his Legion of Honor, removing it only when he went to bed. Perhaps.

Life in the barn was fairly tame compared with the frenzied activity of the previous weeks. The group of heroes spent their days eating well, sunning, and joking, on a well-deserved vacation from the war. Bit by bit the details of their afternoon's work drifted in. They amazed even themselves. Their bold action had turned into an event that heartened the Allies on both sides of the Channel. The Free French broadcast from London called it "a great blow struck for the honor of France." This ragtag group of patriots had dramatically proven that the seemingly invincible German war machine was vulnerable after all.

Those of Sally's companions who had not been sought by the Germans for questioning or taken hostage returned to their homes and resumed the normal life of the occupied French. Two of Sally's barnmates were her roommate Babette and Babette's brother, Arnold LaCroix. The Nazis had come to Arnold's home to interrogate him and his sister. Because they were not at home, they took Arnold's wife, Claire. She was interrogated and released later that day, frightened but unharmed. Babette's brother, Arnold, was an assistant curator of vertibrate fossils at the Musée National d'Histoire Naturelle. Because he commuted to the museum each day and his tiny car was still parked in front of his home, the Nazis reasoned that this young, educated man might be a likely suspect. Neighbors, however, confirmed that this absence was not unusual because "he was always off digging up old rocks in the hills." Eventually the Germans crossed him off their list considering such a bookworm to be harmless.

Hubert Fique, the veternarian, was now the leader of the group. London urged him to avoid any new actions against the Germans for the time being while the situation could be evaluated. Meanwhile the Germans abruptly switched roles from that of visiting tourists to brutal conquerors--an effortless change, for the latter was their true nature.

Hubert told Arnold LaCroix that he believed it was safe to return home. He did, bearing a rucksack of tools and artifacts smuggled to him from friends at the museum. Included was an occipital bone from a Pleistocene Neanderthal skull, a rather rare and remarkable find for his supposed few days of scrabbling in the local hills. He appreciated the joke and the implied approval of his colleagues at the museum.

Babette and Sally were advised to get out of town. Because Babette was on a wanted list and Sally's forged papers would never stand up to scrutiny, their arrest would certainly land Sally in a concentration camp and leave Babette to face a firing squad. There was little doubt that both young women had to leave the area with all haste. The question was whether to go south over the Pyrenees and try for neutral Spain or travel through the north to occupied Belgium and then hope for an opportunity for a crossing to England. They eventually concluded that north would be best because there was a veritable stampede of refugees clogging the mountain passes to Spain.

A resistance group was in Belgium that would be happy to harbor two young women involved in such a major action against the enemy. This confirmed the decision for Sally. It would be north, to continue to fight with the Resistance in Belgium. She had earned her stripes in the organization and she enjoyed the status.

I'm a combat veteran, she realized. I've been in action against the enemy. I can show those hicks in the provinces how to kill the Boche. This was followed by another dreadful thought. I can't believe how bloodthirsty I've become.

13

AT A DESIGNATED POINT IN THE ENGLISH CHANNEL, dangerously close to the coast of Belgium, under the cover of night, a blunt-nosed landing craft was lifted over the starboard side of a war-weary freighter and lowered into the undulating sea. The old merchant ship had recently been fitted with two deck guns and a pair of ack-acks, making the crew of the *Newcastle* downright trucu-lent. In her previously unarmed state the ship had been a sit-ting duck for enemy aircraft or U-boats that elected to engage her. On their many cargo runs across the Channel, including their role in the evacuation at Dunkirk, they had been strafed, shelled, and once even nearly torpedoed--the lethal fish unac-countably veering in the final moments to the amazement and relief of the transfixed deck crew. Now the "castle" had teeth and her crew was itching to bite.

The LCT in the water was bobbing nervously alongside the *Newcastle.* A northeast wind raised a serious chop, making the launching procedure "dicey." Once again the *Newcastle's* big winch growled as an overly large, black automobile was hauled out of the hold and lifted over the side. It made a gentle landing in the unsteady boat--the bloke at the winch knew his business.

When all lines were cast off, the small craft turned and head-ed its flat prow toward the dark, mist-laden curtain that obscured the mainland of Europe. The boat made remarkably little engine noise because of a specially modified exhaust sys-tem--a clumsy-looking arrangement of underwater mufflers running forward along its port side. The contraption caused a significant loss of speed but when one considers that a landing craft is about the slowest beast in the sea anyway, silence for speed seemed to be a fair exchange.

Running without lights along the Nazi-held Belgian coast in search of a specific beach was the equivalent of groping for a toothpick in a haystack wearing boxing gloves. It tested the skill of a British merchant seaman who, until this mission, thought he knew his Channel fairly well. With him was a Belgian corporal who had fished these waters most of his young life. In a remarkable product of British-Belgian cooperation, they found their objective: a small cove sheltering a beach, too narrow and inaccessable to offer a major landing sight and therefore left unguarded by the Nazis.

The twelve-cylinder Mercedes engine roared to life as the front gangplank of the landing craft plopped into the wet sand. The big car sprang forward, damn the noise, and sped down the ramp and up the beach. This was the most critical part of the delivery and had to be accomplished swiftly. As fate and rear-wheel drive would have it, however, the heavy car lost its traction in the soft sand and groaned to a halt. "Oh, merde," was the consensus as a rear wheel spun frantically digging itself in up to the axle until it was impossibly stuck--and this was low tide. There was little hope that three men could push the Mercedes free.

As the skipper was contemplating backing away and leaving this cock-up behind, his crewman ran out of the boat, past the car, and up the beach. He was headed toward the tree line beyond the dunes with steel cable in tow, which was spooling off the craft's winch.

Of course! Why didn't I think of that! thought the English skipper.

The lad was sprinting back with the cable. He had run it around the two sturdiest of the small trees--little more than large bushes--and was hoping the cable would reach the mired car. About ten meters from the vehicle he stopped short. The cable had run out. This time, though, the skipper provided the idea.

"We've got the tie-downs for the car plus the lengths of cable that connected up the four corners of the pallet on which the car was lowered. We'll link 'em together."

They made up the difference with feet to spare and with a clanking of the old, encrusted winch, the big limo was pulled free. Once on firm ground the Mercedes reverted to its competent, teutonic self, easily negotiating the narrow path to the road used by bathers and picnickers. The big, stately car was now on pavement and ready to roll. All tracks and signs of the landing were obliterated and the oilskin packet containing forged registration and motorpool disposition papers were handed to the young Belgian, attesting to his position as driver for the local German motor pool. His orders stated that he was to deliver this recently repaired staff car to some Nazi party mucky-muck. The papers even included a properly signed and stamped repair order for some extensive transmission work.

The men shook hands and took leave of one another like the best of old war comrades. They had been strangers only hours before, but the past half hour had brought them close, each man realizing that he had met a man upon whom he could depend. Such things are not taken lightly.

The strange little craft backed away noiselessly into the gloom as the German car turned inland heading into the familiar European countryside in search of a place to hide until the time its services would again be required.

It was barely an hour later when the gray Horch weapons carrier stopped on the road above the little beach. Its spotlight slowly played along the water's edge.

"Nothing going on," said Gunther to Kurt. "It's quiet tonight."

The searchlight was switched off and the patrol headed for the next stretch of shoreline on their route.

14

THE ADMINISTRATORS OF THE FREE UNIVERSITY OF BRUSSELS were
directed by German occupation officials to prepare for the visit
of the great scientist.   The German Nobel Laureate, Werner
Heisenberg, would be arriving within a fortnight.   The stated
purpose for the trip was given as an attempt to stimulate "academic intercourse" between the countries. In reality, Heisenberg
was there to put his dibs on a quantity of uranium ore that was
presently languishing in the holds of freighters moored in
Belgian Congolese ports.   Faced with the German occupation,
the Belgians cut off the flow of the unrefined ore, rather than
allow the precious material to fall into Nazi hands. Heisenberg
was hoping to obtain the ore with words of reason and thus
spare his Belgian colleagues exposure to the Gestapo's notorious
requisitioning methods.

Word of Heisenberg's visit had leaked out and was passed to
London by one of the radios the British SOE had been supplying
to the resistance.

The information arrived at U.S. intelligence purely by hap-
penstance. During their morning coffee a junior American intelligence officer and his British counterpart were engaged in a
chauvanistic debate over shortwave radios.

"Mine's smaller than yours," maintained the Yank.

"But mine's better than yours," countered the Brit.

The British sets, in fact, were large and cumbersome, nearly the size of a suitcase. They were virtually identical to the commercial transmitters used for years by French and English ham operators as they chatted across the Channel during better times. The diminutive American sets were designed with the properties of lightness, ruggedness, and extended range.

"But surely you can't compare a Rolls-Royce to a Chevrolet, old chap," the Brit said, hoping to at least lose with dignity. "Why, we just had word on one of our sets that some big shot Nazi scientist named Heisenberg is visiting Belgium from Berlin."

A little bell chimed for the young American. He remembered the name from a recent briefing and made a mental note to mention it.

That was a bit of luck as the British like to put it. The information on Heisenberg's trip might never have been revealed to the Americans had it not been for the agreement arrived at by the cousin countries on nuclear experimentation. When England shipped its laboratories and uranium supply to the United States, they insisted on an open exchange of information and regular progress reports, which also came to include general intelligence gleaned from sources in Europe. Accordingly, America kept a small cadre of intelligence liason people in London at this time. These operatives would later become the core of the American OSS, headed by Bill Donovan.

The catcher, the farm boy, and the butcher's little brother took off from Biggin Hill, England, two nights after the news of Heisenberg's trip was confirmed. They sat quietly in fold-down aluminum seats as their camouflaged Dakota burrowed through the gloom over the Channel.

"Say, Moe, did you ever meet Babe Ruth?" Gurney asked over the engine noise, more out of the need to divert his mind from the imminent jump than any profound interest in the national game.

"As a matter of fact, he happens to be a very good friend of mine."

"No kidding," said Ernie, "you know Babe Ruth? What's he like?"

"Oh, he's one heck of a guy, quite easily the greatest athlete I've ever seen, and far more insightful a person than anyone gives him credit for being."

As the twin-engined plane rushed forward into the night, Moe's thoughts slipped back to his early years in baseball. It was a hot afternoon in Chicago in the middle of the 1928 season. The Yankees were in town--Ruth, Gehrig, and company. The count on the Babe went to one and one. Moe thumped his mitt a couple times and settled down behind the plate, taking his time before giving the sign. Two fingers, curveball. Blankenship gave a slow, smug nod and started into his windup. Catcher Berg then moved his mitt slightly to his left, providing a low out-side target. The Babe noticed the movement in the extreme peripheral vision of his left eye and responded by inching his front foot forward and closer to the plate as the pitch was being delivered. The fifty-two-ounce bat interrupted the baseball's trajectory with a resounding crack.

No national anthem ever written can propel a crowd to its feet like the sound of hardwood striking a leather-covered sphere. Twenty-eight thousand fans simultaneously inhaled as the ball streaked into the hazy blue above the right center field fence. The Babe took a few hurried steps up the line, then, as he saw the hapless look on the upturned face of the centerfielder, gently dropped his bat and trotted daintily to first. The Babe toed the bag, then turned and headed across the infield back to the Yankee dugout. As he doffed his cap to the fugue of cheers and appreciative boos, the Yankee batboy raced out of the dugout and circled the bases for the Babe. These were the days when a superstar could hire a lad to do his legwork.

As the Babe jogged off the field, acknowledging the fans, he passed the catcher and said, "Thanks, Berg, I owe you one."

Moe Berg spat and, readjusting his mask, muttered, "We'll get you next time" to no one in particular.

The crowd didn't settle down until a pitch was thrown to
Gehrig, the next batter. He uncharacteristically struck out on
three straight pitches, the desire to duplicate the Babe's feat of
a few moments past overwhelming his judgment on a fat-looking
two-strike pitch at eye level.

A few thousand extra tickets had been sold on that Thursday
afternoon in Chicago in the distinct hope that Babe Ruth would
hit a home run. He had hit a record sixty the year before. The
satisfied murmuring of the crowd was evidence that they had
gotten their money's worth.

Two spectators, however, remained discontented despite the
quality of play on the field. Charlie and Mack were birds of a
feather in that they both disdained the tedium of regular work
and shared a thirst for the alcoholic beverages at present pro-
hibited to Americans by law. This law discouraged few citizens
who earnestly desired to imbibe. Charlie and Mack, sitting in
Mack's brother-in-law's box seats, were consuming the contents
of their third flask, when the catcher, Berg, came to bat for the
Sox.

"Forward Chicago White Stockings!" someone shouted.

Charlie yelled, "Hey, Berg, get a hit, ya Hebe!"

Mack then chimed in, "Yeah! Get a teeny-weeny hit, ya
Sheenie!"

The surrounding crowd chuckled, partly at the attempts at
humor and partly at the drunk act put on by the two characters
in the box seats.

Charlie and Mack took this as encouragement.

"Hey, Charlie," said Mack, loud enough for ten rows to hear.
"Did you know that the Jews sunk the *Titanic*?"

"The Jews?" Charlie responded in mock amazement. "I
thought it was an iceberg."

"Iceberg, Goldberg, Moe Berg, they're all the same."

The crowd got a good laugh at that one.

Moe was trying to focus on the pitcher but he couldn't help
hearing the wisecracks. The anti-Semitic taunting by these two
palookas in straw hats was bad enough, but it really stung when

it appeared that the fans seemed to be enjoying it too. He fought to regain his composure and, succeeding, lined the next pitch down the left field line. Moe, pleased with the solid contact he had made, lumbered around first and slid safely into second for a double. Any other player would have had a stand-up two- base hit, but Berg was slow-footed even for a catcher, so the play was close.

"Get that kike a bike!" Mack barked when the crowd noise died down.

That evoked another belly laugh from the stands. Though he tried not to show it, Moe was mightily disappointed that even a solid hit couldn't win over the crowd.

The Sox rallied and eventually went on to win the game 5-3. The taunts directed at Moe diminished somewhat but nearly all the field-level spectators and players on both teams had heard them. No one said anything. Because Moe was choosing to ignore the taunts, his teammates went along.

On the Babe's last at-bat, he threw an invitation at Moe.

"Say, kid. How 'bout a couple brews after, I'm buyin'."

He promptly slapped the next pitch through the right side for a single. As the Babe took his short lead off first, Moe nodded yes from ninety feet away. It would be an honor to visit with the legendary bambino.

Outside the stadium the two athletes were mobbed by kids waiting in the Shields Avenue parking lot. Moe always tried to be gracious to fans but, in truth, he considered signing autographs a chore. The Babe didn't mind at all. He cheerfully signed and chatted for over a half hour. When Babe's pen ran out, Moe had to lend him his. They finished signing in pencil; someone had lifted Moe's Waterman.

Later in the car, Babe asked, "Where we goin'?"

"It's up to you, Babe, you're buyin', remember?"

Babe laughed and headed the sixteen-cylinder Cadillac down State Street, honking at everyone who turned to look. They wound up at Hattie's place, a speakeasy with a reputation for huge steaks and pretty girls. Moe and the Babe then downed a half-dozen pitchers of beer. Then they each consumed a steak that could have patched the hole in the *Lusitania.*

"You taught me a lesson today," said Moe.

"Me? Teach the perfessor? That's a new one!" responded the Babe.

"I telegraphed the location of the pitch you hit for a homer. I usually wait till the batter's looking for the pitch. But you saw me."

"Heck, Moe, don't feel bad, I got great perfial vision. I can see my earlobes. See!"

Babe tried to make himself look wall-eyed and succeeded only in making the most ridiculous grimace. Both laughed heartily, Moe at how it looked, the Babe at how it felt. When the laughter subsided, Babe continued.

"I'm glad those two rubes in the stands didn't get your goat today," he said as he speared a potato with his knife and swallowed it whole.

"Hmmm, yeah," Moe murmured into his beefsteak. Then as he sliced himself a forkful, he admitted, "To tell the truth, they did start getting under my skin. Just a bit. But I've always felt that it's best to ignore it."

"Yeah," nodded the Babe, draining his beer glass, "you're probably right. Anyhow, it's the way Jews are supposed to behave, right?"

"What do you mean?" Moe stopped eating.

"Well, Jews don't fight back. They always take it. Everybody knows that. That's what makes it easy for guys like those two yeggs in the stands."

"Everybody knows that?" repeated Moe incredulously.

"Sure, everybody I know," assured the Babe. "For instance, you're a pretty tough guy, Moe. You don't sit still for a dirty slide or a beanball. No sir, I seen you bark like a dog and bite like a dog; you let 'em know right off they ain't gonna get away with it. Right?"

"I suppose . . ." Moe conceded.

"But when it's about being a Jew, you're all clammed up. You just take it. Like you did today. Hey, can we get somethin' to drink over here?" The Babe bellowed over his shoulder brandishing the empty beer pitcher.

The insight stunned Moe. Unexpected wisdom from this crude, uneducated boy in a man's body.

They finished off their meal with ice cream and a large chocolate cake. The Babe ate most of the ice cream and at least half the cake.

The enormous meal made Moe drowsy. The Babe, however, was just getting started. As they climbed the stairs to the second floor, the Bambino announced to Hattie, and anyone else within earshot, that he was "gonna fuck every girl in the place!" Several doors opened slightly.

Moe left around 11:00 p.m., after spending a pleasant hour with a lovely, if perhaps vacant, brunette from Ohio. She thought that Moe was in the banking business. When the Babe personally selected her for Moe, he told her that Moe was a catcher. She heard "cashier."

"Put it on my tab," the Babe told Hattie.

Moe could hardly have behaved so gauchely as to reject such largesse, even if it did mean breaking curfew and incurring the wrath of manager Ray Shalk. Besides, she was pretty.

What a remarkable man, thought Moe as the taxi growled through the quiet Chicago streets. He's given himself up to every human excess, yet he's one of the most admirable men I ever knew. He's the antithesis of Jewishness. He never worries about what he should do, he simply does, using his God given gifts to make himself happy. Without suffering. Without guilt. And then his observation about Jews avoiding conflict. Could he

113

be right? All my life I've been encouraged to take the higher road. To avoid belligerence or confrontation. Now a friend tells me that the haters of the world count on this behavior. Could he be right?

As the taxi rumbled around the corner of the nearly deserted Chicago street, the growl of its engine rose to an uncomfortable din. Moe found himself returned to the noisy interior of a twin-engined transport plane heading toward a totally new challenge, one that had nothing at all to do with green grass and neat white lines.

"Yeah, I know Babe Ruth. A heck of a guy, I'll tell you."

The flight engineer emerged from the cockpit area and motioned the three to stand up. He methodically checked each man's chute and managed to tighten the miniscule slack in every harness. The craft was nearing the jump site.

Moe Berg tended to get calm when he was excited. His eyes saw clearer. His mind worked more smoothly. Ernie Kahn got excited when he got excited. He wanted to fling open the door and jump, right now, just to get on with it. Eugene Gurney sat in his seat like a kid going up the slow side of the roller coaster. Boy, is this going to be amazing, he was thinking as the engineer pulled in the cargo door and stowed it. The noise intensified dramatically.

The jump itself wasn't particularly exciting. Once one gets past the idea of leaping from solid footing into a thousand feet of thin air with only an oversized pair of panties slung from one's shoulders, it's really no big deal. Out they went. Moe. Ernie. Then Gene. The flight engineer was prepared to provide assistance in the form of a good shove should one of the jumpers balk in the doorway. None did. Engine noise and wind filled their senses as the three would-be heroes plummeted frantically to earth through the dark sky of the moonless night. No one on the ground observed the three chutes open.

Each man in turn experienced the rude shock of the deploying chute then heartfelt relief as the canopy of silk billowed above them. Now seemingly suspended motionless, the men perceived a disconnection from the world as the aircraft's engine noise faded away. As Moe regained his equilibrium and his heartbeat returned to a normal rate, he could make out the blackness of the earth lazily rising up toward him. It was several shades darker than the blue-black sky he had been falling through.

I sure hope I don't hit something pointy, thought Moe. Then his thoughts wandered to the word "Geronimo," traditionally shouted by paratroops as they leap from their aircraft and wondered if the word was Indian for the phrase "I hope I don't hit something pointy."

Moe hit the ground backward and bent double with the impact. Touchdown had come up surprisingly fast. As he sat on the ground struggling to untangle himself from the harness, he was startled as he felt hands on him. This at first caused a jolt of panic, but when the hands said, in Flemish, "Just relax, we'll have you out of this in a jiffy," Moe managed to relax. When he was finally clear of the chute Moe undid the special snag-free coveralls worn for the jump. They zipped all the way from shoulder to ankle for quick removal. His ankle hurt having been given a good wrench by the large canvas bag of clothes and equipment strapped to his leg, but his athlete's body assured him that he would quickly walk it off.

No one spoke. Moe was put in a motocycle sidecar, his luggage placed in his lap, and quickly whisked away into the night. The motorcycle's painted headlamp was providing very little illumination and Moe concluded that the driver must either know the road very well or be equipped with the new radar they'd been talking about in London.

Finally after a jarring ride they slowed as they approached a house in town and stopped around back. Gene and Ernie were already there. Aside from the scratch on Gene's jaw, both had survived the jump none the worse for wear. In broken English, the man who seemed to own the house where they found shelter said, "You," pointing now to Gene and Ernie, "you. Stay here." Pointing to the floor with both index fingers. "You, safe here."

Moe responded with "thank you for your kindness. We appreciate your help greatly" in perfect Flemish. Everyone's shoulders relaxed at once. Perhaps these brave men weren't idiots after all.

The three men had their first good night's sleep in days on the surprisingly comfortable bunks in the attic. Early the next morning they had a visitor, Bernardus Ijzerdratt, head of the Dutch resistance, who had recently returned from London to help coordinate the effort against the Germans.

"We must be patient," he said. "Rash actions, while perhaps temporarily satisfying, will only be self-defeating in the long run. I am here to convey this message to our comrades in the Low Countries. And also," as he turned to Moe, "to inform you that your 'package' is ready and will be delivered tomorrow just a few kilometers north of here."

They then all partook of a sumptuous country breakfast of eggs, bacon, sausage, and black bread with plenty of butter and honey while the Dutchman and Belgians spoke of gathering intelligence on troop placements and communication centers. There was also talk of the recent great coup of the French Maqui in which an entire Luftwaffe air group was destroyed.

Moe, Larry, and Shemp, as they had been called by the pilot of the Dakota that dropped them in Belgium, simply listened and continued eating. Before Bernardus left he handed Moe a folded piece of paper. It was the itinerary for Heisenberg's trip to Belgium, which ended at the Free University of Brussels where he was scheduled to confer with Dr. Julian Van Otten on uranium ore from the Congo.

These people are thorough, Moe thought to himself.

116

The next morning, the team traveling by car took a circuitous route north, stopping short of a small town called Hoboken. The name got a good chuckle from Moe and Larry. Shemp had no idea of the joke. Neither did the Belgian driver and his wife, who simply exchanged glances. Fortunately they encountered no Germans on the road. The only hitch came at a rail crossing where they were forced to wait while a long train carrying troops and supplies passed through. Relieved to be on their way again, they turned off onto a dirt road and followed it for about a kilometer; then they traveled up a rough overgrown trail for another thousand yards or so. There, in a wooded area, under a camouflage tarp propped up by branches, sat an enormous black Nazi staff car decked out with little swastika flags on each front fender and a whip antenna bolted above the right rear fender. To see this sight in the woods one would think that Goering himself must be in the bushes nearby having a pee. The Belgian partisan and his wife having completed their mission said their goodbyes and quickly left.

Under the forest canopy each man pulled a German uniform from his pack, correct down to the underwear. There was a regulation Wehrmacht radio transmitter built into the car, which also contained within it a cleverly disguised Allied shortwave set. Another disguised compartment in the trunk stowed their civilian clothes. Those intelligence guys knew their business. In a few minutes the metamorphosis was complete; Moe, Larry, and Shemp had turned into a high-level Nazi party official, his aide, and his driver. Meet Deputy Gauleiter Manfred von Dahlheim. Charmed. Lieutnant Ernst Gaiser. Enchanted. And Dieter Stolper, corporal. A pleasure. The three Americans couldn't resist clicking their heels and heiling at each other in response to the uncanny transformation. Two Jews and an Americanized Scotsman had just joined the Nazis to see Belgium.

117

One final problem was solved. Gurney, who was courageous, resourceful and a natural flyer, unfortunately couldn't speak a word of German. Nodding and grinning seemed to be a lot less of a good idea than it was back in London. The scratch on Gurney's face gave Moe the idea.

"You've been wounded, shot in the jaw. You're ambulatory, so they gave you to me as a driver. See, with your jaw wired shut you can't talk. Now nodding and gesturing will work, especially from a hero."

They wrapped Gurney up with gauze from the German first-aid kit in the car, carefully staining it with iodine and yellow salve to make the wound appear fresh and especially nasty. Few would want to get too near.

The Mercedes roared to life and they rumbled down the dusty trail to the main road. The first order of business was to arrange a test of the respect their get-ups would earn them. On a German map Moe located the Belgian fertilizer plant that SOE said had been commandeered by the Nazis to be turned into a munitions factory.

Here, spent shells from the recent campaign were reportedly being reprimed and reloaded, presumably for the coming assault on England.

The big car rolled to a stop at the front entrance to the Fabrique d'Agriculture.

"An inspection!" Lieutenant Gaiser announced to the gate guard.

To his credit, the soldier remained calm, asking to see identification, as if the staff car weren't enough. After credentials were checked, the soldier swung open the gate and waved them in. He immediately phoned the office of the facility to give the managers a few precious seconds of warning.

Moe's entrance was reminiscent of Siegfried in Wagner's *Ring of the Nibelungen*. He strode forward haughtily, looking over the room and the flustered major who was simultaneously attempting to heil and button the collar of his tunic. In a Hochdeutsch so laden with pique that it surprised even his own aide, the gauleiter announced the inspection of the facility. This man sounded as if he had places to go and people to kill.

"This way, Herr Gauleiter."

The inspection was thorough and meticulous. This von Dahlheim seemed to know his way around munitions and their associated chemicals. Under the openly hostile glances of the Belgian workers forced to operate the factory, the inspector general left no chemical bin, no lathe, no measuring device, no primers unchecked. At each stop, he murmured a few inaudible words to his aide, who dutifully wrote them down. At one point, he turned and spoke to the major in charge.

"It is good strategic thinking to have an alternate means of supply. Berlin is always receptive to good ideas and the resourceful men whose initiative furthers the interests of the Reich."

The major couldn't think of a response to this and simply nodded. When the inspection was over, the gauleiter asked to see the production reports. Someone was sent scurrying to the office for the latest figures. Moe looked at the papers, then at the major, then back to the paper.

"You must do better" was the only comment.

He then handed the data to his aide, offered a blasé heil, turned on his heels and headed toward the courtyard. Obviously the inspection was over. As the gauleiter's aide was placing the production report in his briefcase, he leaned closely to the major and in a confidential tone advised him that the gauleiter was pleased and would report accordingly to Berlin. And could he provide the correct spelling of his name so there can be no mistake as to who gets the credit in the report to Berlin. Major Auftucheim spelled his name slowly and carefully. The Mercedes horn sounded. The relieved major shouted the last three letters to the lieutenant as he hurried to the car.

As the Mercedes roared past the gate guard and onto the blacktop road, the two German officers inside were laughing till their sides hurt. The driver was mumbling "wa hppnnd? Teh mi." They laughed even harder at poor "Mumbles" with the gauze over his mouth.

Finally Moe reached forward and placed his hand on his driver's shoulder. "We just passed our first inspection, Gene."

15

SALLY CARLISLE AND HER SISTER IN SABOTAGE, Babette LaCroix, rode *L'Exprès Belgique* as far as Brussels. A new set of identity papers was provided, which gave her name as Odette Szabo, a Belgian national. The evening before they once more boarded the train in Paris, the pros and cons of the two women traveling together were discussed at length. In the end it was agreed that the disarming effect of two attractive young women traveling together would be enough to deflect suspicion and closer scrutiny. Their cover story was that they were both secretaries at the Philips Electrical Appliance factory in France. Odette was returning to Belgium to visit her ailing mother. Babette was accompanying her friend.

Smiles and giggles helped them ease through the many spot checks on the long and tedious train ride. When they at last reached Brussels they endured one final identity check, then walked the short distance to the canal at Molenbeek-St. Jean where their instructions directed them to travel north where they would make contact with the T'égal resistance group and its leader, "Etienne." The recognition word was "T'égal," a slang way of saying "ça m'est égal!"--"it's all the same to me!"--the American equivalent of "six of one, half dozen of the other." Hitchhiking by canal was common in Belgium and the two pretty girls had no trouble securing a ride on a brightly painted old barge decorated with clay pots of bright red geraniums fastened to its low gunwales, laden with farm produce, a pair of swaybacked horses, and a large orange cat.

They hadn't been informed of their destination nor told how far they should travel and the old pipe-smoking captain failed to respond to "T'égal" both times the girls spoke the phrase. All they could do is wait to be contacted. At dusk it began to rain but the weary young women slept through the shower under a waterproof tarp with two horses, a cat, and the toothless skipper guarding their rest.

The girls wakened to the smell of coffee, which was vying with the smell of horse as the barge pulled to the side of the canal allowing them to avail themselves of a nature call. Once under way again they breakfasted on black bread and coffee while being serenaded by local songbirds. As they moved steadily northward with the current, they waved to early morning fishermen stationed on the canal's banks while the sun rose to dispel the morning mists that loitered at the surface of the putty-colored water.

Life seemed remarkably tranquil as the lumbering barge made its way down the waterway. After a while, as the sun hung nearly overhead, the ungainly craft slowed and eased itself into another canal siding. The girls hopped off the barge to stretch their legs as the skipper worked the handle of a pump and began to wet down the horse area with a hose. Then, after the old fellow off-loaded several bushels of turnips, he abruptly cast off his lines and pushed off into the current leaving the surprised girls stranded on the dock. Sally and Babette shouted to him but his only response was a wave and a toothless grin as he and his barge and his horses and cat continued to glide northward. The girls discovered that their belongings had been unloaded and left behind on the dock. The old skipper obviously couldn't or wouldn't take them any farther. Sally and Babette resignedly sat down on their luggage to ponder their predicament. They had been abandoned on a deserted canal dock along with the turnips deep in the countryside somewhere south of Antwerp.

"If you have money you can buy food at my mother's house," a small Flemish voice chirped behind them.

"Wherever did the kid come from?" Babette turned to Sally and shrugged.

"Uh, thank you, but no, we've already eaten, thank you," Sally said to the boy in halting Flemish.

The boy shrugged and said, "Ça m'est égal" and walked up the dock toward a road and the distant farmhouse beyond. The two women turned to each other, recognition simultaneously clicking on in each other's eyes, and hurried to gather up their belongings to follow the stealthy little urchin up the road.

The boy led them to a house where a sad-faced man with thinning red hair sat smoking a clay pipe at the window while a rotund, cheery-eyed woman behind him fussed in the kitchen. Invited in, the two women entered and sat down. Coffee was served and eventually the small talk turned to specific questions. After a strained and guarded exchange of background information that must have satisfied the pair, three men and another woman joined the group. After several more minutes of questioning, their reserve disappeared and they extended a warm welcome to the girls.

Etienne introduced himself and immediately wanted to know, "Did you two young women really destroy half the Luftwaffe?"

"Well, maybe not half," said Babette, "but a goodly fifth for sure."

"Now, the question is," said Sally, "when do we start harassing the Germans in Belgium?"

Everyone looked toward Etienne.

"Our orders are to avoid direct confrontation and gather information."

"Oh," said the French girls in a slightly superior tone as they nodded unconvincingly. "Our orders come directly from London. They need us in place for when something big comes off."

"We did set fire to a building full of documents," said the youngest of Etienne's lieutenants. Everyone looked at him.

"That's good," said Babette.

"They put it out," he then added.

"Oh, too bad."

That night, when Etienne made radio contact with SOE in London, he conveyed his impatience at being held in check. The reply was terse. "Message received. Will advise. Stand by for new information. V for victory." By the time the Germans managed to pinpoint the place of transmission, Etienne and the radio were off the air and kilometers away.

In the days that followed, Sally and Babette acclimated themselves to their new surroundings. Confined to the few homes considered safe by their resistance colleagues, they busied themselves with chores, learning Morse code, and cleaning weapons. Babette took to her new surroundings and companions with ease, but Sally grew solemn and more withdrawn with each day. She seemed morbidly preoccupied and elected to spend much of her free time sullen and alone.

Then one of the men returning from town with supplies announced that "some big shot Nazi from Berlin is inspecting factories here in Belgium. Ernst Millaud saw him. He drives around in a big German car like he thinks he's Hitler himself."

"I wonder how he'd like four flat tires?" someone mused.

I wonder if the gentleman from Berlin could meet with a motor accident, Sally muttered to herself.

16

———— ⊠◊⊠ ————

"THE BOCHE ARE LUNCHING AT THE CLERMONT," announced Madame Bode.

"How do you know?" Sally asked.

"My cousin just called. She saw them. Big as life."

"What road is that on?"

"The south road to Brussels."

"Is there any place along that road where they could be intercepted?"

"Intercepted? Hmmmm, it's fairly wide near the city but it's slow going around the cemetery near Berchem and then there's the little bridge across the Netre."

"Little bridge?" The wheels started turning in Sally's head.

"It's at Lierre where the Germans have put a headquarters in the old police barracks. But if you are thinking of trying anything . . ."

"Couldn't we at least take a look? Just a look. What could it hurt?"

They drove out to Lierre in a small car fueled with recently siphoned German petrol. A picnic basket with some cheese, blood sausages, and a bottle of wine was on the rear seat. Traffic on the bridge at this hour was light, mostly German, a few small vehicles and motorcyles. Sally watched with an icy intensity. Etienne was concerned. He had been a captain in the Belgian infantry and had seen the look before on front-line soldiers--a bravado that manifested itself in a mindless disregard for safety and an irrational desire to make the worst happen, thereby getting it over with. This brave young woman might be a danger to herself.

The narrow ancient stone bridge was only two lanes wide. The roadway was planked with wooden beams, which rumbled noisily as the traffic passed over it. On the outer edges a pedestrian walkway was cantilevered, protected by a low and delicate iron railing. As Etienne was chattily describing the medieval history of the bridge and its many refurbishings, Sally was wondering how deep the water was.

"You see," said Etienne, "it's impossible. Hundreds of Boche within spitting distance and lots of townspeople coming and going all the time. Now, if you'll please remain here, I must make a call to let our people know where we are." He left her sitting on the blanket on the gentle slope by the river. In the distance Sally saw a black staff car driving along the river road toward the bridge. It had bright red flags on the fenders, which flapped in the breeze. It must be the Nazi big shot. It had to be. She rose and walked briskly to Etienne's little deux cheveaux, got in, and gunned the engine.

Gene Gurney instinctively slowed the Mercedes when his front wheels made contact with the noisy wooden planks of the old bridge. His heightened sense of wariness was due to the increased civilian traffic around the bridge and the concentration of Germans in the area. It was then that he noticed the tiny maroon car on the far side of the span. He watched as it lurched erratically into the oncoming lane, then slow down and finally accelerate to an inordinately high speed. As the small car swerved directly into the path of the Mercedes, Gene managed to jam his brakes and avoid a major collision. The small vehicle merely grazed the Mercedes front bumper, glancing into the wrought iron pedestrian railing and knocking a large section of it into the water.

"Damn it!" cried the driver of the small car. "Damn it!" she repeated loudly. Not in Flemish or French but in arch Brooklynese. "Damn! Damn! Damn it to hell!" she repeated through the open window as she frustratedly pounded the steering wheel.

A crowd began to gather. Several witnesses exchanged their versions of the mishap. One of them held the larger vehicle totally at fault. A team of bystanders, directed by a Belgian policeman, hauled Sally's overhanging car back onto the roadway where it was started up and driven to the base of the bridge. The small car's bumper was torn off, the fender was crumpled and impinging on the left front wheel, which had acquired a distinct wobble, but otherwise the little car was still serviceable.

Sally was sitting grimly in the Belgian police car furious with herself and her failure.

When the German military police arrived, the officer made a big show of checking everyone's papers, most likely trying to show off his efficiency to the occupant of the big black staff car. When it was discovered that Sally could not produce a driver's license, it looked as if she were going to be taken into custody by the German military policeman. As she was being escorted to the German MP's car, the gauleiter stepped out of the Mercedes.

"Hauptmann, your name is? . . ."

"Mueller, Herr Gauleiter."

"Mueller, I think you'd agree this is nothing more than a trivial traffic accident. Hardly worth taking a frightened and hysterical young woman to jail for. We should really let the locals deal with her. It's their lookout if they are so foolish as to license scatterbrained females to drive."

Knowing chuckles.

"And frankly it has occurred to me to do some questioning of this young woman personally . . ."

He nudged a lascivious elbow into Hauptmann Mueller's ribs.

"With your agreement, of course."

Mueller got it. Clicked heels, heiled, and took off.

Sally was ordered into the car. Having regained a semblance of composure, she was now demanding to know where she was being taken even before the door slammed. Once inside the car she quieted as she sat next to the gauleiter and across from the lieutenant. The big car drove off the bridge and continued slowly down the road. She was thinking that this was a pathetic way to end when the lieutenant said to the gauleiter in German, "She said, 'damn' several times. And then threw in a 'damn it to hell'. What do you think it means, sir?"

"That's what we're going to find out, Lieutenant."

Sally understood the German words. She also understood that she was in bigger trouble now than she originally thought.

In perfect French the general turned to her and said, "You deliberately tried to ram us with your car. Why?"

Sally sat in silence, her mouth a tight thin line.

"And when you botched it, you said, 'Damn it to hell!' In English. American English. My driver and I both heard you. Explain, please."

Sally said nothing and stared straight ahead.

"Pull over here," he instructed the driver in German.

They drove up a small overgrown road where they were hidden from passing traffic.

This is it, thought Sally. I'm done for. If I get the chance I'm going to run for it. It's now or never.

"Who are you?" demanded the gauleiter, speaking French once more. "Might you be a Belgian girl who has lived in America long enough to pick up some slang . . . and who happens to hate Nazis? Am I warm?"

The last he said in English. It caused Sally's eyes to flicker. Now the pig was talking perfect English, thought Sally.

"And from the sound of the 'damns' and the 'damn it to hell!'" the Nazi continued in English, "I'd bet on the Brooklyn side of the Hudson."

This fellow was good, thought Sally, trying desperately to maintain the expression of indifference on her face.

"Were you trying to kill yourself? Is this some sort of resistance action? Or are you free-lance? It isn't likely to be T'égal. Etienne is much to smart to pull a dumb stunt like this. Yet you are acting like a captured enemy. In any case, cut it out! We've got our own job to do and we can't afford to be obstructed by the pranks of the locals--the very people we're trying to help."

Oh, sure, thought Sally, giving him a sideways look.

"Tell us a convenient place to let you out."

She turned to look at the Nazi in disbelief.

"Yes," the big German nodded, "we're letting you go."

The car was backed out of the cover onto the main road, facing in the direction they'd come.

"Pick some place from where you can walk home but won't be seen with this car."

Sally said, "Make a right turn here."

"A right turn, got that?" repeated the gauleiter.

The driver nodded. It must have been at least five kilometers from home but Sally was taking no chances.

"Right over there," said Sally, indicating a fenced-off dirt road. The car stopped. The door was opened. Sally got out and just stood there, her curiosity struggling with the urge to run for her life. Nice legs, Moe remarked to himself, as he looked over the young redhead trying bravely to appear unperturbed. After a brief pause with Sally and the men in the staff car simply looking at one another, the young German lieutenant leaned over, grinned, reached for the door handle, and pulled it shut.

The gauleiter rolled down the window and said, "You can tell them that we tried to sexually assualt you but you got away."

As the car began to drive off, the lieutenant leaned out of the window and gave her a little wave.

"Wait! she shouted. "Come back!"

The Mercedes skidded to a halt on the gravelly road and backed up to the girl.

"Who are you people?" she said in English.

The window rolled down again and the big Nazi leaned forward, smiled and said, "We've come full circle, haven't we?"

Sally climbed back into the car.

If you had pressed your ear to the rear window of the black Mercedes, this is what you would have heard.

"We're Americans."

"Me too."

"I'm from New Jersey."

"The Bronx."

"Missouri."

"Brooklyn!"

"Brooklyn? Oh, my gosh!"

"What are you *doing* here?"

"Why are *you* dressed as Nazis?"

"What are you doing trying to run Nazis off the road in Belgium?"

"Why are you running around in those getups?"

"We can't tell you and you can't tell anyone about us. And you? Are you Belgian? So what *are* you doing here?"

"I can't say. And you musn't tell anyone about me either."

"Mum's the word."

"Our lips are zipped."

"So what's happening back home?" Sally asked. "Is America still ignoring what's happening in Europe?"

"No, Americans are beginning to realize that we'll be in it soon. We're sending lots of supplies to England. Tanks, guns, food, everything."

"Well, it's about time," said Sally, nodding her head in response to the news. "The Germans are awful, or should I say *you* Germans are awful."

Laughter.

"Hey, you'd better go."

"I know. It's getting late."

"We've gotta go, too."

"Okay. Good-bye."

"Stay out of trouble."

"You too."

"Don't forget about being molested."

"I won't."

"Good-bye."

"Bye."

"Bye."

"Good luck, boys, good luck!"

The car drove off as Sally stood at the edge of the field watching it raise a cloud of dust and disappear into it along the rural road. What a glorious sound, those American voices. Like home. For the first time she realized how weary she was. So very weary. Of being scared. Of being brave. Weary of being a ruthless terrorist.

Wouldn't it be lovely to be Sally Wiener again. Instead of Joan of Arc? Who the heck do I think I am, anyway. And those three fellows were nice. Especially the tall one. He seemed older than the other two. Not by a lot. Maybe five or six years. Thirty-five? Maybe thirty-eight tops.

She arrived home just before dark. All she wanted to do was sleep--and dream of waking up in her bed, in her little room, back on Pulaski Street, Brooklyn, New York, U.S.A.

17

⊷ ⊰◈⊱ ⊶

SO MANY STOPS, grumbled Werner Heisenberg to no one in particular as he sat in his private compartment on the *Belgique l'Exprès.* The trip to Brussels once took less than four hours. Now it will take at least eight. Perhaps it's just as well--catch up on my journals and get rid of some of this paperwork.

Precious little reading or paperwork was ever completed. Professor Heisenberg had pitchblende on his mind. The führer had charged him with the chore of developing a nuclear-explosive device. Now everything seemed to conspire against the completion of that task. The complex process, which was expected to produce enriched uranium, wasn't working, the plants to make the heavy water necessary to facilitate the chain-reaction experiments weren't producing in enough quantity, and now that idiot Von Runstedt has refused to release the uranium he grabbed from the Czechoslovakian deposits.

The fool wants to tip his cannon shells with uranium so they'll penetrate the thick skins of enemy tanks. I cannot believe the imbecile wants to throw uranium at the Allies. I will never understand the military mind.

In his heart, however, he knew it wasn't the military mind that troubled him. It was the political mind. Ambition had driven him to the top in German science. If Niels Bohr was god of this new physics, then he, Werner Heisenberg, was at least pope.

But to what end? Some of the finest minds in Germany are lost to me simply because they are Jews. A troublesome race, to be sure, but exceptions should be made. Some of my finest students were Jewish. If I had them with me, these problems would surely be solved by now. And then there is the matter of the nuclear weapon. In the hands of these unstable and politically insatiable men--the carnage would be horrific. And my place in history would be forever the man who served as the mindless pawn of killers.

It was a long ride to Brussels for Dr. Heisenberg.

"Bruxelles! Prochaine d'arrêt, Bruxelles!" the conductor announced.

Brussels at last. I hope Van Otten can arrange for a free flow of ore from the Congo. And any new ideas on refinement would certainly be welcome. Where the devil is my car? Are you my driver?

Heisenberg . . . berg! You don't know who I am? You idiot! Did you never attend gymnasium? Ah, there you are. Just this one bag. I'll carry both briefcases.

The maroon and black Citroen whisked the scientist away from the train station and toward the university.

Werner Heisenberg ascended the steps to the Applied Science building of the Free University of Brussels in deep, murky thought. Politics, ambition, idealism, good, evil; all those abstractions were suddenly beginning to wobble like the spinning plates of a Chinese magician. Once he had been able to keep them all turning smoothly. He hated the situation in which he found himself. I am damned if I do and damned if I don't. As he approached the ornate wooden doors of the academic center, they swung open to reveal dozens of adoring students and faculty respectfully awaiting him in the entrance hall. Ernst Van Otten, the head of the Applied Science department, stepped forward and made a little welcoming speech declaring that the university was honored by the presence of such a revered and esteemed scientist. Heisenberg bowed graciously to the welcome and accepted the applause of the professors and students. Now that was more like it. In the frenetic pursuit of science for war, he had nearly forgotten the respect due a world-class scientist and Nobel Prize winner. "Ahh" went the little ego figure inside Werner Heisenberg. It felt good, like a massage for tired muscles.

"Nice to meet you."

"A pleasure."

"You're so kind."

"Delighted."

"Enchanted."

Shaking hands with fawning students and obsequious instructors had never been so enjoyable.

He was led to a large room where white cloth-covered tables were arranged into a C shape. Heisenberg sat, in the center position of the center table, as guest of honor. It was the room where the traditional weekly tea was served for senior department scientists. The "tea" description had been recently dropped on the recommendation of the occupation administrators as sounding too British, but the weekly gathering was continued to afford the scientists a chance to exchange ideas and compel them to take a break from their experiments.

As Heisenberg sat he whimsically noted the visual analogy to da Vinci's *The Last Supper*, with himself presiding as Christ. He chuckled privately because he rather enjoyed the amusing observation. Tea and coffee were served with little pastries and sandwiches. Until then he hadn't realized how hungry he was. He ate ravenously. Between bites he genially answered questions and generally impressed everyone in the room with his insights and observations. Some are even taking notes, he observed. As well they should.

When the tables were cleared, Van Otten clinked the side of his glass with his pipe and asked for attention. He then rose to toast the honored guest in a vintage Belgian wine. They drank and then the students shouted three loud hurrahs, the Belgian equivalent of a hip hip hurray. Van Otten then announced that they had taken up enough time from their guest's busy schedule and that he and Heisenberg would now repair to the director's office to discuss the important matters that had brought Dr. Heisenberg to their university. Heisenberg, a bit disappointed to cut short the adulation, rose slowly from the table to join the director; he knew business must inevitably take precedence. Their exit was delayed, however, by several students rushing forward with pieces of paper, franc notes, and calendar pages for Heisenberg to sign. Van Otten started to shoo them away but Heisenberg interceded and genially agreed to the autographs-- especially when a few of the students offered for his signature a copy of his monograph describing his "Uncertainty Principle," published over fifteen years ago in the science publication, *Naturwissenschaften.* He obliged every one of them with a signature. A great man who hasn't lost the common touch was the consensus of the room of scientists.

Now down to business.

"Are you still receiving uranium ore from the Congo?"

"Yes, we've recently received two hundred tons. That's half the quantity of a year ago."

"You were instructed to make the ore available to us?"

"Yes, yes, as far as I know the new supplies are to be set aside for Leipzig."

Heisenberg nodded. "Good, good."

But the director continued, ". . . and eighty tons for Berlin-Dahlem."

Heisenberg fought for composure. "Berlin-Dahlem? I know of no order to send ore to Dahlem."

"Yes," Van Otten replied. "It was in the latest requisition from your quartermaster people. See," pulling the order from the folder and holding it for Heisenberg.

This was mortifying. Pitchblende ore, the unrefined uranium as it came out of the ground, being sent for refining to the facility at Berlin-Dahlem without Heisenberg's knowledge could only mean that Hitler was putting a second team on the project.

Hedging his bet. That second team had to be Diebner and his group. Kurt Diebner was primarily an experimental physicist but he had worked with Otto Hahn, Strassman, and Liese Meitner, the scientists who had first succeeded in splitting a uranium atom.

Yes, Diebner could possibly achieve the breakthrough in creating a sustained chain reaction. And he would get all the credit and the undying gratitude of the Führer--leaving me standing stupidly in the wings like an understudy. What unethical swine these Nazis are.

The remainder of their conversation related to the refining process. The Brussels group was engaged in the separation of Uranium 235 from 238 by a centrifugal process, the same course taken by his team in Leipzig. The results were identical--some glimmers of optimism but little real success. It would seem that Brussels had little scientific insight to offer and only a small quantity of uranium ore to contribute to the solution of Heisenberg's problems.

"Excuse the interruption, please," the aide from the outer office said as he stuck his head into the room. "There is a German captain with a message for Professor Dr. Heisenberg."

"Very well," said the scientist wearily.

The Luftwaffe officer, all spit and Prussian, entered, clicked, and presented Heisenberg with a note.

Heisenberg read it, sighed, and said, "Well, that's it, I guess" to Van Otten. "I've been summoned to an audience with the Führer tomorrow morning. I will have to leave. Unexpected and unfortunate . . ." he was saying as they walked through the open administration offices. "I was so enjoying my stay and your bright young people."

Van Otten beamed at the compliment.

"Now, if you have success in sustaining a chain reaction or enriching a quantity of uranium you will let me know, won't you, Van Otten? Thank you again."

"Herr Professor Doctor," the captain was hurrying him.

"Yes, yes, I'm coming. Good-bye, everyone," he said as he walked through the reception hall. "Would someone fetch my bag."

Out the door and down the steps they went.

Where the hell is he going, thought Moe as he watched from across the square.

Professor Heisenberg entered the car and sat down wearily. The door was slammed shut by a German Luftwaffe officer.

This doesn't make sense. He was supposed to leave tomorrow.

When Heisenberg's suitcase was put in the trunk and the car sped away into the evening, Moe concluded that for some reason Heisenberg's stay had been cut short.

I've got to find out some more about this, thought Moe as he sauntered up the steps of the science building.

Moe was dressed unobtrusively in a dark suit. He had a talent for selecting clothing and all the little details that go with it, allowing him to fit easily into any situation. He would change his walk, the way he carried himself, even the expression on his face. The result often caused total strangers to regard him as someone vaguely familiar.

When Moe entered the building, the scientists and students were still milling about the main hall, chattering about Heisenberg's sudden departure. There was to have been a dinner later with senior faculty and an entertainment, a student string ensemble to play a short program of Beethoven and Ysäye. Everyone was disappointed.

"He didn't seem rude."

"He was very gracious at tea."

"He really seemed to be enjoying himself."

"I heard he was ordered to Berlin."

"Yes, the Boche officer was taking him to the airport."

"A meeting with Hitler himself, that's what I heard."

"The car was taking him to the airbase at Ghent."

The gossipy chatter overheard by Moe was fairly consistent. Heisenberg evidently had been ordered to leave unexpectedly. His presence was urgently required. An emergency? At his research facility? Probably not, because he was summoned by a Luftwaffe officer. The flight to Berlin would take over two hours. Being summoned to meet with Hitler is very plausible. Now, what else can I learn?

"There'll be no new ore. We'll have to stop work soon."

"It's all being shipped to Germany."

"You realize they are stealing it from us."

"What do you expect, they won the war, didn't they?"

"My cousin is a captain in the Belgian Army, he was in the bottom third of his class at gymnasium.

"That figures; it takes an idiot to be a soldier."

"If he would have been last in his class he'd be a general by now."

That was a good one. Moe laughed heartily along with the others. Now he had a fair picture of the situation. All that was left was to find out the destination of the Belgian Congo ore.

This might require a little snooping in the administration offices, after lights-out, thought Moe.

When someone said "Leipzig," Moe eased over to the group of students where someone had mentioned the town near Berlin.

"I saw it on a shipping order with all their silly swastikas and eagles stamped on it. Our trucks, their drivers to haul the shipment to Leipzig when the ship docks. I was there nearly all morning trying to find out about my scholarship money."

I'd prefer to view that document with my own eyes, thought Moe, but because I already have the information it would be foolhardy to risk everything simply to verify. I think I have what I need considering I missed out on Heisenberg.

As Moe walked the several blocks to where the car was parked he tried to formulate a plan that would somehow resurrect a mission about to be aborted. He also was surprised at his nostalgic feelings toward the young scientists and students he had just encountered.

They're the same all over the world; they just love to talk and talk and show off how bright they are.

He also gave a brief thought to Odette, or whatever her name is, back in Lierre. Just a kid, really, but, got to admit, she had nice gams.

"Back to Lierre." The order was met with a groan from both the gauleiter's aide and his driver. "If I was a real Nazi general officer I'd have you both shot for that disrespect."

"Well, you're not," said Gurney. "Thank goodness for small favors. So why are we retracing our steps?"

"We need a place to repair the bumper," Moe explained, "come up with a new plan, and I want to talk to that girl again."

"Oohhh!" the aide and driver said in unison as they made a show of nodding to each other in mock understanding.

"I understand now, " mumbled Gurney to Ernie through his bandage.

"Perfectly clear," said Ernie to Gurney.

"I think I'll shoot you two mugs anyway," said Moe, surprised at the realization that his cheeks were reddening.

From a deserted side road outside Brussels, Moe sent a late night message to London. In a code based on the Jabberwocky lines in Lewis Carroll's *Through the Looking-Glass* Moe communicated the fact of having missed Heisenberg because of his sudden recall to Berlin--worth verifying. No breakthroughs yet or imminent in creating chain reaction--welcome news. And the Belgian Congo uranium ore to be trucked to Leipzig when unloaded at Ostend--request aerial reconnaissance. London responded with "Message received. Do you want out?" Moe countered with "Not yet. Will advise. Not ready to give up on 'H'. V for victory."

18

—•—⊨◊⊨—•—

PROFESSOR DR. HEISENBERG WAS ESCORTED by the young Reichschancellerey aide down the 480-foot-long corridor to the führer's study, a virtual Avenue de Gilded Bronze. The echo of his leather heels was resounding stridently on the dark red marble floor. Once he fell into step with his escort the echoes rebounding from the 30-foot ceilings clattered a bit more contentedly. The sound of men marching in step was a comforting noise to these halls.

The pair stopped at a large set of double doors flanked by two helmeted sentries standing at parade rest. They wore black uniforms with white gloves and white leather strappings. These were the führer's personal lifeguards. Specially recruited by Borman, every man was over six feet tall.

The closed mahogany doors were high enough to serve a cathedral. Perhaps that was the idea. Above the door was a stone placard upon which the ornately carved initials A. H. were incised.

Heisenberg took a seat in one of the four large chairs set up as a little waiting parlor outside the doorway. The chairs were upholstered in a dark fabric upon which the shields of the city-states and regions of Germany were embroidered. Rather a homey touch amid all the gilt and marble, thought Heisenberg, as he looked at his watch. His appointment was for 9:00 and it was already 9:45.

"Well, after all, the führer is a very busy man."

The door to Hitler's study opened and the sentries snapped to attention. Speer came out--Reichminister of Armaments Prof. Albert Speer, who happened to be the architect of this modern, classical-style edifice. Speer nodded politely to Heisenberg as he walked briskly past. With Speer still in sight, the door opened once again and a tall, pretty, blonde, young woman addressed him as Herr Professor Doctor and asked him to please go in. She then exited as he entered.

So this was the throne room. It was a large rectangle of about fifty by a hundred feet with a ceiling at least thirty feet high. The World War I corporal had done very well indeed. To the left the führer sat at a wide, ornate desk and rather austere red leather chair. Three men sat facing the führer--Goering, Milch, and Schumann.

The führer said, "Ah, Heisenberg, I am so pleased you could come. Sit down, here," gesturing to a chair upholstered in gold brocade, by far the most ornate-looking chair in the room. Hitler seemed genuinely happy to see his chief scientist, as he leaned over to shake hands. The three, Goering, Milch, and Schumann, didn't look quite as cordial. As Hitler made the unnecessary introductions he took a handkerchief from his pocket and wiped his hands.

Goering was in the full regalia of Reichsmarshal, the title Hitler had invented for him. Milch wore the uniform of a field marshal of aviation. Schumann's uniform was that of a Wehrmacht colonel. In marked contrast, the führer wore a gray jacket with no rank at all save his party badge and the Iron Cross, first class.

"You had a good trip, I trust?" the führer inquired politely.

"Thank you, my Führer. Excellent flight. Extremely efficient."

"Good, good!" was the führer's response.

Goering took time out from appearing bored and fluffed his ample self at the compliment.

"So," continued the führer, "it is always pleasant to chat with a fellow professional."

Professional? thought Heisenberg. What's he talking about? He's a housepainter.

"You know, of course, I myself was pursuing a career in architecture until the fatherland's needs took precedence. Speer is a fine architect. He was just here. You saw him, perhaps? Speer and I designed all this, the new chancellery. Do you like it? It's the envy of every nation. Young Speer could become the world's greatest architect if I had the time to give him . . . But as you know, our present task is taxing . . . so much time must be devoted to military issues. My soul aches to build, to create, but for now my day is spent with these military types," he gestured to Goering, Milch, and Schumann.

The two field marshals and colonel pouted in unison at the remark.

"But make no mistake, these are men possessed of great courage. Heroes to a man."

They brightened at the führer's pronouncement.

"My dear friend Goering here is the most decorated man in the Reich. A true paragon of the Aryan ideal."

Minus a few pounds, thought Heisenberg as the führer continued.

"The vision is mine but the deeds are carried out by men like these. But enough of that. What do you have for us today, Herr Professor Doctor?"

"As you know, my Führer, we are working to exploit the energy holding together the nucleus of an atom of a heavy element. We feel that the element uranium offers the greatest potential. At present we are building a uranium machine. The difficulty lies with the choice of moderator to slow the neutrons . . ." He could see he was losing the führer's interest. "But we expect a breakthrough any time. Then we will be able to sustain a chain reaction that will produce enormous quantities of energy. Power to light cities, for industry. For undersea boats. For aircraft."

"The device, what about the device you spoke of?" The führer leaned forward hungrily.

"Aside from the energy that could be produced in electrical power, thus freeing us forever from dependence on coal and petroleum, an explosive device could be constructed."

"Yes?" The man was almost drooling.

"It would need to be no larger than the size of a pineapple and would have the explosive power of a hundred squadrons of bombers dropping all their bombs at once."

Goering rolled his eyes in unshielded skepticism.

"To be more specific, this pineapple-size device could explode with a force of some twenty thousand tons of conventional explosive."

"When?" the führer shouted excitedly. "When will we have your pineapple, Dr. Heisenberg?"

"We are working night and day, my Führer, and with the new ore from the Congo, we hope to make our breakthrough soon. Very soon. But it will require an increase in resources devoted to the effort. We need the money to build a new supercyclotron and we need more scientists and technicians. We are breaking new ground every . . ."

"And the British and Americans?" the führer interrupted. "Are they capable of making their own pineapples?"

"I really don't think so, my Führer. Their makeshift efforts cannot compare with German science. We stand years ahead of the rest of the world." He searched the führer's eyes for any recognition that his last statement was a lie. With all the scientists forced to leave the Reich in the past five years, a coordinated utilization of their talents could very well produce the breakthrough necessary to produce an atomic weapon. But it would require a gargantuan effort, enormous financing and commitment, and even then such results would be highly improbable. He was indeed telling a lie to the führer, but then why needlessly worry a man with so much on his mind.

"Herr Heisenberg," said the führer, "I dearly want to supply the English with all the fruit they can swallow. You understand me? Greater effort! *Practical* science. *Practical* applications. Not daydreaming. You will see to it? I know that you will. Thank you for your time, Herr Professor Doctor."

As Heisenberg stood up to shake the hands of Goering, Milch, and Schumann, he was thinking about asking the führer if there was another team working on the project. He decided against it and heiled instead. The führer returned the heil and did not shake hands.

As Heisenberg exited the room, Kurt Diebner was sitting outside the office. He fidgeted uncomfortably in his chair as his eyes met Heisenberg's. They nodded to each other and Heisenberg walked briskly down the long marble hall to the reception area, his footsteps reverberating stridently against the polished marble as he went.

19

"SEEMS YOUR GERMAN IS BACK," Madame Bode announced casually to Odette.

"Where?"

"His favorite hotel, the Claremont. He's also having his car repaired, probably looking for you to pay for the damages."

Etienne had witnessed the entire incident from the auto repair shop about a hundred meters away from the center of the bridge. When the girl took off, he knew she was either crazy, or suicidal, probably both. Then when it looked like nothing serious had occurred, he started walking toward the accident only to about-face and attempt an unhurried getaway when the German military police arrived. He heard later that Odette was taken in the staff car and hoped she wouldn't give them all away under coercion or torture. Plans for dispersing their group were already being made when Odette showed up physically no worse for her encounter and strangely uncommunicative about it.

Her story was that the Nazi had amorous intentions but that she managed to run away. None of it hung together--the reckless girl, a bumbling Nazi general, and the distinct feeling that Odette was holding something back, plus the fact that London has no record of a Sally Carlisle from Park Avenue, New York, U.S.A. She didn't seem like a spy. She had courage but she was definitely an amateur or perhaps a very clever infiltrator. Such things are not impossible. And she's not really one of us; I mean

145

we don't really know her. One thing I know, she's not to be trusted until these questions are cleared up. And definitely not till the Nazi general leaves the area.

That evening Sally Carlisle strode boldly into the dining room of the Claremont Hotel. She had borrowed a red dress from one of the girls, heels from another, and had her hair fixed up by her friend Babette. A white gardenia set off her reddish chestnut curls. If her intention was to attract attention, she would certainly succeed. Makeup, somebody's last pair of silk stockings, and a jangly charm bracelet, provided by Madame Bode of all people, completed the very fetching composition. A movie star had come to town.

Albert Perot, the owner and maître d'hôtel, seated her and lit her cigarette with a gallant flourish. Madame Perot, who had observed the entrance from behind the hotel's front desk, now glowered as she observed the action through the glass of the swinging doors that connected the lobby to the dining room. Whatever the Flemish word for bimbo was, she was thinking it at that moment. A woman simply didn't go to a public place alone and smoke cigarettes. Certainly not to a reputable hotel restaurant. Definitely not in a red dress.

"We may not be the Ritz but we still must insist on a semblance of propriety in our establishment." That was the gist of the tirade directed at her husband when she at last managed to catch his attention with her hisses through the glass partition. "She finishes her Pernod and she's out. See to it." She then humphed at poor Albert and strode back to the lobby to her post at the front desk.

"But, Butter Bun," he implored (Butter Bun weighed in at well over one hundred kilos), "don't you understand? She's here to confront that Boche officer who attempted to impose himself on her. She has come here to show her defiance. She dares him to face her."

Butter Bun stopped in her tracks. Her shoulders drooped. Her features softened. She turned to Albert and for an instant the face of the slender nineteen-year-old girl he had eons ago wooed and won flickered before his eyes.

"You would do no less," he said to her.

"Oh, Albert, sometimes I forget I married a very sensitive man."

Sally sat for hours nursing her drink. It was difficult not to show her disappointment. Madame Perot even came over and replaced the drink with a fresh one and a new pitcher of cold water.

"Don't feel rushed, my dear, you are quite welcome with us," she said, patting Sally's hand.

"Merci," Sally responded, not quite knowing what all the sudden warmth and friendliness was about. She was there to see those American boys again. By sitting so prominently in the dining room she hoped one of them would notice her and find a way to get together. No point in not looking good when it happens, she rationalized.

The driver of the staff car dropped the gauleiter's aide off in front of the hotel. The front bumper was missing--still in the shop where it was to be hammered straight and the bracket welded. They had elected not to leave the car in the shop overnight. The fender had been hammered out and the ripples leaded, smoothed, and primed. Tomorrow, when the fender would get its paint and the restored bumper would be installed, everything would hopefully look as good as new. As the driver parked the car where it could be watched from the window of the gauleiter's room, the aide walked into the lobby of the hotel to tell his chief of the progress. As Ernie entered the lobby, ignoring the cold stare from the fat woman at the front desk, something else caught his eye. It was in the open doorway to the dining room. Something red. Something girl. Ernie stopped on the second step of the staircase and went through the motions of patting his pockets as if he had misplaced keys or the like. As he did, he sneaked a second look at the girl in the dining room.

147

Brooklyn! She's here. Gotta tell Moe.
Then "finding" his room key he bounded up the stairs.

"Aren't you going down?" Ernie asked.
"Of course, but not until she leaves. And I hope she waits till it's dark."
"She will, Moe, she's smart."
"She is, isn't she?" said Moe, thinking that he liked the idea that this moxie young woman was also smart.

Venus was the only star evident in the evening sky as Sally left the hotel. The vestigial glow in the west prevented the lesser stars from making their entrances. As far as the citizens of Belgium and their German occupiers were concerned, it was night. Sally headed up the road, regretting the decision to wear the borrowed high heels, which were already creating a matched set of blisters on each foot.
Well, I tried, thought Sally, as she slowly headed home.

The laden dinner cart was wheeled into the German's room by one of the kitchen apprentices. The regular bellboy refused to do it, but the practical-minded apprentice chef didn't mind; the German did tip nicely. When the lad left the room, Ernie and Gene came out of the bedroom and pounced on the tray of food. Extra portions had been ordered.
As aide and driver set upon the feast, Moe climbed out of the window, walked lightly across the porch roof, and dropped silently to the ground. She went west on foot, his driver had told him, and west he went at a determined jog. Moe wore a fedora and a suit jacket, bought several days ago at a ready-to-wear store a few towns east, and appeared for all the world like a

Belgian office worker on his way home. Several cars passed him but none stopped or slowed. After ten minutes, he caught sight of the girl and called, "Mademoiselle! Mademoiselle Szabo!"

"Yes!" she turned, knowing immediately who it was.

They shook hands and grinned at each other like old school chums reunited. Moe was puffing a little and finding it difficult to grin and catch his breath at the same time surprised that his athlete's body had so quickly lost its tone.

"Let's get out of the road," he managed to say between grinning and puffing. He helped the girl over a low stone wall and into an orchard. She took care not to snag her borrowed dress.

"What are you doing back here?" she asked as they sat down on the grass between apple trees. He helped her to her feet again and put his jacket down for her to sit on.

"Bad timing, bad luck. Perhaps a bit of both, but I've got to decide on trying again or giving up and returning home."

"Oh, I'm so sorry," said Sally.

"Don't be. It gives us a chance to see you again," said Moe.

Us? she thought. I don't see anybody here but you. She savored that private thought. Sitting out in the evening air enjoying the attention of this dark, attractive man was a pleasant and flattering diversion from the upside-down world in which she had been living for the past . . . God, it seemed like forever.

"I need to ask you something," said Moe. His tone had turned serious. "If we decide to get out, we can take you with us. Is there any reason that you can't go?"

"I can't just leave," she replied, trying to think of a good reason. "I'm needed. Until the Germans are driven out I couldn't possibly . . ." She was neither convinced nor convincing.

"Maybe it's time you left and you don't yet realize it," Moe offered.

"No! We have a duty. Don't you see . . ." Sally went on.

"Raise your hands and don't make a sound. If you do you will die here," a voice ordered from the dark. Three men rushed forward and grabbed them. Sally was searched roughly and her hands were tied behind her. Moe was frisked and the .32 caliber automatic was discovered in the holster under his arm. Tied and gagged, they were shoved into a car that appeared from nowhere. They were then whisked away into the Belgian night.

At precisely the same time several kilometers east, two men entered the German's room under the pretense of retrieving the food trays. Four men walked out of the hotel and climbed into the black Mercedes. The hotel lobby was strangely deserted. There was no one at the front desk or even in the restaurant to see them leave.

As the car disappeared into the night, the two rooms occupied by the Nazis were cleaned and straightened. At the rear of the hotel, the little room assigned to the German driver was likewise stripped and remade. As far as the Hotel Claremont was concerned, the three Germans and the black limousine never existed.

"We are Americans," said the big fellow.

"They are, truly," put in Odette.

"And your mission? Passing the names of patriots to the Gestapo, perhaps?" The question was asked by an unshaven man whom Odette had never seen before.

"No. We're here for information."

"Ah, intelligence gathering--but for whom? That is the question."

"You found the documents and transmitter in the car, didn't you?" said Moe.

"Those papers can mean anything," came a voice from the dark at the side of the basement room in which they were being held. Tied back to back in the center of the room, it was hard for Moe and Sally to tell how many people were in there with them.

"You people have made a mistake," Moe said calmy to his captors. "We came by parachute. We were met by some of your own resistance people."

The response was cynical laughter.

"What's so funny?" said Moe.

"And I suppose they used a great zeppelin to land that monstrous large automobile of yours?" More cynical chuckles.

"No, the car was provided as a cover. Look, can't you contact Bernardus? He's the one who set us up and sheltered us." The room grew quiet.

"Of course, you didn't know Bernardus was taken and executed by the Nazis. The one man who could vouch for you, conveniently dead."

"Kill them!"

"The talking is a waste of time," another voice rasped from the dark.

"Then call London for God's sake." Moe was still sounding like a man in the middle of a misunderstanding. No panic. No pleading. No loss of composure.

This fact had not escaped Etienne, who quietly stood off to the side in the dark. There was no evidence of traitorous behavior, but there were glaring inconsistencies. Odette and her friend suddenly appear from France. Supposedly they are wanted saboteurs. Next, one of them tries to run a German officer off the road. Then she and the German are caught together. Lovers? Could they fall in love in the aftermath of a car crash? Romeo and Juliet have no place in T'égal. And this so-called gauleiter and his two stooges--Americans? The Americans are not even in this war. To kill them all and dispose of the car would be the safest course. But, if he is an American agent, it could mean the Americans are about to fight on our side. If I impeded their entry by killing one of their operatives I might be guilty of prolonging the stay of our country's invaders. I would be as bad as Quisling.

"We'll call London," the voice that Odette recognized as Etienne's said. "A short message. And you'll be extra quick tonight about moving the transmitter. Who in London can confirm your story?" he said to the trussed-up pair.

"Send the message to the SOE in London. I'll give you the frequency."

"Oh, no, you are not giving us any monitored frequencies to give us all away. We'll call. You just give us the message that can confirm your identity."

Moe thought for a moment and shuddered. The lack of openness between branches of intelligence operations based in London could get us killed.

Odette became even more nervous at Moe's hesitation.

"Tell whoever you speak to in London, 'Confirm that the catcher plus two is with us.'"

"Or against us?" someone said.

Someone else wrote it down.

One of the other men said, "Catcher? You're not a catcher. It is we who have caught you. You and your accomplices. *We* are the catchers!" They laughed their skunky laughs as they exited. One man remained. He cradled the old 8 millimeter Mauser army rifle in the crook of his arm as if they'd been lovers for years.

"They will confirm, won't they?" asked Sally in English.

"They'd better, " was Moe's reply. "I can't see why they wouldn't," he added to soften her concern.

"Talk Flemish or not at all," their guard announced, a bit annoyed at their chatting in English.

They continued in Flemish. "What are you doing here in Belgium?" she asked.

"I can't talk about that."

"Even if they shoot us?"

"Even if."

"But they won't, will they? London will tell them not to, won't they?"

"They'd better. Of course they will," affirmed Moe.

They sat silently for a while. Then Sally said, "I blew up dozens of Luftwaffe planes."

"Really?" said Moe. "No!"

"Yes, I did. Not all by myself. With friends in the resistance outside of Paris. I even killed a man, a German soldier, with a hand grenade. After he shot a boy who was with us."

Sally had never talked freely about that afternoon. Short, smart-aleck allusions to it had seemed to satisfy anyone who had wanted more details. But now for some reason, the whole story came gushing out. The bravery had vanished in the retelling. Only the sacrifice remained--the lives cut short and the innocent people who just happened to be in the wrong place at the wrong time. She had rehashed her actions every night and a realization was becoming more and more clear: she wasn't half as tough as she had been painting herself.

"I heard about that operation in London," said Moe.

"Most likely in Berlin," injected the guard.

"That was quite a show. You certainly caught the Germans with their pants down."

The remark brought a chuckle to the grim face of the guard. Moe, however, was trying to ease the pain of the young woman to whom he found himself tied.

"You ought to be able to retire with honor after a job like that," he said. "Go home. Help America win its own inevitable war with Germany."

Home, thought Sally, there's no place like it. Where did I hear that before?

"What's your name?" Sally asked her trussed up companion. She was trying to change the subject, mainly to keep from blubbering, but she also wanted to know.

"My real name? . . . It's Morris Berg. People call me Moe."

He's Jewish! Sally nearly laughed out loud at the irony.

They all heard the car approach. They'd been gone nearly two hours. Now they were back. They entered the room, grim, noncommital.

"They don't know you," said Etienne.

"Did you send the message exactly?" Moe asked.

"Just as you said it. They answered, 'No knowledge of catcher'. They even repeated it."

153

Moe was trying to think. Why not acknowledge? Was this a procedure? A precaution?

"Was there anything else?"

"No. Just, 'No knowledge of catcher', they repeated it to be sure. And there was some gibberish letters transmitted."

"What was the gibberish?" Moe asked.

"Stop it, will you?" said Etienne. "You are wasting our time."

"What was the gibberish?" Moe asked again.

Etienne thought, what the hell, humor the man. They'll all be dead in an hour, anyway.

"Paul, you wrote it down. What were those letters?"

The young man pulled a crumpled piece of paper out from behind his belt buckle and read, "B-A-J-O-B-R-E-W-C-Y-K."

"Bajobrewcyk?" said Etienne. "Sounds Polish."

"Let me see the letters, please," said Moe.

Etienne held the scrap of paper before him. He really didn't like the idea of killing these people. They didn't seem like vicious Nazis but his duty was clear. He must protect the integrity of his group at all costs. Had he not provided them every opportunity to be recognized? London didn't know them. And clearly Odette was somehow connected. They would be taken out just before dawn. We would also need to bury the car but we could take our time doing that. But these four would have to be under the earth before sunup. The girl's companion, Babette--we will decide later about her. She may be one of them also. Those hard thoughts were disturbed by a shout.

"Jabberwocky!" Moe said it again. "Jabberwocky! Those letters are an anagram for a code I use. Jabberwocky."

"What in hell is Jabberwocky?" they all were thinking.

"It's a character from *Through the Looking-Glass* by Lewis Carroll."

"*Through the Looking-Glass*. I have read it to my children many times," said the guard. He lowered his gun slightly for the first time that long evening. "The fearsome Jabberwock. I know him too."

"But," Etienne jumped in, "that doesn't prove anything."

"They sent a coded message and we unraveled it. That certainly does prove something."

"Paul," Etienne said wearily, "go get your book. Everyone please be quiet." No one was talking. "This may mean nothing at all."

As the car started and pulled away, a transmitter in another room beeped for attention. The coded message declared, "Catcher plus two friends. Repeat. Catcher plus two friends. Offer all support." The message was repeated. "Acknowledge with a V." Two men ran to the transmitter to make the V, three dots and a dash that confirmed message received and understood.

"They couldn't be sure exactly who was contacting them so they stalled us with the first message and sent the second on our special frequency."

"What a relief."

"What a day."

"I'm going home, my old lady is going to think I'd had it."

"A good day's work, men."

"Hey," said Odette Szabo, once again in her cocky French saboteur voice. "Isn't anyone going to untie us?"

They did, with apologies.

When Paul returned with the Flemish language *Through the Looking-Glass* version, he was surprised to discover the lights still on in the kitchen of the farmhouse. Inside they were all sitting around the table talking, drinking wine with bread, and eating some canned kippers opened for the occasion.

Etienne pulled Paul's daughter's book from his hand and fingered the pages till he found the Jabberwocky. He then began to read the stanzas aloud. Everyone leaned forward in rapt attention.

> *"And hast thou slain the Jabberwock?*
> *Come to my arms, my beamish boy!*
> *Oh frabjous day! Callooh! Callay!"*
> *He chortled in his joy.*

"And is it you who will slay the Jabberwock?" he said to Moe.

"No, it won't be me who slays him. I rather think it will be you."

The Partisans around the table nodded. They thought so too.

"At least we know the place of the Allied invasion," said one of the unshaven patriots.

"Where?"

"Calais, of course."

They were behaving like a pair of lovesick teenagers, reluctant to leave each other's company. They had been very close to death. Sharing that had brought them close. They received warm smiles and knowing looks from the farmhands, most of whom were also members of the Resistance. It was logical; who but a true romantic would commit to such a risky occupation? The Belgian farmer and his family were enjoying the company of these nice young people especially in the light of the extra hands being put to many of the "one of these days" chores always found in farm work. There was good food, cameraderie, and useful work, the best kind of R&R. In addition, London was urging them to avoid all contact before the promised counteroffensive. So, for the time being, T'égal's sole assignment was to gather information for the impending action.

There is no glory in it, thought Etienne, but a soldier is bound to his orders.

Babette and Ernie seemed to be getting along very nicely. They always volunteered for chores together.

Bet there's something going on there, thought Moe. I wonder if any of the others have noticed. In fact, Moe was the last person to have noticed.

Moe was preoccupied with two problems; should he give up on Heisenberg or plan a second attempt and how to get Odette to safety. The coast of Belgium and Holland was hot. The many border incidents had caused the Germans to increase patrols in an attempt to seal off the Channel.

Perhaps Spain? A long trip. But possible. I could take her. But what about the atomic weapon? We need to know. A trip like that would waste time. We've wasted enough of it already. Could somebody else take her? I wouldn't trust anyone else. You've gotten emotional about this, haven't you, Morris? Yes. So what? So think. What's the solution?

"These apples aren't ripe," said Odette.

Moe looked down at the basket he had just helped fill and could only manage a weak "sorry." On the ladder he'd been picking fruit mindlessly. He was trying to come up with the plan that would win the war, rescue this girl, and get himself and his partners safely back to London.

Babette was giggling in the next tree. From the ladder, she was accusing Ernie of trying to look up her dress. Knowing Ernie he probably was guilty. And I'll bet Babette was encouraging him. What was she saying? When winter comes she would take him skiing. She would teach him. It was easy. She had grown up in Oyonnax in the Ain province of alpine France, only a few kilometers from Geneva. As a child Babette had learned to ski almost before she could walk. Ernie understood most of what Babette was saying and was properly impressed. In his best tourist French plus a bit of sign language, he told her that he couldn't wait to start his ski lessons.

A little voice shouted "focus" in the movie theater of Moe's mind. The image of snowy Alps went from fuzzy past sharp to fuzzy again and finally returned to sharp. Switzerland. A neutral country. German-speaking. Probably relaxed security. And one of the scientific centers of Europe. With Odette and her friend safely in neutral territory and my team having access to sanctuary, I've lots more choices than I have here in Belgium. Switzerland! There must be some people who can help us there. I've got to find out.

157

Moe scrambled down the ladder and went looking for someone to take him to a remote spot where he could call London. He was reminded that "we never initiate radio contact in broad daylight, wait till dark." Moe hated to wait. He needed to make travel arrangements for a ski holiday in Switzerland. Right away.

That evening Moe got off a short message to London requesting contact with American intelligence. When a communication in Jabberwocky code was received by SOE, it was immediately directed to the Americans. Only Donovan, William Casey, Robbie Roberston, and a clerk named Ollie Jordan could translate the messages. These were "the catcher's" contacts while he was in the "field." Either Donovan or Casey would always remain in London available for a transmission while the other was away. Two nights passed before Moe received his reply; it was short and gave only the precise time for the transmission three nights hence. When the contact was finally made, Moe outlined his plan in Jabberwocky code.

Several nights later the coordinates for an airdrop were conveyed and two nights after that contact a large well-padded bale was dropped from a single-engined Westland Lysander to the waiting resistance team. The bale contained one wooden box of hand grenades, two large metal cylinders that resembled over-sized Thermos bottles, and a briefcase packed with three hundred thousand German marks.

There was also a letter. "These bottles are to be delivered to Dr. Paul Scherrer, Federal Institute of Technology, Zurich, Switzerland. He is a good friend." It was signed, Robbie. There was a postscript. "Do not open bottles. Contain highly toxic substance. D2O. Destroy this note."

Two days later, after saying their good-byes, the five young people piled into the big car and headed southeast toward the picturesque crags of the French Alps.

As the trip began, the American girl, Odette, made an odd request.

"From now on, I'd like you all to call me Sally, okay?"

"Okay by me."

"Sure."

"Okay Sally," said Moe, "make yourself comfortable, by late tonight our little safari should be in Switzerland.   Neutral Switzerland."

Part 3
Regroup

20

THE BIG BLACK MERCEDES AND ITS FIVE PASSENGERS skirted the city of Reims as they headed south making for Vichy-controlled territory. Moe reasoned that French troops would be less likely to impede a German staff car and its occupants. They were stopped at several checkpoints along the way, but in each case, after a superficial check, the car was allowed to proceed. Once south of Lyons, they turned toward Albertville and the Little Bernard pass. Now the stops became less frequent and they made better time.

As the car began to climb into the foothills, the snowcapped French Alps rose before them in the distant haze. The road turned and switched back on itself more frequently as the elevation increased. It began to rain when they finally negotiated the pass to the Swiss frontier, where they were delayed for a few minutes as French and then Swiss border officials inspected their vehicle. When it was found to harbor no contraband, the gauleiter and his entourage were welcomed to the Republic of Switzerland. The only requirement of the Swiss border authorities was that the red swastika party flags be removed from the front fenders of the car and that the male passengers change into civilian clothes at the earliest opportunity. The men changed into civvies at a nearby rest stop and they continued into the Swiss countryside. A heavy, wet snow began to fall, which turned their surroundings into a lovely picture postcard as it blanketed the road behind them and covered their tracks completely.

During the German aggressions in Europe, the Swiss cities of Bern, Zurich, and Geneva became centers of international intrigue. Switzerland was referred to as Europe's phone booth. Businessmen and foreign agents posing as businessmen filled Swiss hotels. Their stock and trade was the buying and selling of war-sensitive products and information. When information was not available, rumor was readily accepted in its stead. Neutrality had created a boom economy for the Swiss.

After driving all day, through the night, and most of the morning, the big car pulled in for petrol near Bern. German marks and French francs had bought fuel in the German-occupied countries with the help of a high- priority gasoline allocation card thoughtfully included in their packet of credentials. The Swiss gas station attendant adamantly insisted on Swiss francs but eventually settled for double the price in reichsmarks.

"See what happens when they see a big car?" said Gurney, relieved to be driving without the encumbrance of that annoying bandage over his mouth.

On the Höchstädt road to Zurich everyone finally relaxed. It was snowing more heavily now, but the big car held steady and true. They had left the war behind them on the other side of the Jura Mountains. There, every checkpoint or the slightest misstep could bring capture and execution. It was exhilarating to be able to breathe the danger-free air of neutrality.

As the mood of the car's passengers brightened, "ninety-nine bottles of beer" broke out. Gurney started it but before the third bottle fell, everyone in the car was singing. Even Babette, who thought the song was idiotic and said so, eventually joined in. About fifty bottles of beer someone said "I'm hungry." As if on cue, the Gasthaus Romanus came into sight around a curve. The parking area at the side of the inn was shoveled clear and there were several vehicles in the lot. One of them was a Mercedes with civilian German license plates.

164

"Boss?" said Gurney to Moe, indicating the German car.

Moe's initial instinct was to pass up the Gasthaus and find another farther along. Then he thought, what the heck, this is Switzerland. We've got as much right here as anybody. "But remember, we're still Germans. And Gene, keep your mouth shut, okay?"

"Okay."

Inside, the elderly proprietor and his wife welcomed their newest patrons cheerfully. It was turning out to be a better than average luncheon crowd despite the bad weather.

When Moe glanced into the roomy dining room he abruptly turned to the old gentleman and requested "two separate tables, please." He could make out a family of three, a young man and woman with a curly top toddler sitting at a far table. At another table, a younger man and his sweetheart were gazing dreamily into each other's eyes. A third, larger table was occupied by a party of six. This table worried Moe. Three attractive young women and their escorts, three Wehrmacht officers, noisily enjoying their luncheon. They all turned to observe the entrance of Moe and his crew. Moe realized instantly that he and his friends would have to be on their guard. Ernie and Gene were seated together at a far table while Moe shared his with the two young women. Little flashes of disdain passed between the eyes of the three young females at the Germans' table and the two women with Moe. The German officers turned away and resumed their own conversation, obviously discussing the new arrivals.

Moe reached into his pocket for the gold-circled Nazi party pin that he had earlier removed from his uniform. He pinned it to his lapel. All NSDAP party members wore similar pins but this slightly larger version with a wide gold wreath circling it meant that the wearer was someone special. The gold-encircled badge could be worn by only two types of persons: either one of the first one hundred thousand who had joined the Nationalsozialist Deutsche Arbeitpartei (Nazis, for short) and who were with the führer at the very beginning or someone who had performed some act of heroism or service of great importance to the Reich. In other words, that gold circle around the swastika meant that you had the führer's unlisted phone number and that if you called it you could make things very unpleasant for anyone you didn't like. When the Germans spotted the golden glint of the pin, a sudden softening of demeanor overtook them. Pleasant nods were offered and exchanged. Even the three girls joined the effort to be friendly. They'd obviously been instructed to do so.

Lunch was excellent. Today's spécialité de la maison was veal stew with noodles, a very meaty stew in a rich sauce loaded with vegetables. Just the thing to ward off the winter's chill. Each had a generous portion ladled over yellow noodles and some grainy bread with which to polish the platters. First, however, there was the soup, a rich chicken broth with dumplings that looked remarkably like the matzo ball soup Moe's mother made back in New Jersey. Sally caught his response and savored it. She herself had the very same thought. The men had beer with their lunch while the ladies ordered the house wine.

The Swiss proprietor showed remarkable agility as he served courses, removed dishes, and replenished the drinks.

Three more people entered the dining room and were shown to their table, an older couple and a teenage boy, most likely their son. The family also looked German, most likely a middle-level army officer on leave with his family.

After the spring campaign through France, Belgium, and the Netherlands, the Germans had been unaccountably inactive. The Vichy government was entrusted to control the south while the industrial north was left to the Germans. The Vichy government deactivated the French warships all over the world keeping the navy in port while German U-boats were free to harass Allied shipping in the North Atlantic. Although the Luftwaffe was responsible for regular bombing missions over Britain, the army, which had taken only days to subdue Czechoslovakia, Poland, and Austria, weeks to overrun France, Belgium, and the

Netherlands, seemed to be taking a holiday from the war. Leaves were being granted and soldiers were encouraged to visit home and family.

Moe observed that here in this very restaurant at least four German officers sat lunching. Could this mean that Hitler was content now that he had conquered Europe? Was he bombing England to coerce them into some sort of "hands off the mainland" treaty? It was possible--if they didn't yet have an atomic weapon. But Einstein had warned that "such a weapon would make Hitler insatiable. Nothing less than world dominance would satisfy him."

Moe felt a sudden pang. You, helpless oaf, blithely sitting in a cozy Swiss restaurant swilling beer while the whole world was waiting for you to confirm one single fact. Moe drained his glass. It had a guilty taste.

Both girls noticed a changed in Moe during lunch. He had become lost in thought somewhere between the stew and the apfel kuchen. He failed to notice the trouble brewing at his friend's table. To fully understand what happened next, one must go back several weeks.

Young Lt. Gene Gurney was coming to think he had grabbed the scratchy end of the toilet brush. First he went from fighter pilot to limousine chauffeur, a definite demotion. Then there was the stupid bandage over his mouth, which chafed and humiliated him. And--and this was a big and--there was the situation with the girls. Ernie had Babette, a great gal with a marvelous set of maracas. Moe seemed totally hooked up with the American girl, Odette or Sally or whatever her name was. And I'm left to fly solo. Is that fair? In his heart he knew he was being childish. No one planned this. And he knew that Moe was working hard to accomplish their mission and get them out safely. He also knew that it was an important mission. But why me always on the short end? The answer inevitably came back-- because we each have to do our part. This job is bigger than any individual. Complain later. Get yourself together and do as you are told. Stop thinking about only yourself and be a man.

The five bottles of beer and a complimentary glass of Rhine wine completely blocked the little speech with which he had so often rallied himself back to reason. It simply didn't come. What was left was a very annoyed young American soldier in a room full of Nazis. He and the alcohol had a terrific urge to punch someone. But who? Certainly not his friends. What if he slugged a Kraut? Moe wouldn't like that at all. And it might screw the mission, although how it could be screwed further he couldn't fathom.

So he stood up at the table and in a surprisingly clear tenor voice began to sing. It was to the tune of the Australian "Colonel Bogey March."

> *Hitler, he only has one ball*
> *Goering has two, but they are small*
> *Himmler has something similar*
> *And Goebbels has no balls at all.*

Everyone turned and stared.

He then sang the second verse, which was the same as the first, only louder. The three Americans could only watch in stunned surprise with more than a little panic percolating within them. Ernie attempted to pull Gene down into his chair but Gene shook him off. Moe began to rise to swat some sense into his driver when the darndest thing happened. The three German officers began to sing along. They were faking most of the words, but they were well familiar with the key word in each stanza. Hitler, Goering, Himmler and Goebbels. They thought it was an English version of a Third Reich victory song. And they sang it. Loud.

"Goering hadoo buddey fershmall."

Soon everyone in the dining room was singing, including Moe, the German officer and his family, the three women with the Germans, the two girls with the party official, Corp. Ernie Kahn, the young Swiss couple, the young Swiss papa bouncing his son on his knee, and ma and pa proprietor.

"Himmler hat some sing simlah."

The only person not singing was the wife of the young Swiss fellow with the toddler. She taught fifth grade at an elementary school in a nearby village. English was one of her subjects. She spoke haltingly but understood fluently. She also understood just how crazy the floor show at the Gasthaus Romanus was.

"Goebbels hat noble an tall!"

Moe and Sally couldn't believe it. Everyone was enjoying the sing-along. Glasses were raised and the older German guest bought a round for the house as his wife and son beamed. As the various groups finished their meal and left, they stopped at Gurney's table to slap him on the back good-naturedly. He wisely acted too drunk to answer, which initiated another good laugh all around.

The decision was made to spend the night at the Gasthaus Inn because of the snowy roads and the indisposition of the chauffeur.

Sally and Babette took one room and the three men shared another. A cot was set up for the very tipsy driver, who began snoring even before he was horizontal. After Gene was undressed, Moe walked over to the girls' room to see if they were set up okay and to say good night. Babette answered his knock, gave him an odd grin, then called Sally.

She stepped out into the hall and closed the door. When Moe leaned over to give her a little kiss, she threw her arms around his shoulders and turned it into something more. That good-night kiss released the feelings and desires that the couple had been suppressing during the past weeks. Now they stood, recklessly entwined in a dimly lit hotel hallway, oblivious to time, place, duty, and mission, aware only of each other.

After a while, Moe said softly, "I've got to go."

She replied, "I know." She then took his hand and placed it on her breast and said, "Good night, my dear," then turned and disappeared into her room, leaving Moe standing alone in the quiet of the hotel corridor with the sound of his own heartbeat in his ears.

Luckily Moe had his room key in his pocket because as he walked down the hall he realized he had forgotten his room number.

21

AMERICA WAS IN IT NOW. While the world watched Hitler, the Japanese attacked Pearl Harbor and essentially destroyed the Pacific fleet. The next day President Roosevelt addressed Congress to declare "December 7th, 1941, a day that will live in infamy," and that as of this date "a state of war exists between the United States and the Empire of Japan." Three days after the president's announcement, Hitler and Mussolini declared war on the United States.

Americans were stunned by the vulnerability of its seemingly invincible military forces. Admiral Kimmel and General Short, the two Pacific commanders, were criticized for their apparent negligence in permitting ships and planes to be deployed in a way which made them extremely vulnerable to attack. The careers of both these officers were irreparably damaged as a shocked America asked, "How could it happen?"

There was also the question of the Third Avenue El, the steel structure for the elevated subway line running the length of Manhattan. It was dismantled along with several other steel structures throughout the United States, and alleged to have been sold as scrap metal to Japan. Americans were outraged that this same scrap iron had been thrown back at them in the form of bombs and bullets.

There were many questions, much confusion, and even a little panic because of the events of late 1941. New Japanese submarine sightings were reported every day off the coast of

California. Americans were frightened, hurt, and confused all at once, but slowly a single emotion rose to supersede the others: anger. Americans plain got mad. Few people in the history of civilization responded quite the way the Americans were about to respond. They set aside their differences and self-interest and rallied to a single objective: Beat those rats.

The Swiss had always viewed Hitler with disdain. Most citizens likened him to a posturing comic opera villain attempting to be arch and malevolent behind his ridiculous postage stamp mustache. Now that the United States was taking him seriously, the Swiss could do no less. The dictator, after all, lived right next door. Not only are the Swiss realists, they are also a tough people. The world thinks of the Swiss as watchmakers and bankers. This is true. However, every adult male is in the army and keeps his rifle in a closet of his home along with his allotment of forty-eight rounds of ammunition. It has been said that Switzerland doesn't have an army, it *is* an army. And those picture postcard Alps? A warren of gun emplacements and artillery with the targets well zeroed-in. Any incursion by a foreign enemy would meet serious oppostion. As one of the world's oldest democracies, the Swiss are realistic about what it might take to preserve their sovereignty.

The café in the Hotel Züricher was buzzing with the latest war news. Germany had recently imposed rationing on its citizens. There were few shortages at this stage of the war but with typical teutonic logic the leaders of the Reich decided that it would be prudent to put limits on consumption of necessities like food, petrol, coal, and clothing. The popular joke going around asked: What is the difference between India and Germany? In India one man starves for millions, referring to Gandhi; in Germany, millions starve for one man, the führer.

The talk was also of Germany's new law requiring that all adult Jews wear a yellow cloth star on their outer garments. Someone quipped that this mandatory star should be called the

"Pour le Semite," making a punster's allusion to the "Pour le Mérite," or Blue Max, the highest imperial German decoration of World War I. This gallows humor usually garnered a chuckle from the Zurich café crowd, who sat, drinking their schnapps, wiling away the hours in discussion of current events and worst fears. In the relative safety of Swiss neutrality, they nervously awaited the next moves of this world-stakes chess game.

When Moe registered as a party official of the Reich he noted that the Swiss desk clerk acted as if deputy gauleiters checked in every day. If indeed they did then, Moe thought, it would be necessary to stay alert. Sally signed in as Sally Carlisle, Park Avenue, New York, and companion. Ernie and Gene took rooms at the Pension Schlichter, a small nearby inn. It was clean, quaint, and not nearly as posh as the Züricher but certainly welcome digs after the many hours spent on Mercedes upholstery.

So here they were, an improbable band of spies and saboteurs, lounging about in nice rooms in a neutral country with plenty of good food and money, immune from the danger they had come to accept as a constant companion. It felt good to finally let down one's guard.

"Hey, that's Moe Berg!" the young attaché assigned to the American Consulate blurted out to his dinner companions. The party of three was dining at the Züricher. With him was Ashley Inness, deputy to the American consul in Zurich, and a handsome, dark-haired American woman, not the deputy consul's wife. The young attaché's assignment this evening required a degree of diplomatic skill. He was to leave with the woman after dinner, escort her to her hotel, see her safely to her door, and then leave. Presumably the deputy consul would discreetly arrive a bit later.

As the three were having their dinner, the younger man was saying, "That's Moe Berg. I went to school in Boston. He was on the Red Sox. Great with the young pitchers. Kept 'em loose in the bull pen. That's Moe Berg, I'm sure of it."

The dapper Inness gestured for the captain and quietly inquired as to the identity of the big, dark-haired fellow his young aide had pointed out.

"Oh, and Kurt, if you could tell me the name of the young woman with him," Inness added as an afterthought.

Kurt dutifully returned with the names. The man was Manfred von Dahlheim, deputy gauleiter from Berlin.

Inness chortled at that. "You picked a high-ranking Nazi for your Berg look-alike, Tyler." He spoke as if he were addressing an idiot child. Inness and the woman had a hearty laugh at the expense of the reddening young man.

"And the young woman is Miss Sally Carlisle of Park Avenue, New York."

Inness stopped laughing. "I won't keep you, Celeste dear. I know you wanted to get to bed early. We'll have our check, Kurt."

"At once," said their captain.

Damn, no dessert, thought young Tyler Vaughn.

No coffee, what's his hurry? thought Celeste as she collected her gold cigarette case and rose from the table.

She's a lovely little thing, thought Inness, as he stole a furtive glance at the table in question, but what's she doing with a Nazi?

"Good night, Celeste dear," said Inness as he rose and kissed the hand of the exiting woman.

"'Night, Tyler." And they were gone.

"Kurt," he said when the captain arrived with the check, "I think I'll have coffee after all and some of that wonderful apfel strudel of yours."

"Very good, Herr Inness. Will that be mitt schlag?"

"Of course."

A message was delivered to the deputy gauleiter's room early the next day. It read, "Imperative we meet. At your convenience." Signed, Ashley Inness, Senior Attaché, American Consulate.

174

From Inness's point of view, there were four reasons the meeting was imperative. First, when a high Nazi official appears on one's turf, albeit neutral turf, a good operative finds out why he's there. Second, if by some faint chance Tyler is correct and this fellow is indeed Moe Berg, it behooves a son of old Nassau to seek out a fellow alumnus. Inness, Princeton class of '16, master's program, had heard of Berg, class of '23, the bright Jew who became a professional baseball player. Third, what in hell is a former American baseball player doing here in Zurich posing as a goddamn Nazi bigwig, if indeed it was he. As Ashley Inness was slated to become European chief of the newly formed Office of Strategic Services, he wondered, why the diddly damn hadn't he been informed of the project and its objective? Operations behind my back won't be tolerated, by God, thought Inness.

He unriled himself slightly as he came to the fourth reason for the note. She was the delicious redhead with the haunted green eyes dining with the gauleiter. Miss Sally Carlisle, Park Avenue, New York. Yes, she was a tasty tidbit indeed. Her every gesture bespoke her breeding. There was something exotic about her too. Fresh and exotic. Perhaps someday she might find herself in need of the assistance of a man of influence. Quite possibly. Gad, how I love my work.

Deputy Gauleiter Moe Berg read the note, slipped it back in its envelope, and placed it in the little drawer in the hallway table. There are no reasons at all for me to reply, he thought. At least not until I conclude the issue of Heisenberg, one way or the other.

Prof. Paul Scherrer, Moe discovered, was away for a three-week holiday at his sister's home somewhere near Bern, which meant there was little else to do but relax and enjoy the coming 1941 holiday season in the congenial atmosphere of Swiss neutrality.

22

—————✦—————

"Happy Hanukkah, Moe," said Sally as he opened the door to his room one morning. They had arranged to meet for breakfast and she was a few minutes early. Sally looked especially pretty today with her hair up, wearing the stylish new dress she had bought the day before. Her eyes sparkled as she offered Moe a small, brown paper-wrapped package.

"This is for you. A present."

Moe grinned and said, "Give it here. What is it? It's heavy."

"Open it."

The crinkly tissue paper parted to reveal a menorah. A Jewish Hanukkah candle holder. The small brass object seemed to stun Moe.

"Uh, thanks, but what am I supposed to do with this?"

"Well, you are Jewish, aren't you?"

"Yeah, and I'm also a card-carrying anti-Semite in case you've forgotten. You've got to get rid of this thing," handing the thing back to her.

Of course, Sally thought. Moe was right. What was I thinking? By buying this nostalgic symbol of normal home life she had given in to an irrational impulse. The rules of this game permitted no slipups.

"I realize it's a stupid idea but I thought we could light candles tonight. In honor of Hanukkah. I found it in a little stall at the flea market. It shined up nicely, don't you think?"

176

As she spoke of her find and her prowess at bargaining, Moe began feeling like a rat. An ungrateful rat. But the thing had to go. They both knew it.

"And I bought it because I have something to tell you." Her voice became raspy with emotion. "I thought I'd tell you tonight. When we light the candles. My name is really Selma Wiener, not Sally Carlisle. I'm Jewish. I thought you should know. I've wanted to tell you for a long time. I don't know why I didn't."

Moe understood that this "revelation" was obviously a big deal to Sally so he put his arm around her in an effort to console her.

"Hey, it's okay Sally, er, you said Selma?"

She nodded into his chest.

"Selma. We'll light the candles tonight and get rid of the thing tomorrow. Okay?"

Again she nodded and snuffled. He gallantly offered his handkerchief. She took it and continued snuffling into it.

"Selma," Moe said softly, "your being Jewish makes hardly any difference at all."

The girl listened quietly, her breathing becoming more regular.

"You know, from the start I felt a kind of pleasant familiarity, a comfort factor; felt it right off. I'm relaxed with you. Can be myself. Not Gary Cooper or Clark Gable, but me. I don't feel I have to be dashing. I don't have to be witty. Though sometimes I can't help it."

Sally responded with a damp chuckle but still held tight.

"So if you're some do-gooder debutante or a nice Jewish girl from Delancey Street, it doesn't matter. See. Right now, personal things, things that have to do with family and happiness, they have to ride in the rumble seat. I've got a job I have to do. Understand?"

She nodded yes, but he could tell she didn't really understand.

177

"Although, I've gotta admit, my mother back in Newark would've breathed a happy sigh at your disclosure. Now, do I call you Selma or Sally? How about I stick with Sally? Okay?" A small nod in the middle of a shuddering sigh indicated assent. "Okay! We'll keep it Sally!"

Moe guessed that he'd said the right thing because she was daubing at her nose with his hankie and beginning to smile. I'd rather face a low outside curveball any day, thought the lifetime .248 hitter.

That evening Moe ordered up a birthday cake with eight candles and put them in the crude little menorah. Selma Wiener spoke the ancient blessing to the best of her recollection and lit the candles. The Nazi party official took note of the fact that the French resistance fighter looked especially pretty in the candlelight. As they savored the Hanukkah cake with their champagne, it occurred to Moe that they might've stumbled on an improvement on the several-thousand-year-old ritual.

Until now, keeping tabs on the woman had been a boring assignment. She shopped with the blond, spent a lot of time with the Nazi. She was chauffeured around in that black limousine. She went for frequent walks. No sign of outside contacts or anything suspicious. Ah, but now his patience had paid off. He had observed an actual drop. After waiting for an appropriate time, long enough for the street to clear, he casually, nonchalantly, picked the package out of the trash barrel. It was small but heavy. He could feel the weight in his coat pocket. A new sort of gunsight, perhaps? Safely back in his office at the embassy he closed the door and unwrapped the paper. It looked like a candle holder. Brass. Funny writing on it. Some wax still in the holes. There's a promotion in this for me if I can present the object *with* its meaning. Are the holes spaced equally apart? Aha. There's a slight varience between them. Could mean something. Surveillance Agent Aymar Wentworth III, nicknamed "Trip," pondered his brass prize all weekend. His bombsight theory was checked out by the technical chaps and dismissed. Finally, when a secretary serving cocoa identified the object as a menorah, a Jewish candle holder, the find was dismissed as a coincidence totally disassociated with this subject. Instead of a reprimand for the wild-goose chase prompted by his naïveté and overzealousness, Trip Wentworth was commended for his tenacity. Men like Wentworth often occupy safe middle-level jobs in the business world. In the State Department, such men are promoted. By the war's end he had been elevated to assistant director of operations for central Europe with fifty-odd operatives reporting to him--proving that intelligence is no prerequisite for success in the field of intelligence.

23

―――•—• ⊠◇⊠ •—•―――

"I WILL SEE YOU," grumbled a rather reluctant Prof. Paul Scherrer into the telephone, "out of courtesy to an old friend. But I must prepare you . . . I can offer you no assistance. Your purpose here is of no interest to me."

"That is fair enough, Herr Professor Doctor." Moe used the precise and correct title of the esteemed physicist aware that such subtleties of propriety often have inordinate importance to some men. "I will see you tomorrow, then, at ten. I thank you for your courtesy."

The next day at 9:50 a.m., the black limousine crossed the Limmat Bridge and discharged Moe Berg one block from the administration building of the Zurich Federal Institute of Technology. Moe was wearing a black leather coat, black homburg, white silk scarf, and was carrying an oversized black briefcase. He looked like the devil himself after closing an enormous deal in Swiss souls. The overstuffed briefcase was nearly bursting at the seams.

Moe quickly found the physical sciences department and was given directions by a hurrying student to Professor Scherrer's office. When Moe reached the glass door bearing Scherrer's name and title, it was two minutes to ten. Moe then turned away and slowly walked the length of the long corridor retracing his steps back to the front entrance. One minute and fifty-eight seconds later, Moe returned to knock at the professor's door.

Scherrer glanced at his watch, acknowledged the time with a nod, and said, "You may enter."

His visitor's appearance surprised Scherrer. A big, dark man, younger and far more physical a specimen than the embassy bureaucrat he expected.

Moe made a slight bow and said, "Thank you for seeing me, Herr Professor Doctor."

Scherrer politely rose from his seat and extended his hand for a tentative handshake, then gestured to the chair in front of the large, cluttered desk. He was a slender man, in his early forties, graying at the temples. He had a large aquiline nose and piercing blue eyes that bored into his visitor over small steel-rimmed reading glasses.

"So what is it that makes this visit so imperative, Herr von Dahlheim?"

"Sir, I must first apologize for misleading you. My name is not von Dahlheim, my name is Berg, Morris Berg."

"Morris Berg?" The professor repeated the name. "I was told there'd be someone . . . but, Berg you say? Berg? That's very humorous. No disrespect intended, I assure you, but Herr Berg, you must be aware of a certain irony."

"Yes, sir, I am, now if I may continue."

"First," opening the black briefcase, "I bring you greetings from Dr. Robertson in London and Professor Einstein in America."

Scherrer gave Berg a sidelong glance at the mention of the names. He greatly admired Einstein, having met the renowned mathematician once, and Robbie Robertson was an old friend. Now slightly less aloof, Scherrer was paying a bit more attention to his visitor. If this Berg was telling the truth, and bringing word from two of his most esteemed colleagues, then he was obliged to hear the fellow out.

Moe could see the effect he was having on Scherrer and judged that it was time to press his advantage if he was to make an ally of the Swiss physicist.

"These are for you, sir," Moe said as he pulled the two large cannisters from his briefcase. The leather case sighed in gratitude at having been relieved of its burden.

Thermos bottles? the professor wondered to himself. Schnapps, perhaps? Or maybe good French vintage?

"What is it, Herr Berg? Thank you very much," hefting one of the containers, "but what is it?"

"Deuterium," replied Moe.

The older man was speechless. He licked his lips and still he couldn't speak. How did you come to it? How did you get it here? How did you know I was in need of . . . that, that my work had come to a virtual standstill for lack of it? All these questions raced through his mind while his mouth refused to produce the words. Finally he managed to say, "Deuterium?"

"Yes, sir," said Moe. "I was given to believe it would help you with your work. I'm sorry there's so little, but it's the most that I could safely carry."

There were tears in the old fellow's eyes as he sank back into his chair cradling one of the bottles in his arms as if it were a newborn babe. "I visited my little niece at Christmas time. When I first arrived she informed me that her mama and papa had said there would probably be no Santa Claus this year because of the war. I told her not to be surprised if Santa managed to get through in spite of the searchlights and antiaircraft. You see, I had brought her a lovely little doll that one of my assistants had found for me in Bern. Sir, I now know just how she felt when she found that doll beneath the tannenbaum."

He then rose and placed both cannisters on the floor, looked at them for a while and then turned to Moe.

"Now, tell me Herr Berg. How may I help you?"

Moe filled him in. From his meeting with Albert Einstein, his cram course in atomic physics with Robertson in London, to his parachute jump into Belgium and his near miss of Heisenberg at the university. Then his auto tour of occupied France, and finally his arrival here in Switzerland and the strange message from the American Consulate.

"It reads like the Odyssey of Ulysses," said Scherrer, finally. "An amazing journey through untold dangers. For whatever help it may be, I can tell you that no breakthroughs have occurred that I know of. Till now no one has yet managed a sustained chain reaction. Such news would be difficult to keep secret. Physicists are a vain and competitive lot and would risk even the anger of Hitler to be able to crow of such a success."

"That's comforting, sir, but not enough," said Moe. "I need to know if a breakthrough is imminent and I need to hear it from the source."

"Heisenberg," nodded Scherrer. "I understand. But you are certainly not going to walk up to 'His Emminence' and ask, how are you coming with the nuclear bomb, Herr Heisenberg."

"That's precisely what I intend to do, Professor Scherrer. And I need your help to find a way to do it."

"I'm hungry," said Professor Scherrer, looking at his wristwatch. It was nearly one o'clock. "Come. Join me for a nice lunch and perhaps we can solve your problem."

"Thank you, sir," said Moe. "But should we be seen together? I mean would it compromise you?"

"Ach, don't worry about that. I'm already on record for denouncing those Nazi gangsters. If Germany invades Switzerland they are sure to lock me up. So let's eat. I'll introduce you as a new graduate candidate from Göttingen. Come, I'll take you for a kalbsbrust like you've never tasted before."

The picturesque Kronenhalle did indeed serve an extraordinary stuffed breast of veal. At an out-of-the-way table, the teacher and student lingered over their luncheon with a dry white wine and several tankards of the restaurant's fine beer.

The two men ate and talked for hours. Only when the headwaiter began erasing the luncheon specials on the slate blackboard and lettering in the dinner fare did Moe bring the conversation back to business.

"Sir, under what circumstances would Heisenberg see me?" asked Moe.

"He'd see you if you brought him two cannisters of deuterium," the professor chortled.

"No, we are fairly certain he's not short of heavy water," Moe replied. "Would he see me with a letter of introduction from you?"

"I doubt it," said Scherrer. "He sees me as the opposing team. He would give no aid to the opposition. Especially if that opposition is both scientific and political. No, Berg, I think it must be arranged that you and he meet as if it were inadvertent. That would be your best course. Something like a casual encounter. But for that you would need to know his itinerary and you have little chance of obtaining that. I understand he has a small experimental atom smasher in Berlin-Dahlem, smaller than the one at Göttingen, but I couldn't say with certainty which he was working with. My guess would be that with limited resources of uranium, he would be concentrating in one location. And that, in my opinion, would be Göttingen. Further, there is a school of thought that contends that the metallurgy necessary to build an atomic chain reaction chamber would tax the capabilities of Germany at this time. The production of pure chromium and special alloys would require an industrial center of major proportions. To my knowledge, no such facilities are in operation. But this is not to mean that it is impossible. Every physicist today believes that we are living in the eve of the atom, and yet I'm afraid no clear picture can be projected of Germany's, or anyone else's, progress toward the making of an atomic bomb."

Ach, they are always so serious, thought headwaiter Emil Schnitzer, as he observed the two men at table 14. Scientists plumbing the depths of the universe. He had seen it many times before. The older fellow was a regular, Scherrer. Big cheese professor. The younger one he didn't know. Probably some budding genius student whose work the professor is especially pleased with. Well, wait till they plumb the depths of this. He was carrying the house dessert on a platter. Saltzburger nockerl--a sweet soufflé of butter and egg whites served on a warmed plate of preserved whole strawberries and syrup. Guaranteed to lift all but the already dead from down in the dumps. See. It was working already. Both men ceased their conversation and eyed the dessert as it was ceremoniously presented. Two perfect mountain peaks, light as a feather, aromatic and golden brown. Almost too hot to eat. Certainly too pretty to disturb. Scherrer was no stranger to this dainty. He plunged his spoon into his soufflé's middle and began to devour the deflating alp.

"Go ahead, Berg. It's very light. They're famous for this dessert. I know you'll enjoy it.

Moe plunged in, piercing the confection as the professor had. Scherrer was right. It was delicious.

"You know, Berg, or I should say von Dahlheim, this gives me a thought. If Mohammed can't go to the mountain, then the mountain must come to Mohammed. Yes!"

"Yes?" Moe repeated quizzically.

"Yes! We shall hold a seminar. A gathering of what is left of Europe's great physicists."

"And invite Heisenberg?" Moe put in.

"Ja, we invite Heisenberg," Scherrer affirmed as he scooped an errant strawberry from his plate and plopped it into his mouth.

"In the past we would hold our meetings at least once a year. Often twice. We were, after all, the apostles of the new physics," Professor Scherrer explained. "Then politics set in and it has never been the same. Oh, some of us still meet now and then. But the free exchange is missing. Rank has supplanted fellowship. And race takes precedence over scholarship. For an uneducated workingman to accept doctrines of racial superiority may be understandable. For a man of science to embrace such nonsense is unforgivable. Our little seminars are usually well attended and sometimes the old fire is rekindled. But most often the 'good Germans' revert to doctrine, refuse to share, then heil Hitler and leave."

"So you don't have much hope that Heisenberg will come," Moe added.

"Hope?" said Scherrer, as he leered mischievously over the remnants of his dessert. "A scientist does not hope. He creates a set of conditions that will induce a desired effect. Our challenge, Berg, is to compel the high priest of quantum mechanics to visit us in Zurich."

Several days later, across the city at the American Consulate, a late night briefing was in progress.

"He's a student. He's attending classes at the university. He's moved into the students dormitory."

"What? Nonsense!" Ashley Inness shouted at young Teddy Eddington, the consulate attaché assigned to shadow von Dahlheim.

"No, sir, he goes to classes every day."

"Who's he seeing at the school?" asked Inness, reluctantly accepting his man's report.

"Besides his teachers and classmates, a Professor Scherrer," Eddington read from his notes. "Head of the physics department. The guy checks out. Outspoken anti-Nazi. I'm telling you, von Dahlheim is really a student. Bought himself books, notepads, and everything."

"Hmmm," mused Inness, "this could be big."

In a secret communiqué to London, Ashley Inness had requested information on the identity and business of a Deputy Gauleiter von Dahlheim or Morris Berg, a former player on the Boston Red Sox baseball team. He had to wait several days for an answer. When the coded reply arrived in the mail via Lisbon it was not particularly satisfying. It said tersely: Aware of individual. Functioning highest P. Provide any assistance. That made Inness do a face-grabbing slow burn identical to the frustratingly frazzled expression comedian Billy Gilbert executed so archly in his films. Only Inness's wasn't funny.

"Am I not to be named OSS director for Europe? Do I not have the right to know about operations in my area? All operations! Not some. But all! Just who the hell do they think they're screwing with? And now with this new wrinkle. Science. This could be big! This bird either works for me or he doesn't work on my continent. That's my final word. Got it?"

"Yes, sir," replied the terrorized agent, understanding very little of the basis for his chief's outrage.

That evening at his villa as Ashley Inness was receiving oral sex from Celeste Bankton, the elegant American socialite, he was still seething over the monstrous affront that had been accorded him.

Celeste looked up from her task and said, "Ashley, darling, this 'head' business requires just a wee bit more concentration on your part, I fear. That is, if we have the slightest hope of getting anywhere."

Ashley Inness achieved no climax that night. He felt he would not achieve another until that dark stranger was either out of his territory or under his thumb.

The date for the seminar was set for the second week in May. Moe didn't like waiting that long but Scherrer rightly pointed out any earlier date was likely to conflict with busy schedules and, therefore, increase the number of "unable to attends." An expensive Zurich printer engraved the invitations and produced a very elegant job. Dr. Heisenberg received top billing as "guest of honor." The seminar was described as "the annual gathering of the colleagues of the New Science"--a blatant allusion to the good old days when the scientists were young, their minds crackling with insights that probed the mysteries of the atom only now beginning to open to them like a willing and beautiful young woman.

Once addressed, certain invitations received a handwritten note from Scherrer. "Could we prevail upon you for a few words during the session, Herr Doctor?" Or, "We would be honored if you could prepare an address to the group during the conclave."

Asking these prima donnas to speak was equivalent to suggesting that Jack Benny play his violin at a party. Even before one said "please," the squeaking would begin.

"Will this bring Heisenberg?" Moe asked.

"We cannot be sure," answered Scherrer. "We can only create the optimum conditions. Hmmm. I wonder. Can the conditions be improved?"

"How do you mean?" asked Moe.

"Provide a carrot," replied Scherrer. "I have recently heard from my friend, Klaus Clusius in Germany, who has been working on a heat-evaporation process for enriching uranium. It seems that they have reached a, how do you say? . . . dead end. The Germans would be grateful for a new direction. Then there is the scarcity of deuterium. Any new insights into the production of the stuff would be jumped at."

That very day a letter was sent to Robertson in London via Lisbon and a coded message was forwarded to SOE from France. Both communications made the same request. Translated from Jabberwocky, they read: "Need piece info to trade. Something H would travel for. Consider advance in refinement of U or production of D2O."

"Now, if you'll excuse me, sir, I've got to run. I'm late for my quantum mechanics class."

Scherrer nodded approvingly as his thirty-seven-year-old physics prodigy gathered up his books and hurried from the room.

Moe's classmates, some of whom were nearly twenty years younger than he, accepted the "old fellow" easily. Most were prodigies in mathematics or physics drawn from various schools in Switzerland and Europe. A few couldn't help wondering why this rather pleasant but backward old fellow had managed to become the pet of Professor Dr. Paul Scherrer.

All the invitations had been posted, except one, Heisenberg's. It was stamped and addressed and waiting to be mailed. All it lacked was a carrot. But it couldn't wait too long. Both Berg and Scherrer knew that. They would wait just one week more.

24

⚜

It was the afternoon of December 2, 1942, a glowering overcast day with just a hint of the winter to come, swirling in the air. Albin McCreedy, the assistant coach of the University of Chicago "Maroons" soccer team, had just blown the whistle on the next-to-last practice session before the Christmas vacation. The boys looked awful. Worse than awful. The new kids who were trying out--not a prospect in the bunch. The older lads who ought to know better played listlessly and without enthusiasm. They've got their minds on mom's roast turkey and apple pie, Coach McCreedy surmised. The team had recently lost several key players to the service and more were expected to join up at the end of the semester. McCreedy would be forced to play freshmen who were rough as a cobb. But that didn't mean they could sleepwalk through practice. A little special motivation was in order.

"Ladies, in case you didn't notice, that was a pretty sad effort," McCreedy told the boys who had sheepishly gathered around him. "So instead of the usual ten laps we are going to really get your blood pumping and run the stadium steps. Up one section, down another. That should hold yer attention, awright. Awwright, let's go!"

Regular spectators at Alonzo Stagg stadium had learned to bring seat cushions when they came to watch an event. The concrete seats are high, deep, and very hard. That afternoon, the steps looked exceptionally high, particularly deep, and sadistically hard to the weary young men. Up was difficult. A bit like high hurdles going up hill. But down was frightening. Momentum in collusion with gravity threatening a headfirst spill onto the rough concrete surface. It took only three sections, on the average, for even the dullest lad to conclude that it was well worth a bit of extra effort during practice to avoid this postpractice penance.

Directly beneath the concrete stands the sound of running athletes would have given the impression of distant thunder to the white-smocked scientists who were tending America's largest and most advanced atomic pile. Most of them were oblivious to the noise as they focused their full attention on the experiment in progress.

Prof. Enrico Fermi was preparing to produce a sustained chain reaction of the heavy element, uranium--something theoretically possible but till now, never before achieved. The contraption, called an atomic pile, was built upon a doubles squash court directly beneath the stands. It resembled a blockhouse of black bricks supported by a wooden framework. The rows of bricks were of the purest graphite with alternate layers hollowed out to house a pair of rounded hockey pucks of nickel-plated uranium. The highly purified graphite served as an excellent modifier substituting brilliantly for the rare and difficult to produce heavy water. Fifty-seven courses rose from the wooden floor of the squash court to the rough underside of the concrete stands. There was not enough room for one more course of graphite bricks.

As he focused intently on the Geiger counters and scintillation chambers that measured neutron emissions, Fermi gestured to his assistants manning the cadmium-clad control rods and safety dampers. Slowly they were withdrawn, first the cadmium sheets suspended from pulleys anchored to the framework, then all but one of the cadmium control rods. The clicking Geiger counters increased their tempo and then segued to an agitated buzz. The recording stylus traced a wild be-bop of scrawlings on the graph paper, then settled down to a more regulated oscillation.

"When do we get scared?" asked Dr. Leona Woods, one of the scientists manning a counterweighted safety rod.

It was a question on the mind of every one of the scientists in the cavernous room. There was concern that once the chain reaction began it could no longer be shut down and the resultant energy release would escalate uncontrollably till the very atmosphere surrounding the planet was consumed. The end of the world might well be at hand.

When Dr. Fermi smiled and answered, "Not yet," a wave of reassurance washed over the team.

Fermi glanced up to the top of the pile where three scientists stood poised with containers of cadmium sulphate solution. These were the so-called suicide squad with orders to douse the pile with the neutron- absorbing material if the reaction accelerated out of control.

At a nod from Fermi the last rod was withdrawn in six-inch increments as the Nobel laureate observed the gauges for the telltale increase in neutron multiplication. The counters now no longer clicked but were producing a disquieting, high-pitched whine as the blurred tip of the recording stylus scratched insanely at the paper. Everyone in the room was suppressing the urge to flee except Dr. Fermi, who calmly directed the technician to "withdraw the rod another six inches."

An unsteady hand withdrew the rod six inches more as the core temperature pegged at over two thousand degrees. As Fermi declared his expectation that the pile "will now stabilize," the shrieking Geiger counters inexplicably calmed. There had been an enormous spike on the chart that registered neutron discharge but then as if catching their collective breaths all the indicators paused and normalized attesting to the fact that the reaction had indeed stabilized. While the tracings on the graph paper indicated a staggering output of energy, they also showed that the emissions were regulated. Core temperature slowly decreased, an indication that the coolant was maintaining the system.

For nearly thirty minutes, the scientists stood motionless, barely daring to breathe as the world's first sustained nuclear chain reaction purred obediently for its master. Professor Fermi asked an assistant to note the precise time for history's sake and then ordered the control rods replaced into the heart of the pile. The chain reaction slowed, then ceased, as the Geiger counters now found little to measure besides the stray background radiation of the universe. The nuclear age had officially dawned at 3:55 p.m., December 2, 1942, in Chicago, Illinois, U.S.A.

Ferdinand Maggiore, an overweight freshman who aspired to the position of defensive back, was gasping frantically as he thudded his way down the last section of the concrete stands. His more agile teammates stood and shouted encouragement as he neared the end of his harrowing run. "Go, Ferdi," they cheered and, then, applauded as he managed the final vault from the concrete edifice to the relatively soft and level cinder track.

At the precise moment that the world's first controlled nuclear reaction began to stabilize, a scientific breakthrough that rivaled manned flight, fire, and the wheel, the overweight freshman, Ferdinand Maggiore, had been galumphing less than a foot from the pile. He was closer to the scientific milestone than Dr. Fermi himself.

After the holidays, Coach McCreedy cut the fat Italian kid from the team.

"Bad enough they're gonna laugh at our play. I don't need 'em laughing at our players."

One year later Maggiore took his physical and was declared 4-F. He had hoped to be a pilot. Fat chance. He remained instead at the university to earn a degree in electrical engineering. In later years he would specialize in nuclear energy.

25

＋＋ ▣◇▣ ＋＋

THE BASSO DRONE OF THE LONE, FOUR-ENGINED BOMBER caused the morning rush of students to interrupt their hasty scurryings to their classes and look up to the sky. The mysterious new student, von Dahlheim, also happened to observe the unusual sight as he took his early morning constitutional around the university grounds. At first some feared an air raid, but as the aircraft drew closer it was obvious that the lone plane was in no condition to bomb anyone. Its landing gear was lowered, one propeller was windmilling helplessly while two other engines trailed black smoke. It appeared to be limping toward the Dübendorf Airfield to attempt what was obviously to be an emergency landing.

With both his radios inoperative, Flight Lt. Clive Bainbridge hoped the Dübendorf tower was sufficiently alert to clear the air and permit the crippled B-17 a straight approach. He and his British crew were one of the first to check out on one of the lend-lease fortresses sent to the RAF via Newfoundland from the Boeing plant at Seattle, Washington. Gad, what a beauty she was. Handled like a charm. Ample power thanks to those big supercharged Wright Cyclone R-1820 engines. Sleek and roomy inside. Great leverage on the controls--not at all like the arm wearying tug-of-war one was forced to endure in the Stirling and Halifax bombers he had flown previously. And those cleverly designed throttle levers made power control a bally cinch. But not today. Today, the *Excellent Lady* wallowed in the air like a drunken hippo. Her name was painted in large bold letters near

194

the pilot's side window. The British tended to decorate their planes less flamboyantly than the exuberant Yanks, but because this fine bird was on loan from the States, the crew decided she rated a highly visible moniker.

Upon the bomber's delivery to RAF Bomber Command, a package was found taped under the radio operator's table. It contained eleven baseball caps with the instruction that they were to be given to the first British crew of the new fortress. The red caps were emblazoned with a capital S with a small t and a capital L, all entwined. Someone said it stood for St. Louis, which didn't make much sense to Lieutenant Bainbridge, St. Louis being a French saint and all, but after takeoff the crew members removed their service caps and donned the new head-gear--a sort of esprit de corps thing. Considering this crew flew their first twelve missions without a scratch, it was possible that St. Louis was indeed their patron saint.

In she came, the American B-17 bomber with British mark-ings and British crew, wearing St. Louis Cardinals baseball caps, attempting to land on one good engine while two others sput-tered and popped and the feathered fourth simply bummed a ride. To make matters worse much of the vertical stabilizer was shot away and the flight controls were binding intermittently. Pilot Bainbridge fired two red flares indicating his intention to land as he made his approach and was relieved to see an answering green flare spiraling skyward from the runway's edge indicating that the tower had cleared his landing. Thank God for at least that. Now Bainbridge's problem was not to prang the crippled craft into the Dübendorf runway. This was highly inop-portune time for the *Excellent Lady* to refuse to answer the con-trols.

"Try for the grass between runway and taxiway, Clive," said the copilot.

"Trying. Still crossways. Rudder pedal to the firewall. Coming . . . coming around."

At the last possible moment the sidling lady straightened her seams and quit misbehaving, touching down daintily on the frozen turf between the main runways like a ballerina with sore feet. She rolled casually to a stop at the far end of the field.

"Top hole, old man," declared the copilot.

"Bang on, Clive!" Toby shouted from the navigator's compartment.

"Piece of cake!" replied Flight Lieutenant Bainbridge, whose woolen shirt was soaked with sweat despite the chill air.

The German Consulate, the British Consulate, and the Swiss government all demanded custody of the plane and its crew. In the end, the Swiss prevailed, setting the wartime policy for belligerent aircraft landing in neutral territory. The craft and crew would be interned for the duration. The craft's armament would be removed and the crew would become the guests of Switzerland, their stay supervised by the International Red Cross. The airmen would be forced to endure good meals, warm bunks, no shooting, no inspections, no dying. For the duration.

26

THE HALF-PAGE AD IN THE *ZÜRICHER TAG-PLATTE* announced the All-Star International revue to be presented by America's favorite comedian, Bing Higby. It would be a limited engagement of only two performances held at the State Musikhalle one week hence. The show was assembled under the auspices of the Red Cross and was intended primarily for the entertainment of the many Allied internees now residing in Zurich. However, admission was open to all nationalities.

That same day a messenger brought an envelope addressed to Manfred von Dahlheim to the office of Dr. Scherrer. It contained seven complimentary tickets to the All-Star International revue.

"Guess what, we're going to the show," Moe announced to Sally over the telephone. "We'll meet at the theater on Saturday evening. I think we should not all sit together so I'm having some of the tickets exchanged for others, seating us a few rows apart. But this is a pleasant surprise. It'll be a taste of home."

On the night of the show, as Moe and Sally took their seats in the plush gilt and red velvet hall, Sally looked as young and lovely as Moe, in a dark suit and party badge, looked dour and ominous. His demeanor matched the other German officials in the hall.

"Good evening, ladies and gentlemen. This is Bing, 'Nobody's More Neutral than Me,' Higby, here in Zurich on the behalf of the International Red Cross. We've got a great show tonight and we hope we can provide the entertainment and some laughs to keep your morale waaay up there."

The audience began to laugh, then applaud. The comedian was puzzled for a moment, then realized his "nobody's more neutral than me" line had taken a few moments to be translated. Well, that was a relief, he thought to himself. Still, it was a bit disquieting to have a joke laughed at about ten seconds late.

"Yes, I can see many of you are here on R&R. That's not rest and rehabilitation, you know. More like you've been *rail-roaded* to Switzerland." Nothing. All he could hear was breathing.

"Ah, Switzerland. The land of Swiss cheese and milkmaids. Which reminds me of the story about this Swiss milkmaid who . . . sorry, folks. Better not tell that one." Polite chuckles. Most were still working on the railroad joke.

"Did you hear about the fellow the other day who was caught smuggling ball bearings to the Allies? He put 'em in the holes in the Swiss cheese. Got caught when one of your customs guards broke a tooth." Oh, God, he wondered desperately, do I wait or keep going. Keep going. The first rule of show biz.

"At the airport, this fella wanted to trade a genuine Swiss watch for our Jeep. I told him it was a bad deal. Our Jeep doesn't run. He said, that's okay, the watch doesn't run either." A laugh reared up and filled the room. "Ball bearings in the cheese . . . customs man broke a tooth." HaHaHaHo. Most of the audience was exactly one joke behind.

Von Dahlheim and his party were laughing at the jokes, then again at the belated audience response and once more at the poor comic, who was obviously thrown by the situation but coping bravely.

"I was told by a friend of mine that in Zurich they bury Swiss bankers ten feet deep. Why ten feet deep? I asked. He said, Deep down they're not so bad."

Hahhahhahhohohohah!

"The watch doesn't run either."

"You know they've got a new prime minister over in England. Fellow named Churchill. He smokes those long cigars, you know. Has to, the ashes from the short ones keep burning his stomach." Ha Ha Ha. "Deep down they're not so bad."

"The previous British prime minister was named Chamberlain. Didn't work out. The French, Czechs, and Belgians were positive his name was spelled 'J'aime Berlin'." Hohohahaha. "Burning his stomach."

It took a few minutes but Higby eventually took charge once he finally got into the rythym of his audience. When they at last caught up with him, he received a standing ovation from the delighted crowd. After several minutes of basking in the enthusiastic applause, Higby signaled for the applause to end so that he could introduce the next performer. It was the French singer, Marcel Pitelaire, who came on and sang a popular song in every European language but German. At the end of his performance he received an enthusiastic hand from everyone in the theater but the Germans.

Next, Higby introduced Germany's Tiller Girls. A troupe of twenty-two leggy frauleins who tap-danced and high-stepped sexily in their scanty costumes with all the zest and precision of a Prussian drill team. When they went into their high-kick finale, the audience roared with delight. These internationally famous girls were oft imitated, most notably by the Rockettes of New York's Radio City Music Hall.

Finally Hansi Mueller, the German comic, came out and did an insane act in overalls with paste bucket, ladder, and brush, attempting to wallpaper the theater curtain. To the howls of the audience, he repeatedly stepped in his bucket, fell off his ladder, and papered his body to the curtain. The biggest laughs came as he feigned anger at the audience for laughing at his ineptitude and in retaliation flung the contents of his gloppy paste bucket at the cringing front rows. Of course, the bucket was filled with confetti, much to the relief and delight of the folks in the front rows.

Bing Higby then came out with two leggy Tiller Girls, one on each arm, thanked the audience for their fine reception, then brought out the French singer and the German comic for a final curtain call. They were followed by the rest of the Tiller Girls. It was a stellar evening of entertainment, which effectively took its audience away from the concerns of war for a brief time.

After the show some of the performers came out and mingled with the audience to shake hands and sign autographs. The French singer was the most forward, bussing the young girls and leering lasciviously at the women in the crowd who were no longer girls. He carried a stack of sheet music under his arm, copies of the songs he had sung that evening. He signed them and handed them out as souvenirs. Stopping in one aisle he gave an exaggerated heil Hitler to a tall fellow in the company of a pretty redhead. People nearby quieted. They were wondering how the Nazi would respond to the man. Moe wasn't quite sure how he should respond either. The singer saved the situation when he pulled out a page of his music, signed it, and with a smile handed it to Moe. He then kissed Moe on both cheeks, to the relief of the applauding spectators. Then he leapt to the next aisle where he continued his clowning with a group of interned airmen.

As Moe folded the autographed pages of sheet music and slipped them into his suit pocket, the realization struck that he might have just received his answer from Robertson in London.

Later in the hotel, when the lines of the sheet music were examined under an extremely powerful glass, miniscule instructions detailing the condensation process for the refinement of uranium 235 were revealed.   That same evening a handwritten note was placed by Professor Scherrer in the lone unmailed invitation. It read: One of my students, who until recently has been studying in America, has knowledge of some advanced techniques in the mass spectrometer process for the refinement of U-235. He is anxious to meet you and would be honored to discuss it with you. Look forward to seeing you, sincerely, Paul. A nice juicy carrot, indeed. The envelope was sealed and would be on its way to Göttingen by tomorrow's post. The Swiss Postal Service was second only to the German Postal Service in efficiency.

27

ELISABETH SCHUMACHER HEISENBERG was a strikingly handsome woman: tall, slender, chestnut haired, with piercing gray eyes harboring a mischievous glint that generally disarmed anyone who happened to gaze into them. A dozen years younger than her Nobel Laureate husband, she provided the missing element in the physicist's solitary life. As a girl, she grew up in an intellectually active family; her father was a respected professor of political economics at Bonn and her brother lectured at London University in economics. Elisabeth chose a career in the wholesale book business and became a successful dealer despite the myriad obstacles encountered in this male-dominated trade.

The couple met at a piano recital in Leipzig. Werner had consented to participate in an evening of chamber music at the home of Otto Bucking, a local publisher of textbooks. Elisabeth was an invited guest. Werner was to perform Beethoven's Trio in G Major on the piano, accompanied by his host on cello and Erwin Jacobi, the Leipzig University chemistry professor, on violin. The moment Werner saw her he was taken with the bright-eyed Elisabeth. As their eyes met, the neutrons flew, splitting their respective nucleii at nearly the speed of light, resulting in an uncontrolled reaction of emotions. A fitting manner for a great physicist to fall in love. They were married six months later.

Today Frau Heisenberg was in her kitchen contemplating the bird sent over from the metzgerei. A fresh-killed, remarkably plump duck, considering the growing scarcity of such delicacies as the two-front war was pursued. This was not the first bird ordered by Frau H. There had been another, but there was every hope that this one was going to erase the ignominy of that former fowl. On that previous occasion Elisabeth had eschewed the aid of AnnaLise, her housekeeper, electing to author the duck dinner, one of Werner's favorite meals, entirely on her own. She was determined to display a domestic side heretofore unrevealed to her new husband.

Armed only with the information gleaned from a quick glance at a cookbook, she prepared to roast the bird. After it had been in the oven a short time, Elisabeth took a peek at the bird. Its skin looked perfect, a uniform golden brown color, which assured the eye that it was evenly roasted and nearly done. The aroma, which permeated the kitchen of their cozy university cottage, confirmed the observation. When the handsome bird was removed from the oven and regally presented on its platter to her beaming husband, the physicist eagerly leaned forward to carve. The initial incision foretold of the disaster. The flesh ran red. Underdone! It practically quacked. Elisabeth fled from the dining room in tears.

Werner, hoping to salvage the situation, continued carving. Perhaps it looked worse than it was. He sliced off a sliver of breast meat and tasted it. Ach. Cannibal dinner. He was hoping to comfort his distraught bride in the upstairs bedroom by telling her that the duck tasted devinely and only needed a bit more time in the oven. But this was vile. Fatty. Raw. Completely inedible. So he did what any man would do if he loved the woman who had cooked such a bird. He lied. He returned the corpse to the oven, turned down the gas, and climbed the stairs to his inconsolable mate. And lied.

"Delicious! Just a bit undercooked. But what an aroma. Merely a slight miscalculation of cooking time. A good cook learns to ignore such minor setbacks. Let's eat out."

Smart women know when a man is lying. Very smart women know when to let him. Elisabeth Heisenberg let her Werner lie and allowed him to think she believed him. This is the basis of many good marriages and the genesis of many of the world's heroes. Men often achieve greatness simply because women allow them to, thus all humankind benefits and civilization continues its forward march.

My next encounter with a duck will be different, thought Elisabeth Heisenberg, as she coldly contemplated the supine form of her latest nemesis. A consensus of professors' wives determined that Elisabeth had neglected to prick the bird with the sharp tines of a fork, thereby allowing the abundant fat to run off, a most important step in the roasting process. Armed with this new information, Elisabeth vowed that this bird will be delicious because it will be both well pricked and well done. Inside the 220°C oven, the bird was oozing fat into its roasting pan. None of the professors' wives had bothered to mention the need to continuously draw off the highly flammable liquid fat to prevent an oven fire.

Earlier that afternoon in the basement laboratory of the Leipzig University physics building, Werner Heisenberg and his assistant, Robert Döpel, were adjusting valves on the perimeter of a five-foot-square aluminum box, which housed a sphere containing five concentric circles of uranium tile-like plates and a quantity of heavy water. The small scale-model atomic pile took the shape of an aluminum beach ball-size sphere. The entire apparatus was lowered into a tank filled with circulating tap water. In the center of the sphere, a neutron source of radon-beryllium was unshielded and began plinking at the nearly fifteen hundred pounds of uranium that surrounded it. The reaction was moderated by approximately three hundred pounds of heavy water. This was audacious science--in the vein of "let's put it all together and see what happens." There were no controls or dampeners, except the ordinary water expected to cool the contraption and inhibit the refined uranium's pyrophorous nature and propensity to ignite.

The Geiger counters told the story, clicking excitedly at the production of neutrons at a rate greater than either the air or the aluminum casing could absorb. Both scientists smiled at the reassuring noise, which meant that the experiment was proceeding as expected. Neutron bullets were dislodging multiples of neutrons as the bombarded uranium atoms split creating a limited chain reaction. A working reactor would be just a matter of upsizing this little beach ball. He, Werner Heisenberg, would be the first to sustain an atomic chain reaction. Perhaps even a second Nobel Prize would be his.

"Döpel, what are those little bubbles? Is there a leak? Raise the sphere from the water. Check for pressure loss."

As the valve was turned, the hiss of a pierced coffee can could be heard. "Check to see if our vacuum is still intact." Suddenly, in several places on the sphere, small jets of flame, as if from a miniature welder's torch, flared out. Döpel immediately yanked on the chain of the hoist, dropping the sphere back into the water tank. As the eruptions subsided he quickly started the pump, which siphoned the precious heavy water out of the breached aluminum sphere. This was a bad move. With the cooling properties of the heavy water no longer in effect, the heat intensified. Under water, the sphere glowed and shuddered. More bubbles appeared. The pulsating sphere seemed to have a life of its own, heaving and undulating in the water, or was it the visual distortion of refraction? The temperature gauges on the walls of the tank continued their climb until they pegged at 1500° C. Döpel took an ax to the sphere in an attempt to ventilate and depressurize it. All he got for his trouble was a steel ax head that caught fire. It burned with a white searing flame. Now the sphere in the roiling water seemed to undulate in angry spasm. Werner Heisenberg and Robert Döpel turned to look at each other, then fled from the laboratory as if the devil himself was at their heels. In truth, the devil appeared moments later in the form of a geyser of molten uranium, which burst through the sphere and up through the lab ceiling to the floor above.

The Leipzig fire department rushed to the scene to extinguish the strange laboratory fire. Once the components of the pile had been separated, the intense heat generated by the uranium could dissipate and the fire was easily put out. In his report the fire chief assessed the damage to the building as severe but because the blaze had been confined to a limited area, the structure was considered repairable. He chose not to mention the steel ax head, which stubbornly continued to glow with a hot, eerie light even as it lay in a steel drum filled with water. After all, who would believe such a thing?

When the fire was out and the damage to the laboratory was assessed, the physicist dragged himself home. There he was greeted at the door by his teary-eyed wife.

"Oh, Werner, I've had such a terrible day. Nothing went right. And the bird I was making for supper--all burned up. And what's more, the oven caught fire and the firemen were here and the kitchen is a mess. It will have to be repainted. And I'm sure the stove is ruined . . . Oh, Werner!"

He put his arms around his Elisabeth and smiled to himself.

"I know exactly how you feel, mein schatz," he said lovingly.

Later that evening Werner told his wife about his little laboratory disaster. When she sensed that it was all right to laugh, she laughed. They laughed together. At ruined ducks and uranium experiments gone awry. It made them both feel much better.

"This came for you dear," Elisabeth said to Werner. It was an invitation to a seminar in Zurich.

"From good old Scherrer. I always liked Scherrer. But a seminar in Zurich? I'm much too busy. It's impossible."

"I think you should go," said Frau Heisenberg.

"How can I possibly go?"

"I really think you should go."

"You do?" he replied.

"Definitely!"

28

—◄—≡◆≡—►—

WHILE MOE HAD VIRTUALLY DISAPPEARED, immersing himself completely in university life, Sally and Babette offered their services to the International Red Cross. The Swiss director of the overworked Zurich operation looked upon the two women volunteers as sent from heaven. They were put to work immediately translating the many requests for services. The few hours of volunteer work they had anticipated grew to become a six-day-per-week job.

At the end of the first week during their lunch break at the canteen, a distinguished-looking, neatly dressed man presented himself to Sally.

"Miss Carlisle, good afternoon. I'm Ashley Inness with the American Consulate. I wonder if you could spare a moment?"

Sally smiled weakly, glanced at her friend Babette, then nodded a tentative assent as she put down her sandwich.

"This is Miss LaCroix," Sally said, indicating her friend beside her.

"I'm pleased to meet you, Miss LaCroix," Inness said charmingly. Then he turned once again to Sally. "Well, Miss Carlisle, what brings you to Zurich? If you don't mind telling me. We at the Consulate like to keep up on our own, you know."

He oozed with sincerity and paternal concern. Sally was impressed and a bit flattered. Inness spoke of his desire to help those who had been caught up in the maelstrom--all of the uprooted and displaced people, not merely the Americans. He

207

was just an ordinary man doing his part as best he could, wishing he could do more. What a decent man, thought Sally. We are certainly fortunate to have people like this in our foreign service.

As they chatted over coffee Sally divulged a sketchy outline of her circumstances: her work with refugees in France after her graduation from Columbia, her flight to Switzerland after the German occupation, and her relief at finding sanctuary here in Zurich.

"How the time flies," said Inness, after a glance at his pocket watch. "I've enjoyed our getting acquainted so much I completely lost track of the hour. Duty calls, my dear. We should speak again. And soon. I must insist. Good afternoon, my charming Miss Carlisle, Miss LaCroix." A courtly little bow and he was gone.

Such a nice man, agreed the two young women.

So far, so good, thought Ashley Inness. "I've still got it, don't I?" the lunch hour Lothario chuckled out loud to no one in particular.

The car picked him up on the Bahnhofstrasse and drove back to the American Consulate. On the ride his thoughts returned once more to his luncheon encounter. Gad, her tits are high. Couldn't take my eyes off those young cupcakes. Practically at her collarbone. Celeste's must nearly be at her waist. And my wife's back home in Virginia? Can't even remember. I can't wait to unwrap those firm young titties. Patience, Ashley, patience. First rule of intelligence work. Don't try for too much at first contact. Inness liked to think he was one of the men who wrote those rules.

That night there was a party in the gauleiter's suite. It was Sally's idea. Why not, said Moe, who had elected to risk a night away from the dormitory. Sally bought another new dress, the third in a week. This one was a maroon velvet off-the-shoulder thing that made her look like a starlet at a Hollywood premiere.

Babette was a knockout in a backless blue number that criss-crossed in front and pinched at the waist, showcasing her rather remarkable figure.

Moe ordered up food and drink for a reception for eight. He then overtipped the room service captain enough to guarantee that they wouldn't run out of champagne and hors d'oeuvres. Everyone dressed to the nines and looked great. This was going to be a proper New Year's eve party, even if it was a month late. But where was Gurney? Gurney was late. Hell of a thing. When Gene finally showed up, it was worth the wait. He made his entrance with one of the Tiller Girls on his arm. The sly wolf had met her after the Bing Higby show and somehow made the connection—an impressive feat considering the girls were virtually imprisoned at night and scrupulously chaperoned. Yet there she was, a beautiful blonde amazon fraulein standing at least a head taller than Gene.

"Everyone, this is Helena."

As Helena was introduced to all, her smile faded and she grew quiet and dejected. Sally finally figured out the problem. The girl felt that her plain dress didn't fit in because everyone else was dressed so elegantly.

"We can fix that," said Sally as she and Babette whisked her down the hall to their room just as Professor Scherrer and his wife arrived. When the girls returned, Helena was all smiles. She was wearing Sally's dress, a green satin number that bared one shoulder, but the tall girl's proportions created an entirely different effect than when Sally had tried it on. Now replete with costume jewelry, hem at least four inches above the knee, the leggy Helena rejoined the party. The imbecilic grin remained on Gene Gurney's face for the rest of the evening.

As the party got rolling, an old fellow in the suite next door came over to complain about the noise. When Ernie invited him to the shindig he left, returning with his wife a few minutes later in their night clothes, and later amazed everyone with their mastery of the Charleston. Professor Scherrer did some sleight-of-hand magic tricks and Gurney taught Helena to jitterbug. It turned out she was a natural-born trucker. There were toasts all around and a special one "to our dear friend 'H'," whose acceptance to the seminar had prompted the celebration.

The party finally broke up around 3:00 a.m., when the hotel refused to send up any more food or drink. Moe and Sally slipped away to her room down the hall. Luxuriating in the quiet, they just sat and talked. About Gurney's tall girl. About what a nice party it had been. And about two lucky people who somehow found each other during terrible times like these.

"And one more thing," Moe added, turning slightly serious. "That fellow Inness, you told me about? Please don't trust him just yet. He's probably all right, but in our situation it might be smart to offer as little information as possible. Got me?"

"I've got you."

"I know you have."

Moe drew her to him and Sally could feel that his interest even at that late hour was not directed toward sleep.

"Wait a minute. Hold on just a minute," she said, putting her arm against his chest. "First I've a right to know who I'm going to bed with."

Moe didn't follow.

"Well, are you the arrogant Nazi party boss?"

Moe smiled.

"Or are you the major league athlete of mythical prowess?"

Moe's smile broadened.

"Or are you the freshman student learning the fundementals of nuclear physics, who," she continued, "would benefit from an experienced and well-rounded tutor? Well, who?"

It was nearly dawn when they fell asleep in each other's arms. Safe and contented. For a little while forgetting the many beings on this planet who slept neither safely nor content on this night.

29

THE LECTURE HALL WAS PACKED--literally standing room only. The small auditorium bustled with students and physicists from all over Switzerland and Germany. The first row of seats was reserved for a virtual who's who of European science. Schroedinger was there. Pretz, Weizsäcker, Langmuir, even Schumann, the Nazi supply chief. Standing around the circumference of the hall like a platoon of sore thumbs were Gestapo agents, Swiss plainclothes police, and university security men all intently observing the crowd with one eye and one another with the other.

Heisenberg came directly from the bahnhof. He was to be chauffeured by a driver from the university but the Gestapo insisted that they provide the guest speaker's transport. On the short ride to the school the Gestapo man implored Heisenberg to cancel his talk on the grounds that it would give aid to the enemies of the Reich. As they drew closer to the university, the Gestapo man's pleas became threats with insinuations of treason if he didn't immediately return to Germany. This last pitiful attempt to bully him only served to confirm the helpless position of the Gestapo thugs. It was a bluff and both parties knew it. However, although Heisenberg's fervent belief that science outranked politics remained unshakable, he was also no fool. He would confine his seminar lecture to pure physics. Nothing strategic, nothing controversial, and certainly nothing about atomic fission. Now that he had flouted the will of the Gestapo, it wouldn't be prudent to provide them with any substance for further criticism.

As the lecture hall's seats filled, Gestapo agents were busy attempting to identify every attendee. In an identical hall next door they mapped the room. On a large sheet of graph paper every seat had its square. The object was to identify the person occupying each seat. Soon only a handful remained unaccounted for. One of them, a third-row seat near the center of the stage, in which sat a youngish, dark-haired man. Big fellow. Not a professor or well-known scientist. Certainly not one of the guest scientists--they had all been accounted for.

"Who is that fellow?"

One of the clerks in the administration office made the first identification. "Oh, that is Manfred von Dahlheim, a student in advanced physics."

"A student? A bit old for a student, wouldn't you think?" the Gestapo man asked suspiciously. "Who is in his class? I would like to speak to someone in the same class."

They quickly produced one of von Dahlheim's classmates, who verified that he indeed was in the physics class.

"Thank you, that will be all," the Gestapo man said to the lad.

One more seat verified; only a few more and all the bodies in the room would be accounted for. He barely listened as the student went on about how that von Dahlheim fellow was not particularly adept at physics and therefore really shouldn't merit an invitation to such an august gathering. The agent simply wrote the word *überprüft* in the square representing Moe Berg's seat.

As Moe sat waiting for the entrance of his quarry, he shifted his shoulders slightly, partly to relax his upper body and partly to reassure himself that his .32 caliber Beretta was still nestled in its holster under his arm.

Heisenberg swept into the hall and walked straight to the lectern with all the resolve of the man who needs to read the gas meter. During some polite applause he perfunctorily acknowledged his audience and his host, Professor Scherrer, who accompanied him into the hall and quietly took the front row seat he had reserved for himself.

With nary a "gee, it's a great pleasure to be here at Zurich Tech," Heisenberg began his lecture. S-matrix theory applied to quanta and the mathematical implications of the Zeeman effect. No more than three minutes into it, Moe was lost. The delusion that he possessed a rudimentary grasp of the new physics was utterly shattered. Now his task was to at least appear to be following. Some in the hall were taking notes, among them, a Gestapo stooge with scientific credentials who was there to find something in the lecture that could later be used against the physicist. As theoretical physics is part mathematics, part philosophy, part poetry, nothing incriminating turned up.

From his demeanor Heisenberg appeared aloof and remote--a god condescending to share some simple wisdom with mere mortals. But that was his game face. Inside he was delighted to be there, enjoying the opportunity to bask in the adoration of his fellows. Since he had become a scientist for the Reich, Heisenberg's world had changed radically. To his new employers he was merely a technician like a plumber or a dentist, a tradesman to be sent for and asked "when will it be ready?" and "how much will it cost?"

Today he was back in his element. Being brilliant among brilliant men. Until now, he hadn't realized it was the camaraderie that he missed the most. The company of this cultured and elite band of brothers made the striving to know worthwhile. At one time, in the early days, there were only twenty-odd people in the world who could even claim to understand the new physics, and he, Werner Heisenberg, was one of the brightest. He'd proved it so many times in countless jousts with his contemporaries--a brilliance duly recognized by the Nobel Prize. Now, only after his position was secure, did he realize that the fun was in the running. Here he was, once again running at the head of the pack, showing off his intuitive leaps of brilliance, amazing them all with his finishing kick.

Well into his lecture he began to look around the room. He recognized old friends and yearned to speak with them. There were also some new faces, young upstarts who presumed to carry forward the cause when men like himself, Scherrer, and Weizsäcker would be bouncing grandchildren on their knees. He also observed lots of police. They were easy to spot by their alert eyes yet lack of attention to his talk. Germany, alas, was turning into a nation of policemen. Then there was the youngish fellow in the third row. His gaze didn't waver. He was inhaling every syllable. Should I know this fellow? Perhaps he's a mathematician? They are a notoriously intense lot.

Heisenberg lectured for two uninterrupted hours. No one coughed. Few blinked. When he was finished only a single formula remained on the blackboard: $E = E_i + gmhv\ 6$.

"I would be happy to answer any questions if I am able," brought enthusiastic applause from the group. There were no questions.

Scherrer then rose, thanked the speaker, and called an intermission. Refreshments would be provided in a nearby assembly hall. Now it was time for old friends, beloved rivals, introductions to adoring colleagues, and general kissing up. Inevitably they separated into small groups and as the conversation turned to more current topics and politics, the Gestapo grew even more uncomfortable. Moe was introduced to Heisenberg by Scherrer as the student recently from America who was versed in advanced methods for the enrichment of uranium, information he'd picked up at a recent semester at Princeton.

"Is there a place we can talk away from this din?" Heisenberg asked.

"Of course," Scherrer said, leading them to an empty lab a few doors down the hall.

While Moe Berg, alias Manfred von Dahlheim, was bringing one of the world's great scientific minds up to date on the mass spectrometer process for separating the rare and highly fissionable U-235 isotope from common U-238, five Gestapo agents were becoming apoplectic at the disappearance of the scientist they had been charged to protect. When rudely queried as to the whereabouts of Professor Heisenberg, the institute administrator observed that even a Nobel laureate had to go potty now and then.

In the hallway as they were returning to the reception room, von Dahlheim casually asked Heisenberg a question: "There's also been much talk of a weapon, some kind of nuclear explosive device. Is such a thing feasible? Do you think?"

Heisenberg responded with uncertainty. "Yes, theoretically it is possible. But we know so little about controlling the uranium machine required to create such a reaction. It might well be years before we learn how. And I speak only for German science. The rest of the world is decades behind us. We really must be getting back."

With that, Heisenberg reentered the crowded reception area to the relief of the nearly frantic Gestapo men.

It sounded good. I mean, it sounded bad for Heisenberg. Good for us. No breakthrough! As yet. But was he lying? I don't think so. The man is too vain not to hint about success. But he's also smart. Don't forget, Morris, old bean, this is a very smart character. Don't allow wishful thinking to cloud your judgment. The Beretta in the holster under his arm felt heavy once again.

"It's a little dinner for a select few of us. We've commandeered the school dining room. It gives us an opportunity to visit with each other. If you're not too fatigued from your trip I hope you can join us. You are, after all, the guest of honor."

"Of course, Paul. I shall be delighted to attend. And, by the way, would you mind inviting the student from America. I enjoyed talking to him."

That afternoon three more dissertations were delivered. Heisenberg sat at the desk to the side of the platform serving as moderator to the gathered scientists and offering polite interjections and much appreciated praise for the speakers. When the floor was once again opened to questions, there were many, with Heisenberg charmingly presiding as master of ceremonies.

Some of the world's foremost scientists delighted in becoming students again. The banter was exhilarating and many of the arguments brilliant. The policemen who were intruding into their world were all but forgotten. Science once again reigned. At least for the remainder of the day.

That evening sauerbraten was served for dinner. A traditional German dish of specially marinated beef. In a note to Frau Heisenberg a few days after his acceptance of the invitation, Anna Scherrer had inquired as to Werner's gastronomic preferences. Elizabeth Heisenberg wrote back that one of Werner's favorite dishes was sauerbraten. She did not mention roast duck. Frau Scherrer informed, the faculty chef, who, unsure of his sauerbraten recipe, suggested that he prepare a trial meal. The professor, Mrs. Scherrer, and three teaching assistants and their wives were impressed as guinea pigs. The meal was politely received but it was clear to all that the dish lacked something. Everyone was too polite to acknowledge the disappointment. Frau Scherrer, however, came right out and said it.

"This is good sauerbraten, but I'm sorry to say, not *great* sauerbraten. I wish I knew what was wrong. What is missing? The chef is French, you know."

The students and their wives looked at one another nervously. One does not fault the dinner at one's superior's home. Young Isabel Hametner, recently wedded to the assistant director of the mathematics department, was not yet fully versed in faculty protocol. The slender, dark-haired young woman said simply, "Gingersnaps." All heads turned toward her.

"What was that?" Frau Scherrer said, turning to better hear the comment.

"Gingersnaps. The problem is in the sauce. There is no ginger taste. Crumble some broken up ginger cookies into it. That's how my mother makes it. And she's famous for her sauerbraten."

Herr Hametner was contemplating enlistment in the Russian Army just then, when Frau Scherrer said, "Ginger, of course. My dear, you are absolutely right. Come with me, child. We must tell chef."

The young woman was correct. With the addition of the missing ingredient, the dish came to life assuring that the sauerbraten served to their guest of honor would be acceptable.

"Excellent sauerbraten," Heisenberg observed to his host upon tasting his meal. "My compliments to your chef."

Scherrer was elated. Anna Scherrer was relieved. The chef was ecstatic. Frau Hametner was delighted. And her mathematician husband was the proudest man in the room. Moe Berg, on the other hand, thought the concoction vile. Nothing like this would ever come out of his mother's New Jersey kitchen. He smiled, however, and dutifully ate his portion, only slightly distracted by the cold heft of the pistol nestled under his left arm.

There was little access to Heisenberg during the dinner and the many flowery toasts. As the evening's visit was concluding, Moe offered to walk with Heisenberg to his hotel. The scientist eagerly accepted and thanked him for the company. It would give them a chance to clear up a few points on the spectrometric refinement process.

It was a cool spring night. Clear but no moon. Heisenberg wore his overcoat. Moe carried his. As they chatted, stopping to watch the water flowing under the old Limmat bridge, Moe put on his coat in the realization that he ought to have both hands free.

"When I was a boy I loved the mountains. The sheer power of it all. Walking alone in those hills relaxed me and invigorated me at the same time. I was able to think with such clarity."

How do I kill this man? I suppose I put the gun to his head and pull the trigger. Do I shoot once or several times? I guess at least three. They taught us to shoot three times in close contact.

217

"Of course, Zurich is much too flat. Really just a floodplain for the Rhine. I wouldn't like to live here. Not when there are so many mountains nearby."

Do I need to kill him? If he's no threat I'd be killing an innocent man. And he seems decent enough.

"We have a place in the hills near the university. In Urfeld. My family stays there while I spend the work week in Leipzig. Like a commuter. A regular businessman."

But Einstein said Heisenberg was the man. If anyone in Germany could figure it out he would be the one. That's what he said.

"You know, von Dahlheim, it's important where you bring up your family. Especially when the children are no longer babies."

"I suppose that's true."

It's really murder. I never thought of myself as a killer. But then we're at war. The whole world is at war. And this man may be the key to the enslavement of the world. But is it right to punish a man for what he *might* do?

Moe Berg then turned to Heisenberg and flatly asked, "Do you think you are going to do it? Build an atomic bomb?"

Heisenberg was stunned. His mind had been far away. Lost in much pleasanter thoughts. Now he had been rudely jerked back to reality. How should he respond to such a provocative question? He attributed its blatant directness to zeal and naïveté. How much like himself over twenty years ago? He surprised himself as he answered with equal directness.

"Von Dahlheim, such a device is possible but I think not at all in the next few years. Certainly the war will be over by then. We have not even properly solved the problem of the moderator, which must be deuterium oxide. I would have thought that carbon in graphite form would suffice, but tests in Heidelberg have proved otherwise. So we have to rely on heavy water, but there are not sufficient quantities available. And our ability to produce enriched uranium in any substantial amount further prevents our progress. Until we can surmount these serious obstacles my estimation is that we will not even produce a sustained chain reaction by 1945. If the war turns against us and materials are even more difficult to obtain, it won't be until '47 or '48. Which reminds me, when we spoke of uranium refinement you mentioned electromagnets of great size to guide the trajectories of the uranium oxide gas. Would this not require enormous quantities of copper? Is the U.S. so rich in copper they can tie it up in physics experiments?"

"I was told, sir, that they don't use copper," Moe explained. "They use silver, borrowed from the U.S. Mint reserves. Pure silver, extruded into wire and wound into the coils for the electromagnets."

"Of course," said Heisenberg. "The silver isn't altered. Oh, that's rich. It's so like the Americans. Such clever tinkerers. What a charming story. Now, to give you the true answer to your question about the atomic weapon," his tone took a more serious note, "the führer has said he will not consider any project that will not bear fruit within six months. One does not so lightly promise Herr Hitler a weapon and fail to deliver. Does that help answer your question, my curious friend?"

Moe nodded. "It does, sir," and, he thought, at the same time saves your life.

They walked a bit further without speaking when Heisenberg, as if thinking out loud, added, "Of course, I can only vouch for myself. The führer has seen fit to assign Diebner to the same project. Perhaps the great Kurt Diebner will prove me an ass and develop the weapon for the führer."

Uh-oh! Another player on the scorecard.

At the hotel steps the two men said good night.

"Have a good trip home, sir."

"Thank you, I enjoyed our talk."

Nice fellow, thought Heisenberg. Mathematician? Or did he say?

I'm glad I didn't have to kill him, thought Moe, as he walked briskly to the university dormitory. I honestly believe he's nowhere on the bomb. But now we've got to locate this Kurt Diebner and go through the whole damn process again. Damn it!

The Gestapo man sitting in the darkened car observed the physicist enter the hotel alone and watched the student walk away into the night. He wrote in his pad: 2340, Heisenberg walked to his hotel accompanied by student. Student then left. Nothing out of the ordinary occurred.

"Do you know a Kurt Diebner?" Moe asked Professor Scherrer.

It was the morning after the seminar's end. Everyone seemed to agree it went very well. Very little politics. Lots of pure science. The Knights of the Round Table had convened once again with Scherrer in the role of Arthur and Heisenberg as Merlin. During the past days, the Knights had renewed their vows of fealty to the chivalrous laws of science. It felt good to see their armor glistening in the sunlight once more.

A message, in Jabberwocky, was sent to London via Marseilles and Lisbon. It read, "At last did business face to face with company principal. Have reasonable assurance product not preempted. However, have discovered new competitor. Need to negotiate. Send money. Love and xxx's. C."

Wild Bill Donovan notified President Roosevelt immediately upon receipt of the message. When FDR read it he said, "Well, at least that's something, isn't it? Oh . . . and please send my best regards to the catcher."

Ashley Inness indignantly demanded a translation of the coded message and its answer. He knew about the scientist's convention and surmised a connection but he had no idea of the specifics. Donovan told him flatly that there was no need for him to know and that von Dahlheim was operating "ex cathedra," outside the organization's normal chain of command. This caused Inness to seethe all the more.

Meanwhile thank you's and congratulations were streaming in at the university even before the seminar had concluded. Scherrer and his staff were bombarded by handshakes, appreciative notes, and phone calls. Scherrer sat at his desk beaming like a man who had bagged his limit of grouse on the first day of the season.

"Diebner? Of course I know him. Bad scientist. More of a technician. Cuts corners in his work. Plus he accepts all that racist kvatch. He's a Nazi, an actual Nazi party member. I know all I want to know about Kurt Diebner. Why? His boss, Schumann, was here at the seminar. Diebner works for Schumann in the munitions procurement ministry. Probably cooking up new ways to kill people . . . Diebner?"

Scherrer put it together.

"He is working on a nuclear device?"

Moe filled the professor in. His conversations with Heisenberg, first at the school, then on the walk to the hotel. Moe felt that all evidence pointed away from the imminent development of an atomic device. When Scherrer digested Moe's almost verbatim reproduction of Heisenberg's words, he concurred. And then, out of the blue, the mention of Diebner, which changed everything.

"We've got to pursue it. At least, I have to. I've got to know how advanced he is. I will ask him, I asked Heisenberg . . . but first I've got to find out where he's working."

"I can tell you that," said Scherrer. "Schumann told me."

Moe's jaw dropped.

"Gottow near Leipzig. Something about I. G. Farben installing some new equipment there."

"Wow!" said Moe. "What a stroke of luck. Well, I guess that means a trip is in order. To the lovely village of Gottow."

"Von Dahlheim?"

Moe turned at the change in tone.

"Yes, Professor?"

"If you had discovered that Heisenberg was close to making an atomic weapon . . . ?"

"Yes?"

"What would you have done then?"

"Why, I would have drawn my pistol and shot him several times in the head."

"Ja, you see? A typical American response. Always with the jokes. Come, I have a map; we'll find Gottow for you."

30

　⋯⊱⊰⋯　

WHEN MOE RETURNED TO HIS HOTEL AFTER THE SEMINAR he was hoping to find Sally waiting for him.   Strange, he thought. I was half expecting her to be wearing an apron and greet me with, "Hi, honey, here are your slippers. How was your week?" Instead there was a note. "Gone to Red Cross with Babette to help out. Boys playing baseball." Now, what's that all about? Moe wondered as he tossed his coat on the chair and dove for the bed managing to flip one shoe into the air as his head sunk into the down pillow. He was asleep before the shoe hit the floor.

The crew of the *Faithful Floosie* went out to the ramp each day in an empty ritual of tending to their B-24 bomber. In fact, there was no work to do. The oil lines, severed by the flak over Kael causing the two port engines to overheat and thus prompting their detour to Switzerland, had been replaced on the second day of their internment. Number two ran a bit rough at 2200 RPM but pilot and engineer concurred that they'd both flown missions with worse. Some sheet metal had been chewed up around the main gear doors but that damage had been hammered straight--not a very pretty repair but nothing that would offer any significant resistance to the airstream. In every other respect she was airworthy.

"So tell me again, boss, why can't we fly this thing outta here and back to England?" technical sergeant "Shorty" Hobart demanded from his pilot.

First Lt. Warren Rogers rolled his eyes, then bent his lanky six-foot-four frame over his diminutive crew chief, rested his forearms on the smaller man's shoulders, and looked him in the face.

"I told you. We are in a neutral country. We are guests. We can't leave, at least not with the Floosie. They made a deal. An international deal. If we go, they'll shoot us down. We're not allowed to fix the plane, we gotta off-load any ammo or bombs. We even had to give up our side arms. You know those cut hoses you replaced?" He nodded. "Well, they'd o' had a cow if they knew you did it. We're here for the duration, Shorty. It stinks but we gotta make the best of it."

It was about the third time he'd explained it to his crewman but Shorty Hobart was the best, most resourceful B-24 mechanic that he'd ever flown with and if Shorty asked the question again five minutes from now, Rogers was prepared to provide the answer anew. They'd flown fourteen missions together and this diminutive grease monkey had patched, rigged, and contrived ingenious repairs upon at least five different occasions when it looked for sure that they'd have to abandon the Floosie and hit the silk.

"You want me to explain it again?"

Shorty shook his head. "Nah." Then brightening. "Regular maintenance?"

"Yeah, no repairs, only upkeep."

"Engine run-ups?"

"That's regular maintenance."

"Taxiing?"

"Only with permission and not on main runways."

Shorty was simply looking for a loophole. The pilot understood. They all owed their skins to Shorty's persistence so let him scheme.

The Red Cross had provided them comfortable quarters; officers were assigned two to a room and the enlisted men slept in barracks. There was good chow, plenty of hot water for showers, and clean uniforms to replace their grimy flying togs. Ping-Pong and painting lessons were available, even sight-seeing trips into town and the countryside. In effect, they were on unlimited R&R. The Red Cross made sure their families were notified that they were safe and they were even beginning to receive mail. The war was over for these airmen.

For some strange reason the flying crews stayed together. They seemed to have a need for each other's company, to remain a unit even though the unit had no function. They often could be found near their aircraft. Most crew visited their ship nearly every day.

One day a couple of flyers produced a baseball and pair of gloves and started having a catch. Miraculously, other mitts appeared and the grassy flat behind the parked bombers began to look like spring training camp. Soon more gloves, balls, and several bats were provided courtesy of the Red Cross, who hadn't produced the equipment till now because they had no idea what it was. Recently one of the volunteers, an American woman, observed that "this is baseball equipment; the boys might want to use it now that the weather is getting warmer."

Thus began the Swiss Baseball League. At first, a few men turned out to have a catch. Soon others joined in. Next a pepper game. Then a choose-up game. Then a game between two airplane crews. With the availability of more equipment, squads were built from several crews, the managers competitively cadging the best players for their teams. Soon there was a game being played every day.

Ernie and Gene noticed the familiar but out-of-place activity from the road one afternoon. The many U.S. aircraft parked on the ramp was an inviting sight by itself, but the boys didn't think Moe would approve of mingling with the flyers. Eventually the baseball activity proved impossible to resist. Parking the Mercedes a respectable distance away, they walked over "just to

225

watch." They were soon shagging flies and playing catch, which of course led to Gene Gurney becoming the left fielder for the Zurich Yankees. Ernie Kahn wasn't selected for any of the aircrew teams. He privately suspected that the fellows felt uncomfortable with his accent. The truth was that he just wasn't a very good ball player. He did know the game and so qualified as an umpire. "Yer out" forcefully delivered in a German accent makes for an indisputable call.

The next evening Baron von Berg's flying circus gathered in Sally's room for dinner. It was a reunion of sorts, for Moe had been spending nearly every day at the university. Moe hoped to establish himself as a student and therefore defray possible suspicion that could prevent his access to Heisenberg. But he was back now and there was much to catch up on. Moe announced that he had accomplished his primary objective but unfortunately some new information had come to light that indicated there were still some "loose ends." Gene and Ernie weren't quite sure what "loose ends" meant but didn't press it. Obviously Moe would explain later in private. Sally and Babette told of their Red Cross volunteer chores and how Sally was especially useful as there were more than three hundred British and American airmen interned here in Zurich. There were now at least two Allied planes every week seeking the refuge of Swiss neutrality.

"And, by the way, that nice Mr. Inness came down to the Red Cross offices again yesterday just to visit."

"That was very thoughtful of him," said Moe, with just enough insincerity in his voice to make Sally think he might be jealous.

Next, the boys shared their baseball news. They told of how they had discovered the grounded American airmen accidentally and joined them as they played ball in the fields near the airport.

"Fellas, I don't like it," said Moe, after listening patiently. "It's risky. Too many people involved."

"Aw, Moe," said Gene. "They're Americans."

"And British," added Ernie. "They're our guys."

"Yeah."

"And all we do is play baseball."
"That's all! We never talk about our jobs."
"You oughta come down."
"See for yourself."
"If you don't like it, we'll quit."
"Just see it."
"Okay?"
"You comin'?   C'mon, just see it."
"Okay. But if I don't like it you quit, right?"
"Right."
"Right."
"Okay."

There was no game today. Only practice.

Lieutenant Rogers, who was scheduled to pitch tomorrow's game, was stroking grounders to the infielders. Behind first base, Thibideau, the Floosie's waist gunner, was muttering to himself as he vainly tried to hit fly balls to his outfielders, one of whom was Gene Gurney. His efforts resulted only in weak dribblers.

The entire team felt the presence of the big man in the dark suit who had been watching them play for over a half hour.

"What's he want? Some wierd Swiss fascinated by baseball? Or is he interested in the planes parked behind us?"

Only Gurney saw the humor of the situation before him.

"C'mon, Thib, can't you get it up?" he shouted as the ball rolled to a stop at his feet. Instead of tossing it in, he waved at the ominous observer in the black suit. "Hey, Manfred, how about hitting us some fungoes."

You son of a bee was all that went through Moe's mind. You got me, didn't you. Moe was smiling as he stripped off his jacket, loosened his tie, and walked toward the bat lying on the grass. Thibideau trotted out to his place in the outfield, happy to relinquish the chore. If he had looked a little foolish it was nothing compared to how the suit is going to look when he tries hitting a baseball.

Moe swung easily. CRACK. The fungo went sailing over the head of the deepest outfielder.

CRACK. The fellows started backing up.

CRACK. As they ranged back to the proper distance, each man was hit a challenging high fly ball.

"Where'd that guy learn to hit fly balls?" one of the outfielders asked no one in particular.

Someone else said, "He was probably on the Heidelberg University baseball team."

CRACK. "Mine!" yelled Thibideau, who made a nice running catch. When they came in they shook hands with Manfred.

"Nice hittin'!"

"Yeah."

"Good goin'."

The infielders, who had stopped to watch, came over.

"So where'd you learn to hit fly balls?" asked Lieutenant Rogers.

"I played some ball back in the States," answered Moe.

"Can you hit? Pitching, I mean."

"I hit a little."

"Would you mind if I threw you a couple?"

"Nope," said Moe, suppressing a grin, "not at all."

Rogers threw three pitches. Moe hit each one solidly, far over the outfielders' heads. They found only one of the balls; two were lost in the scrub beyond the field.

"Manfred, whoa, we can't afford any more baseballs. I guess you can hit, all right. How about joining our team? We've got a big game tomorrow."

"Oh, thanks, but I couldn't possibly. I mean it's . . . there's no way I could . . . "

"Well, you think about it, will you?" said the pilot. "We could certainly use you. And by the way, what position do you play?"

"Catcher."

"Catcher! We could definitely use a good catcher. Ours keeps ducking his head. Getting konked with foul tips. Game's tomorrow at eleven. We play the Interns."

"No, I really couldn't."

"Their pitcher played college ball, too."

"No. I really don't think . . . "

Ernie and Gene got chewed out on the ride back to the hotel. They kept silent, managing to keep a straight face until Moe said, " . . . and they want me to play ball tomorrow against a team called the Interns? What are they, a team of doctors?"

With that, all three gave in to the absurdity of the situation and laughed. It was true that all these men were interned, but it was still a stupid name.

Moe was let off at the Züricher and Gene and Ernie continued to their digs.

"I bet he plays," said Gene.

"No bet," said Ernie. "Did you know I'm the umpire tomorrow?"

"Oh, jeez," was Gene's response.

31

⊷ ⊠◈⊠ ⊶

ROWS OF PARKED ALLIED BOMBERS formed the backstop for the three baseball fields, which were arranged side by side east of the Dübendorf airport. The diamonds were set far enough from the aircraft so that they weren't continually pelted by foul balls, but the planes were still close enough to loom supportively. A new B-17, the *Say Goodnight, Gracie,* had arrived on the previous afternoon with her tail shot to shreds and several wing tanks punctured. The pilot brought her in safely with the fuel gauges reading empty. The Gracie's navigator had taken a few slivers of flak in his side and arm and looked kind of gray as he was carried from the plane, but the latest word from the hospital was that he was going to make it. The Gracie was towed into place beside her sister ships--another sentinel to guard the baseball fields. Gracie brought the total of Allied aircraft to twenty-seven.

"You gonna play, or what?" The gruff, cigar-chomping manager of the Yankees asked Moe. The players had told Major Bradley about the American with the Kraut name in the black suit who had the day before shown that he might be a good prospect.

"If you don't mind, I'd prefer to watch a little," the big man told Bradley. "Put me in later on. If you need me."

"Suit yourself," Bradley grumbled back, "uniform's in the plane. Cookie'll show ya. I hope you really can play, fella. College? You play in college?"

Moe nodded.

230

"Well, at least that's something. Watch him. Don't let him touch anything in the plane," Bradley ordered the young corporal who accompanied the big man.

Moe was led to a B-24 named *The Faithful Floosie* where he was given a "uniform" to put on.

Moe enjoyed being a spectator, watching the boys warm up and go through infield practice. It even felt good wearing the makeshift baseball outfit. The "athletic costume" consisted of a gray sweatshirt, gray woolen knickers that buttoned below the knee, heavy woolen socks that came up over the calf, and black high-topped sneakers topped off by a green fatigue cap. The pants were gifts of the Swiss Army. The sweatshirt, caps, and sneakers came from the Red Cross.

Better judgment, Moe realized, went right out the window when he decided he would play if the opportunity arose. Perhaps it was the spring weather--for so many years a circadianlike cue to begin catching and throwing a baseball. His body seemed to yearn for the activity. Risky, risky, he admonished himself, but aw, what the heck.

Moe sat on the bench for most of the game, but when Hobart had the wind knocked out of him in a play at the plate, Moe was asked to substitute. He donned the "tools of ignorance," as he had years before named the catcher's gear, and settled in behind the plate, amazed at how good it felt to play at a boy's game once again.

Moe stroked an easy single in the Yankee victory, which gained the team the right to play for the Zurich championship in one week's time. They would play the Cardinals, the only other team without a loss. The Cardinals were very good. They also had the advantage of playing in real St. Louis Cardinal baseball caps. Nobody knew where the caps came from but there were rumors that they were left by an American baseball team that had played an exhibition game here before the war.

As the teams packed up and the sixty-odd spectators began dispersing, two airmen in the stands were engaged in a vigorous debate.

"It is."

"Oh, it is not."

"I tell you, it is.   That's Moe Berg."   The sergeant was adamant.

"No, it's not," said his companion.

"I'm tellin' ya, it's Moe Berg. My grandpa took me to a spring-training game in Florida. Years ago. I got his autograph. That's Berg."

"Whyn'cha ask him."

"Awright, I will. Hey, Moe. Moe Berg!" he shouted towards the group of players. There was no response. The big man didn't turn around. He just continued walking with the other players.

"I guess not."

"See, told ya."

Gurney stole a nervous glance at his teammate; Moe kept his eyes straight ahead. They changed back into street clothes in the Floosie, four at a time.

On the ride back to their respective hotels, Moe informed Gene and Ernie that the mission was not yet over. There was still another bird to be flushed.

"Get your German uniforms brushed off. In a couple of days, we're hittin' the road back to Germany."

No one spoke for the rest of the ride.

Part 4
Return to the Reich

32

IT WAS HARDLY A SECRET. By this time every physicist in the world was aware of the two likely paths to a nuclear weapon. If a sufficient mass of the rare and highly unstable 235 isotope of uranium could be refined, one could create a bomb. Or, if a sufficient quantity of the newly discovered transuranic element, plutonium, could be created in an uranium pile--this substance would likewise produce an explosive device.

The difficulty facing the world's scientists was the complex and tedious enrichment process and the design of a functional uranium machine in which a sustained and controlled chain reaction could be achieved.

Kurt Diebner and his associate, Erich Bagge, were given the latter problem to solve. They pursued their experiments in a fine new laboratory equipped with the most advanced technology, including high speed air and water pumps and remote control material-handling systems. It was housed in a reinforced concrete structure with walls two meters thick designed to survive fire or bomb attacks, though at the time it was designed few Germans believed that there would be any serious bombing threats so deep in the Reich. The facility was piggybacked to a civilian shelter built for the citizens of Gottow. Diebner was well connected in the party and when a friend in the ordinance ministry mentioned the proposed new bunker, he requested and received the approval to expand the shelter for his new laboratory.   Not only were the latest advances in technology put at Diebner's disposal, he also received two precious metric tons of heavy water for his pile.

"Poor Heisenberg, that Jew-loving naïf has been pleading for additional heavy water at the ministry. I would love to see the look on his arrogant Nobel laureate face when he learns that I have as much as I need. You see, Erich," Diebner leered at his assistant, "this party pin counts far more these days than any Nobel Prize. It's not what you know, it's who. Heil Hitler."

It wouldn't be long before he expected to call his chief, Schumann, and announce that the führer could be informed of our breakthrough, which will result in the wunderwaffen, which will strike the fatal blow against the cringing enemies of the Reich. Not long at all.

Diebner's optimism was justified. He was further along in the development of a working uranium pile than Heisenberg and not merely because he had access to quantities of heavy water. He had chosen to arrange his uranium core in an array of four-inch cubes, precisely milled and closely spaced for optimum neutron exchange.   Each cube was independently suspended from a graphite-lined lid by an aluminum wire. The elements were then to be immersed in a cylindrical tank of heavy water and surrounded by a cloak of pure graphite. This arrangement proved to be far more efficient at neutron multiplication than Heisenberg's pile, which employed an overlapping lattice of uranium plates.

The entire pile was set into a pit hollowed out of the concrete floor of the concrete bunker. When filled with circulating water that served as the coolant for the pile, it resembled a small swimming pool. All was deemed ready for their initial attempt. The try for a sustained chained reaction would take place tonight.

The first tier of uranium blocks was lowered into place by Bagge from the top of the cylinder. Diebner took his spot by the Geiger counters. Each cube was suspended from its own wire marked with black tape to indicate proper positioning. A ring at the end of the wire was secured to a hook bolted to the graphite lid. As the cubes were lowered into position, a hemispherical mass of uranium began to form in the water. When the lower half of the hemisphere was in place, a radium-beryllium neutron source was lowered to a position at the center of the forming sphere. The Geiger-Müller counters began to click announcing the discharge of neutrons.

They were now ready to proceed with the more complicated part, the assembly of the top half of the sphere. Because so many wires already crowded the lower half of the semicircle, the top hemisphere would have to be much wider and more irregular. Diebner's calculations, however, promised that the geometry should still work. As Bagge began lowering the uranium cubes to form the top hemisphere, the Geiger counters increased their tempo. From a steady faucet drip, the clicks upped to four-fourths time. A good sign. Diebner was pleased to hear the encouraging clatter. Bagge, however, on top of the pile, was having difficulty. Some of the cubes were not lowering to their markers. They were becoming entangled on one or more of the myriad suspension wires or had come to rest atop some other cube and refused to drop into place. He jiggled the wires. First lightly, then violently, to no avail. Bagge then unhooked the wires that suspended the cubes closest to the balky ones and jiggled.

"What is happening?" shouted Diebner.

The radiation counters began clicking at an erratic pace. The temperature of the pile was rising.

"I'm having difficulty lowering the phase-two cubes," answered Bagge.

"Stop at once," shouted Diebner. "Retract the top hemisphere cubes."

The erratic clicks and neutron surges told Diebner that something was very wrong. Inside the pile, five cubes were swinging side by side and striking against each other. Each collision in the presence of the heavy water moderator and the neutron stream resulted in a small but brilliant flash. An erratic energy discharge was produced as the chorus line of cubes collided with each other. With all Bagge's jiggling, he had inadvertently set the cubes swaying despite the damping effect of the heavy water. Bagge was now frantically pulling up the uranium blocks and securing them to their respective hooks. Amid his panic, he managed to regain his wits. Reaching over, he grasped the wire from which the neutron source was suspended, yanked it from the midst of the pile, and secured it to its hook. The clicking stopped abruptly. Core temperature immediately began to drop off. The beast quieted allowing the uranium cubes to be raised in relative safety.

"I'm sorry, Kurt," Bagge said to his chief. "It's my fault the experiment didn't work."

"Nonsense, Erich," Diebner responded jovially. "For the experiment not to work, nothing should have happened. As you can see," displaying the sheet of graph paper covered by erratic scribbles, "lots of exciting things have indeed happened. We came close to multiplying our neutrons. When we refine our geometry a bit, I am certain we will have our sustained reaction. Drain the heavy water and secure our uranium. And, we had better see if any of the cubes have been damaged. When you finish I will treat you to a nice dinner at the Gasthaus in the town. They make a wunderbar goulash."

Diebner's generous offer sounded mighty good to Bagge, whose hands were still trembling.

33

"Do you have any idea how long you'll be?" Sally asked as she handed Moe some shirts for his valise.

"Can't be sure," said Moe, managing to avoid eye contact. "Not long. I don't think we'll be long. Just need to check on another scientist; not long."

"Are you going to miss me?" she asked reaching up and locking her wrists around the back of Moe's neck. As he straightened, the full length of her pressed against him.

"Nah," he said, "prob'ly not," wrapping his arms around her waist and pressing her body even closer.

The largest single organ of the body is the skin, serving its wearers as a watertight covering and sensing receptor. Obstacles, such as trousers, shirts, dresses, panties, and neckties are known to inhibit the flow of especially delicate information. When these impediments are removed a truly remarkable and sensitive communication process will usually commence. This process, guided by an age-old imperative, often relieves the participants of coherent thought as it functions to assure the survival of the species. In a short time this intense condition inevitably dissipates and the participants are returned intact to the realm of coherent thought.

"Wow," said Moe.

"Definitely, wow," agreed Sally.

"I wanted you to have something to remember me by." Moe grinned and leaned over and kissed the point of her hip bone as he rose from the bed.

"Moe?"

"Yeah?" beginning to retrieve his hastily castaway clothes. "Where the heck is that sock?"

"Moe!"

"Yes?" The sound of that last Moe suggested the need for full attention. "What?"

"I didn't want to bother you, but . . . ," and she then told him about Inness. How his initial attentions had been friendly enough; fellow American and all that. About his thoughtful visits over at the Red Cross. His praise of their good work.

Moe listened attentively.

"But then he kept asking me to lunch. He was so insistent. He took us both out. It was pleasant, but somehow I felt strange. Then he wanted to go without Babette. I didn't really want to but he was so . . . insistent. And I didn't want to appear rude. It was at the Schweiss-Regent Hotel restaurant yesterday. He asked me to go upstairs to a room with him. That old man. I told him no and started to leave. That's when he told me that I was acting 'negatively'." And if I continued to act 'that way' he would be forced to take certain 'steps' because he had checked up on me and discovered that there is no record of a U.S. passport issued to a Sally Carlisle. I didn't want to tell you, but I guess he frightened me a little. Moe, why is he doing this?"

"I don't know, girl. Some people behave like rats just because they can get away with it. But don't worry. He can't harm you. Just avoid him. I'll take care of it."

"You? Won't it compromise you and your mission?"

"Mission? You make me sound like a saboteur. You're the only saboteur in this family. I'm just here to do research. Let me handle it. You don't have to give it another thought, I promise."

Moe then kissed Sally on the cheek, trivially, as if he was an ordinary husband leaving for another day at the office and the information she had just shared with him was truly not anything to be concerned about. The strategy worked, Sally was able to relax as the anxiety left her. She even managed a carefree smile as he closed the door.

Tuned up and running smoothly, the big Mercedes reveled in her shiny new wax job as they headed out of town. The two busboys at the Pension Schlichter had done a superlative job. They earned themselves an extra five marks each for the effort.

There were to be two stops before the car and its three passengers left the city of Zurich behind and headed north to the German border. The first at the university to bid auf Wiedersehn to Dr. Scherrer and his staff. During their good-byes, Scherrer presented his pupil with two large metal flasks. Some special home brew for the journey, no doubt. The big car then crossed the stone bridge and headed up Bahnhofstrasse where it made its second stop in front of No. 550, the German Consulate.

"Be right back," said Moe as he left the car to enter the building with the red flag bearing the black swastika.

"I hope he knows what he's doing," said Gurney.

Ernie Kahn just shook his head.

Moe Berg, the American baseball player, Morris Berg, Esq., the lawyer and linguist, and Manfred von Dahlheim, the physics student, remained outside the consulate. Von Dahlheim, the Nazi deputy gauleiter, strode through the front entrance. As the German aristocrat approached the reception desk one could tell by his manner that here was a man with very little patience for underlings.

"I must see Stauber," he told the seated young diplomat in the wire-rimmed glasses. "You will announce me. Von Dahlheim," handing the fellow his card.

The reception clerk eyed the card and began to explain that Chief Consul Stauber was accepting no appointments this morning, but the man stopped himself in time and then provided a more appropriate response to the ominous presence before him.

"At once, Herr von Dahlheim. I'll announce you immediately."

Escorted upstairs and through ornate gilded doors, von Dahlheim was directed into the consul's office. A short man in frock coat and striped pants rose from the thronelike chair behind a huge mahogany desk and glowered at the intruders. As he set his monocle to his right eye, his dour expression left him. It softened further as the visitor strode forward.

"Herr Stauber, I am in need of your assistance. But first may I present my credentials."

Moe produced a folded piece of paper and offered it to the consul, who stiffened as he recognized the signature at the bottom. It was the product of the best forgers at SOE in London, who had held a competition to see who could do the most authentic Heinrich Himmler. Heinrich's own mother would have taken it for genuine. A diplomat sitting out the war in a plush office at the time so many of his countrymen were fighting on two fronts could do no less.

"I am at your service, Herr von Dahlheim," he said, clicking to rigid attention. He hadn't even completely read the note yet. The typewritten memorandum stated: To all government officials: the bearer of this order is on an important secret mission for the Reich. You will provide to him any assistance that is requested. Signed, Heinrich Himmler.

"How may I help you, Herr von Dahlheim?"

"First no mention of my presence here must be made. Is that clear?"

"Clear!"

"It is a matter of some sensitivity. I can only tell you that it is of a high-level political nature. And that knowledge is for you and you alone, Stauber."

242

Stauber nodded gravely, as if he had just been made privy to the invasion plans for Britain.

The big man continued. "It concerns the assistant attaché to the American Consulate here in Zurich."

"That would be Herr Inness," Stauber offered.

"Correct. Now, this is what I require."

Outside the consulate, the two young Americans squirmed in their seats. Passersby couldn't help staring at the impressive car. Some even crouched to look inside, perhaps to catch a glimpse of Albert Speer or some such big shot. People entering and leaving the building did only slightly better at disguising their interest. The discomfort level of the car's occupants rose steadily until the consulate door opened and Moe finally stepped out. He was accompanied by Stauber, who shook his hand vigorously as he exited. Ernie jumped out of the car and opened the door for his chief who entered without breaking stride. Stauber was even further impressed, if that was possible.

"Where to, boss?" said the driver, who too soon would be silenced by a slightly stained bandage wrapped around his lower jaw.

"Head north," came the instruction from the back seat. "To the fatherland! And we'd better get back to sprechen Deutsch."

"Ja woll," said Ernie.

"Ja woll," repeated Gurney.

The car turned at the bahnhof and headed north into Germany. The vacation was over.

Inside the consulate the chief diplomat was addressing two of his subordinates.

"You idiots. You have been keeping a surveillance on an important agent of the Reich. I want all your records and the file destroyed. It must be as if he never existed. Is that clear?" Not waiting for their confirmation, he continued, "When you have completed that little chore, report to me. I have an errand for you."

At the border, the uniformed Swiss officer politely noted the names of the occupants, then bowed politely and waved them past. Fifty meters north stood the German border. One look at the car and the official simply ordered his sergeant to raise the barrier. The Mercedes didn't even have to slow down.

34

⊱━━◈━━⊰

THE CAR CRUISED EFFORTLESSLY NORTHWARD, all twelve cylinders humming contentedly at the prospect of being back in the fatherland. They paralleled the Danube for a time, then headed in a slight northeasterly direction toward Nuremberg. The tranquil German countryside betrayed no evidence of military presence. Their goal was to make Leipzig before dark. There they would formulate a plan to find the laboratory of Kurt Diebner in the town of Gottow, less than an hour's drive away.

Once they had crossed the Main River, the country opened up into farmland divided by patches of woods. In one of these stands of forest the team changed into their "nasty suits" as Gurney liked to call them. The red and black party flags were secured into the fixtures on the inside curve of the front fenders and the three Americans were once again transformed into full-fledged Nazis. Progress was slower than planned because of a few wrong turns and the prudent decision not to travel at a speed that might draw undue attention to themselves. As a result they determined they would not make Leipzig before nightfall. In Zwickau, they were fortunate to find a rather nice and virtually empty inn. Von Dahlheim registered, requesting rooms for himself and his aide and the simplest accommodation for his driver. These days there were lots of rooms to choose from because the war discouraged travel and Allied bombing had significantly increased in regularity. The factories at Meissen, to the west, had recently been attacked in a cowardly act of desperation by the Allies, the hotel owner explained.

"They flew over us. For a time we thought we might be their target, but they flew past. We will soon be getting a sturdy shelter for the town. The depraved English and Americans have no humanity. Bombing innocent civilians. It's positively barbaric. Here are your keys, Herr von Dahlheim. Heil Hitler."

"Heil Hitler," Moe responded, as he switched the keys to his nonheiling hand.

Later, after changing from his uniform into a dark suit, he entered the hotel's small dining room. It was surprisingly crowded.

"There will be two for dinner," Moe informed the captain.

He was shown to a corner table large enough to easily seat six. Strange, thought Moe, for smaller tables in the dining room seemed to be packed to capacity. Why is everyone gawking and smiling? Germans generally do not consider it impolite to stare but several dozen townspeople just sitting there watching was downright uncomfortable.

When Ernie finally joined his boss, he had the same disquieting feeling about the unusual interest shown them. Ernie was wearing his Wehrmacht uniform and was worried that perhaps he had it on wrong.

"What's up?" he whispered in German. "Are my decorations upside down?"

"I'm not sure, Lieutenant. Near as I can figure, we are celebrities to these folks. My guess is they don't see many party big shots 'round these parts. The desk clerk must have blabbed."

By then, even more people had packed the room. When there were no more chairs, they stood ringing the walls, quietly watching the two seated men. An unctious waiter took their orders and hurried away. He returned quickly with two large steins of beer. Moe and Ernie drank and registered enjoyment, which provoked a murmur of approval from the onlookers. The beer happened to be a local product of which the town's inhabitants were justifiably proud. Knowing glances were now directed toward a red-faced fellow with an enormous belly seated at a far table. It was a good bet that he was the town's braumeister.

Next came the soup, a clear chicken broth with what looked an awful lot like matzo balls. The soup was followed by a salad with a light sugary dressing. Then Ernie was brought his meal, a rich hasenpfeffer--rabbit stewed in a dark brown sauce with vegetables. Moe had chosen venison sautéed and served over a bed of noodles. The food was delicious and despite the dozens of eyes following their every mouthful, they managed to enjoy the meal.

When a second round of beer was served, there was another approving bustle in the audience. For a nervous moment Moe thought they were going to applaud.

Dessert consisted of apple cake and coffee. When the dessert plates were removed, an unordered platter of fruit and cheese was ceremoniously presented. Poor Gurney, thought Moe. He's probably dining on some stale bread and hard cheese in his tiny room.

When they had finished their banquet, the owner appeared and asked if everything had been satisfactory. Moe proceeded to praise every course of their banquet, including the "ausgetseich-net bier und das herliche's bröt." He laid on the compliments to generous excess. Amid the smiles and approving nods of the dining room crowd, which had by now grown to at least sixty people, Moe asked for the check.

"Oh, no check. It's our great pleasure for you sir, to be the guest of the Gasthaus Nekker."

"That is extremely kind of you, Herr? . . . "

"Rausemund."

"Herr Rausemund. I accept your generosity on behalf of myself and my aide."

Beaming, Rausemund then continued hesitantly. "I was wondering, Herr von Dahlheim . . . I was wondering if I may present meine frau. Come liebling," gesturing at the door to the kitchen from which emerged the ample Frau Rausemund. She was the spitting image of the braumeister, sitting in the corner, right down to the pink cheeks and heroic circumference. Moe rose as she was introduced. He gallantly kissed her hand and whispered, "Gnädige Frau. Es freuht mich sehr," punctuating it all with a smartly executed heel click. Moe then presented his aide, who also did the hand-kissing routine. Herr Rausemund was in his glory. Obviously he was very fond of his statuesque mate. Quite deservedly too, for she was the successful establishment's gifted chef.

Now some of the other guests rose and began to edge toward Moe and Ernie's table. They jostled for position, but deferred to one fellow who then introduced himself as the bürgermeister. The town council was presented, several prosperous-looking farmers, their even more prosperous-looking wives, and eventually the braumeister and his rail-thin frau. When the deputy gauleiter had either shaken every hand or exchanged a "heil Hitler" with a who's who of Zwickau society, he assumed the ordeal would be over. But instead of leaving the Gasthaus and returning to their homes, they returned to their chairs. Moe then realized that there was a price to be exacted for the complimentary meal. These people were expecting an entertainment.

"So if you would be so kind, Herr Gauleiter, tell us, how goes the war?" queried the bürgermeister.

"It goes as planned. We are winning."

The audience waited a moment and began to laugh at the terse and confident reply.

"Will there be more rationing?"

"When will the invasion of Britain begin?"

"What about the bombings?"

"What's the Luftwaffe doing about the bombings?"

Moe answered easily and obviously. His assurance was calming to these small-town Germans. They supported their government, which had returned to them their dignity and sense of national pride. There is an aspect of human nature uniquely prized in the Germans: the need to be looked upon as formidable--to be feared and respected. To this end, they gladly proffer obedience and respect to those above them. In these days everyone employed by the state, from postman to streetcar conductor to field marshal, wore a uniform of some sort. Rank was clearly visible. Respect willingly given. Say what you will, it was a system that worked. In recent weeks, however, as petrol had become more difficult to obtain, raw materials and food rationed, and married men with families being shipped to combat units, an unease had crept into their resolve. Then there were those damn Allied bombers. How could our leaders permit such a thing? Now that America had thrown in with the British could they expect even greater hardship? The first faint glimmers of doubt were beginning to erode their early confidence. Could this man, an important and knowledgeable leader of the Reich, reassure us and reaffirm for all the rightness of our path?

"Is there some message, some words of importance, that you could convey to us? Perhaps something of the führer's? His vision for the future? Anything at all?"

Moe realized they wanted a pep talk, a sort of half-time rouser. Well, let's see what I can come up with. Hmmm, I know.

"My friends," said Moe, as he rose to address them. "There is no new message from the führer. As you may well imagine, he is extremely busy personally directing the military expeditions. But you can be assured that he is aware of your sacrifices and he is proud of you. You, the people who have entrusted him with their leadership and their destiny." They ate that up, didn't they? Moe glanced at Ernie, who continued to stare straight ahead, refusing eye contact.

"There is a topic, however, that may be of interest to you. The question of the United States of America. This is a subject in which I am in all modesty somewhat expert."

Ernie couldn't help but look at that.

"Now that America is in the war," Moe continued, "you might be interested in the capabilities of our newest enemy. It is a large country, true. Over ten times the size of Germany. It is rich in resources and has enormous food-producing capabilities.

249

Its industrial prowess is truly great. But it also has a great weakness, a fact the the führer has correctly recognized. Its rulers are weak. Drawn from the ranks of a privileged class, they are spoiled by their lives of ease. America's workers, those who make up the vast middle-class population, are vassals of the greedy bosses who abuse their country's resources and are destroying America's bounty. I will give you examples. In the United States of America, an area of arable land that would correspond to two hundred farms of sixty-four acres each disappears daily. Each year, millions of tons of topsoil are destroyed by erosion. That is enough earth to build six hundred Cheops pyramids every year. The food-producing areas of America are turning into a desert. What were once immense wheat fields, cotton, maize are now enormous wastelands. Storms sweep over the land east and west tearing up the soil and carrying it off. On days when the wind is blowing, automobiles must drive with their headlights on. Grains of soil from the farms of Kansas or Colorado fall in the streets of New York City after being carried more than 1,250 miles, only to be washed into the sea."

The good bürgerin of Zwickau sat in silence at this description. The plight of their enemy was being described here but there was no rejoicing. These people were of the land and word of such devastation was solemnly received.

"But, my friends, no sympathy should be offered to them. They brought it all on themselves. They have been shamefully exploiting America's natural wealth for over a century. Her forests were ruthlessly cleared; once part of one of the most densely wooded continents in the world, today America has scarcely enough wood for her own needs. Forests were treated like mines from which there was to be got as much as possible and damn the future. The profligate wealthy class responded to this crisis by building themselves swimming pools. Every wealthy home has one. It is their symbol of status and contempt. Swimming pools, even in the most water-starved states, simply to show that they are above the laws of nature. All of this ruthless expoitation has resulted in a drastic modification of climate. They now experience Siberian winters and Saharan summers since the forests have been cut down. Nature's own systems of retaining moisture have been forever altered. The continent once so rich is becoming a vast steppe. Treeless and dead. Once an inexhaustible paradise, America is becoming a dried-up wasteland. Soon all that will remain will be empty skyscrapers towering over a barren and exhausted continent."

Silence. No one said a word. No one could. They got their pep talk, in spades. Plus cards and big casino.

What a crock! thought Ernie, but these rubes bought it, hook, line, and sinker. Finally, after recovering their composure, they responded to their guest speaker with enthusiastic applause.

"Bravo, Herr Gauleiter."

"Danke."

"Thank you for sharing your knowledge with us."

As the gauleiter and his aide headed up the stairs to their rooms after shaking nearly every hand a second time, the aide turned to his chief and asked, "Where ever did you get that bullshit?"

Moe winked and said, "I read it in a copy of *Signal,* the official Nazi propaganda magazine."

"Well, then I guess it must be true."

As the townspeople filed out of the inn, they were buzzing with excitement. The supposed juggernaut that was America seemed far less formidable now. True optimism could once again reign in place of doubt. As the groups broke up and drifted toward their respective homes, they were still chattering about the revelation that had been shared with them.

When Emil Krause and his wife, Greta, returned to their neat little cottage home on the other side of town, their twelve-year-old son, Rudi, was still awake. Rather than scold the lad they told him about the gauleiter and how he had shared with them some important information about the Reich's newest enemy. After a glass of milk the boy was tucked into bed and lovingly chided to go to sleep if he knew what was good for him. The lights were put out, darling Rudi was kissed again, and after listening for a moment at the closed door, the Krauses went to their bedroom. They did not hear the click of the official Hitler Youth flashlight under the covers of Rudi's bed where he was searching through the pages of a book that listed all the party officials of the Reich. He could find no gauleiter named von Dahlheim in any of the forty-three provinces that made up modern Germany.

The next morning the team was up at six, hoping to get an early start on the two hundred or so kilometers remaining in their journey. They were also hoping to leave unobserved. No such luck. An impromptu bon voyage party had already begun in the restaurant where stiff good-byes and handshakes were ceremoniously exchanged. Even a picnic basket for the trip was provided. Gratis. There seemed no end to their desire to ingratiate themselves to the party. As Moe edged toward the waiting car, one of the lesser officials of the town offered a piece of information that would undoubtedly earn the praise of the gauleiter.

"You know, Herr von Dahlheim, there were fourteen Jewish families in Zwickau just one year ago. Today I can proudly announce that every one of them has been transported. We turned their names in on the very same day we received the order. Even some names that were slightly suspect--mixed grandparents, remarriages, and the like, all were removed. Our town is one hundred percent clean. I can proudly declare there are no Jews here in Zwickau."

"It is comforting to know of such diligence," Moe responded. "But," lowering his voice to a confidential tone, "one can never be absolutely sure, am I right?" directing the question to his aide.

"Ja voll, Herr Gauleiter," answered Ernie, who closed the door of the staff car and hurried around to the driver's side.

Heading out of town, Moe said softly, "You can't feel sorry for these people. They deserve everything they are going to get."

That same day, Rudi Krause conferred with his Hitler Youth troop leader, sixteen-year-old Helmut Adler. He found the fact of an unlisted deputy gauleiter to be of only slight interest, most likely a clerical error or a recent appointment, but he nonetheless complimented young Rudi for his diligence. The führer himself had warned of the cleverness of the Reich's enemies and the need to report all irregularities regardless of how seemingly unimportant.

"You have done well, Rudi. I will bring this to the attention of our Thüringen district leader."

Nearly half way to Gottow, Ernie Kahn announced: "I'm getting hungry." The other two men agreed, so the black Mercedes staff car pulled off the main road and stopped for lunch. There was wurst and ham sandwiches on black bread in the basket, which also contained several bottles of the excellent beer. They hungrily ate their picnic lunch sitting on the running board of the car. When they finished, Ernie disgustedly flung the basket against the trunk of the tree.

"Yeah, let's get this over with, " said Moe. "This show has been running too long."

They returned to the car and sped north with new resolve.

The relative ease with which Moe and his team had traveled through Nazi-dominated territories had given the men confidence and turned them into fairly good actors. They began to relax, believing that their masquerade was foolproof because it had till now been accepted without challenge. The crossing of Belgium and France had been accomplished too easily. Now they were in Germany and things had changed. Germans had till recently viewed their homeland as a fortress and accordingly directed their vigilance outward. This meant persons coming and going within the Reich were generally not impeded. Now with the increased bombings and reports of successes coming far less frequently, a heightened sense of paranoia could be felt in the Reich as the fear of saboteurs and spies abounded.

Moe and his team were aware that it was into this new state of wariness that they now intruded. The danger was greater than ever before.

"Roadblock up ahead," Gurney mumbled excitedly through his bandage. "What do we do?"

"Nothing," said Moe. "They've already seen us. No choice but to play it out."

A young Wehrmacht private standing in the road pumped his hand downward several times to slow the Mercedes. Two other vehicles were already stopped in front of them. An officer was leaning over and talking to the occupants of the first car. As they drew closer and stopped, Moe and his team were somewhat relieved by the fact that the roadblock was a railroad barrier, but the team was still uneasy at the prospect of being subjected to scrutiny.

"Herr Gauleiter," the officer saluted smartly, then returned to business. "Your papers, please."

The gauleiter produced the documents with a weary gesture and asked the young soldier testily, "What is the delay?"

The lieutenant did not answer immediately as he focused his full attention on the papers. As the young man's eyes strayed to Gene and Ernie, Moe stated obviously, "My aide and my driver."

"Danke, Herr Gauleiter, heil Hitler!" said the saluting officer as the papers were returned.

Only then did the young officer respond to the gauleiter's question. "A train, sir, coupling a new locomotive. See, it comes now. You will be soon on your way."

A string of wooden boxcars slowly backed into the crossing and stopped. From the opposite direction a squat, black locomotive belching grimy gouts of smoke appeared and backed hurriedly toward the rearmost car. The engineer miscalculated his speed slightly and as engine and train coupled, the impact sent the boxcars lurching rearward. Shouts and distressed wails could be heard emanating from the wooden freight cars.

There are people in there, Moe realized. He then turned to the lieutenant and asked, "What's that all about?"

"Juden," was the young officer's dispassionate reply. "Jews!"

"Ah!" Moe responded knowingly, marshaling every ounce of self- control to disguise his rage and revulsion.

When the train had passed and the barrier was raised allowing them to continue on their way, Moe finally broke the silence.

"Do you know what that was back there?"

"Yeah," said Ernie. "We know."

"Those Nazi bastards," murmured Gene into his bandage.

No one spoke again for the next hour.

Their mission seemed to take on a new clarity. Even the car plunged forward with a renewed sense of purpose. Gottow! Do what we have to do and get the hell out of there.

35

⹂━◈━⹂

THE SLANTING RAYS OF THE LATE AFTERNOON SUN glinted off the grace-
fully curved fenders of the big black Mercedes as it turned to
enter the outskirts of the small village of Gottow.

"Keep your eyes open. We're looking for a new facility," Moe
reminded Gene and Ernie. "A fairly large laboratory of some
sort. Made of concrete. Fortified. Schumann bragged about it
to Scherrer. Built by I. G. Farben. That's a big outfit. So look
for something new and big."

Their first pass through the small city turned up nothing.
They continued into the outskirts for a bit, scrutinizing every
side road for a newly bulldozed driveway. They found none.
Doubling back to town, they drove over an old stone bridge that
crossed a stream and followed the road, which paralleled the
stream. Still no sign of a laboratory. They then returned to town
and parked conspicuously in the square near a fountain.
Unusually whimsical even for a German fountain, it took the
form of a bronze goose girl on a stone pedestal coyly rebuffing
the amorous advances of a bronze shepherd boy while three
loyal bronze geese hissed at the presumptuous young man.
Three streams of water spewed from the open beaks of the
guardian geese to form a single arc of crystal clear water that for
generations had filled the water casks of the Gottow townspeople.

"What do we do now, boss?" said Ernie.

"I guess we ask."

"I'll do it," said Ernie, getting out of the car. "A poor lost gauleiter is a pathetic sight to behold."

"Scientifiche laboratory? Nein, Ich ken sie nicht," said the innkeeper.

The three other occupants and the cook were likewise unaware of such a place. Ernie stood there and shook his head, utterly dejected.

"My chief is in that car outside."

Two of the patrons went to the window and observed the impressive car.

"He's going to have my ass if I can't locate the installation we are scheduled to inspect."

The Germans have never really developed the art of hyperbole or satire. The expression "having one's ass," therefore, could only have two meanings. The first, too degenerate to consider. The second, and most likely, was that the officer who rated such a car was also capable of putting his young aide against a wall and shooting him dead for his incompetence. A shame. He seemed like a nice young fellow.

"There were two professors in here the other night, come to think of it. Quietly ate their dinner. They're not from these parts though. They're from Berlin, I believe. They've been in several times before."

"Thank you, sir, at least now I can give him some information. You're sure you don't know where they are employed?"

"No." "No." All around.

"That doesn't help much," said Moe at the sparse information. "It simply confirms what we know. The facility may be hidden. But how do you hide a thing like that?"

Chief of the Hitler Youth, Baldur von Schirach, was proud of his boys. They were the future of Germany, to be molded by his able hands. Inculcated to the sacred principles set down by the führer. Past generations had been so easily infected by the viruses of liberalism and cosmopolitism. This new generation would be raised on the manly virtues of nationalism and total fealty to the new world order. Beginning with their very first school days, they are imbued with the Aryan ideal and the utterly irrefutable fact of its superiority. These young men, upon coming of age, will be the worthy inheritors of a cleansed and pristine new world.

So dedicated were these young people that they would regularly report their friends and family members for behavior detrimental to the precepts of the Reich. In fact, they were encouraged to do so. Very often the report, upon investigation, became a matter for the Gestapo. Occasionally a report proved completely erroneous, an outright fabrication, or a case of youthful imagination concocted out of a desire to display loyalty and win approval. Even such cases had value, if only to help spread the word that wrong thinking in any form would not be tolerated however innocent the context. And it will be our policy to continue encouraging such vigilance, mused von Schirach as he read the odd report recently placed on his desk for consideration.

It had been taken down verbatim from one of his youth leaders in Zwickau. Apparently some party official who recently visited the town is in question, a deputy gauleiter, of what district it does not say. The man does not appear in any of the most recent party staff directories. A suspicious deputy gauleiter? Highly improbable, but . . . credit it to the enthusiasm of youth. A simple phone call to Berlin will undoubtedly set the issue to rest. I'll have my secretary call later this morning. Von Schirach placed the note on the table behind him after jotting down a note: "Helga. Phone Schlichter at party headquarters and confirm this name." He drew an arrow to the name and then circled Manfred von Dahlheim, deputy gauleiter.

Ah, now for important matters. On his desk was an elaborate sketch of the new Hitler Jugend ceremonial dagger. It had been argued that youngsters shouldn't wear such a dramatic decoration. But Baldur felt strongly that there should be a device sufficiently impressive to honor the outstanding boys in the HJ. Besides, boys of this age would literally kill to wear such a dagger. And isn't that precisely our goal?

36

⟶ ⊰◊⊱ ⟵

THE TOP BRASS OF THE SWISS AIR CORPS had been seen arriving this morning at the headquarters building at Dübendorf Air Base. That many brass hats meant that something big was going on. As the meeting extended into its third hour, Wachtmeister Franz Schramer and Oberst Karl Högger were summoned and ordered to stand by just outside the conference room.

"What do you suppose is up, Franz?" asked Högger.

"Can't be sure, but I'll wager it has something to do with all these British and American planes we've been collecting lately. In any case, I have a feeling we will find out very shortly."

The platinum blonde secretary with the cornflower blue eyes looked up at that moment and smiled at the seated men. Both airmen, flipping their caps nervously, returned her smile. She was a very attractive young woman. Just then, the intercom light flashed and the secretary flipped the lever. A barely audible gravelly voice made an abrupt statement. The secretary, still smiling, cocked her head toward the conference room door and the two airmen rose briskly and went in, caps properly tucked under their arms.

"Hey, somebody's messing with the Floosie!" shouted Shultz, the waist gunner, as he jumped to his feet and pointed to the rows of aircraft.

260

Lieutenant Quinn, the Floosie's navigator who was lying on the grass, raised the cap from his face and squinted at Shultz, annoyed at having his nap disturbed. He and the rest of the crew had come to the field to watch today's ball game. Two inept teams, the Fighters, made up of mostly fighter pilots, and the Knights, who led the league in errors, were locked in a 3-3 tie with the ignominy of last place at issue.

As Quinn rose to observe the source of Emil Shultz's concern, he saw that someone indeed was messing with the Floosie.

"Hey!"

The crew members sprinted to the aircraft and demanded to know why a tug was being hooked up to the nose wheel and where the hell she was being dragged to.

The English-speaking Swiss mechanic told them that all he knew was that the lacerated sheet metal around the left wheel well was to be repaired. The work to be done near the metal shop in one of the larger hangars on the other side of the base.

"They're fixin' her up?"

"That's okay, ain't it?"

"Yeah, but why?"

"Yeah, why?"

No one could provide an answer nor could the mechanics say when they were bringing the ship back. The crew pressed Lieutenant Rogers to register a formal complaint to their Swiss "hosts," which was politely received with the assurance that someone would certainly look into the matter. The Swiss provided no more explanation. They did, however, remind the flyers that the fenced off section of the base was Swiss Army Air Corps and the hangars on the other side of the active airfield were off limits to the airmen. They also made it abundantly clear that internees could easily become prisoners if they began behaving like spies.

So the crew of the *Faithful Floosie* was forced to accept the fact that they were now a crew without a plane. There were several crews in a similar condition--flyers whose ships had crash landed and were too shot up to be repairable. For these crews internment was a bit more difficult. They were, in effect, men without a country, the disenfranchised. Crews that retained access to their aircraft still had hope. All the flyers understood they were here for the duration but those without a plane, be it Fortress, Liberator, or pursuit ship, were essentially unemployed. Any child of America's Great Depression despised being unemployed.

Schraner and Högger had been given their assignment to get themselves checked out on all these aircraft: fly them, evaluate their capabilities, and in turn check out other Swiss airmen. The biggest aircraft in the Swiss Air Force was the twin-engined Junkers JU52, a toy compared to the B-17s and 24s. What an opportunity! thought Shraner and Högger. It was like spending the night in Pfefernick's toy department a week before Christmas. While the sheet metal repairs on the Floosie were under way, the two airmen familiarized themselves with the cockpit and the manuals of the Liberator. The more they learned, the more in awe they were of American technology. Until now it had been a foregone conclusion that Germany would prevail in the present conflict. That view began to change as they experienced the elegance of these American-made machines.

They soon felt competent enough to begin taxiing the big bird. The steerable nose wheel was a pleasant surprise. Steering had traditionally been effected by engaging one or the other of the main wheel brakes, a method that was inefficient and tough on the brakes. There seemed to be no end to the technological wizardry of the Americans.

After several days of run-ups and taxiing, they felt ready to take her up. Down the runway, one-ten, one-fifteen . . . at 120 knots, the yoke was rotated and she fairly leapt into the sky. So *that's* what those big wings are for. And the power! Lord love those supercharged engines.

Word of the flight got back to the crew of the Floosie.

"They're stealing your plane."

It pissed the crew off. It pissed all the internees off. But what're ya gonna do?

Eventually the big white cross of the Swiss Air Force was painted on the fuselage over the U.S. star insignia. Smaller white crosses were painted on the wings and vertical stablilizers. Confiscated .50 caliber machine guns were installed at all positions. Even a Norden bombsight that had managed to survive a crash landing was installed and removed each evening. It was a very rare gadget indeed because so few remained intact. And considering the Germans had offered a one hundred thousand marks reward for a workable example--that made it rarer still. The Floosie was once again complete . . . but . . . she was now the newest aircraft in the Swiss Army Air Corps. *Faithless Floosie!* For the Swiss airmen, it was pleasant to know they possessed a plane that hadn't been purchased from the Germans or French.

The matter of the name came up. Wachtmeister Schraner was reluctant to remove it. And he rather liked the scantily clad Petty girl with the bee-stung lips who brazenly winked from the fuselage. She had undoubtedly been lucky for her previous crew. The only problem was the word "floosie." Faithful translated just fine. Floosie didn't appear in any of the German-American dictionaries. No one could translate the word. He eventually got his translation from a young American Red Cross worker. When he first asked, she responded with a strange expression. After he explained the context, she smiled and told him it was a sort of slang that meant frivolous. Faithful-frivolous. There was nothing particularly untoward in that. He thanked the young woman, bowed smartly and left, thinking that she was a rather attractive young woman, that Fraulein Carlisle.

The sudden shriek of an air raid siren shattered the tranquility of the drowsy Gottow afternoon.

"My God, where's that coming from?" said Ernie, wincing from the din.

"German only, Lieutenant. Don't forget again," was Moe's stern response.

Accompanying their new concrete and steel air raid shelter, the good bürgerin of Gottow had also received a superdeluxe air raid siren. Because the shelter was built to specifications appropriate for a city much larger than Gottow, the siren they received was accordingly designed to alert a much larger population. This was the way of German procedures. In strict accordance to specifications, the siren had to be matched to the size of the bunker. No matter that the town of Gottow had fewer than two thousand residents, minus the few away for war-related service. It would be easier for Goering to fit into Goebbels's trousers and button them than to alter German procurement procedures once a system had been set down. So the small city of Gottow was sent an air raid siren appropriate for Mannheim.

From the outside, the shelter built into a hill on the edge of town looked small and unimpressive. The steel door had been observed with little interest by Moe and his cohorts during the several pass-bys the big black car made as it continued on its frustrating search for a new concrete laboratory facility.

"Uh-oh, what's he want?" mumbled Gene referring to the elderly policeman who gestured and waved as he hurried over to the Mercedes in a creaky and comical trot.

"You must go in the bunker. An air raid has come. It is the rule. There are no exceptions. You must go in the bunker. You must obey the rule."

The elderly schutzmann recently recalled from retirement so that younger men might serve in the army, took his reinstatement very seriously.

"What about the car?" Ernie demanded as the men dismounted from the vehicle.

"It is safe here. No one will molest it. You must immediately go in the bunker. It is the rule."

They had no choice but to abandon their car and allow themselves to be herded into the bunker by the old copper while the blaring siren made it difficult not to seek shelter. Barely one hundred meters away, up in the church steeple, young Hansi Glock, the assistant fire marshal of the town, was gleefully cranking the siren. Fire engines made lots of noise and Hansi had always delighted in the whoops and clangs the vehicle made on its way to emergencies along the local Gottow roads, but that noisemaking was tame compared with this. This sound was exquisite. This sound was like the götterdämmerung. Because of his partial deafness he had been turned down by the army. That suited him perfectly because right now he was on top of the world.

At the entrance to the door of the shelter someone waved. That was Hansi's signal that the shelter was about to close and the siren could stop. "Sheise!" said Hansi to himself, and gave the crank a few extra turns just for spite. With the noise still echoing amid the bruised air molecules of downtown Gottow, the teutonic Quasimodo hurried down the worn, stone stairs and sprinted for the bunker. The sound died out just before he reached the big steel door. He vowed to one day win that race.

"I'm curious," said Moe. "Perhaps you can enlighten me?" He was addressing the person who seemed to be in charge. A big, red-faced man with thick farmer's hands who was dressed a bit better than the other townsfolk. Probably the mayor.

"Do you expect Gottow to be bombed? I can't imagine why this place would be a target."

"You are correct, Herr Gauleiter. Gottow is not a target for bombing. But Dresden, eighteen kilometers to our east, is. Coal, you see, and the antiaircraft implacements that defend it--the debris of their shells. If they are shooting at the planes in a westerly direction, well, you understand, it would fall on

Gottow. Several roofs have been damaged and some livestock lost in an early test of the batteries. That is the reason we have been given this strong bunker."

"I see," said the gauleiter. "And when was it completed, if you don't mind me asking?"

"In May, I think it was. Built by I. G. Farben. A most impressive structure, is it not?"

"Yes, indeed it is," said Moe. "Thank you for explaining it to me."

The big country gentleman nodded and walked over to talk to a group of villagers in the corner.

"Moe, Moe!"

"Shhh. Later!"

The light bulb had snapped on for all three men.

"Was that an explosion?"

"I thought I heard a noise."

"I heard it too."

"Shhh. Listen."

"I don't hear anything."

"Shhh, how can you hear anything if you're talking. Shhh."

Inside the bunker, the eighty-odd townsfolk sat in nervous contentment. On the one hand they were worried about their homes and fellow Gottowen outside. Still, they enjoyed the concern their government had shown them by providing this substantial shelter. Why, it even had a flush toilet--an objective example of the largess of the new order. Here, bürgermeister could sit cheek by jowl with town drunk in the protective embrace of all that thick concrete. (Actually, the town drunk sat as far from the bürgermeister as he could.) Here, all men were equals, including a visiting gauleiter and his retinue.

The gauleiter heard the muffled bang. The eyes of Ernie and Gene acknowledged that they too had heard it. They were all seated on solid wooden benches. Plenty of room. Almost too much. The furthest of the three sections wasn't occupied at all.

Candles, food tins, and first-aid supplies were stocked in abundance on shelves near the steel entrance. There was even electric lighting. Powered by who? The town? Or some nearby generator? Near the high ceiling were ventilation ducts. The faint sound of circulating air could be heard during lapses in conversation. There was obviously quite a sophisticated ventilation system installed here.

The gauleiter stood up. To stretch his legs? Or, as it seemed to the others in the bunker, the big important fellow was getting a bit edgy. Back and forth he paced, taking full deliberate steps. He's nervous, all right. Trying hard not to show it. So he's human after all. After a few minutes of watching the Nazi pace, the townsfolks returned to their conversations, their thoughts. By then the Nazi official had reclaimed his seat on the bench and was patiently awaiting the all clear.

Fourteen paces. With my stride that's about, say, thirty-five feet, Moe calculated in his head. It made sense. Yes. There could easily be another, larger section on the other side of that wall. It's got to be Diebner's uranium laboratory.

Bang. Bang. Bang. Someone outside was knocking on the steel door. When it was opened, a gray-haired man stuck his head inside and grinned.

"Alles klar! Hansi!"

Hansi darted out the door past his fire chief and sprinted for the tower. He was eager to begin his next gig.

As the occupants of the shelter filed out into the early evening, Moe and his men lingered behind. When they were finally alone, Moe and Gene gave Ernie a boost up to the vent.

"See if you can see anything."

Ernie stood on Gene's shoulders trying to reach eye level with the grating. He had to step on Gene's head to see into it. Moe moved to check the door. It was fortunate that he did. The elderly town cop was approaching.

"Come, come. You must go out. Out!."

Moe blocked the door, smiled his most amiable smile, and informed the old fellow that one of his men had got a bit nervous and was availing himself of the toilet facilities.

"Ja, ja, also. He must hurry. I am required to assure that all have exited from the shelter. He must hurry."

As the old fellow walked away he was thinking, ha, the big one doesn't want to come out of the bunker and the other has most likely wet himself. What a bunch of sissies, this new generation. In my day we had guts. In my day our officers would have such chickens shot. Imagine being afraid sitting in a shel . . . As he trudged stiffly past the church, the din of the all clear drowned out his thoughts.

Ernie was able to remove the grating thanks to the screwdriver in Gene's Wehrmacht-issue pocket knife. The screen was thrown to Gene, who caught it as Ernie pressed himself into the two-foot-wide opening. He was gone for what seemed like a week. Moe stationed himself at the door to check on the old policeman's whereabouts. Looking up at the empty vent, Moe and Gene exchanged nervous shrugs and "where the hell's he gone" looks. At last Ernie's grinning face reappeared in the opening. He emerged headfirst and dove out into the arms of Gene. He was covered head to toe with gray dust. After replacing the grating and securing it with one turn of each of the mounting screws, they exited the bunker. Ernie looked utterly disheveled as they walked toward the car.

One of the locals, standing in a group nearby, gestured to the three men as they strode past.

"That must be the one who wet himself in the shelter."

"From the looks of him, he barfed his guts and rolled in it."

A good, rural laugh was had at the expense of the bespectacled young lieutenant.

Once they got in the car, "Well?"

"Did you see anything?"

"I found it," Ernie blurted through the broadest of grins. "It's a lab. Big. Even bigger than the bunker. I saw three people working. There were at least three. One was writing. The other two working at a machine--a metal lathe or something. Big tanks all around the walls and in the middle of the room, a huge tank on its end sitting in a kind of swimming pool. Built right into the center of the floor. Then there was all this stuff hanging from a round plate near the ceiling. It was right over the big tank in the center of the floor. Once one of them looked right up at the vent. I tell ya, I thought for sure he saw me, but then he went back to his work. Does that sound like what we're looking for, or don't it?"

Moe looked at Gene and then at Ernie and then with a broad grin said, "You found it, all right. That's what we're looking for. Drive, Gene. Let's get out of here. We've got to figure out what to do next."

The black Mercedes made a U-turn and headed back to the town square a few blocks away where there seemed to be a crowd and a traffic jam. What's all the commotion?

A Wehrmacht half-track was about to leave. In it sat a German officer, two soldiers with rifles, and the driver. Between them, three bedraggled American airmen. The hauptmann had their names. Capt. Richard Mumma, pilot; Technical Sgt. R. B. Medford, engineer; and First Lt. Alan Goldman, bombadier.

"Is this one a Jew?"

"No, his tags say he is Catholic."

Their bomber had been damaged and the crew had parachuted. There were at least seven more to be rounded up. Captain Mumma had landed in a field. When he hit the ground he felt something snap in his right leg. It hurt like hell too. As he was attempting to untangle himself from his chute harness, he received the initial thump from the hayfork handle. An angry farmer had been the first to welcome Captain Mumma to Germany. He was venting his frustrations on the poor, gimpy pilot when the Wehrmacht arrived.

They had been searching for the downed airmen in their motocycle and sidecar when they came upon the comical scene. They let it go on for a bit, but eventually rescued the Yank. They gathered up the chute, took his pistol and his cigarettes, and helped him walk to the sidecar and climb in. The three men shared the American cigarettes and had a smoke as the grim-faced pilot sat awaiting his fate.

Mumma asked, with sign language, how many bailed out, using his cupped hand as the symbol for parachute. The soldiers didn't understand at first but the farmer got it and indicated eight chutes open and two streamers, shaking his head and saying, "Kaput."

Oh, God, I've lost two of my crew, Mumma was thinking as he was driven off. A bedraggled Goldman and Medford were sitting in the German half-track when the pilot arrived. They looked as if they had either both plopped in mud or had been roughed up upon capture. Mumma joined his men as they sat in the village square. There they sat as local Germans were permitted to view the vanquished enemy. At first, a few fists were shaken at them, followed by some curses none of them could understand. Finally one old fellow rushed the vehicle and reached over to punch Medford. This was followed by several of the townspeople surging forward and pummeling the American airmen. The guard permitted the beating. Blood trickled from Goldman's brow as he vainly attempted to dodge the blows. The nearest guard looked to his officer for direction but none was offered.

Few noticed as a big black Mercedes staff car drove into the square and stopped a few meters from the scene. The beating of the prisoners was increasing in viciousness when a gunshot rang out and froze the action. It was the occupant of the staff car, a general officer of the party, who had fired into the air.

"Calm, calm," he said softly amid the emotionally charged atmosphere of the square. Then walking toward the vehicle, he called to the officer. "Hauptmann, if you don't mind, a word."

The Wehrmacht captain hurried over to Moe and heiled smartly. Moe returned it casually and calmly.

"I see you have captured three enemy officers. Well done. It would be a shame if these prisoners were incapable of providing us information at their interrogation because of injuries received while in your care. Would it not?"

"Yes, Herr Gauleiter!" The captain said.

"Good. Good. Now, see that you don't spoil your already fine work."

"No, Herr Gauleiter."

"Excellent, you may carry on!"

The officer made a brisk about-face and ordered his men to form a protective cordon around the half-track.

Capt. Dick Mumma sat in dazed disbelief as he observed the improbable scene unfolding before him.

I'm not sure, but I think we've just had our skins saved by a Nazi. And a really mean-looking one, at that!

37

IN THE FADING LIGHT, Ernie climbed the hill above the broad tunnel into which the air raid shelter had been set. His steep climb was rewarded by a beautiful sunset and a commanding view of much of Gottow and the surrounding countryside. As the sky grew dark he carefully made his way down the opposite side of the small mountain he had just conquered. In negotiating an obstacle course of several hundred yards of gloomy pine, scrub, and loose boulders, Ernie then entered a wide area appearing much brighter by contrast. It consisted of newly deposited rocks and dirt, the tailings of an excavation, no doubt. Scrambling over and around the loose ground, Ernie could make out the meandering line of a recently cut road. In the failing light he followed it away from the hill for what seemed to be nearly an hour, increasing his pace as his eyes grew accustomed to the gloom. The road dipped and curved for over a mile and finally intersected a wide paved road, most likely the access to the main Gottow town road. To any passerby, the path would look more like a turnaround than the road to a sophisticated physics laboratory. Having discovered its outlet, Ernie now turned to search for the road's destination.

After another hour of backtracking, Ernie thought his eyes were playing tricks. Lights up ahead, flickering. He then heard the motor noise and sprinted for cover. A vehicle rushed past him, heading out to the main road. Probably workers from the lab leaving for home. When the car was well out of sight he continued his march toward the bunker. The moon, which now began to show itself above the treetops, provided ample illumination as Ernie headed toward the lab at an easy trot.

Uh-oh, another light coming this way. From his hiding place behind a tree, Ernie observed a man on a motorcycle leaving the lab. He's no fool, thought Ernie, he's taking it nice and slow.

After only a few more minutes of walking, Ernie's quest revealed itself. The road ended at twenty-foot-high steel doors built into the face of the hill. Set into one of the doors was a small, man-size opening. Ernie found that both large and small steel doors were securely locked. As he put his ear to the door and listened he could hear only the low drone of of an electric motor, most likely the ventilation system.

Abandoning the steel doors, he scrambled back up the hill as quickly as the darkened terrain would permit, anxious to bring Moe and Gene the news that he had found the entrance to the hidden lab.

Ernie found his compatriots in the dark just outside the shelter entrance. They had managed to get the locked door open, thanks to a bit of persuasion provided by a tire iron. Ernie told them of his discovery and the big steel doors with the serious-looking locks. They concluded that their best bet would be to attempt to gain access through the ventilation system in the shelter.

Once again Ernie went up through the grating and into the duct. Gettin' my exercise today, he thought, as he wriggled as quietly as he could toward the vent leading to the lab.

The laboratory was faintly illuminated by two dim light bulbs. It appeared to be deserted. With the small pliers of Gene's utility knife, Ernie quietly unscrewed the vent's fasteners and removed the grating. Then confirming that the large room was unoccupied, Ernie whistled a signal and Moe and Gene followed him up into the duct. First Gene, then Moe, who was cradling a rucksack under his arm. Moe and Gene then dropped lightly to the table under the vent opening to join Ernie, and the three men stood quietly viewing the room in the silence, three Americans in Nazi Germany's most advanced nuclear laboratory.

"Let's wreck the joint," said Gurney as he climbed down to the lab floor.

"Whoa, fellas, we'd better think this out," Moe said as he eased himself down. "Let's look around first, size up the place. Look for tanks of water," he instructed as he walked over to inspect the crazy mobile in the center of the lab.

"There's a cot and clothes. I think somebody lives here, Moe," Ernie called from the far corner of the room.

"That means somebody might show up. Better rig that door to make a noise if it opens," Moe ordered.

"How's this?" asked Gurney as he leaned a thick wooden beam against the small steel door.

"There's water in the pool," said Ernie, pointing to the pit in the floor in front of them. "That the water we're looking for?"

"No, that's ordinary water. We're looking for 'heavy water' . . . deuterium, probably in those tanks against the wall."

"Shall we flush 'em down the drain?" Ernie asked as he ran to the valves at the base of the three large tanks.

"Maybe," answered Moe, "but first let's figure this gizmo out. According to Robertson, a uranium machine requires, first, uranium. Those metal cubes up there, hanging from the plate, they must be uranium. See, they're suspended from wires of all different lengths. They probably stack at different heights when they're lowered into the tank. Next you need a moderator, that's the heavy water--see, here's the pump and the valves that fill the tank. The water in the pit is ordinary well water to cool the contraption. And that big holding tank must store the extra coolant. Okay, so far it makes sense. Now we need a neutron source. That funny gray box hooked up at the center of the lid, that's got to be the radioactive material that shoots the neutrons. Yup. It's all here, just like Robbie and Scherrer predicted."

"I wonder if we've got anything like this in the works?" Gurney put in.

"I sure hope we do," said Ernie. "These Germans are smart, aren't they?"

"I wouldn't say that," said Gene. "You're German and you're not smart."

"Guys!" Moe preempted the imminent rejoinder. "We've got some decisions to make. They're my decisions, but I want your input."

Gene and Ernie got serious.

"As I see it, we've got a couple of options. First we could wait for the scientists to return, probably in the morning, kill them-- we might even get Diebner; then wreck the lab, drain the deu- terium, and run for it. High probability of getting caught on the way back, though. Or we could wreck the lab, drain the juice, and run for it--we'd give ourselves a little better chance, but still, it's a long way to Switzerland. Then there are these jugs of pow- dered boron that Scherrer gave me. Supposed to absorb neu- trons, foul up a fission reaction."

"What do we do with it?" asked Ernie.

"Scherrer said put it in the heavy water. It'll ruin it. But we can dump the deuterium down the drain so there's no need for it."

"Why not screw things up in a way they can't tell right away? Drive 'em nuts trying to figure it out. It might give us the extra time to get clear. I'd rather not get shot if it's all the same to you."

Moe thought for a second. "Gene, you're a genius."

Gene tried to look modest, failing utterly.

A loud motor noise on the other side of the steel doors caused the men to turn and look. Then realizing someone was about to enter, they hurriedly took cover, each in a different part of the lab.

The heavy wooden beam clunked to the floor as the door opened and a leather-coated man with a shaved side haircut and bristling eyebrows lurched into the lab. His arm was draped around a slightly overweight, thirtyish blonde who was wearing lots of rouge on her rounded cheeks. The two were laughing and

275

giggling, obviously a bit drunk. The woman was pretty in a frowsy way, wearing a dark red dress with a revealing oval cutout in the front.

This must be the caretaker of the lab, who had this evening brought a companion home to help him wile away the hours of darkness.

He led her to the corner where his cot stood and produced a half-full bottle and two glasses from a cabinet. He poured out two generous drinks, offered her a glass, and they toasted each other, then, laughing, downed the liquid. Even before she lowered her glass, he lunged forward, wrapped his arms around her waist, and buried his face in her bosom. Giggling, she pushed him down, loosing his grip on her middle, and stepped away from him. Poor fellow was kneeling on the ground trying to imagine where she had suddenly gone. Refocusing his eyes with great effort, he located her again, standing a few feet in front of him. She, in turn, began to undo the back of her dress, stepping out of it with all the sensuous grace her tipsy condition would permit. The caretaker, grinning stupidly, sat back on his haunches enjoying the private striptease. His jaw dropped open into a gaping grin as she pulled her slip up over her head and threw it aside.

The three American men in hiding silently observed the bizarre engagement in fascinated discomfort.

As the brassiere came off, allowing gravity to usurp control of her goodly breasts, the poor fellow leapt to his feet and charged, uttering a short yelping noise as his outstretched hands reached for those remarkable orbs. Giggling sadistically, she swatted him in the face with her bra, sidestepping him with the ease of an accomplished matador. Then, all bare feet and knickers, she turned and ran from him choosing to hide behind some large metal cylinders. They happened to be the very same cylinders behind which Moe had elected to hide. When she saw Moe, she screamed.

The thwarted lovers lay face to face on the cot with their arms and legs trussed together. They were warned not to attempt to free themselves or call out or they would be gagged and their bonds would be tightened. The only consolation given was the woman's request that her dress be set aside so that it would not be creased or damaged. A nightshirt was provided for modesty's sake.

Pulling the curtain on the trussed-up pair, Moe turned once again to face the lab.

"Let's start smashing those atoms," said Gurney.

The team set to work. They pumped a small amount of heavy water into the big tank, threw two handfuls of the boron into the fluid, and then reversing the pump, sucked it back into the holding tank. They did this three times, once for each of the three deuterium storage tanks. It appeared that each tank held enough heavy water to fill the experiment tank. That meant Diebner had three times the deuterium he needed. Now it was all going to be spoiled. They then tainted a quantity of coolant water, just for the hell of it. Next Moe wondered if there was a way to spoil the uranium. But how? Could we coat the uranium blocks with boron? Think guys! Ernie came up with the idiotically simple solution: smear the bottom of each square of uranium with oil or grease. Then dust on the boron. If the water wasn't turbulent, the oil and boron would adhere. If it washed away, it would simply further contaminate the deuterium flowing around it. It might be days before they figured it out. The most important thing would be that the largest stock of deuterium in Europe would be poisoned--that's the word Scherrer used, poisoned. Permanently.

"Let's get to it, guys. We've got a long drive ahead of us."

"What about Fred and Ginger?" asked Gurney.

They checked the pair behind the curtain. The bonds were still secure. They were then forced to finish the bottle of cognac, each consuming three nearly full glasses. As an extra measure, the couple's hands and feet were tied to the steel cot making breaking loose even more difficult. The curtain was once again drawn on the pair.

"It'll take a few hours for them to free themselves," said Moe. "We'd better be far gone by then."

After one last look around the lab, back up to the vent they clambered, carefully replacing the laboratory grid. Then after crawling the length of the duct and dropping down into the shelter, they securely replaced the grating. The three dusty burglars used the tire iron once again, this time to pry the door back to its locked position, and hurried to their car hopeful that their night's work would not be discovered till they were well on their way to Switzerland.

38

ASHLEY INNESS HAD PUT IN A TOUGH WEEK. The wholesale information trade, which normally did a brisk business, had recently picked up significantly. There were countless operatives reporting in and requiring aid in the form of radios, weapons, food, money, and sanctuary. Now that the momentum of the Nazi expansion seemed to be slowing, more dissenters were encouraged to organize and resist. The job of the newly created Office of Strategic Services was to foster those organizations along with existing resistance groups. This meant an ever-expanding intelligence and counterintelligence network. There were hordes of refugees to interrogate, many of whom felt their information was worth reward or special favors. Ashley Inness himself would determine the disposition of these requests.

Inness loved his work and knew he was good at it, but being so involved meant devoting long hours at his Bern headquarters. This weekend he promised himself a break. He would leave his offices at 6:00 p.m., no matter what, and drive the 130 or so kilometers to his apartment in Zurich, where he was determined to reward himself with a relaxing weekend--perhaps even spend part of it with Celeste. And then there was that fresh little morsel, Sally Carlisle. Or whatever her real name is. Her protector, Moe Berger, had left Switzerland, according to a report; perhaps with the fellow out of the picture she'll be a bit more compliant. Yes, compliant. That's the word. He repeated the word aloud, "compliant," as he drove east in the big Daimler that had been provided by the American Embassy. It stays light so much longer these days, he thought to himself. How "compliant" of nature. He laughed out loud at the broadened context of the word. The unique qualities of intellect, assertiveness, and daring would make the world compliant to Ashley Inness. Who knows how far it would lead? A cabinet post? Perhaps, even-- dare I say it?--the presidency. It certainly wasn't beyond him. It's clear that I've outgrown the job of OSS chief of Europe. I should be in London directing the entire OSS operation. No doubt I will when Donovan moves on. My years with the State Department eminently qualify me for the job. We insiders are the true heroes of this war. And while the dreary working-class types driving the tanks and planes will be given medals and parades, as good public relations dictate they should, the inevitable victory will be won behind the lines of combat by men of my stripe, gentlemen with the prerequisite background and breeding to make the truly important decisions.

The kilometers slid effortlessly past as the picturesque Swiss countryside was bathed in the amber light of the late summer sun setting in his rearview mirror. Inness sat in his car feeling in control and confident. Contented as any man who sees himself as master of his fate can be.

It was dark when he arrived at his apartment. The concierge greeted him with a gracious, "Good evening, Monsieur Inness." He nodded in return.

A short ride in the lift and he was at last in his suite of rooms. They were lavishly appointed even by peacetime criteria. Ashley Inness believed in maintaining one's standards. He undressed and called Celeste while the tub was filling.

"What would you like to do this evening?" he asked.

"Oh, you must be tired after that tedious drive. Why don't you just come over and I'll fix us a nice supper."

"Sounds great," was his response. "I'll be over as soon as I change."

A quiet evening amid gentle comforts was exactly what he was hoping for. Celeste understood. Celeste was compliant. As he walked past the full-length bedroom mirror, stark naked, he stopped, sucked in his belly, and struck his best Charles Atlas pose. Not bad for a fifty-two-year-old man. Then, as he slowly settled himself into the hot water, he noticed through the open door the picture of his wife, Grace, smiling from the window of the silver frame on the dresser. Ah, good old girl, keeping the home fires burning, Ashley mused as he soaped under his arm. If subjected to closer scrutiny, Grace's smile would reveal a resignation that seemed to say, yep, he's a jerk all right, but he's my jerk.

Ashley parked the Daimler a good fifty yards from the gated driveway of Celeste's villa. Not parking close was standard OSS practice. Of course, there was also the lady's reputation. His gallantry and circumspection in this case proved to be a mistake.

As he walked along the fifty or so secluded yards of street toward Celeste's front gate, two men rushed out of the darkness and assaulted him. A fist in the stomach doubled him over. A second blow to the chest straightened him up. Then an arm circled his neck from behind as a hand was clamped over his mouth. He tried to concentrate. Is it a robbery? He elected not to struggle. Let them take what they want. As a hand undid his watch he thought, sure, take it. They next removed his wallet. The bills were removed and the billfold thrown to the ground. His tiepin was pulled free. Oh, rats! he cringed. That's a real diamond. Now one of them grabbed for his ring! It wouldn't come off. Inness was revolted as the brigand spit on his finger and twisted the ring free. It was his father's. Oh, God, he thought, just don't hurt me. One of them struck him in the face. Smack! He could taste the blood. What else do these animals want?

Then one of them, a thick brutish, ugly man, looked Ashley Inness in the face and shook his head with his finger over his lips. Inness understood the man wanted him to keep silent.

While he was in their power he had no choice. Inness nodded that he understood. Then the goon did a strange thing. He took a small slip of paper from his pocket and read, or tried to read, "Shtay avey von Sally Carlisel." What? The man repeated the message. "Shtay avey von Sally Carlisel." Sally Carlisel? Sally Carlisle! Fright and comprehension crept into Ashley Inness's face. The two thugs threw their victim down to the ground and tugged on his left leg. What the hell now? Aahh! The pain was excrutiating. His assailants had placed his ankle on a rock and stamped on the bone of the lower leg. Oh, my God! thought the writhing Inness. I heard it snap. It sounded like a piece of kindling. The pain! It was unbearable. When Ashley Inness realized his tormentors were gone, he began to shout for help. The pain that coursed through his savaged limb imparted an odd squeaking sound to his frantic cries.

Several hours later in the apartment of his friend Celeste, his leg in plaster, Ashley Inness was interviewed by the Zurich polizei. A mugging, obviously, but strange for it to occur this far from town. Still, all they got was a Gerard Perigaux watch, twenty-two hundred and some-odd Swiss francs, a small diamond tiepin, and a worn gold ring of little but sentimental value. Then to the matter of the assault and broken limb--most likely the result of a hurried departure by the criminals or perhaps Herr Inness offered greater resistance than he had thought. No question, a robbery, plain and simple, with the unfortunate result of a compound fracture of the tibia. It was all in the polizei report. There was no mention of any message or the name Sally Carlisle.

Ashley Inness was accorded the tender loving care worthy of a triumphant war hero. Celeste even offered to drive him to his offices in Bern later in the week. She was happy to do it--what a swell gal. The only thing that rankled was that Inness knew exactly who had maimed him. That goddamned Jew bastard, Berg. And there was nothing, not a thing, that he could do about it. At least not right now.

39

ㅡ·ㅡ ⟨◇⟩ ㅡ·ㅡ

ON THE OUTSKIRTS OF AUGSBURG the black car passed a sign that read Bodensee, 122 km. The spirits of the three saboteurs were buoyed at the thought of safety less than three hours away but they were also aware that the most dangerous part of the journey lay before them now that they were traveling in daylight. They had been moving at high speed for nearly five hours and made good time during the night stopping only once to gas up from the spare cans stored in the trunk.

"We're practically home free," Gurney announced hopefully, but as he spoke the green sedan he noticed in the rearview mirror a few kilometers back reappeared.

There were three men in the car trailing the Mercedes: a young driver, a soldier, both wearing helmets and the tan uniforms of the Hitler Jugend, and an older man in civilian clothes. His name was Baldur von Schirach, administrative chief of the Hitler Youth. He was shouting at his driver.

"Put your foot down, you idiot, they are pulling away."

"I am, I am, sir," said the driver. "It's these hills. They have a very powerful car."

"I don't want excuses, just overtake them," von Schirach snarled through clenched teeth. The Hitler Youth leader was dressed in a black trench coat and dark slouch hat, a costume he deemed appropriate for this type of undercover work.

Von Schirach had picked up the trail of the imposter in Gottow where an interview with the local constable revealed that the "gauleiter" had left town heading north.

"North. He let himself be observed heading north. Clever! That means we go south, Gerhard. South on the autobahn to catch a big fish!"

This will change things for me, thought von Schirach, as he sank back into the rear seat of the camouflaged Opel sedan. The führer himself had selected him as Reichsjugendführer, but chancellerey politics in Berlin had seen fit to "kick him upstairs" into a relatively powerless position and allow Artur Axman to succeed him. Axman, the war hero, flapping that empty sleeve like a music hall dandy. When I singlehandedly unmask this counterfeit gauleiter, the führer will see that I have the stuff of a true leader.

In the seat next to him, the helmeted personal guardsman sat rigidly alert, supporting his Schmeiser submachine gun against his knee.

"We are gaining on them, Gerhard. You must put on more speed and we will have them."

"Guys, I think we're being followed," Gurney finally confided to Moe and Ernie.

Both turned to look at the green vehicle some thousand yards behind them.

"He's been in my mirror for at least a half hour, followed us through two turnoffs. For a while I thought we'd lost him in the hills west of Nuremberg. But he's back."

"Do we try to make a run for it?" Ernie asked.

"We're already running. Let's try to figure this out," said Moe. "Those two in the lab couldn't have gotten free this quickly. If they did, there'd be roadblocks. It could simply be another car heading for Munich or southern Germany. When we make the next sharp turn, let me out, then drive on to the next bend in the road and pull over and stop."

Moe hopped out and the big black Mercedes proceeded another fifty meters or so, then pulled over onto the shoulder of the road. Moe made his way through the cover of the woods toward the car.

"There he is! We have him," von Schirach screamed while triumphantly pounding the seat in front of him.

As the green Opel sedan pulled in behind the stopped vehicle, the two Hitler Youth guards bounded out and positioned themselves on each side of the black Mercedes, their weapons poised. Von Schirach then stepped out of the car at an exaggeratedly slow pace as if to savor every moment of his victory. He withdrew a silver cigarette case from his coat pocket, removed a cigarette, tapped the end on the case, and casually lit up. After taking a deep heady drag, he approached the black car.

"Out! You will exit the car, keeping your hands in plain view at all times."

The two occupants of the black Mercedes eased out with their hands raised. The one who emerged from the driver's seat wore a bandage over the lower part of his face just as described by the Gottow policeman. But where is the so-called gauleiter? Von Schirach drew a pistol and gestured for his two captives to move away from the vehicle, then wrenched open the rear door only to find the car empty. He then inspected the large trunk and found only gasoline cans and some suitcases.

"Where is he?" demanded von Schirach.

"We are to meet our gauleiter in Munich," Ernie offered innocently.

"Liar!" raged von Schirach as he leaned close to Ernie, blowing smoke into his face. "He is no gauleiter. He is an impostor, and for all I know so are you. Take them away from the road, into the woods. We want to be out of the view of passing traffic."

A convoy of military trucks carrying troops rumbled past as the group moved into the woods to a clearing about fifty meters from the road. There the interrogation continued.

"Sir," Ernie pleaded, "you have made a serious mistake. Our gauleiter is on the staff of Reichsleiter Borman in Berlin."

Von Schirach nosed closer. "I have spoken to Berlin. They know nothing of a von Dahlheim. Nothing!"

Ignoring the man, Ernie continued his explanation. "He was summoned to a conference in Munich. He was flown . . . "

"You are lying! Impostor!" von Schirach ranted. "You are all impostors! And I *have* you."

After several minutes more of futile questioning, the frustrated Hitler Youth chief completely lost his composure. He placed the muzzle of his Mauser automatic to the side of the driver's head and demanded that the lieutenant reveal the true identity of the so-called gauleiter.

"If you don't tell me who he really is and the purpose of this masquerade, I will execute this man. You have three seconds to begin talking. Eins . . . zwei . . . drei!"

Bang! The pistol shot resounded through the trees surrounding the little glade.

Gurney's eyes were wide, partly at the realization that he was not shot and partly at the deafened state in which he now found himself.

Von Schirach had vented his rage by firing his pistol over the driver's head.

"I have run out of patience," said the HJ chief. "Speak now or this man dies!"

"But, sir, you don't understand . . . "

"Shoot him," von Schirach ordered his two young henchmen.

The two sixteen-year-old boys hesitated for a moment, first looking at their leader and then at each other. They then both raised their weapons. Suddenly, in the woods all around them, the shadowy movement of men with rifles could be detected. A Wehrmacht officer stepped forward and leveled a Luger at von Schirach and his two Hitler Youth gunmen.

"Drop your weapons. Raise your hands in the air," the officer barked as the clearing was quickly surrounded by his men. A high-ranking NSDAP officer stepped forward to stand beside the pistol-wielding unit commander.

"You see, Lieutenant, as I told you, these boy scouts are up to some serious mischief. Would you kindly place them under arrest before they can do any real harm."

"At once, Herr Gauleiter." The Wehrmacht lieutenant gestured to his troops, who disarmed the two Hitler Youth boys and the fellow in the trench coat and herded them toward the road.

"That man is an impostor! He's posing as a gauleiter. He's a fraud! A fraud, I tell you," von Schirach turned and began shouting, only to be silenced by the thump of a rifle butt in the small of his back. The civilian crumpled to the ground at the feet of the soldier who had struck him. As the man looked to his officer for an indication of what action to take next, von Schirach regained his feet and bolted back toward the woods like a panicked deer. The soldiers raised their rifles and awaited the order to fire.

The lieutenant looked to the gauleiter, who raised his hand as he shook his head, 'no', don't shoot. He then, inexplicably, reached to the ground and picked up a turnip-size stone and with an unhurried, fluid motion winged it at the fleeing man. At the distance of approximately twenty meters the projectile overtook von Schirach and struck him squarely on the back of the neck.

The Nazi's fedora flew as both limp arms sprung outward from his unconscious body, which pitched face first into the ground and slid on the damp turf like an aircraft executing a perfect belly landing. The grinning soldiers nodded in appreciation of the gauleiter's feat.

"Lieutenant, I would appreciate your keeping these men in isolation until I can personally interrogate them. Do you think that can be arranged?"

"Ja, Herr Gauleiter," said the troop's commander. "We will take them to our camp at Fürstenfeldbruck. We have a very secure stockade."

"Excellent, Lieutenant," said the gauleiter. "I will return to deal with them this evening. Remember, keep them incommunicado until I can personally question them. Gag them, if you must."

As the soldiers and securely bound prisoners climbed into their truck, the gauleiter thanked the young officer.

"Be assured, Heigler, that your efforts this morning will not go unappreciated."

Heil Hitler and the black Mercedes continued on its journey to the south. In the rearview mirror, Gene watched as the Wehrmacht truck rumbled off in the opposite direction.

Lake Constance lies on the border between Germany and northeastern Switzerland. The shimmering body of water was a welcome sight when it came into view as the big black car crested a small rise. The rearview mirror was clear. No one was pursuing them. They were nearly safe.

But what was all that activity at the lakeside? It looked like a runway under construction. A new airfield this close to Switzerland? The Nazis seemed to be building a runway along the German side of the lake. Something that looked like a large red cross had been painted on the concrete at either end of the construction.

"Did you make out a red cross at the end of that runway?" Moe asked his companions.

The car was descending now, nearly at the level of the construction, making the markers more difficult to see.

"What?" said the still slightly deafened Gene in response to Moe.

Moe raised his voice and repeated the question. "A red cross! Did you see it? . . . at the end of the strip!"

"Yeah," said Gene, a bit too loudly and muffled by the bandage. "It sure looked like it to me."

Whatever it was, its purpose is to be viewed from the air.

"Yeah, some kind of air marker," Gene added loudly.

"But for what reason?" Moe pondered.

"To offer first aid to damaged aircraft?" suggested Ernie.

"But a German plane in trouble could land anywhere."

"True, so it must be a marker for Allied planes."

"Why would they land here if they could be in neutral territory across the lake?"

"That's it!" said Moe. "They want to lure aircraft heading for Switzerland to land in Germany."

"Those rats!"

"Hey, it would work. A pilot in trouble would see that red cross and thinking he'd made it to Switzerland, land his crippled ship. Red cross, white cross; most Americans wouldn't see a difference."

"And he'd become a German prisoner of war," Gene added.

"Those rats!"

Up ahead, the sign pointed to Zurich as the road divided. They were in the homestretch and the fatigue of the long night's ride and their close call disappeared. True to form, Moe became calm.

"Everybody act cool when we get to the border check. Remember, we are the master race."

Ernie got nervous. "What do we do if they try to stop us? Gene, you gotta floor it at the first sign of trouble. Crash that barricade."

"Got it!"

Gene, true to form, always looked forward to a new opportunity for excitement.

"This is going to be easy, bullshitting those border guards. Just one look at this car and they'll be 'heil Hitlering' all over the place."

"He's probably right," said Moe. "No reason to be worried. Let's expect it to be routine. Just act like we do this every day."

There it was. Up ahead. The border shack. As the car came into view, two uniformed officials came out.

"Turn in next to the shack," ordered Moe. "Act like we want to check them out."

Gene pulled in alongside the guard shack. Ernie jumped out and ran around to open the door for his gauleiter. Moe stepped out and affected his most contemptuous demeanor. He walked directly toward the two border guards.

"I and my people would like to utilize your cabin so that we may change into civilian clothes. With your permission, of course."

He asked permission, but his tone implied he didn't need any.

"Certainly, Herr Gauleiter. Sergeant! Show them inside."

"Thank you, Lieutenant. These idiot Swiss play at neutrality but the mere sight of a uniform frightens them. Someday soon they may find the German uniform a very familiar sight, eh, Lieutenant?"

"Yes, sir, most familiar."

As the three weary saboteurs changed clothes in the privacy of the guard shack, some four hundred kilometers north, just outside the town of Gottow, a young woman wearing a maroon dress with a revealing scoop neck was walking down a macadam road. She and her laboratory caretaker paramour had finally managed to free themselves from their bonds in the early morning hours. They worked furiously in the hope that the scientists who usually arrived at eight would not discover her presence. There could be dour consequences for her partner, who had sworn an oath of secrecy about the existence of the lab. Because the lab seemed to be intact--nothing missing, damaged or removed, and the intruders long gone--the pair decided that it would be prudent to say nothing of the incident. Yes. That would be best for everyone concerned.

She began her trek with the morning sun. Several hours later, her feet were raw and throbbing as she neared the Gottow street where her flat was situated.

"He will pay dearly for my pain," she muttered as she hobbled up the front steps.

Once again in civilian clothes, the three men of business headed out to their motor car.

"Herr Gauleiter!" called the lieutenant.

"What is it?"

'Your name. For my register. Would you sign, please. And also the names of your men. If you don't mind, sir."

"Certainly not," said Moe.

He wrote, Manfred von Dahlheim, purchasing agent. Purpose of visit, business. His men put down their names and their respective occupations of secretary and driver.

"Danke! Herr Gauleiter," the border officer popped a very sharp heil Hitler. Moe walked toward him and offered his hand. The surprised officer took it and shook it.

"Businessman!" said Moe, as he winked.

The businessman entered his car and was driven the fifty or so yards to the Swiss border shack. There he was met with typical Swiss efficiency.

"Identification papers! Purpose of the trip." The documents were inspected and duly logged in. "Thank you, Herr von Dahlheim. You are free to go. We hope you enjoy your stay in Switzerland."

The car rolled past the barrier and into the sovereign country of Switzerland.

Whew! Neutrality. It had a fine smell. Nearly as good as freedom.

Part 5
Escape

40

⊷⊷ ⊨◈⊨ ⊶⊶

SALLY AND BABETTE MUST HAVE BEEN VERY WORRIED. It showed on their faces when the men returned. They'd been gone fewer than three days but for the two women waiting nervously in Zurich, time had passed with agonizing slowness. Sweating out some-one else's danger is always a tedious chore.

Sally held Moe close to her as she fought to control the upwelling of emotion. Moe held her away from him, looked into her moist eyes, and said, smiling, "What? What!" She just hugged him again, snuggling her face into his chest. He knew very well "what." He was just trying to minimize the danger they had recently faced. In truth, he was just as relieved to see her as she him. But as a paid up member of the hero's union it was necessary to behave as if it was all in a day's work.

A hot bath, a lot of fussing, and clean, crisp sheets were the reward for Moe's return. Babette drove along with Ernie and Gene, to their pension, ostensibly to fluff their pillows. One could imagine that she intended to give Ernie's pillow a couple of extra fluffs. There was even a letter waiting for Gene. From that tall Tiller girl. Perfumed, too. Plus a message left by his baseball team reminding him of the game tomorrow.

Later that morning, Sally called Professor Scherrer at the university and left word that his prize student had returned safely. Life in Switzerland had once again returned to normal. With the boys tucked safely in their beds dreaming the dreams of the innocent, Sally and Babette went to their jobs at the

295

International Red Cross. There were still lots of refugees to care for and records to initiate. Each day brought more people seeking the sanctuary of neutral Switzerland. They were people from all stations in life attempting to reclaim some dignity from the disruptions of war.

The girls had thrown themselves into their work. They helped translate, expedited paperwork, and, with genuine compassion, provided some semblance of calm to their uprooted clients' lives. Neither Sally nor Babette would admit it, but each realized that she was much better suited to social work than sabotage.

Professor Scherrer was waiting in the hotel lobby when Sally and Babette returned that evening.

"It is most important that I see him," said the professor.

"I don't know if he's awake yet . . . " On seeing the serious look on the older man's face, she reconsidered her resolve to protect Moe's rest. "But let's go up and see."

Moe was awake and had already shaved.

"Nice to see you, Professor Scherrer. I've got lots to tell you."

"Good, Manfred. Why don't we then go somewhere where we can talk."

Moe understood immediately that Scherrer was reluctant to talk in the hotel room when he emphasized the word "Manfred." Moe finished dressing and they went outdoors where they could converse in privacy.

Sally couldn't understand why the two couldn't talk in their nice hotel suite. She had no way of knowing the conversation would be about neutrons.

"Cubes, you say? Suspended by wires! Ingenious! A flexible way to mass the uranium. Any geometry can thus be achieved. Go on, please."

Moe told Dr. Scherrer everything--everything he could remember about the lab, the uranium pile, and the sabotage. He was characteristically precise, recalling every detail, even the nature of the ventilation system by which they gained access to the lab and subsequently made their escape.

"Remarkable," was Scherrer's comment when Moe had finished describing the adventure. "Remarkable. Also you have established two extremely important facts. First, a sustained chain reaction has not yet been achieved. If it had been, the massed uranium would have been locked into place and the neutron source simply removed to shut down the action. Clearly, the proper configuration has not yet been determined. Our boron trick will play havoc with that. But they will eventually discover the problem and continue their experiment. From your description, they are very close.

"The most significant piece of information you have uncovered is the great reserve of heavy water they had available. You say there were three large tanks holding approximately four hundred gallons?"

Moe nodded.

"That is an enormous quantity. Diebner must have considerable influence considering Heisenberg's position as Germany's preeminent physicist--his heavy water supply is severely rationed. Ah, the ugly presence of politics in science! Once it was all so pure."

Scherrer grew wistful for a moment, then returned his focus to reality.

"They cannot proceed without heavy water. You've fouled their supply. I doubt if it can be purified, but even if it can it would require a complex separation process, nearly as difficult as the electrolysis process initially used to separate heavy water from sea water. My guess is that they'll opt for a new supply. If we could somehow prevent them from obtaining any more, they would essentially be out of the uranium chain reaction business."

"Don't they make the heavy water in Norway?"

"Yes," answered Scherrer, "in Rjukan, but one does not jump into a car and drive there. It's virtually inaccessible, a remote plant, on the eastern coast."

"Could it be bombed?" Moe offered.

"Perhaps. It's a long way. I don't really know. But one thing I do know, Germany must be denied its access to heavy water. If we accomplish that, they are effectively stopped in their tracks."

"Then that's what I'll tell London. We've got to destroy their heavy-water-making capabilities, wherever they are. Give it the highest priority, too. I hope I can convince them."

"I hope you can, Moe. Diebner is close. And where Heisenberg might think twice about presenting Hitler with such a weapon, Diebner would not."

41

—•—░◆░—•—

Two sets of stands were erected along the foul line between first and home and third and home. The wooden structures were very sturdy and slightly overbuilt--American airmen/carpenters determined to impress their Swiss hosts with their craftsmanship. Today the Yankees played the Cardinals, the two remaining unbeaten teams in the Zurich Internee League. Neither team had shown any particularl dominance in their initial games, lucking into many of their early season victories as much good play, but as the season progressed both clubs grew stronger and more confident. They changed personnel to improve defense and juggled batting orders to concentrate their hitting.

Both teams also possessed a pair of college-level players. The Yankees ace pitcher was the lanky Lieutenant Rogers, Stanford, pilot of the *Faithful Floosie,* and in center field, Lt. John Dunbar, copilot of *My Gal Glenda,* who only a year ago stalked the outfield grass of the U.S. Military Academy. The Cardinals pitcher was southpaw Lt. Roy Poole, bombadier of *Gotcha,* the B-24 that had executed a near textbook pancake landing only two weeks before. Their shortstop, Algie Pickens, was a Tulane University star, who enlisted during his third year, impatient to drop bombs on the Nazis. He did exactly that for nine missions as lead bombadier of the 344th on the *Immaculate Contraption.*

This matchup had the promise to be one hell of a ball game. The new stands didn't fill up, however; many of the airmen seated along the foul lines assumed the nice new wooden seats were

299

for officers. But in general there was a substantial turnout. The American Consulate staff showed up in force. Not because they sought contact with the American flyers, in fact, for some arcane diplomatic reasons, they had always made every effort to avoid their countrymen. Today was an exception. Baseball on a summer's day was a taste of home that was too luscious for even the diplomatic corps to pass up. Ashley Inness, the number two man at the consulate, was in attendance on crutches, his leg in a heavy plaster cast. Obviously some sort of freak accident, Moe observed. Doesn't look too happy about it either.

Sally and Babette were in attendance. They sat in the stands opposite the consulate staff to the delight of the young airmen who surrounded them. When the "Star-Spangled Banner" played on a hand-cranked phonograph, every American proudly sang the words, including the last two; play ball!

Moe was not in the starting lineup. He had asked to sit on the bench in deference to the regular catcher, Hobart. The diminutive backstop had gamely caught most of the Yankees' victories and certainly deserved the honor. Besides, Moe wanted some time to sit quietly and contemplate his next moves in the imminent bigger game. The first order of business was heavy water. Word needed to get to London about the necessity of depriving the Reich of their sources. Somewhere in Norway sat a sophisticated electrolytic facility that produced the liquid moderator for Germany's nuclear reactor experiments. It had to be put out of business at all costs. Communications to that effect had already been sent--Jabberwocky messages were dispatched, both in the regular Swiss mail to Lisbon and by transmitter to operatives in France, who would hopefully relay the word to London.

Even Paul Scherrer sent similar dispatches to colleagues in Britain via Sweden all artfully worded so that the messages would be indecipherable by anyone but a fellow physicist. Despite all these communications, Moe was still concerned that the vital task of eliminating Germany's heavy water sources could only adequately be conveyed in person.

Which led to Moe's second concern: how to return to England in the speediest way possible? Do we walk out and take our chances crossing the Pyrenees to Spain? Do we rely on diplomatic protection and take a Swiss train to Marseilles where we could catch a boat to Lisbon and then London? Both long, tenuous trips fraught with danger. And haven't I endangered my buddies more than necessary already? What about Sally and Babette? Do they stay here? Sit out the war? Or do they join our breakout? Haven't they also been endangered enough? I'm responsible and I don't want to foul up now, after all we've been through.

When Moe finally turned his attention back to the game, it was the fourth inning of a 2-2 tie. Both pitchers had worked effectively, allowing only two hits apiece. The runs were due to several errors and some sloppy play. At the moment the Cardinals were at bat and had their leadoff man safely on first, the result of a bunt base hit. The catcher, Hobart, had fielded the ball cleanly but his wide throw pulled the first baseman off the bag. The Cardinals realized they had uncovered a weakness and responded with three more consecutive bunts. All were mishandled, two by Hobart and one by the third baseman, who threw over the head of the short catcher thereby missing the force play at home. One run in, bases still loaded. None out. "Time," called the manager. He walked to the mound but really wanted to talk to his catcher, who disheartenedly followed him out.

"You're killing us, Shorty."

"I know, I'm not good at those."

"Will you be sore if I put in the ringer?"

"You mean Manfred?" He knew Bradley meant Manfred.

"Yeah."

"He's good at bunts and we want to win, right? Bring him in, it's okay."

"Substitution, Ump! Von Dahlheim for Hobart, catcher."

"Got it," said umpire Ernst Kahn, barely able to suppress a smile. The venerable master of nuclear saboteurs was about to don mask and chest protector to chase bunted baseballs about on the coarse green turf of a Zurich meadow.

Two hours earlier, on the far side of the city, a senior German diplomat was ushered into the office of the Swiss foreign minister. He was imperious to the point of insolence. The Swiss minister received him cordially. He had orders to be gracious and conciliatory when entertaining the entreaties of the Reich's representatives. The reasoning was simple. If Hitler really wanted Switzerland he would take us. We are sovereign only so long as it remains inconvenient for Germany to invade.

"What a pleasure to see you again, Herr Brutman. How may we be of service to you?"

Brutman was typically direct. "There is an individual named von Dahlheim presently here in Zurich. He is neither a German nor a Swiss citizen. We demand the immediate arrest of this person along with his companions and we further insist on their extradition to Germany. These persons have commited crimes against the fatherland and must be returned to the Reich to face charges."

Brutman allowed his demand to sink in and then with dramatic pause delivered his ultimatum.

"We require immediate action on this issue. If you fail to comply, I can only warn you that the existing relationship of neutrality that presently serves our countries will be seriously jeopardized. I trust the implications need not be explained further. Heil Hitler!"

With that, he turned about smartly and strode from the minister's office, leaving the nervous diplomat sitting in his chair wondering exactly what this von Dahlheim could have done to infuriate the Nazis so.

302

The bunt was still on. It had been effective till now, why change it merely because they put in a new catcher? Big clumsy-looking mug, too, observed the Cardinal's manager. The redbird's third-base coach confirmed the play by wiping the front of both thighs. Then he ran through the signals for the batter, touching his nose on the fourth sign. Fourth inning, fourth sign. Squeeze play. The next pitch was duly bunted up the third-base line. This time the new catcher overtook the horsehide in two strides. The runner coming from third pulled up short as he saw catcher with ball bearing down on him. He skidded to a stop, then reversed his field, back to the safety of the third-base bag. Once the runner had commited, Moe threw to third, forcing the runner from second. When the confused base runner saw the base occupied by his sliding teammate, he reversed direction once again and sprinted toward home. The third baseman made the short, easy throw to his catcher now halfway up the line where the tag was slapped on the passing runner. Double play. Two out. Runners on first and second. The bunt was taken off and the next batter lofted an easy fly ball to Gurney in left. The rally was cut short but the Cardinals had taken the lead, 3-2.

On the third floor of the Tonnhalle the Swiss minister found his chief, the foreign secretary, taking coffee in the private lounge set aside for senior officials. The unnerved minister spoke of his visitation by Brutman. The older man listened quietly, sipping his coffee and allowing his subordinate to thoroughly vent his concerns. Finally the minister asked, "What do you think we should do, sir?"

The foreign secretary responded, "Obviously we must make every effort to comply with the German envoy and apprehend this fellow and his cohorts and turn them over."

The minister's face fell. " But . . . "

"But if these persons are no longer within our borders the Germans can't very well expect us to arrest them, can they? Clearly they are Allied operatives--French, German, American, perhaps even Russian. We must allow the news of the German ultimatum to be spread to all Allied embassies. They will warn their operatives and we, in the meanwhile, will move very deliberately to arrest these wanted men, who, unless they are complete nincompoops, will have long since fled our borders. Then, it will be our extreme regret to have to report that the persons in question have eluded us. You see, my friend, diplomacy has always been the art of saying 'nice doggie' to a vicious cur until which time you can find a tree to climb or a stick thick enough to brain him with."

In the seventh inning, after the shortstop grounded out, Moe hit a single. Unfortunately the next two batters popped up and flied out stranding Moe at first. As he trotted in to put on his gear, Moe noticed the odd emotional state of his team.

"C'mon, guys. We gotta win this game," implored Shorty Hobart, from the bench.

"Yeah, for the Floosie."

His teammates seemed upset. At first Moe hadn't taken notice. He was so immersed in his own problems, but now as he looked into their faces he could see they didn't seem to be enjoying the game as they should. It was more like a funeral than a baseball game.

"What's with you guys?" Moe said. "Something wrong?"

Lieutenant Rogers explained, "They took the Floosie. Our airplane. She was the crew's identity, kinda."

The Yankees were made up of five players from the Floosie's crew. With their aircraft confiscated, they felt disenfranchised. The Cardinals' players were drawn from several flight crews and still regarded themselves as functional combatants because they still had daily access to the winged symbols of their trade. The aircrew was forced to watch as the Swiss callously appropriated the Floosie. To rub it in, they even painted the Swiss Air Corps white cross on her wings, fuselage, and stabilizers. She became a painfully familiar sight in the air above Zurich, brazenly flaunting her new nationality. Eventually several craft would be commandeered by the Swiss; at least three B-17s, a second B-24, and a half dozen fighter planes were turned renegade and shamelessly decorated with white crosses. Even an ME 109 was seen to have been converted: one of the new G-models with the enlarged spinner and more powerful engine—most up-to-date Luftwaffe. It was little consolation that the Swiss Air Force "borrowed" from the axis too.

This practice angered and demoralized the interned aircrews.

"Those douche bags stole the Floosie! We gotta win this game. For the Floosie!"

So, that's what's been eating these guys. Now Moe understood. Certain things give meaning to men's lives. Belonging was such a thing. It was family, nationality, and cause rolled into one. For Moe, these men had lost their portion of the war. To also lose their plane simply rubbed salt in the wound. To point out the irrationality of it all would be futile. Next at bat, Moe vowed, I'll try to do more than simply meet the ball. My team needs a better effort.

"We want a hit! We want a hit!" Sally started the chant and the animated crowd of airmen, Allied escapees, and Swiss spectators chimed in.

"We want a hit! We want a hit!"

There were two on and two out.

Moe shook his head as Schultz, the next Yankee batter, popped up to the infield for what would certainly be the third out. But the Cardinal infielders did an Alphonse and Gaston, "after you," "oh, no, after you" on the ball and Moe was saved an "up." He strode resolutely to the batter's box.

At that very moment a junior official approached the American Consulate group sitting in the stands and handed a folded piece of paper to Ashley Inness.

The chant of "Let's go Manfred" grew louder as the count went to two and two. Even spectators rooting for the Cardinals got into it. The fans thought that chanting the unusual name was great fun. Three persons, however, found the chanting an annoyance. Moe Berg, Ashley Inness, and Tyler Vaughn, who now believed in the correctness of his initial observation: that this fellow was indeed the former Boston Red Sox ball player, Moe Berg.

Moe pulverized the next pitch, a drive that flew past the pitcher's ear and kept rising. The center fielder moved to his left to align himself with the ball but the white sphere just continued to climb. He backpedaled frantically, but the ball was now at least twenty feet over his head. And rising. It finally landed in the distant scrub beyond the playing field, at least 150 meters from home plate. Moe trotted briskly around the bases. He displayed no sign of jubilation or satisfaction. Just a businesslike home run to put his team in the lead.

"What a blow!"

"Did you see!"

Even the Swiss and British spectators who were struggling to make sense of the game were impressed. All applauded loudly as Moe followed the runners around the bases.

Ashley Inness took time to read the message delivered to him by the consulate courier. Surprisingly, it concerned the man who had just struck the home run.

"He's a remarkable athlete, don't you think, sir?" said the still applauding Tyler Vaughn.

"You could say that," Inness replied. "See here, he is wanted by the Germans. They're demanding the Swiss arrest him and his thugs and deport them to Germany."

"Does he know?" the younger man asked, indicating Moe's team with a slight tilt of the head.

"I doubt it," said Inness testily, "and we're not going to inform him."

"But if he's one of ours . . . "

"We don't know that for sure."

"But, sir, London confirmed that they knew him!"

"Well, I don't know him and that's what counts around here! Case closed. So stop looking so wounded and let's enjoy the game. Maybe the Cardinals can rally."

306

The Cards got a leadoff hit in the last of the ninth but it went for naught. The next three batters made out quietly giving the Yankees the victory, 5-3.

Handshakes all around. A picnic with sandwiches, cold chicken, and lemonade provided by the Red Cross. It wasn't exactly a Sunday in the park back home, but it was close. As for the Yankee team, the new champs, the winners of the Zurich World Series trophy, the victory provided meager satisfaction. The men were still far from home, on the sidelines of their country's fight, and most miserably, without their plane--a plane not damaged, not destroyed, but kidnapped, sitting over on the ramp across the runway contritely wearing a prissy white cross and being flown daily for the satisfaction of Swiss crews and Swiss purposes.

"Excuse me," said the young diplomat as he extended his hand to the Yankee ball player, von Dahlheim. "I'm Tyler Vaughn. That was quite a homer you hit today."

Moe responded warily with a weak smile and nod.

"You're Moe Berg, aren't you?"

Moe's face made no response to the question.

"Well, if you won't acknowledge it, that's your business. I know you're Moe Berg. I saw you play in Florida. But never mind that. I'm with the American Consulate and we were informed only a few minutes ago that the Germans have demanded of the Swiss that you and your associates be turned over to them. The Swiss have agreed. I just thought you ought to know. My chief is against informing you but I thought you should know. That's all I wanted to say."

Moe was searching the man's eyes as he spoke. They were clear, blue, and truthful.

"I've got to go," the young diplomat said. "Congratulations on your victory. Good day."

He then turned and briskly walked away. He had walked almost ten steps when the ball player spoke, "Mr. Vaughn."

The younger man stopped and turned.

"Thank you," said Moe.

The young man made a small nod, the strain leaving his face. He then continued on his way only now there was just a hint of swagger in his step.

"Lieutenant Rogers!" Moe called. "May I have a word with you? Over here, away from the crowd. I've had a thought. I was wondering how you'd respond to it."

Lieutenant Rogers called his men together and put it to a vote. Bug out or stay? It was unanimous on the first ballot.

Moe Berg put the same question to his team. They likewise agreed.

Next came the really difficult part. Steal a B-24 bomber from the Swiss Air Corps and inform Sally and Babette that under no circumstances could they come along. Eventually the two women accepted the decision but they made no effort to hide their displeasure. Moe explained that he, Gene and Ernie were likely to be arrested at any moment and therefore it was necessary to leave immediately. Sally and Babette concurred but still didn't feel that justified their being left behind.

"We're going tonight."

"It's as good a time as any," someone said.

"We'll need extra chutes," Lieutenant Rogers reminded them.

"And flying suits."

"Yeah."

"Some better charts," George Quinn, the navigator, added. "I'll scrounge those."

"Some food," said Hobart.

Everyone chuckled at that but Shorty was right. Something to eat would keep them sharp on their flight to Spain, if they ever managed to get off the ground.

"Everyone scrounge what you can and we'll meet at the fence at, say, oh-one hundred hours. Manfred and I will reconnoiter the plane."

"How about me comin' along?" said Hobart.

"I was about to say, Shorty, you come too. We've got to check out the Floosie. If she looks okay, we'll come back for you guys. We meet at this exact spot at the fence. Oh-one hundred."

The airmen returned to their billets where they settled in to eat their evening meal. They talked about the game and received the praise and good-natured ribbing of their comrades. No one noticed the unusually high consumption of bread, rolls, and fruit this night. There was also a brisk trade in chocolate bars and cigarettes. Then too, fleece-lined jackets, pants, and electric boots, which had been stored and all but forgotten during the warm summer months, were unpacked and stuffed into bags for the imminent departure. Bed check was at midnight. Not a very strict affair. The flyers themselves took turns at CQ, charge of quarters, making sure that everyone was accounted for. The officers had a similar system with an enlisted man acting as concierge and checking the officers in and out as they passed the front desk.

Moe said his good-byes to Sally in a field adjoining the road within sight of the Dübendorf air base. It was decided not to return to the hotel. Too risky.

"There's plenty of money," Moe said. "You know where it is."

Sally nodded.

"And there's Paul Scherrer if you run into any difficulty. Under Swiss neutrality, you should be able to get to Madrid by train. From there to Lisbon and then to the states by boat. It should be safe. Vichy has no reason to detain you. Neither has Franco. With money you should be able to get home without any trouble. There's a man at the American Consulate named Tyler Vaughn, he seems like an honest fellow, and I think he'd help you if you needed it. Tyler Vaughn, got it?"

Sally nodded.

"And I'll see you soon? Okay?"

Sally threw her arms around Moe's neck and held him close. Realizing that in their brief relationship there had already been too many good-byes. It was no longer an exciting adventure, no

309

longer a noble crusade. Let it be someone else's turn to save the world. This man is dear to me and once again he has to leave. I may never see him again. Why can't they just leave us alone?

Moe held her face in his hands and said, "I'll see you real soon, you'll see."

"Yeah, real soon! Take care of yourself, Moe," she said and then she threw her arms around him and kissed him. Very hard and then softly.

"Gotta go," said Moe and then turned and jogged into the unmowed field that separated them from the air base fence. Some yards away Ernie bade a similar farewell to his girl. Babette waved a white handkerchief. She continued waving it long after both men had disappeared into the night. The two young women then looked toward each other. Neither spoke. There was nothing to say.

Gurney intruded upon them with an overly cheerful, "Come on, ladies, your last chauffeured limousine ride is waiting. And I don't want to miss my plane, you know."

They drove into town and stopped several blocks from the hotel. There Gene and the two women stepped out of the car and bade Gene farewell and safe journey. Any passing Zurichers would undoubtedly have raised an eyebrow at the unusually affectionate relationship these women had with their chauffeur.

The Floosie sat solemnly chocked outside a large hangar, the ribbon from her pitot tube cover fluttering in the breeze. The ramp looked deserted. Moe, Lieutenant Rogers, and Shorty Hobart lay in the grass across the runway beyond the ramp and quietly observed the scene.

Two floodlights near the hangar roof bathed the area in a harsh glow. A hundred yards away a lone pursuit plane stood, its canopy covered with a tarp. In the distance the dim outline of several single-engine fighters could be made out in the gloom.

Beyond the smaller hangar, the wooden structure of the control tower rose above the scene. Except for some lights in the tower, the area appeared deserted.

As their eyes became accustomed to the poor visibility of the ramp, Shorty observed, "No guns. Probably remove them after each flight. That's proper procedure according to the manual, but we usually stowed them in the plane and just replaced the ammo. Saves schlepping."

Moe reminded himself to someday ask Shorty where he'd picked up that word.

After at least a half hour of quiet surveillance there was still no sign of movement anywhere on the ramp.

"So far, so good. They obviously don't work nights in the Swiss Air Corps."

"No! Can't be," said Rogers. "There's got to be some kind of security."

As the words were spoken, the sound of a motor vehicle intruded upon the relative quiet of the windblown ramp. Then headlights swept into view as an open vehicle turned up the ramp toward the slumbering aircraft. The soldier on the passenger side played a searchlight over the darkened bomber as the vehicle slowly circled it, then drove off in the direction of the fighters.

"One thirty," said Rogers, checking his watch. "We've got to time their rounds. Moe, you go get the guys. I'll keep watching."

"How about I go see where that patrol winds up," said Shorty.

"Okay, but be careful, will ya."

The three men separated. Hobart trotted after the guard vehicle. It stopped at a door in the side of one of the low storage buildings built alongside the smaller hangar. Shorty peered into the room through a grimy window. Inside the two guards had already stowed their weapons in the rack and were settling down at a table to resume their card game.

A pair of fuck-offs, thought Shorty, as he began the return trot to the parked bomber. Looking back over his shoulder, he noticed there was movement in the glassed-in tower.

311

"Uh-oh. Someone's on duty. Better tell the skipper."

Corporal Basch, the tail gunner, led Moe, Ernie, and Gene to the B-24's open bomb bay where they climbed onto the central rail and entered the belly of the aircraft. They were followed by Thibideau and Shultz, the waist gunners, each burdened by a canvas bag stuffed with flying suits and a chest-pack parachute. It would be too risky to depend on finding chutes in the hangar or in the craft. The radio operator, bombadier, and copilot entered next. As they made their way along the narrow beam running the length of the bomb bay and dispersed to the fore and aft compartments, they shared an eerie feeling brushing up against all those two hundred pounders in the dark.

"So far, so good, huh boss?" said Shorty, as he plopped to the grass next to his pilot.

"I don't know . . . we're pretty far from the runway. Soon as we start these engines, the cat's out of the bag. That's a lot of taxiing. They could stop us easy by blocking the runway. I really don't like it."

"Hey, skipper, how 'bout we go?" said a voice from the dark behind him.

"Yeah, right," Rogers said to George Quinn, his navigator, belly gunner Pekula, and copilot Benson. "Almost forgot. You guys go ahead, but keep your faces out of the Plexiglas."

As he spoke the three men sprinted for the ship.

"Boss?"

"Yeah, Shorty."

"What if I towed us out to the runway?"

"Towed?"

"Yeah. I saw a tug and a tow bar over by the hangar doors. I'll just hook us up and haul us out. The tug won't make much noise. Especially in this wind."

"Okay, do it."

"I could use a hand."

"Sure, take someone from the plane. I'll get aboard now. I've got to do the check list. We go right after the next sentry round. Got it?"

"Rog," said Shorty over his shoulder as he sprinted across the grassy infield toward the plane and then to the darkened hangar. A figure exited the craft and followed.

When they were out of sight, Lieutenant Rogers trotted toward his Floosie. She sat expectantly, keen to fly now that her rightful crew was being restored to her. As her pilot entered through the nose wheel compartment, she now lacked only her favorite flight engineer to complete her crew.

The airmen and passengers were attempting to settle into more comfortable positions, being careful, as ordered, to stay away from the Plexiglas. Though it was a cool night, all perspired freely. Lieutenant Rogers asked that no one talk and briefly explained that Shorty was going to tow them out to the runway to give them a running start.

"We go as soon as the patrol makes its next pass. If they don't come soon, to hell with 'em. We're leaving anyway."

Moe Berg sat in the dark tunnel aft of the gunner's bay on a bag of leather flying clothes and contemplated the adventure of the past two years. Would it come to an end here in this aluminum cocoon? Helpless. Placing total trust in strangers? No! Teammates! That was fitting. Moe felt a bit better thinking of these young flyers as teammates. It was always appropriate to put one's trust in teammates. *But I wish we'd get this rodeo on the road.*

The light from the twin beams of the patrol car flashed against the hangar wall before the vehicle came into view. Everyone hunkered down, away from windows and held their breath. The floodlight swiped at the underside of the big aircraft as the open car slowly circled it. It slowed for a moment causing a dozen skipped heartbeats but then hurried off down the darkened ramp out of sight. Even before the sound diminished, a tug was backing up to the nose gear of the bomber. A figure hefting a tow bar jumped off and hooked it up, then ran to kick out the chocks. The bomber lurched forward then rolled

313

smoothly down the ramp and turned onto the taxi strip. Benson ordered Hernandez to start the gas-powered putt-putt in the aft compartment to supply juice to the Floosie's electrical systems while Lieutenant Rogers began flipping circuit breakers and checking fuel and hydraulics. One of the figures on the tug jumped off and ran toward the hangar.

They were nearly at the runway--so far, so good. Hell, thought Rogers, I'm going to start number one. Hope I don't frighten Shorty.

Like an old man in the morning, the left outboard engine coughed itself to life. Rogers worked the control surfaces and lowered the flaps as Benson monitored the gauges for fuel and hydraulic pressure. Number one, meanwhile, was building oil pressure and RPMs. Then two, three, and four were started. Enough noise to wake all of Zurich. The tug was disconnected and ditched off the runway onto the grass. As the engines idled, Rogers could make out Shorty running toward the plane. He was burdened with some heavy object he had lifted from the tug. Pilot and copilot stood on the brakes while Rogers spread his fingers and pushed the throttles to takeoff power.

When the RPMs had reached acceptable numbers, Rogers shouted back into the craft, "Let me know when Shorty's aboard."

"I'm here, boss," a slightly breathless voice spoke a few inches from his ear.

"Then, let's go! Now!"

Pilot and copilot popped their brakes in perfect unison. They had practiced this many times during their dozen missions together. They hadn't lost their timing. The Floosie jumped straight out of the starting gate and dove down the runway, seemingly elated to be reunited once again with her American crew.

Rogers peered out of the windscreen into the blackness, hoping not to see some obstruction that would abort their escape.

"Oil pressure stinks," shouted Benson.

"Can't sweat that now," replied Rogers. "Close the bay doors, Durkee!"

The bombadier had already thrown the lever setting the garage doors in motion. They made an unpleasant, grating sound as they creaked shut.

"Eighty! Ninety, one ten. One fifteen," called the copilot.

"Rotate!" shouted the pilot as both officers hauled back on the yoke together. The Floosie was airborne.

"We made it! We're flying!" Rogers smirked as he turned to his second officer and said, "Undercarriage up," in a dreadful parody of an English accent.

"Undercarriage up," acknowledged the copilot, snapping the gear lever into the up position, then tapping the brakes to stop the wheels rotation. The undercarriage thing had been their little private joke. British airmen referred to their landing gear as undercarriage. It was a source of humor and confusion the first time they heard the term. Isn't a carriage a conveyance for babies? Eventually the crew of the Floosie adopted the term and referred to their own landing gear as undercarriage. It sounded so much classier.

As the bomber headed into the western sky there was no alarm. No fighters were scrambled to pursue them. The two sentries in the guard shack were preparing themselves a hot snack of venison hash. Its delicious odor permeated the air as it sizzled in the pan. It made so much noise they had to open the doors of the gramophone much wider to hear the new Marlene Dietrich song.

In the tower, the wachmeister on duty could only stare out at the dark shape as it took flight. He held his hands behind his head at the behest of the man behind him brandishing the pistol.

315

Dozens of Zurich citizens, awakened by the engine noise, muttered to themselves at the lack of consideration of the Air Corps in choosing such an ungodly hour to operate their aircraft. With a groan, they punched their pillows and groggily rolled over to attempt to reclaim their rest.

Two young women in the heart of Zurich were also awake to hear the racket. Sally and her friend Babette embraced and wept tears of relief as the engine sounds faded into the distance and stillness once again reclaimed the night.

"I need a heading!" bellowed the pilot over his right shoulder.

"Steer two fifty," was the navigator's immediate reply.

"Two fifty it is," the pilot confirmed, smiling at the quick response. His navigator's usual reply to any request for course adjustment, was "wait one." Quinn had obviously plotted this one before take off. "Landmarks?"

"Water. Big lake. Lake Geneva in about twenty minutes."

"Got it!"

The city of Geneva was on the western tip of Switzerland. Once beyond it, they would be over the mountainous portion of occupied France--in occupied France the Luftwaffe owned the skies.

"Get into your leathers and plug in, people," Lieutenant Rogers ordered. "Then I want an oxygen check and a roll call. Somebody help our distinguished passengers."

They suited up as the bomber clawed for altitude. At nine thousand feet, each man strapped on his oxygen mask and checked in.

"Gene! I didn't hear Gene," said passenger Berg.

"He's not in the bomb bay," someone said.

"He left with Shorty."

"He's not with me. Didn't he come back?"

"He's not on the plane."

"You mean we left him? How the hell could that happen? How could we leave without him? Huh? How could you people do something like that? Can somebody tell me? Dammit! I'm asking."

Everyone was silent. Only Moe was talking. He was nearly frantic. The tension of these many months was inevitably finding release. Only the climb to twelve thousand feet subdued him, running him out of breath and forcing him to put on his oxygen mask or give up breathing altogether.

The plane flew in silence through the blackness. At this altitude the stars were twinkling brightly. Below, the land was dark. The daring hijackers used the time for quiet contemplation. Only the men in the cockpit were busy, smoothing the throttle settings and keeping precisely on course.

"I'd really like to get rid of that bomb load," said Benson.

"We can't very well drop on the Swiss, can we? We'll salvo over Lake Geneva, okay?"

"Right."

"Our fuel is good. We could make it all the way to London," remarked Mutt Benson casually.

"Yeah, well, let's get out of German air and into neutral territory first. Then we'll worry about London, okay?"

"You're the boss," said the copilot, popping his gum nonchalantly.

"Make sure everyone's clear in the bomb bay. I think we're over Lake Geneva," Lieutenant Rogers said to Shorty.

Shorty looked out. "Jeez. That looks like the Atlantic. Lieutenant Quinn, you didn't screw up, did you? That's some big lake."

"It's Lake Geneva, all right," Quinn affirmed, "right on schedule."

The bomb bay doors that slid in a track on each side of the fuselage like a rolltop desk rumbled open and then stopped dead. They had moved approximately fourteen inches. The door switch was recycled to "close" and when the doors moved three or four inches more they once again shuddered to a grinding halt

317

and refused to roll further. They had jammed against two .50 caliber shell casings that had rolled into the trackway during some recent Swiss test firing. American crew chiefs had learned to check for these errant hulls of brass but the Swiss crews had no such experience to guide them. The doors were jammed tight and refused to move. Opening and closing the switch only wedged the doors tighter. The flight would have to be made with the full bomb load.

At the edge of the lake the lights of the city of Geneva could be seen.

"Course change, skipper," announced the navigator. "You got a choice. South to the Gulf of Lions--gets us out of France but takes us over the water--or the shorter direct route to Spain over the mountains."

"We'll take the direct route. I want to keep away from any occupied coastline," was the pilot's answer.

"Rog, new heading two twenty!" replied Quinn.

The plane made a slight left turn to accommodate the new heading, which would minimize their time in the hostile air of occupied France. There would be at least three more hours of darkness to cloak the Floosie's audacious bid for freedom.

42

━━◄◆►━━

AS THE FLOOSIE'S ELEVEN-FOOT HAMILTON STANDARD PROPELLERS CHURNED THROUGH THE STAR-SALTED BLACKNESS, Lieutenant Rogers glanced over his right shoulder and noticed the first pale intrusions of dawn in the sky behind them. He shuddered slightly at a strange thought: the dark offers refuge while behind us the advancing daylight threatens us with failure, capture, or worse. Even this mighty aircraft running at full power couldn't hope to outdistance the oncoming day. The Floosie was doing 3? . . . 330 miles per hour at the richest of carburetor settings, guzzling fuel shamelessly, but even at full power our engines are no match for the thousand-mile-per-hour advance of the sun.

"It's gonna be light real soon. Let's hope our luck holds out," the pilot told his right-seater.

"Skipper!" It was Shorty. He'd been clunking around in back somewhere.

"Yeah? What's up?"

"I just slung us a gun in the right waist position."

"A gun?!" said Rogers as both pilots turned to acknowledge the resourcefulness of their engineer.

"It's okay, ain't it? I mean, it's not against some rule about escaping or anything?" the diminutive mechanic intoned sarcastically.

"Sure, it's okay," said Rogers, graciously accepting the crack.

319

"We got four hundred rounds of ammo. I carried the gun. That guy Gurney brought the ammo. We found it in the hangar. I thought he was going back for another gun; never saw him after that . . . Schultzie is gonna test fire the gun, just thought I'd let you know."

"Go right ahead. Just let me clue in the crew on the intercom first."

Three bursts of three rounds each were fired into the rarefied air over southern France as the gun checked out. Nine spent .50 caliber slugs tumbled impotently to the dark farmland below. From the place they harmlessly struck the ground, four distinct contrails could be seen cutting a vivid pink swath high in the cloudless, predawn sky.

Squadron commander Emil Dummler couldn't believe his eyes. He and his flight of five Me109 fighters were aloft on the first sorties of the day, the dawn patrol. There in the faint opalescence of the encroaching dawn, he could clearly make out the unmistakable signature of a multiengined aircraft. An enemy bomber over southern France? What luck! It had to be an enemy aircraft. The Luftwaffe operates few four-engined heavy bombers. It could be two aircraft in tight formation. Well, we shall know soon enough.

"On me, gentlemen!" he called to his hounds. "To the hunt!"

In single file each Me109 raised one wing and wheeled up toward the improbable object in the morning sky.

"Tourist at three o'clock low," someone shouted into the intercom of the B-24.

Oh, Christ! thought Rogers. We're in for it now.

Moe and Ernie looked at each other.

"Tourist? What's going on?"

The waist gunner turned from his vigil at the Plexiglas port and said, "We got fighters comin' up after us. At least one I can see."

The two passengers rose and moved to the port for a better view.

"Hey," the gunner complained, "you gotta stay out of my way. Sit down and don't move around."

Moe and Ernie contritely returned to their places at the rear of the gunner's bay.

"I can make out four more climbing. About one o'clock."

"Got 'em," said the copilot. "Probably waiting for the lead guy to check us out."

"Here he comes," said the gunner.

"Don't shoot," Rogers ordered. "And secure that gun. Remember, we've got neutral markings. Maybe we can bullshit 'em."

An American B-24 heavy bomber, observed the German squadron leader hungrily. It was the first he had ever seen and its size impressed him. He silently hoped the Americans didn't have many more of those! Then he noticed the Swiss Air Force markings. What is the meaning of that, he wondered. A Swiss aircraft heading for Spain? A neutral visiting another neutral in an Allied warplane? Smells fishy. Yet, he observed, the gun in the right waist hasn't moved. He flew a bit closer to the gun to see what would happen.

The maneuver took courage. If the bomber was hostile this would be a perfect time to initiate attack. Dummler was making himself an easy target.

"Skipper!" Thibideau shouted into the interphone.

"I see him, Thib. Just ignore him."

At the slightest movement of that muzzle, Hauptmann Dummler was poised to pull up out of its field of fire. Hmm, strange, he thought. I can see only the one machine gun.

The German then pulled his fighter forward to align it with the bomber's flight deck. He signaled "down" with his hand, then pulled up in front of the craft and banked into a lazy turn across the big aircraft's path. The bomber's crew ignored him and continued on their course. Now Dummler was joined by the rest of his flight. They bracketed the bomber with their commander taking the forward position just a few meters from its nose. The American airmen watched as the Germans executed a slow banked turn to the right. The Swiss-marked American craft continued to ignore them.

"Our best chance is to stay on course and hope the Luftwaffe is low on fuel" Rogers announced over the intercom.

Hauptmann Dummler's response to being ignored was to order his men to re-form above the bomber and have them each fire a burst across the nose of the obstinate aircraft. The Floosie didn't flinch. She continued plowing forward, unwaveringly on course for the distant mountain range that served the Iberian peninsula as a natural barrier from the rest of Europe.

Suddenly all the fighters pulled away and climbed. The German commander ordered his men to assume an attack formation. Emil Dummler did not appreciate being snubbed by the big American-built bird. Besides, this would be an excellent opportunity to practice gunnery with live ammunition and a real target. He first warned his men of the lone gun protecting the right flank of the bomber and instructed them to fire only at the left wingtip. Despite his frustration at the bomber's refusal to acknowledge him, it was still wearing the markings of a neutral and had taken no hostile action. Therefore, Dummler reasoned, it might be an overreaction to destroy the offending aircraft. A few bullet holes, however, might well induce a more respectful appreciation of the situation.

The German commander deployed his men.

"Heinz, Werner, Egon, then Wolfie follow, close interval. Only the right wingtip. We attack only to wake up those idiots. Clear?"

Three "klar's" and a "ja wohl" indicated they understood.

Inside the bomber the Americans were searching the skies in all directions.

"They're back! One o'clock high!" shouted Durkee, the bombadier who spotted them first.

He had a prime view, up front amid all that Plexiglas. No guns or ammo cans to impinge on him, no Norden cramping his legs. Now with the fighters heading right at him, Durkee felt naked and helpless.

"I see 'em!" shouted Rogers. "They're either trying to turn us or kill us."

The first fighter expertly turned and dove at the left wing executing a roll to make the wingtip fly through the stream of tracers. The Floosie's left wing took several plunks on its outermost portion. The unarmed left waist gunner watched helplessly.

"Skipper, we took some hits in the left wing."

The second fighter executed the identical maneuver but his burst missed completely. Now the third 109 came in, this time punching a few more holes in the wing.

At the first burst of hostile fire, the right waist gunner untethered his gun and stepped up to anxiously await a target. None appeared in his field of fire.

"C'mon, bastards. Come out where I can see ya," he shouted into his oxygen mask.

The fourth and fifth plane's attack missed also--no new punctures appeared in the already ravaged wingtip.

"These guys stink," announced Shorty, who was standing in the empty top turret wearing his flak jacket and helmet.

"Uh-uh," said Rogers, "they just want to show they're not foolin' around. If they've got enough gas for a next pass it'll be for real."

It was real enough. The time for subtlety was over, the entire plane became the target. One by one they came in, encouraged by the lack of return fire. For the German pilots it was a lark, like popping at a towed target at very close range. Inside the Floosie, the helpless crew cringed at the sound of every hit but could do nothing but sit it out in the hope it would be over soon.

Ernie and Moe were crouched helplessly in the tunnel under the large oxygen bottles aft of the gunner's bay. They stared at each other in bewilderment, finding the bizarre predicament in which they found themselves barely comprehensible. They couldn't shoot, they couldn't hide. They could only try to keep out of the way. A strange way to fight a war. They watched as Thibideau and Shultz were frantically affecting the switch of their single gun to the left side of the craft. In the move, the ammo container was knocked over. As Ernie reached forward to right the can for the gunners, his helmet fell off and rolled a few feet forward. Crawling to retrieve his steel hat, a portion of the fuselage beside him disintegrated. Light streamed in from three jagged thumb-size holes. Ernie picked up his helmet and put it on, looking alternately at the perforated aluminum and at Moe. If he hadn't moved at that moment, the sunlight would be now shining through parts of his head.

"They're comin' again," Shorty shouted from his top turret vantage point. The gunless turret made him feel like a nudist standing in a greenhouse.

Once again the attack concentrated on the left side of the now well- perforated bomber.

"Hey, Shultzie, don't fire till you've got a sure thing. All we've got goin' is surprise."

"Rog', Skipper," acknowledged the waist gunner.

Ping, ping, katchung, ping. Here we go again, thought Ernie, as the lead fighter made his second pass.

The next aircraft came in from the front and slightly below the Floosie, a tactic that would have been ill advised had the bomber been armed with its normal complement of guns. This craft, however, carried only the one gun mounted in the right waist opening. The fighter's guns raked the nose of the American bomber shattering the Plexiglas. The bombadier's scream was heard by everyone on the flight deck. The German continued firing along the left side of the bomber's fuselage but he was missing high as he instinctively raised his nose to avoid a collision course. He corrected slightly and brought his tracers back on track. The big white cross proved an excellent aiming point. Switching his thumb position, he fired his 40 mm cannon, which caused his fighter to shudder at each burst. He was very close now, time to break off. He could almost see into the gunner's port, the one without the gun, but . . . there was something in the opening now. The odd, winking sparkle in the dark rectangle was the last thing Lt. Werner Lutz would ever see. The Me109 disintegrated in two separate explosions. Men of both sides watched the debris that had once been a fighter aircraft and a live human being tumble to the earth.

Inside the fuselage of the bomber, Moe and Ernie cringed in terror as the world was whited away in a storm of hissing vapor. One of the large oxygen bottles directly above them had been ruptured and the pressurized gas covered both of them in a frosty white icing. As the cylinder emptied, Moe and Ernie looked at each other and wondered silently, who could that gray-haired old man be, who is now sitting in my friend's place.

The German squadron leader helplessly followed the dissipating cloud of black smoke and falling wreckage of his comrade's aircraft, but no parachute blossomed in the air below him.

"Our fuel is low," Dummler announced over the radio to his remaining charges. "I will finish him and we will return to base."

Inside the Floosie, the navigator and flight engineer were busy attempting to treat the bombadier's bloody wound. The radioman, Corporal Hernandez, was also hit and slumped unconscious at his position. Because there was no visible injury, bombadier Durkee's obvious wounds took precedence.

"I can't feel my dick! Did they get my dick?"

Frantically struggling and trying to sit up, he was thwarting the attempts of first aid by his comrades. Shorty held him down while Quinn cut away the leather flight suit to inspect the damage.

"One hangin', two clangin'," announced the navigator.

"Oh, God," said the bombadier, "I thought I was killed."

The back of both thighs were torn up pretty bad--two separate wounds, both bleeding profusely.

"You gotta turn over on your belly so I can get the bleeding stopped."

"Okay," said the bombadier, allowing himself to be flipped on to his stomach. "As long as I'm all right."

He was far from all right. As sulfa-treated gauze dressings were pressed down on the twin wounds, the blood flow seemed to slow. Suddenly the aircraft was once again shaken by several solid thuds of cannon fire. A lone Me109 was firing its nose cannon into the wings and fuselage of the bomber.

"He's right below us," a voice on the intercom reported. "I can see him in the periscope."

The B-24D was equipped with the Bendix remote control power turret. It was operated from inside the craft by a gunner who sighted through an optical device. What had been considered a futuristic idea, providing the ball gunner a relatively safe and armored position from which to fight, ultimately proved to be a failure. Invariably the gunner, when peering through his periscope, fell victim to acute vertigo. Even the toughest, most experienced ball turret gunners in the corps would find themselves sick and retching when assigned to the Bendix. But this time the periscope tipped off the exact whereabouts of their tormentor.

The "thud thud thud crunch" of cannon fire reverberated through the big aircraft. The bastards were firing again. This time the number two engine belched black smoke.

"Feather two!" Rogers ordered. Benson pushed the button that turned the propeller blades of the disabled engine into the airstream. The smoke subsided somewhat.

"Bert," said Rogers, "he still there?"

"Yeah, skip, he's comin' back."

"Does he get under the bomb bay?"

"For a bit--he does a slow loop and we pass over him. We must look like a helluva big target at this range."

"Yeah, yeah, Shorty, get up to the dump switch. Salvo the load when I tell you."

"But boss, the bay doors--they're stuck, remember?"

"We're gonna drop through the damn doors. Bert, you still there?"

"Yeah, skip."

"On your mark. When he's under the bomb bay, say 'now.' Shorty, salvo on 'now', okay?"

"Okay, boss, but I don't know about this."

"Hey, what have we got to lose?"

"My next pass should do it," thought squadron leader Dummler, annoyed and slightly impressed with the amount of punishment the large craft was taking.

"Enough of this! I will aim for the wing root. Perhaps I can sever the wing. Finish it! . . . almost in range."

"Now! Shorty, now!"

All thirty-two, 200-pounders unshackled simultaneously and began their gravity-directed journey. There were practice bombs filled with plaster instead of explosives but when they encountered the corrugated metal of the bomb bay doors they punched through the aluminum skin like a bunch of bananas through wet tissue paper.

The German had no time to respond. The air seemed filled with large malevolent blobs. Both wings of his fighter were sheared off by the salvoed ordinance. His craft nosed downward and the fuselage began to roll in the opposite direction of his still-racing propeller. Working frantically against the intense G-forces of the twisting craft, Hauptmann Dummler pounded at his canopy in an effort to free himself. The wingless aircraft plummeted earthward like a demented auger, its engine shrieking insanely at full throttle. When it struck the ground, all the screams were silenced. Amid the smoke and settling dust only the wind could be heard as it careened through the jagged putty-colored foothills of the French Pyrenees. A playful gust caught a fold of camouflaged silk still strapped to the lifeless form in the cockpit of the shattered machine. It billowed posthumously in the first rays of the morning sun.

The surviving pilots of Hauptmann Dummler's dawn patrol were in shock. They had lost a comrade, then watched as their leader was destroyed in a bizarre and horrifying spectacle. Nineteen-year-old Heinz Sieber angrily wheeled his craft toward the enemy with guns blazing. He threw aside all reason and hours of military training; his anger sought only to bring down this hated enemy. He would succeed even if it meant ramming the monster with his own machine. He began firing well out of range, frantically holding down the trigger of his machine guns, which promptly froze, either having expended all their ammo or jammed from overheating. Realizing that his guns had quit on him, he switched to his cannon and fired off a single 40 mm shell into the bomber. It struck the fuselage to the rear of the gunner's opening, propelling tiny aluminum shards through the area. The impact knocked the gunner's partner to the deck as shrapnel tore through his fleece-lined leather jacket at the right armpit. The shredded leather began to stain red. Ernie Kahn crawled over to tend the injured man. While ex-gauleiter Manfred von Dahlheim helped feed the fifties to the chattering gun, gunner Shultz calmly brought the line of tracers to bear on the oncoming fighter.

"Got you! I got you, you son of a bitch!" shouted the jubilant gunner.

Multiple hits on the fighter's engine and a shattered windshield quenched the rage of Lieutnant Sieber. The craft decelerated as if it had struck a wall. With supreme effort he kept the powerless craft level and then after nosing up slightly he pushed away the remnants of the ravaged canopy and jumped clear. His training and discipline had returned at an opportune time. The slow, unhurried descent to earth under the silken canopy gave him adequate time to contemplate the many inequities of warfare.

Two fighter planes remained. What to do, the young Luftwaffe pilots pondered.

"How's your petrol?"

"Low."

"Mine also."

"Ammunition?"

"Some. Less than one quarter."

"I'm the same."

"Should we return?"

"We should complete what we started."

328

This is insanity, thought Moe. He was probing the jagged tear in his leather flying pants where a metal chard had come up through the floor and out the ceiling. There was a little sensitivity but no blood. I guess I'm okay. Only his trousers had been hit. We've been flying blithely along while those bastards are shooting us to pieces. I don't mind a fight where you've got a chance to defend yourself, but this is crazy. All we can do is sit in this tin can and take it. These Air Corps guys are plain nuts!

On the flight deck of the B-24 Rogers and Benson were busy. One engine had been feathered and another was running erratically, its RPMs fluctuating wildly and requiring constant throttle adjustment. The engine also seemed to be vibrating excessively. It might be wise to reduce power and let her coast. Also, the controls were leaden. The Liberator's normal control surface handling was bad enough. "Positive feel," the Consolidated reps had called it. Fact was that it took King Kong to fly this bird for any length of time. The extra difficulty meant that control cables were binding at one or more places along the length of the plane.

The sound of a renewed enemy attack made these technical concerns irrelevant. "Ping, ping, katching, ping-o," the hailstorm resumed, announcing that the next and probably last round of the fight had begun.

"Hey!" Rogers shouted to his copilot. "Should we turn? Put 'er down? Maybe in those flats over the mountains."

"Nah," said Benson. "I wouldn't give 'em the satisfaction," jerking his thumb at the air outside the craft.

Moe and Shultz were standing in the center of the gunner's bay cradling the unmounted .50 caliber machine gun. The idea was to surprise the attacking fighters. Shultz had the removal and installation down to record speed, but the fighters had elected to sit just aft of the bomber and fire from relative safety.

"Can anyone see the Krauts?" asked Rogers. "Have they bugged out?"

"Don't see 'em," said the left waist.

"Nothing!" put in Ernie from the opposite side.

"Not below," said the remote ball gunner.

"I think maybe they're behind us," said Shorty, looking back from the top turret position.

"Yeah, they're right behind us all right," confirmed Corporal Basch, the tail gunner, "two of 'em."

Basch had stuffed several flak jackets and extra chutes against the Plexiglas in an absurd attempt to protect himself. When he cleared them away and peeked out to view the situation, he found himself face to face with his worst fears. Two fighters attacking from the rear. Right up his nose.

"Oh, God! God! and me without no guns!"

"I'm gonna head for the deck. Maybe find us a field," said Rogers over the intercom.

He knew the creaking Floosie couldn't sustain more damage and remain aloft.

"Wheels down," he ordered his copilot.

"Aw, Warren."

"I said wheels down."

"Okay, wheels comin' down." There was no mention of "undercarriage."

The plane shuddered as the gear creaked into its lowered position.

"Down and locked," confirmed the copilot.

"There, we give up. We tried. Nobody's dead."

"Ping, ping, ping, katching, ping."

"Hey, we've surrendered. Knock it off," the annoyed second officer shouted to the ceiling of the flight deck.

"They either don't understand gear down means surrender or they don't care."

Ping sproink ping ping thunk.

"Son of a bitch!"

"Skipper they're still shootin'," announced the tail gunner.

"Douche bags!"

"Hey wait, one of them's smokin'. He's bugging out. I don't get it. Wait, wait, there's a third. A new guy, comin' up fast. He's firing. I think he hit his own guy. The other one's turned. He's buggin' out too. But the new guy is on us. On the left, Shorty. Left!"

"That's all we need. Reinforcements," Lieutenant Rogers muttered as he strained to see the new menace. "He's pulling alongside. Waving his arm."

Shultz and Moe were working frantically to mount the fifty in the left position. Battle damage had twisted the bracket slightly, making the installation difficult.

"Got it! Now shove in the friggin' pin," Shultzie yelled as he swiveled the fifty into position.

"Hey, that Messerschmidt's got Swiss markings," said Rogers.

Moe looked out of the left port over the shoulders of the gunner. He could see the pilot of the fighter clearly. A young man-familiar. Wearing a leather flying cap. Why is he familiar? He's waving and smiling.

"Let him have it," yelled the injured Thibideau from the floor of the compartment. "What're you waiting for?"

"Don't shoot!" yelled Moe, pushing the gunner's hands off the twin shovel grips of the fifty.

"You nuts?--get outta my way!"

"That's Gurney over there," shouted Moe. "I know it. See. It's a Swiss plane. It's Gurney. I can tell even in that funny hat he's wearing."

Ernie got up to look. He looked, shook his head to refocus his eyes, then started laughing. He laughed and continued laughing in the rarefied air like a crazy man, only stopping when it hurt too much to continue.

It was Gurney. He was waving and mugging and looking very pleased with himself. How he had managed to come by the German fighter plane had to be an amazing story in itself. That would come later. The present problem was keeping the crippled Floosie in the air over the Pyrenees.

"That Gurney, what a character."

With their landing gear returned to the up position, they flew for at least fifteen minutes before anyone in the cockpit spoke again. One and four were running well but seemed overly thirsty. Three was unfeathered then restarted at a prudent RPM. The flight controls were leaden, obviously binding at several places. Shorty was prowling the fuselage hoping to free up the control cables.

"Let's hope they aren't being sawed through every time I move the controls. Better keep corrections to a minimum."

"How's fuel?" Rogers asked his right-hand man.

"Not great. At present consumption, figuring in the leaks, we got about a half hour."

"Hey, George, got any nice long Spanish airfields on your chart?"

"Got one at Zaragosa, but that's about forty-five minutes."

"I'd really prefer to land the Floosie," declared Lieutenant Rogers, stating the obvious. "We got wounded and only two reliable engines."

"First, let's get over these mountains, huh, skipper?"

"You're right. First things first."

Though seriously damaged, the Floosie flew fairly straight avoiding the predacious granite fingers that reached to slash at her unprotected belly.

With the tallest peaks behind her, the Floosie descended to eight thousand feet. Better to see, easier to breathe.

"How're the wounded?"

"Durkee's conscious. Bleeding's stopped, Mex is still out cold," Shorty informed the pilot.

Ernie Kahn sent the message forward that Thibideau's wound had also stopped bleeding.

"I see a valley up ahead," announced the copilot.

"Too steep," assessed Rogers. "Plus, see, there's a stream running down the center of it. Keep looking."

The stream they observed was the Segre River, a tributary of the Ebro, the river which flowed unhurriedly to the sea through the province of Catalonia, the easternmost section of Spain. Neutral Spain.

Young Duke Alonzo de la Müella Maria Anselmo de Escobar had little in his life about which he could complain, even when considering the recent circumstances. The bloody Spanish Civil War had left him and his family virtually unscathed. The ancestral lands and family wealth threatened by the Communists of the so-called Loyalist army had been protected by Francisco Franco and his victorious Nationalists. Franco returned stability and order to Spain. But he could not do it alone. His victory required the assistance of the Germans and Italians. The fact that these were exceptionally brutal Allies was not lost on the generalissimo. At the onset of the European war when the belligerent nations offered Spain the choice of neutrality, Franco wisely accepted. Perhaps payment for Hitler's and Il Duce's intervention might never come due.

Young Duke Alonzo had only recently returned from the United States where he attended Harvard University during his country's war years. He was profoundly influenced by his experiences in America and upon return to his homeland found himself in disagreement with the generally accepted view that Hitler was unstoppable. He prudently kept this point of view to himself.

The young nobleman had an even more consuming passion than politics. Soaring. Here, near his family's summer residence in the hills south of Andorra, a grassy runway had been cleared on an elongated plateau. Beside it, two small hangars housed his precious sailplanes. As a teenager he would soar for hours in the thermals and air currents that deflected off the surrounding hills. The experience was the embodiment of peace and spirituality for the young aristocrat. He felt at one with the gods during his silent and effortless soaring.

Each day he drove up to visit those cherished gliders in his yellow Packard convertible, a trophy of his American college years. There was always something to do, some repair to make on the grounded birds. Perhaps at war's end he could resume his passion but for now he could only sit in the cockpit of his earthbound glider and invoke memories of soaring through the clear, crisp, Catalonian air.

"Those sons of putas stole my tow plane!" Four years ago the new Piper L-16 purchased to tow his gliders aloft had been commandeered by Franco's grimy Nationalists for "reconnaissance." Father said it was the least we could do. Lord knows where my plane finally wound up. Most likely crashed. Those boorish clods.

As he sat in the cockpit of a glider and ruminated over his earthbound condition, he detected the distant drone of an aircraft. Holding his Boston Red Sox baseball cap to shield his eyes from the morning sun, he beheld an impossible sight. An enormous four-engined aircraft was circling the valley, preceded by a small pursuit ship. Be careful what you pray for, the sage once said, you might well receive it. He watched as the strangely marked Messerschmidt flared out, bounced heavily on the grassy field, and taxied toward the low wooden buildings. It stopped on the turf behind the set-back hangars and cut its engine. Now the bigger aircraft turned to make a low pass from the northwest as if to measure the small field. A closer look at the bomber revealed two things: it was seriously damaged and its pilot was determined to land on this tiny mountain airstrip.

Duke Alonzo ran to reattach the stowed wind sock to its moorings in an attempt to be helpful. The pilot of the single-engine craft ran toward the Duke. For some strange reason the young man broke into a broad grin as he offered his hand.

"Mucho hurt hombres," he said to the young nobleman as he pointed to the circling B-24.

Wondering why the German pilot was attempting to communicate in pidgin English, he nodded that he understood.

They backed away from the strip as the Floosie wallowed into its final approach. Its wings and fuselage seemed to fill the sky over the little valley. At the slow landing speed, the Floosie's decimated rudder surfaces provided virtually zero yaw control. She came in crabbing sideways and there was no correcting it.

Only two courses of action remained: slam the throttles forward and attempt a second go-round or retract the landing gear and pancake her in. Rogers chose the latter. The gear indicator registered up and locked at the same instant the crew felt the pod of the belly turret make contact with the grass. Four parachutes, secured to the gun mounts on both waist positions, billowed out and slowed the plane's momentum a bit. The Floosie slid along Duke Alonzo's dew drenched pitch like a greasy hocky puck. A flap tore away along with remnants of the bay doors as all four propellers bent as they dug into the soft turf. The slowing bird slid sideways off the bank of the short, narrow strip and slowed to a grudging stop against the slight upward slope of the bordering knoll. The crash landing had been the easiest part of the journey.

Gurney and Duke Alonzo sprinted to the craft with the large red fire extinguisher from the hangar in tow. Inside the craft, Lieutenant Rogers was flipping switches and ordering everyone out. He needn't have bothered. Most of the crew was already deplaning. The wounded were carefully lifted clear and carried a safe distance from the wreck.

Moe spotted Gene Gurney and embraced him.

"You sneaky son of a gun. You saved us, you know."

"And you thought you left me behind, huh, admit it. You felt bad, didn't you?"

"Yeah, but later for that," said Moe. "We've got to get some medical help for our guys."

"Talk to him," Gurney said, indicating the fellow spraying a smoking engine with CO_2. "He's the airport manager or something."

In his most precise Catalonian Spanish, Moe addressed the fire fighter.

"We require medical assistance. Can you help us, please?"

Duke Alonzo turned and looked quizzically at the big dark airman. Moe thought he didn't understand.

Before he could repeat his request, the Spaniard said in accented English, "Of course. We can take those who can be moved in my automobile."

The three wounded flyers were driven to the home of the local doctor. Most seriously injured was Durkee, his two deep wounds requiring him to spend the next ten days sleeping "over a barrel" on his stomach as the backs of his legs began to heal.

Thibideau was wounded in the armpit. Once treated, he was required to wear a braced frame that held his arm up away from his side. His greatest problem then was having to remember to enter a room sideways.

As for Hernandez, the radioman, he didn't have a mark on him. Simple concussion. He woke on the examination cot in the doctor's office speaking Spanish and complaining of a terrible headache. He remembered nothing of the German fighter attack on the Floosie.

43

⊢┿┣◆⊒┿⊣

"ALL RIGHT! TELL US. HOW'D YOU PULL IT OFF?"

"Yeah! How'd you get the fighter?"

"Where'd you learn to fly?"

"I thought you were a driver out of the motor pool."

The crew gathered around Gene in the courtyard of the duke's mountain villa. They were full of questions for the man who had come to their rescue. Servants were hurriedly setting up a table and providing breakfast for the noisy and exhuberant airmen. There was bread, cold meats, sausages, eggs, and amazingly strong coffee. And few, if any, table manners.

The wounded were in good hands at the little hospital in the valley below and the flyers were slowly relaxing in the giddy realization that they had survived their ordeal. All listened attentively as Gurney recounted his tale.

"I was really going for another machine gun; they were on a worktable in the hangar, when I thought, that guy in the tower--he'll sound the alarm. Soon as an engine kicked over, it'd be all over."

"Yeah, so!"

"Could you pass the sausages," said Gurney, indicating the heaping platter. "They look really good!"

Someone hurriedly passed the sausages. Gurney spilled three onto his plate and then skewering one, took a bite, savoring both the taste and the impatience he was causing.

"Yeah, yeah, come on, Gurney!"

337

"Where was I?"

"The tower, c'mon!"

"Oh, yeah. Nice fellow. Corporal. Spoke English pretty well. I had my pistol so I told him hands up and sit tight while the Floosie takes off. He didn't want any trouble."

"But how'd you get the fighter?"

"Oh, that part was easy. I had my tower pal walk me out to where a Messerschmidt was parked and made him crank the starter spring. Now here's the best part."

Gene lowered his voice for dramatic effect. The crew, Rogers and Berg included, leaned in toward him, barely breathing.

"I jingled the keys to the Mercedes limousine in his face. I told him where it was parked and that it was his if he'd give me about ten minutes before sounding the alarm. I wasn't exactly sure that he was understanding me till he suggested that I tie his hands behind him with some wire to make it look better."

"Holy cow, what a crazy story!"

"Hey, we made it, didn't we?"

"We sure did and you sure saved our bacon."

"I hope he takes good care of my car. That was one hell of a car. Would somebody pass the eggs?"

The eggs were passed with a flourish befitting the feting of a great hero. In a broader view, all these men were heroes, though not one of them would have stood still for the label.

During one of the crew's several return trips to the wreckage, Moe asked the duke if the Swiss insignia could be removed from the aircraft, explaining that the markings could cause confusion and therefore difficulties with the Spanish authorities.

The duke indicated that he understood and agreed--he would order his workmen to remove the white crosses.

"We have the acetone to do it. Now, eh, Moe," the duke began shyly, "I was wondering . . . everyone has heard of the Allied bomber that has crashed. But few are aware of the Messerschmidt. I was wondering, perhaps . . . "

338

Moe and Lieutenant Rogers got it immediately.

"If you can make use of the plane, as far as I'm concerned, it's yours. It'd be my pleasure, except you'd better find a good place to hide it."

"Hmmm, yes. Perhaps in the woods."

"If we took the wings and prop off, you could stash it in the rear of one of your hangars," Shorty kibitzed.

"But I have no idea how to . . . "

The widening grin on Shorty Hobart's face stopped the duke in midsentence. Obviously this fellow could dismantle an Me109.

News of the downed airmen had reached Barcelona. Before the civil authorities could decide on appropriate action, the newspapers published the story. Soon the Red Cross, American Embassy, and Socialist press were demanding their speedy repatriation. Under the glare of world scrutiny, the Spanish government declared the brave crew to be technically considered evadees rather than internees and therefore eligible for repatriation to their own nationals. A special liaison sent by Franco himself would accompany the flyers to Lisbon where they would soon be reunited with their fellow Americans. All this would occur when the three wounded men were fit to travel, for the flyers were adamant about returning together as a unit. Then all twelve would make the daylong train ride across the Iberian peninsula to the Atlantic coast. Included among the names of the aircrew of Consolidated 241989, *Faithful Floosie,* were Lt. Gene Gurney, officer-gunner, and Cpl. Ernst Kahn, gunner. A larger-than-usual crew but it was not uncommon for base personnel to be given unauthorized combat rides.

Several days later, representatives of the Spanish Nationalist Air Corps made the journey up the mountain to visit the wreck. After a thorough inspection, they concluded that although it might be possible to repair the craft, it certainly couldn't be flown out from this strip and therefore she would have to be dismantled and hauled out. But the large flatbeds necessary to do the job were unavailable so the *Faithful Floosie* would have to sit patiently in her mountain meadow for a while.

The Spanish Air Corps officials politely complimented the duke on his gliders as they viewed the two sailplanes in their separate hangars. The Messerschmidt's overpainted fuselage sat in a low wooden frame at the rear of the hangar. Its unattached wings and two spare sets of glider wings screened the Messerschmidt's fuselage and engine. The fighter took up remarkably little space in its knocked-down condition. The propeller, however, was in plain view, suspended from the rafters of the hangar. If anyone happened to look up, they would take it as a decoration. Once the excitement quieted down, Duke Alonzo would have himself one hot little tow plane.

44

GLASSES WERE RAISED all around the table of the grand dining room of the DeEscobar villa. A toast had been offered by the dark-haired American who spoke Spanish so well. He made this toast in English.

"Gentlemen, for most of my years I have been convinced that the single most important goal of a life well lived is knowledge. But as I grow older, and, as I observe that I am the oldest seated at this table, I must insist on being accorded the respect due my seniority . . . " He paused to allow for some hoots, table banging, and a couple of haw-haws.

"I wish now to revise my formerly held view. Gentlemen, camaraderie is the goal of a life well lived. It surpasses the most profound learning. You men seated before me; we, together, functioning as a team, rose to overcome impossible odds. For any one of us to have come through required the actions of each of the others.

"I have learned that when individuals offer their uniqueness rather than hold it aloof, truly amazing things can happen. I have seen it on a smaller scale in the field of sport but my education was truly incomplete till I saw it function in the face of real danger.

"My comrades, teammates, I drink to you and I trust you agree with me when I include Duke Alonzo as part of the team. He may have been the last to have joined us but he certainly arrived in the nick of time."

The crew of the Floosie rose from their chairs, pointing their glasses toward the young nobleman, urging him to rise. He threw his shoulders back and lifted his glass in acknowledgment, touched at having been so honored.

"To us," Moe continued, "the best team in the league."

The duke then took everyone by surprise when he threw his empty glass into the dark fireplace. For a beat, the airmen thought he was crazy. Then, as understanding registered, the air was full of glass projectiles shattering and tinkling amid the laughs and shouts of the men.

Lieutenant Rogers rose and ceremoniously pinned his pilot's wings on the young duke's chest. Alonzo was deeply moved at the gesture. He had spent over four years among Americans, coming to admire them and their philosophy of optimism, but he had never truly felt like an American until the moment when those wings of silver were affixed to his shirt.

Later, Moe whistled for quiet and continued his farewell speech.

"All you fellows have dog tags. They'll get you through and eventually back to our side. I don't have any tags. I'm strictly civilian and I can't afford to delay--there are some vital reports I've got to make so, gentlemen, I'm leaving in the morning. The duke has graciously offered to drive me to Madrid. From there I can get a train to where I need to go. Good-bye. Good luck. You are the best team I ever played for. If any of you ever get to New Jersey . . . "

It's strange how New Jersey, of all the forty-eight states, can provoke a chuckle at even the most solemn of moments.

Moe arose early the next morning to leave with the duke but Ernie and Gene were up to see him off.

"Hey," Moe said as he wrapped his arms around his two compatriots. "It looks like the three musketeers are gonna have to split up for a while."

Porthos and Athos stared at the ground.

"I need to say something to you two."

Both men looked up into Moe's face.

"You two are something, you know that?"

"You're pretty okay yourself, Moe," said the subdued Gene, while Ernie nodded in assent.

"Well, later for that," said Moe. "I just want to tell you that you two are the finest and bravest men I ever knew."

"Awww."

"I mean it. Now here's what I really want to tell you. I want to arrange a reunion. For after the war. On the first day of May when it's all over, we'll meet in the bar of the Astor Hotel in New York at six p.m. Got it?"

"Got it."

"Got it."

"And I want you to be wearing your medals."

"Medals? What medals?" asked Ernie.

"Yeah, what medals?" repeated Gene.

"Listen," Moe intoned in mock confidentiality, "I've got friends in high places. There'll be medals. So long, fellas."

The three shook hands quickly and Moe turned and walked briskly to the yellow Packard convertible where young Duke Alonzo was waiting to drive his American friend to the train station.

In a civilian corduroy jacket and a black beret, the dark-haired man who boarded the Madrid train for Gibraltar looked more like a Spaniard than the Spanish conductor. Moe hoped to reach the British base at the southern tip of the Iberian peninsula before dark. Before boarding, he gave two letters to the young duke to post for him. One was to London, written in Jabberwocky code reiterating the importance of destroying the Germans' supply of heavy water. The other was to a Sally Carlisle in Switzerland, informing her of his safe arrival in Spain and urging her to extricate herself from the uncertainties of central Europe.

As he sat in his train compartment heading south, a dozen newspapers littering the seat beside him, Moe would have been pleased to know that his letter would never reach his beloved Sally. The morning after the men's escape, she and Babette bought tickets on the Swiss Express to Spain, with scheduled stops at Andorra, Zaragoza, and Madrid. She had sought the help of Tyler Vaughn at the American Embassy as Moe suggested. Vaughn personally arranged for the expeditious processing of the two women's exit paperwork with the Swiss authorities. The Swiss director of the International Red Cross thoughtfully provided them with the additional credibility of Red Cross credentials, which attested to the fact that the two women were traveling under the auspices of the world-renowned organization.

45

—•—⊏◊⊐—•—

THE "NEUTRAL" EXPRESS TO MADRID was a train filled with businessmen, diplomats, refugees, and spies. Sally and Babette shared a first-class compartment.

Armed with travel papers from Swiss immigration and credentials from the International Red Cross, the young women were treated like V.I.P.s.

At the French-Swiss border, the American woman, Miss Sally Carlisle and Mlle. Babette LaCroix, were welcomed to La Belle France by the customs official and reminded not to leave the train until they had completed their journey to Spain. After an uneventful daylong ride, they reached the Spanish checkpoint high in the mountains. They were now only a few minutes away from the refuge of Spanish neutrality.

The Spanish border official scrutinized their papers and Red Cross credentials, looked them over once again, then bowed and wished them a pleasant stay in Espana. As he closed their compartment door, he winked and gave his impeccably trimmed moustache a lascivious twirl. The two young women embraced, as tears of relief ruined their mascara. They had once again brazened their way out of danger. Hopefully, this time would be the last time. They drank a toast together with Spanish wine, first in thanks for their own good luck and then in the hope that the young men on the aircraft were also safe.

Changing trains at Madrid, the two women traveled to Lisbon where Sally attempted to arrange passage to America. She presented herself as Sally Carlisle to the visa office. From the nervous look the clerk gave her she realized something was wrong. The clerk insisted on holding her passport until the next day when there would be "adequate time to perform the complicated paperwork entailed by her request."

The delay was prompted by a communiqué from the American Embassy in Bern. When Ashley Inness was informed of the Carlisle woman's exit from Switzerland and her intention to reach Spain, he sent a wire requesting that U.S. authorities in Madrid, Barcelona, and Lisbon detain her on the grounds that there were "irregularities" concerning her documents. Therefore Sally Carlisle, Park Avenue, New York, should not be granted an entry visa to the United States of America.

His leg itched like blazes under that cast and Ashley Inness was by nature a vindictive man.

Sally was by now fairly adept at smelling a rat or recognizing a stall. She wisely took immediate action toward an alternate plan. Brazil was accepting refugees--many with no papers at all. Political escapees and Jews were freely offered refuge. As Selma Wiener, she could certainly qualify with the Brazilians.

Sally never returned to the U.S. immigration office to reclaim her passport. She had, in fact, succeeded in booking passage on the *Karquelen*, a grimy cargo ship with limited passenger-carrying accommodations scheduled to sail for São Paolo by way of Casablanca this very evening.

Sally and Babette said their good-byes at the dockside. These two women had shared a great adventure, each providing strength to the other in time of travail. Now Sally had to leave her "bosom buddy" as she liked to call her amply endowed friend. Babette had decided to return home to France. She felt that she had to go back and continue the fight to free her country. Sally argued halfheartedly against her decision, knowing her friend was determined. Babette even joked about the life of luxury she would lead with her portion of the money left them by

346

Moe. They embraced once again and Babette watched Sally walk briskly up the rusty gangplank of the squat merchant ship. A final wave and both turned away.

Sally was shown to a tiny stateroom with a small fold down cot sadistically designed to serve the most junior ensigns of the Brazilian merchant marine. To Sally, it looked like the Ritz.

Heck, once I'm in South America, I can walk back to Brooklyn, thought Sally, as she unfastened the bunk and lay down without bothering to undress. She was sound asleep even before the vessel had engaged the harbor tugs that would nudge her through the long neck of the bay to the open sea.

Just one more escape in the life of a young woman who had already made more than her share.

46

※—✦—※

A BRITISH PBY FLEW MOE FROM GIBRALTAR TO LONDON. There he was debriefed by the OSS chief, Bill Donovan, and Professor Richardson. They informed him that both his and Professor Scherrer's messages had been received and that Germany's heavy-water manufacturing capability in Norway was even now being targeted for destruction.

After a detour to a London tailor shop where two new suits were miraculously cut for him in four days, Moe flew to New York and then to Washington on Donovan's personal plane. He went directly from the airport to the Executive Office Building where Donovan, Gen. Leslie Groves, and physicist Leo Szilard were waiting.

They asked hundreds of questions about Heisenberg, Diebner, and Diebner's atomic pile. Szilard asked many technical questions, intent on gaining insight into the progress of the German nuclear program. He laughed out loud when Moe described the vandalism he and his team had wrought upon it. When the long day of interrogation was over, they finally seemed satisfied, having asked every one of their questions at least twice. When at last they adjourned, Groves extended his fleshy hand to Moe and declared with uncharacteristic vehemence that he thought Moe "was just about the ballsiest, of your type," he had ever met.

"What exactly do you mean by that?" asked Moe, coldly.

"Huh?" said Groves.

"When you say 'your type'," Moe repeated, "what do you mean?"

"Well, you know, brainy types--intellectuals," Groves stammered.

"C'mon, General," Moe persisted. "There's not much intellectual about me. Heck, I'm just a ball player. So what do you really mean?"

Groves's expression betrayed his discomfort.

"Well, you know, your type. It's unusual for you people to . . . to, you know," stammered Groves.

"No, I don't know," Moe said close to his face. "Do you mean it's unusual for a Jew to attempt a mission like this?"

"Yeah, kinda. I guess that's what I meant," Groves offered, hoping to have cleared it all up.

Moe was wrestling with the impulse to haul off and shove his fist through the general's moustache when Donovan, sensing Moe's agitation, stepped between them.

"C'mon, gentlemen, we're all on the same side. So relax."

"My enemies are the Nazis, General, are they yours too?" Moe asked as he stepped back from Groves.

"Of course," answered the brigadier.

"Well, to listen to you one might think otherwise."

"Hey, I didn't mean anything, really," said Groves as he offered his hand.

"Okay, if you say so," Moe responded.

It had been a long journey and Moe elected to let it go, satisfied that this time he hadn't dodged the issue as he had so often in the past.

At his hotel there was a message at the desk; it said to please call Nelson Rockefeller and gave a number. At 9:30, Moe dialed the number. The famous man answered the phone himself.

"Yes, Moe, thank you for returning my call."

It turned out that Moe had been recommended to Rockefeller by no less than Franklin Roosevelt himself. Rockefeller asked Moe if he would like to join the staff of his special South American ambassadorial contingent.

"The president is concerned about the growth of fascism on the South American continent. Especially in the light of so many Nazis fleeing Europe. We'd be there to promote democracy and keep an eye on the opposition. We'll be based in Brazil but our responsibility will cover the entire continent. It's an important job. Otherwise FDR wouldn't have given it to a Republican. Please think it over Moe, I need your help. Now get home. Get some rest; I understand you've just returned from a difficult mission. Call me next week with your decision."

Moe promised he would consider the offer and get back to Mr. Rockefeller. What is the world coming to, Moe pondered, when a Rockefeller seeks to hire a Berg?

Moe awoke early the next day and set out into the still quiet Washington streets to buy his habitual pile of newspapers. He turned a corner to find the old stand looking exactly as it had ten years ago. Moe crouched to look inside. As he did, the ruddy face of Henny Eckstein appeared before him. Though he was sightly fleshier in the cheeks and sported a much grayer head of hair, Henny's wise and contented grin hadn't changed at all.

Without betraying the slightest sign of surprise, Henny said, "So, boychick, if you'll wait a couple minutes I got your papers right here."

"Sure," said Moe, "I've got all the time in the world."

"Here you are," said Henny as he placed a stack of newspapers on the counter. "That'll be two bits, a dime, and four pennies. Prices have gone up, you can see."

Moe put the change on the counter and gathered up the papers.

"So, boychick? You're not running today? How come?"

"You know I've always got time to schmooze with you, Henny."

"Ah, go on. Get oudda here," said Henny as he waved Moe to be off.

Moe smiled at his old friend and turned to go.

"Hey, boychick, you look good."

Moe nodded, accepting the compliment.

"Could be you found something to do that's really important."

47

THE FINAL LEG OF MOE'S RETURN JOURNEY brought him home to the New York area. After a brief visit with his sister, Ethel, and brother, Sam, he set off across the Williamsburg Bridge to the borough of Brooklyn.

The yellow cab rolled to a halt in front of the tired-looking Pulaski Street brownstone. The taxi sat at the curb for several minutes. Moe didn't get out.

He was watching a slender, dark-haired boy on the sidewalk throwing a rubber "spaldeen" against the worn stone steps of the "stoop." The boy concentrated on hitting the rear corner of the center step to produce a "killer," which resulted in a fast, eye-level rebound.

Moe Berg leaned forward in the rear seat of the taxi watching appreciatively as the boy caught and threw the ball with fluid grace.

"The kid's pretty good," Moe remarked to the cigar-munching cabbie.

"Yeah, yeah, a regular Cookie Lavagetto. So, you want me to wait, or what?"

"Yes," said Moe as he handed the driver a five and climbed out of the car. "I want you to wait."

The big man walked toward the boy and said, "I'm looking for Wiener."

352

Without looking up or changing his rhythm, the boy answered, "Third floor."

"Thanks."

Moe took the steps two at a time, found the button marked Wiener, and pressed it. He was rewarded almost immediately with a return buzz that unlocked the door.

The boy meanwhile followed in behind him saying, "My mother, she prob'ly thinks it's me."

Moe turned to look into the face of the young man. "You must be Kenny."

The teenager nodded vaguely. When the big man in the dark suit smiled and extended his hand, the boy shook it tentatively.

"My name's Berg. I met your sister in Europe. Is she home?"

"Nope. She ain't home."

Upstairs, Moe knocked at the apartment door but Mrs. Wiener, seeing a stranger in the peephole, refused to let him in. She thought he was selling something. After a brief exchange, she finally understood and the door was flung open accompanied by flustered smiles and a gracious "please sit and be comfortable." In a few minutes the bustling Mrs. Wiener covered the table with dishes of strudel, fruit, challah, coffee, and Friday night wine. My God, thought Kenny, you'd think it was Eddie Cantor that just dropped by. When Mrs. Wiener offered some strudel, Moe told her, "No, thank you." She cut a generous piece and handed it to him anyway. Then she poured him a cup of coffee and the avalanche of questions began.

"So tell me, when did you see Selma last? How is she? How does she look? Is she thin?"

The plump Mrs. Wiener finally ran out of questions and permitted Moe to speak. He told her about their journeys through Europe and Switzerland and how he was forced to leave her in Zurich. And how she looked when they parted. Mrs. Wiener then produced a shoebox of letters and began to read parts of them to Moe. She started with the stack from Switzerland. In a short time, Frieda Wiener and Moe Berg became friends. These two strangers had much in common.

In the meantime, Kenny had been fidgeting in the next room of the railroad flat apartment. He repeatedly looked in on his mother and the strange man, wondering, I know this guy. Where do I know him from? Berg? Moe Berg? Could it be? The boy ran to his sock drawer and dug out a thick stack of baseball cards. There it is. It's him! Moe Berg, Washington Senators, 1933. Nobody would trade me for it. Now he's sitting on our sofa. Oh, my gosh!

Back in the parlor, Moe and Frieda Wiener were still happily chatting about Sally. When Mrs. Wiener produced Sally's most recent letter, postmarked, São Paolo, Brazil, Moe shook his head and began to laugh.

"Brazil? I can't believe it. Brazil!"

From the other room Kenny wondered, what's so funny about Brazil?

"Mrs. Wiener," Moe asked, "may I have her address. I'd like to write her."

As she copied it down for him, Kenny entered the parlor and offered Moe the baseball card.

"Uh, Mr. Berg . . . Moe, would you please autograph my card?"

"It would be my pleasure, Kenny."

With his own fountain pen, Moe wrote; "To my good friend, Kenny Wiener, a sure bet to make the major leagues, Best regards, Moe Berg."

Moe and Sally's mother continued to chat for at least another hour.

When he finally rose to leave, Mrs. Wiener reached up and gave him a kiss on the cheek.

Turning to the boy, Moe said, "So long, Kenny. Maybe you and I can have a catch sometime."

The taxicab, of course, was long gone. Kenny walked with Moe to DeKalb Avenue where he could catch a trolley in case they couldn't find another cab. But as Moe stopped at a newstand to buy a paper, Kenny hailed a cruising taxi. The big man opened the cab door, smiled at the boy, then reached out and ruffled the young man's hair. He then slammed the door and the yellow DeSoto Skyview accelerated out into the traffic heading toward the city. It was just getting dark.

In the folded newspaper on Moe's lap, buried on page five, a curious story appeared:

> A bright flash of light reported by dozens
> of local residents as having illuminated
> the predawn desert sky near Alamagordo,
> New Mexico, yesterday was explained by
> military authorities as an accidental
> explosion of a large stockpile of ammuni-
> tion. The army spokesman said that no
> injuries had been incurred as a result of
> the blast.

48

THEY WERE STACKED THREE DEEP AT THE ASTOR BAR on the evening of May 1, 1946. The bartenders had given up trying to keep up with the boisterous crowd and just kept it coming as best they could. There were lots of uniforms among the thirsty throng, but when a soldier or sailor inched forward to pay, more often than not, a nearby sport in civilian clothes made him put away his money and settled the tab.

The Hotel Astor stood on the southwest side of Times Square where it overlooked all the ads and the lights and the thirty-foot replica of Miss Liberty, which, through the war years, reminded New Yorkers to buy bonds. On their way home from the ETO, the boys invariably took time to visit this world-famous cross-roads. Many of them stopped for a drink or two at the bar in the Hotel Astor.

Moe arrived about 5:45. He looked around, didn't see his friends, and, as he was a bit early anyway, decided to work his way toward the bottles and mirrors to order a drink.

"Hey, Moe!" someone shouted from the edge of the crowd. "Moe, over here."

Moe turned to see Ernie Kahn, raised above the crowd, waving both arms wildly from a far corner of the room.

Moe worked his way through the crush to his friend and found him standing on a chair.

"Ernie, you sawed-off son of a gun! It's so good to see you."

"You too, Moe," said Ernie, clasping the big man's shoulders while still perched on the furniture.

"You look good!"

"So do you, old friend."

Ernie jumped down to the floor and the two embraced again.

"Any sign of Gene?" Moe asked, stepping up on the chair that Ernie had vacated. "Wait, there he is," shouted Moe. "Gene! Hey, Gene! Gurney!"

The three found a vacant booth and began their reunion.

"Both you fellas look great," said Moe.

"You too," grinned Ernie.

"Did you grow?" Gene asked Ernie. "I think you got taller. And look at all those stripes!"

Ernie covered his tech-sergeant chevrons with his hand and smiled self-consciously. But not for long.

"Look who's talkin'," was Ernie's comeback as he flicked at the gold oak leaves on Gene's shoulders. "You've been doing your share of ass kissing, I see."

"Moe, isn't that the same suit you had in Zurich?" Gene asked, hoping to get Ernie off the subject of epaulets.

"No," said Moe solemnly. "Different suit. But I had it made to look just like the other one."

The two soldiers nodded knowingly.

"What's this gaudy piece of cloth?" Moe counterattacked as he fingered the first ribbon in the line of three that Ernie wore over his left uniform pocket. "I see you've got one, too," turning to Gene.

"Distinguished Service Medal," Gene explained. "I was told to report to the CO's office one afternoon and while I stood at attention, the old man pinned a medal on me. 'For the successful completion of a dangerous mission,' he said. Then handed me the box and made me swear never to spill a word about it."

"That's the same way I got mine," Ernie added. "Only I received it in an empty mess hall."

"Standard procedure," said Moe. "Our little escapade was an OSS operation, though the OSS wasn't officially in business when we started. What we did and what we saw is still classified top secret. To make sure you two didn't blat, they couldn't decide whether to kill you or give you a medal."

"How about you, Moe?" Gene asked. "They give you a medal too?"

"Oh, there's been some talk, but I'm not really sure I want it. I'm a civilian, where would I wear the darn thing? Not on this lapel--much too flashy. Now, if they had a nice dark blue medal . . ."

Gene told how he had rejoined his old fighter squadron near London, escorting the "big friends" to their bomb runs and eventually being promoted to commander of a squadron of P-51s.

Ernie explained that he was still officially a mess sergeant but had spent much of the last four years on loan to intelligence where he helped interrogate German prisoners.

When they looked to Moe to fill in the years, he just shook his head. "Let's just say I've been busy. Beyond that there's not much I can talk about."

Ernie suddenly grabbed his beer and stood up. "Heil, Herr Gauleiter," he shouted, giving the Nazi salute.

Gene followed and likewise heiled.

Moe then rose and raising his beer, shouted, "Heil, my incompetent driver. Heil my inept aide!"

They then drained their glasses and fell back in their chairs laughing. Their laughter swept away the residue of recent years and connected them once again. It was the uninhibited laughter of boys on a spree. While they laughed, a waitress with a Veronica Lake hairdo appeared. Without a word, she placed fresh lagers on the table, snatched up a dollar bill along with the empties, and hurried off toward the bar.

"Hey, Moe," said Ernie, dribbling his first sip of the fresh beer, "you have any idea what happened to Sally and Babette?"

Moe looked down into his glass. "Sally's fine. She made it to South America. I saw her there. We had our own reunion in Rio. What a time. She's some swell gal, I'll tell you. Some swell gal. She looked just great . . . tan . . . I didn't think redheads got tan . . . she was working with the Red Cross down there."

"Was . . . Babette with her?" Ernie asked hesitantly.

"No, Ernie, Babette didn't go with Sally. They made it to Spain together, but then she returned to France. Sally tried to talk her out of it, but you know Babette."

Moe could tell that Ernie sensed the rest of the story.

"There were some reports, Ernie, in London, that Babette was killed fighting with the Underground. I'm sorry, Ern."

"Yeah," Ernie said softly. "I'm sorry too."

"That's tough, Ernie," said Gene, reaching to place his hand on his friend's shoulder.

The three men sat quietly for a while, watching the foam dissipate in their glasses.

"Hey! Sally must be back by now," Gurney said, almost too loudly. "Let's give her a call."

"I'm afraid we can't do that fellas," said Moe. "When Sally left South America she went to Palestine. I received a letter last week; she's back in the refugee business."

Gene told of his decision to stay in the Air Corps and make a career of it. Even without a war, he'd be able to fly. Ernie, on the other hand, was due to be discharged in a few weeks and planned to join a relative in the real estate business in Florida.

"Real estate in Florida? You've got to be nuts," said Gene, as tactfully as his blood alcohol level would allow.

"Florida's nothing but mangrove swamps and alligators."
"And mosquitoes! Don't forget them," Moe added.

Even tales of mosquitoes the size of hummingbirds couldn't dissuade Ernie from his venture.

"How about you, Moe? What're your plans?"

"Oh, I don't know, haven't given it much thought. Something will come up, I'm sure." Moe didn't mention the scores of German scientists recently abducted by the Russians. Someone was going to have to find out what they were up to.

Amid the polished mahogany, plush carpeting, and glistening brass the three friends joked and laughed and recounted the adventure they had shared. This seemingly frivolous evening of reunion represented the closing of an important circle in their lives. They could now part contentedly, secure in the knowledge that the special camaraderie that sustained them during the most crucial test of their lives was for all time affirmed.

There are as many heroes in the world as there are angels in the firmament. And, like angels who appear to us in varied forms--as lordly archangels or stately seraphs or ebullient cherubim--we often find ourselves indebted to the most unlikely of them. An over-the-hill Jewish baseball player, for instance.

The End

Afterword

In the Baseball Hall of Fame museum in Cooperstown you will find, displayed in a glass case, a small bronze medal suspended from a red ribbon. It is the presidential Medal of Freedom, our nation's highest civilian honor. The citation displayed beside it reads:

> *Mr. Morris Berg, United States civilian, rendered exception-*
> *ally meritorious service of high value to the war effort from*
> *April 1942 to January 1946. In a position of responsibility*
> *in the European Theater, he exhibited analytical abilities*
> *and a keen planning mind. He inspired both respect and*
> *constant high level of endeavor on the part of his*
> *subordinates which enabled his section to produce studies*
> *and analysis vital to the mounting of American operations.*

Moe Berg died in 1971. I would like to believe he would be pleased to find himself in the company of the greats of his beloved game.